W

THE
BAKER

THE
BAKER

A Novel

PAUL HOND

RANDOM HOUSE NEW YORK

W

This is a work of fiction. All characters and dialogue are imagined, and not intended to represent real people, living or dead. Any such resemblances are entirely coincidental.

Library of Congress Cataloging-in-Publication Data
Hond, Paul.
    The baker / Paul Hond.
      p. cm.
    ISBN 0-679-45673-2
    I. Title.
    PS3558.0466B3   1997
    813'.54—dc21   96-52566

Random House website address: www.randomhouse.com
Printed in the United States of America on acid-free paper.
98765432
First Edition

ACKNOWLEDGMENTS

This book could not have been written without the support, guidance, vision and expertise of many people. I am especially indebted to my family; to Henry Bean, Nanette Burstein, Ann Hood, Michael Mandel, Jean-Isabel McNutt, Jim O'Connor, and Lynne Robertson; and above all to my editor, Jon Karp, and my agent, Barbara J. Zitwer.

THE
BAKER

1

Mickey Lerner pressed his nose to the glass at the top of the front door. Where was Benjie? He'd run out this morning with his basketball—the day had been warm—but now it was past dinnertime, it was dark, it was cold. You had to be a fanatic to play ball on a cold autumn night, and Mickey would sooner deliver his son to an all-consuming fanaticism than think about what he *might* be up to, on this night before Halloween. Not that Benjie was capable of perpetrating the sort of vandalism you often read about this time of year—the slashed tires, the grave markers defaced and tipped over, the car windows streaked with eggs, with soap, the scattered bonfires; no. Not Benjie. He was crazy for basketball: his bedroom walls were covered with life-size posters of ferociously airborne NBA stars, whose sleek young bodies and hateful scowls could prompt in Mickey a strange jealousy, such was the sway they had on the boy's imagination.

Still, Mickey'd been proud as hell when the kid made the high school team in his sophomore year. It was a marvelous thing to watch—Benjie's white face in the huddle, nodding at the coach's instructions, his eyes full of an attentiveness that bespoke, Mickey thought, a firm, old-fashioned upbringing; here was a coach's dream,

a workhorse, the kid who set an example. On the court, though, it was
another story: Benjie never did live up to his potential, or rather, the
potential itself never really coalesced; and so it was a bittersweet moment when the coach plucked him from the bench and started him at
guard in the final game of his career, a gesture of respect toward a lumbering senior whose previous appearances had come chiefly in the
waning seconds of lopsided contests. Mickey was in the stands that
day (he'd closed the bakery early just to be there), and as he watched
his son get buried by a flashy black kid from Columbus—thirty-six
points this kid scored—he was haunted by reminders of his first and
only amateur fight some forty years earlier, at a small, smoke-filled
arena in Dundalk.

The ride home from the school—Benjie looking vacantly out the
window, the faded fingerprint of a moon pursuing them overhead—
had been pretty quiet. Mickey tried to put things in perspective. "My
old trainer was a lot like your coach," he said, a touch of humor in his
voice. "Tough as nails, a real son of a bitch. I ever tell you about him?
Lou Glazer?" In fact he'd been compelled to tell the Glazer story
many times during the course of Ben's career. But never, ever did he
mention what happened in Dundalk. "Don't let it get you down," he
told his son. "There's more to life than a ball game."

Now he considered turning on the porch light to give Benjie a bea-
con, but decided against it, not wanting to encourage to his door the
evening's trick-or-treaters, who would be getting ready to make their
annual assault. Twenty, thirty years ago, Mickey would have been prepared, would have gone so far as to fit his mouth with toy fangs and
hand out bags of cookies, maybe even hunch his shoulders and laugh
in a sinister way upon answering the door. Back then, the kids—a glit-
tering, paint-smeared, sheet-covered dwarf race in sneakers—would
occupy the neighborhood, patrolling the streets and alleys, their orange plastic baskets filled with candy that sparkled under the street
lamps like the jewels of a vanquished people; it was fun to play along,
to frighten them as they wished to be frightened, or jump back in
mock horror when they raised their little bloody hands and roared.
These days, though, you'd get maybe a dozen kids all night, strictly
chaperoned, looking victimized in their store-bought costumes; it
seemed there were more parents on the street than kids, and you
might well have a lawsuit on your hands if you tried even in a very be-
nign way to scare one of the little creatures.

Mickey could hear the squeal of Emi's violin down in the basement; she'd been at it all day, and the scratchy, seasonably macabre

sounds (Berg? Bartók?) were like an extension of his anxiety. In the last two months she'd either been on the road or sequestered downstairs, up till midnight and risen before dawn. All he had of her, it seemed, was a spot on a bedsheet, a strewn article of clothing; at times he found himself with a shred of linen in his fists, clutching it insensibly, as though it were something recovered from a wreck. Things had changed between them since the summer, he thought; she was putting him off. Was he just imagining it?

He went to the kitchen and finished cleaning up the meal he'd eaten alone—a Mediterranean salad made from the dregs of his garden, his beloved garden, which had just yielded its last desperate fruits: gourd-shaped cucumbers, bulbous tomatoes nesting in dirt, skinny green beans curled like the fingernails of the dead; each one a bumper afflicted with a huge yellow-green unripeness. Mickey could be depressed by the final harvest, by the pallor and rubbery give of things, as though he were in some bumbling way responsible; so that while most folks dreaded a steamy Baltimore summer and were happy to see it go, Mickey—brushing the dirt from a whopping, jaundiced eggplant, or examining the bent knuckles of a carrot—was always sad to inhale, in late August, the first gentle changes in the air, knowing that in a short time his little Eden would be dried up, and the big silken leaves from his neighbor's sugar maple would sail onto his lawn, turning the whole yard red as blazes.

Ah, the leaves. A beautiful sight on someone else's lawn. On his own property it was like an attack, an invasion, and often he raked until it seemed he'd make the ground bleed. Only afterwards, the leaves bagged and set by the curb, would he realize that it was the beauty he resented, the carelessness of it, the way it revealed itself on its own terms and gave you only a short time to admire it. He did not like to be dazzled.

And yet he rejoiced, every autumn, in the increased activity at the feeders out back, where he had learned to identify the birds that gathered there—cardinals, blue jays, starlings, chickadees—by song. A few summers ago he had even painted one of the feeders red to attract hummingbirds, though he had yet to see one. Perhaps he liked the birds because they came daily, without fail; they were reliable. And it was to their credit that they couldn't be held in one's hand and examined, like a bright dead leaf. There was nothing tragic about them.

Mickey put the salad in the refrigerator. Benjie could have some later—a double-sized portion, seeing as how Emi wasn't in the business of eating these days. Sometimes she'd get that way before a big concert—nerves, she said—though Mickey couldn't help but feel, this time, that there was something more to it.

He washed his hands, dried them on his trousers. What now? Maybe he'd take a walk over to the bakery and enjoy a little quiet among the oven and mixers before the bakers arrived for the night shift. He'd been doing a lot of that with Emi away—lurking in the dim tranquillity of his store, trying to cheer himself with the idea that he was, after all, a pretty lucky so-and-so, that it was but a happy accident of birth that he ended up *owning* the bakery instead of being up to his elbows in dough at three and four in the morning like the men under his command. Maybe he wasn't a world-class violinist, but then he wasn't a simple baker either. He was a businessman, and in a small way—he wasn't embarrassed to think it—an emperor; and it was in the spirit of forging this image that he'd long since stopped baking bread in the house, lest anyone—his wife, his son, the neighbors within smelling distance of his kitchen door—begin to imagine that it was somehow his true vocation.

Silence downstairs. Was Emi taking a break? Mickey decided to drop in for a visit.

He went to the basement door and knocked. "Emi?"

"Come down," she called.

Mickey turned the knob. He could remember a time, in the early days, when he wouldn't have dared to knock, when he'd have just stood by the door like an obedient pet, waiting. Funny. He'd always had the deepest respect for her privacy, and now, years later, he could become physically aroused by the very act of infringing on it.

He went down the steps. "Em? You taking a break?"

"A short one."

"Good."

She was seated in her chair, the horsehair bow in her lap. Mickey regarded her: dark hennaed hair wrapped in a tight bun, cheekbones drawn up high, mouth turned slightly down at the corners; hers was an increasingly severe beauty, like that of an aging ballerina: the concaveness of the cheeks, the perfect fermata of eye and brow.

Mickey walked over and stood beside the music stand. "Benjie hasn't come home yet," he said.

"Where is he?"

"I don't know." It pained him to admit this; by a tacit arrangement prompted by Emi's career, Benjie had become his father's responsibility, and Mickey had long been too proud to share with Emi his parental concerns. But now, with Benjie out of school and verging on adulthood, Mickey felt a weakening of his resolve: he would need help—a young man's life was at stake. "This morning he went out with his basketball," Mickey said. "I haven't heard a thing since."

"He'll be fine," said Emi, her eyes still intent on the score.

Mickey scratched his cheek; he wanted to trust in Emi's words, but lately he'd been considering such remarks less a statement of a mother's intuition than a glaring symptom of her indifference. How could she be so calm? But in the next moment there came a sound from above: the click of the lock, followed by the squeal of the door, the heavy footfalls on the stairs.

Emi pretended not to notice—a rebuke of sorts, Mickey supposed. He laughed, feeling vindicated, as though Ben's arrival, late and un-explained though it may have been, was evidence nonetheless of a solid rearing. He had at least come home at all. "Of course he's fine," Mickey said, with a touch of irony. "He's eighteen, he's indestructible." And he himself felt invincible: he wanted to revel in this small ac-quittal, celebrate it with his body. He took a step forward, and was met by the end of the bow, thrust out like a sword at his belly.

"Mickey."

"What?" Mickey said. He reached for her breast; the bow struck his hand.

"It's a bad time," said Emi.

"A bad time. It's been a bad time since the summer."

"I'm sorry," Emi said. "Please just bear with me."

Mickey barked a laugh. "What does that mean?"

"Please. Okay?"

"Christ." Mickey shook his head. "Three months," he grumbled.

"Tomorrow," Emi said. She looked up at him. "Okay?"

Mickey laughed, less savagely than before. "Is this the new arrange-ment?" he said. "A schedule?"

"It's only temporary. I promise."

"Tomorrow," Mickey said. "Tomorrow, in case you don't remember, we have a date out back. That gardening has got to get done."

Yes, the garden. Was there a greater, more enduring monument to their union? Over the years they had transformed it into a small par-adise: heavy rocks of brown, umber, gray and ocher (Mickey had driven to western Maryland and collected them himself) now lined the side of the house, with pink and blue creeping phlox growing out from the cracks. The two beds near the patio boasted yellow tulips, reddish lilies and pink begonias. Along the back fence was the veg-etable garden, which this year had featured two kinds of tomatoes,

tasty but wildly deformed carrots (the soil had been too heavy), arti-
chokes, cucumbers, green beans and giant bell peppers shaped like
weird, sunken faces. The harvest recalled a mutual feeling of parent-
hood: the pulling up of the carrots from the ground, slowly, in anticipation of length and shape, and the timid plucking of the tomatoes
from the vine, leaving both gardeners amazed by their frank redness,
the shock of ripe testicular discovery in all that fuzzy, bristly green.

"Okay," said Emi. "Tomorrow night then."

"Yeah?" said Mickey. He planted his feet, folded his arms. "What do
you have in mind?"

Emi smiled, and for a moment she looked thirty years younger. She
raised the tip of the bow to her parted lips and tickled the shaft with
her long, pointed tongue: a parody of seduction behind which she
concealed the real thing. She laughed, then gave a stroke to the E
string to indicate she was ready to resume her work.

Mickey felt a sudden despair. It was all so easy for her; she chan-
neled everything into her music. He was the one with the needs, the
big dumb urges. He longed for an outlet, a means of expression. How
could he ever explain it?

He excused himself—Emi had begun playing—and went upstairs,
where he stood confused in the living room before deciding to go up
and talk to Benjie.

Ben's door was closed, and Mickey rapped on it lightly. Other fathers might have to bang on their kid's doors, to compete with the
rock music. Not Mickey. Nothing but quiet behind this wood. Such
quiet, in fact, that Mickey could almost imagine the room was empty;
that the kid, like everyone else in his high school class, had gone off to
college.

He rapped again. "Benjie?"

"I'm busy," came a voice.

Mickey took a breath and counted silently. He could make splinters
out of that goddamned door if he wanted. "I'll give you until three to
open this door," he said. "One." In fact he'd never actually reached
three; at two and a half he always got his results. The realm of three
remained a mystery to both of them. *"Two."*

The door opened, and, as often happened, Mickey was jolted by the
sight of this young man in a T-shirt and undershorts, with a few
whiskers on the chin, of whom people would remark, "He looks just
like his father." Mickey wasn't so sure. For one thing, the kid was
skinny, almost gangly. A featherweight. His dark hair—darker than
Mickey's hair had ever been, and without the touch of gray that had

singed Mickey at the temples during adolescence and left him with a virile silvery head by the time he was thirty-five—was buzzed close to the scalp, and he wore a tiny gold stud in his right earlobe. Oh, there'd been a heated battle over that ("What's next—lipstick? Mascara?"), but Mickey eventually threw in the towel.

"What are you doing in there?" he said, searching the face for signs of trouble.

Ben shrugged. "Nothing. Just playing *Empire.*"

Mickey wanted to tell him that if he'd used the computer for his studies instead of goofing off with games, maybe he'd rule a *real* empire someday, or at least be a productive citizen of one. But there were other issues at hand. "And where were you today," Mickey said, "that you couldn't pick up a phone and call?"

"Playing basketball."

"All day?"

"Then I went to Nelson's."

Mickey raised his eyebrows: Nelson was the delivery man at the bakery, a ghetto kid from a broken home whom Mickey had hired nearly a year ago. "You were down in that neighborhood at night?" Mickey said.

"It's not so bad."

"Don't tell me it's not so bad. I don't want you running around down there. At *any* time. You understand?"

"No," said Ben. He looked hurt. "I don't."

"It's dangerous."

"You grew up there."

"A long time ago," said Mickey. He sighed; he didn't have the energy to argue, he'd take it up later. He said, "There's a salad downstairs. You hungry?"

"I ate already."

"Where?"

"Nelson's. Miss Donna made pumpkin fritters."

"You invited yourself?"

"No. Donna offered."

Mickey was suspicious. He didn't know Donna Childs too well, could barely remember what she looked like, but he got the feeling she was trying to curry favor with him on behalf of her son. It was only natural, of course, for her to fear for Nelson's job; times were hard, and Nelson, given his circumstances, might slip up at any moment. Mickey resented Donna's tactics, and was embarrassed that he could see through them so easily. Worse, she seemed to feel indebted to him, and there was no telling what she might do in the way of pampering Ben in her desire to pay him back.

"She always asks how you are," Ben said. "Says she remembers you from the old bakery."

Mickey ignored this. "I don't want you going down there," he said. "Nelson is welcome to come here—" He stopped himself; he didn't mean it. Not that he had anything against Nelson personally; it was just that Benjie ought to be spending time with, well, other kids. Kids in college. Kids from good families. "I need you to do something for me," Mickey said, hoping to change the subject. "Tomorrow. I'll need you to run the store."

Ben smirked. "Why? So you can spend the day with Mom?" There was a hint of high school jeer in his voice.

"Just do what I tell you."

"How much are you paying?"

"You're working for the privilege of keeping your room," Mickey said. He'd spelled it out for him over the summer: either you get a job and pay rent, or you help me out when I ask you. "Any questions?"

Ben shrugged. "I could drive the van if you want."

Mickey took a breath. They'd been through this a million times since Ben got his license, and Mickey'd had about enough. "Is that what you want to do with your life?" he demanded. "Drive a delivery van?"

"You wouldn't say that to Nelson."

Mickey's neck got hot. "Leave Nelson out of this."

"Fine," Ben said. He looked bored all of a sudden. "Am I excused now?"

Mickey thought for a moment. "Yes," he said. "You're excused."

"Good," said Ben. His door slammed shut.

Mickey stood there, unsure what to do next. The basement door, too, was closed; Mickey found himself alone, a stranger in his own house. He had a mind to get in his car and drive somewhere, anywhere. Or maybe he'd call Donna Childs and let her know that here was a father who gave a damn about his son's comings and goings, and who would furthermore appreciate it if she would call and inform him, or, better yet, ask his permission the next time she felt like inviting his son to dinner.

He decided to go to bed early, thinking that what he really needed was a good night's rest. He lay in the dark waiting for Emi to come up, but within minutes he was asleep; and when he awoke the following morning—he'd slept deeply, as if buried at sea, dreaming of women he'd never seen—the house was already empty: Emi was down at the conservatory, teaching her morning class, and Ben—it took Mickey a moment to remember—Ben was keeping shop at the bakery.

Mickey yawned, swung his body upright. Nothing had changed: he felt as confused and anxious as he had the night before. He needed to do something, to act. Motion was the key. Keep moving. He showered and dressed and went outside.

The sky was blue as a hydrangea in midsummer. Blue-jay blue; the blue of bellflowers, of eggshells in the grass. Still, a surprising color to find in nature. Blue? Mickey stood and breathed deeply. The air—warm, burnt, spun through with the gold of leaves, awaiting, like a prisoner draining his last cigarette, the cold cruel blade of night—took him back to childhood, to the smell of pears, of golden crusts of bread. Yes: there was, in this world, a place he could go, a place where he could recall himself. His access to it seemed unreal, like a forbidden skin that he was suddenly free to touch.

He got into his Buick Skylark and started the engine.

2

The old neighborhood. Mickey hadn't come down here in years—
the area had gone to pot ages ago—but as he turned onto Percy
Street (and there was his old house, number 2207), he wondered if it
really was as bad as all that. The streets were deserted, he was safe in
his car; what could happen to him? Nothing. He'd never felt as secure
as when he'd lived here as a boy, and that same feeling washed over
him now. He recalled the snap of laundry billowing on the clothes-
lines, the smell of boiled turnips, cabbage, pickled herring. He could
point to each house and name the family that had lived there: the
Kleins, the Grossmans, the Blanks, the Alters. He recalled their cars,
their dogs, their famous illnesses. He recognized a hydrant, a few
curbside trees; and there, near the corner, low and secret in the gutter
and wide as a monster's grin, the dreaded sewer hole, his old nemesis,
the spot to which he ran so often on tiny skinned legs, in pursuit of
yet another ball that had skipped under his fat pancake of a mitt or
whizzed over it, rolling speedily and with a kind of cruel intelligence
toward the inevitable hole, where it would be swallowed into a plung-
ing darkness.

He turned off Percy onto Washburn, appreciating the chill in the air, the faint smoky smell of leaves, the sturdiness of old, soot-scorched brick. Fifty years ago, he thought. He was getting on sixty; his memories touched the tips of vanished, ancient things. On the corner of Percy and Washburn there had been a grocery, Ruby's, and Mickey could remember the smell of the briny pickle barrels, of the wrinkled black olives and fatty luncheon meats. The storefront itself was long gone, but if you looked closely at the brick facade, you could see a faded advertisement for Singapore Fruit. Now the sign was all but a ghost, the paint like a handprint vanishing from glass.

Mickey stopped his car in front of Nelson's house on Washburn. Nelson would be on deliveries, but Donna might be home, and Mickey did have a few things to discuss with her. Should he go up and knock on the door? He looked around. Garbage cans were bunched at the curb, their tops slanted at impudent angles, like gangsters' hats. Mickey hesitated. A man in a white T-shirt appeared on the front steps two doors down. Mickey felt for the lock, a reflex. Not that he was worried; God knew he'd driven through worse neighborhoods. Years ago, come a holiday (Passover especially, when the bakery'd be closed for over a week), he would drive through the damnedest areas— Fulton Street, Edmondson Avenue—to distribute bread to his credit-book customers. He once went inside a customer's house to use the toilet, and when he came back out his car was gone. That had been the last time.

Now he wondered if he ought to just get out of there, go home. He knew the man in the T-shirt was watching him, and it wasn't unreasonable, given what you saw on the news these days, to imagine himself being pulled from his car at gunpoint, perhaps even shot for no reason and left for dead in the gutter as his car disappeared around a corner. He hated to think that way, but what could you do? As if to disprove his own assumptions, he parked in front of Nelson's and stepped out of the car; and as he braced himself to look over at the man and give a friendly nod, he realized, upon glimpsing the man's puzzled, somewhat guarded expression, that he was being seen for what he surely must be: a cop. What other white man would have any business around here? Yes: Detective Mick Lerner, fixture at crime scenes, a man of burger wrappers and coffee cups and the occasional highball, a solid veteran with the charm of a bulldog and the heat to back it up. This fantastic notion, made all the more vivid, somehow, by the way his tie flapped behind him in the breeze, carried Mickey all the way to Nelson's door, and as he waited for Donna Childs to answer his knock—three times he knocked, just as Detective Lerner might—he watched as the man in the T-shirt went back into his house, looking away, as though not wanting to be involved.

Mickey knocked again, softly, regretting the authoritative raps of a moment before. He wondered how he might appear through the peephole. Would she recognize him? A new confusion set in. What was he doing here? Why not have just talked on the phone? Before he could think, the door opened, and a young, attractive black woman—Donna Childs, no question about it—looked up at him with a stunned expression.

"Yes?"

"You're Donna Childs?"

"Yes." Donna placed her hand over her mouth. "Did something happen to my son? Oh my Lord."

"No," Mickey said. "No, no. Everything's fine. I'm Mickey Lerner."

Donna lowered her hand.

Mickey smiled to ease her fears. "I was just driving through the neighborhood, thought I'd drop by and say hello. I wanted to—to talk about our boys."

"Is everything okay?"

"Everything's fine, nothing to worry about. Is it a bad time?"

"I was just on my way to the bus," Donna said. "I have to go to work." She seemed scattered, unsure of the time, the date. "I'm sorry—otherwise I'd invite you inside." She smiled nervously. "You said you wanted to talk?"

"That's right. Do you want a lift?"

Donna looked at him. "A ride?"

"I don't mind."

"Okay," said Donna. "Let me think." She placed her hand on her cheek, trying, Mickey guessed, to think of a way out; she was off her guard, flustered. "If I get a ride . . ." Her brown face was round and smooth as a bowl. She was forty, Mickey calculated, but she looked ten years younger, what with the dozens of cordlike braids that fell to her shoulders, each one so elaborately woven that Mickey could be exhausted just by looking at them. She wore jangling bracelets and an Indian cotton dress with intricate floral patterns; when she moved there was a quiet rumble of hips, of bosom.

"It's not a problem," said Mickey. "Where do you work?"

"Me? Downtown. On Cathedral Street."

"Let's go then," said Mickey. He smiled, gave a coaxing nod in the direction of his car.

"Okay—okay then." Donna closed her door, made sure it was locked. "Down on Cathedral," she said, fumbling with her keys. "I give shiatsu massage." She had a serious yet musical voice, Mickey thought, a voice through whose nervousness could be heard a slight Southern drawl—a twang that conjured up uncut grass, wildflowers and Sunday picnics in the shade. "Ever heard of it? Shiatsu?" She was overcoming fear. "It's Japanese for 'finger pressure.' It's good for tension, circulation. It cleans your cells. Helps fight disease."

"Sounds like hocus-pocus," Mickey said good-naturedly.

"It works. You should try it sometime."

"Me? I just had my annual physical. Doctor gave me a perfect bill of health." Mickey drew a long breath, his chest expanding with the youthful pride he took in his physique. Standing naked just last month in the cold-tiled examination room as Dr. Abel touched, probed, listened and scrawled glowing notes on a pad, Mickey had become aware of himself as a specimen, a true marvel of fitness; so that now, leading Donna Childs to his car in full view of possibly hostile neighbors, he took refuge in the temple of his health—the thump of his small, efficient heart, the loose, leonine ripple of his thighs—and, from the most discreet portal of this sanctuary, eyed his companion with a mix of wonder and disbelief: he hadn't seen her in years, not since the days of the old bakery down on North Avenue; suddenly, everything came back to him.

"Éclairs," he said. "Chocolate-covered éclairs."

Donna laughed. "My favorite," she said. The nervousness was gone: they could have been old friends. "You remembered that?"

Mickey smiled. "Your mother always warned you you'd get sick. But you insisted."

"And you always backed me up."

Mickey laughed. "Just doing my job." He unlocked the passenger door and walked around to the driver's side, patting the hood of the car on the way. "What were you—nine, ten years old? I never saw such an appetite."

Donna followed him with her eyes. "I'm still trying to reverse the effects."

Mickey laughed as he got into the car. "Aw. Come on now. I'm sure you're just fine."

Donna got in and closed her door. "I've always wondered," she said, and the humor drained from her voice. "When you hired Nelson. Did you know who he was? Or who I was?"

"Well," said Mickey. He buckled his seat belt. "I did recognize the name when he filled out the application. The parent's name. Donna Childs. Sure, it rang a bell."

"I thought it would," Donna said. "Not that I expected it would get him the job. I guess I'd like to think you hired him, you know, on his own merit." She looked at her smooth hands, the fingers ringless, probably on account of her line of work. She said, "He doesn't know that you once knew my father."

Mickey glanced at his passenger. Despite himself, he felt increasingly aware of their differences; was this really the little colored girl with the pigtails and the big front teeth, smiling up at him at the bakery counter? He lowered his window, wanting air. The cultural myth of the automobile as a haven for outlaws and lovers added to his growing sense of the illicit, a sense heightened by the strange apparition of his own whiteness: the pink fingers on the wheel, the sallow face in the rearview mirror; or perhaps it was the features of the interior—the locks, the straps, the buckles, the mirrors—that smacked too strongly of fetish, of leathery pleasures and general sexual peril. He said, "Nelson got the job fair and square."

"Good," said Donna.

They passed a block of decrepit row houses, eroded, leprous. Mickey turned onto Coldspring, heading for the expressway. "Me and your father had one fight," he said. "We really didn't know each other that well. I think we kept in touch for a couple of months, but that was it. We just sort of—fell out of touch."

"He went bad," Donna said. "Wasn't that it?"

Mickey shrugged. "I wasn't too familiar with his personal life. I know he had problems. He got mixed up with some characters. But *you*"—Mickey heard his voice brighten desperately—"you were just a baby."

"He used to talk about you," said Donna. "I remember. Up until the day he died, he talked about that fight."

"Oh?" Mickey dreaded the topic, but he was curious to know what Thomas Childs had said about him.

Donna brushed the lap of her dress. "He said he nearly killed you in the ring." She laughed, as if to assure Mickey that she knew this was an exaggeration, the drunken bluster of a deeply troubled man, but Mickey detected a note of pride in her voice. "Said he messed you up so bad, they had to give you a new nose. I always used to look at your face, trying to see where they operated."

Mickey laughed, but he felt depressed as hell. Poor Tommy Childs.

The fight had ruined him. He never fought again, as far as Mickey knew; the life he'd tried so hard to escape through boxing quickly reclaimed him, and in less than ten years he was dead, shot during an argument over money. Mickey'd always felt bad about Tommy, as if he himself were somehow liable for the man's plight; he often wished he could do something to make up for things, something short of punishing himself, and now, for the first time, he realized why he had stuffed little Donna Childs with éclairs, and why, more recently, he had hired her son—Tommy's grandson—to drive the Lerner Bakery van.

"I never did tell Nelson about my father," Donna said. "It was bad enough his own father was no good. Bad men all around. The child never had anyone to look up to."

Mickey cleared his throat. "I meant to talk to you about our boys," he said. "Ben and Nelson."

Donna didn't seem to hear him. "Been doing everything I can to make sure he doesn't turn out the same way."

"About Nelson and Ben," Mickey said. He paused to make sure he had her attention, then went on. "I know that Benjie's been spending a lot of time at your house lately, and I just want to make sure he's not, ya know, overstaying his welcome. Inviting himself over, that sort of thing. Taking advantage."

"Ben Lerner?" said Donna. "Are you kidding me? He's welcome anytime. But now, if it's a problem—"

"Oh no, not at all. No problem. I just want to make sure it's okay on your end."

"Are you worried about him being in that area at night?"

Mickey laughed too readily. "Why would I be worried?"

"It's dangerous, that's why," Donna said. "I wouldn't want *my* child hanging around that area, night *or* day. But at this particular moment, I don't have a choice."

Mickey felt shamed by her admission; he didn't know what to say. Already he had bungled the point of the meeting, which was to somehow contrive to keep their children away from each other. Now he felt like a goddamned bigot. But why a bigot? Was it wrong to want something better for one's own son?

"We'll move someday," Donna said. "Right now I'm saving to send Nelson back to college."

"Right," Mickey said. "He was taking classes, wasn't he?"

"Two semesters," said Donna. "Took the required classes. Math, history. English. Hated every second of it. Said it was a waste of time."

"Why?"

Donna shrugged. "Too easy. That's what he said. Disruptive students, too, just like high school." She wiped something from her eye.
"He could've gone to a good college on scholarships," she said, "if he
hadn't got mixed up with the wrong people. I told him all through
high school: stay out of trouble. You're a smart child. But kids, they
don't want to listen. He was nearly killed. I'm not even going to go
into that. He's got a job now, and all I can do is pray he holds onto it."
She sighed. "I just wish there was someone who could talk to him.
Someone he'd listen to. Someone he respected."

Mickey nodded, aware that he was being marked for some awful
favor. He wanted to discourage Donna from trying to enlist his help,
but her faith in his fatherly powers was strangely flattering, prompt-
ing him toward a rosier account of his own son than the facts allowed.
"Yes," he said. "Fortunately, as far as Ben is concerned—" He stopped;
he couldn't do it. He couldn't tell a lie. He decided to go with the
truth, hoping that a more sober profile of his son might yet sound like
a father's modesty—as if, out of tact, he were quietly downplaying
Ben's prospects. "What I mean," he said, "is that Benjie's the same way.
I call him an underachiever. We decided it was a good idea to wait a
year before he went anywhere. Too many kids jump right into college,
they're not ready." He paused, then said, "You got an impressionable
kid, believe me, college can do more harm than good," hoping, as he
tapped the wheel with his fingers, that this subtle reference to drugs—
colleges being notorious hotbeds for every drug you cared to name:
cocaine, pep pills, marijuana—would ease them into the topic and
allow Mickey to wonder aloud if their boys were perhaps indulging
together in the harder stuff—reefers, crack, angel dust, Mickey
couldn't come up with all the names—endemic to many of the poorer
areas, such as the one in which Donna happened to live. But Donna
didn't seem to catch his drift. "The way I look at it," Mickey said, now
focusing on his previous point, "a kid shouldn't be pushed too hard
one way or another. Into college, I mean." He took a breath, satisfied
that he'd rung the very bell of fatherly reason.

But Donna seemed agitated. "I don't know," she said. In her reluc-
tance to contradict him she betrayed a soft disappointment. "They
don't always know what's good for them. They *need* to be pushed."

Mickey bristled; he hadn't counted on having to argue his point. "I
agree," he said. "I only meant that they shouldn't be forced into anything." This was, Mickey knew, a bit of hypocrisy; for hadn't he been

pushing Ben toward the bakery? Wasn't Ben behind the counter right this minute, under threat of eviction from his room should he refuse to comply? "What I mean is," Mickey said, "you have to give a kid direction—" He broke off, disgusted by the sound of his voice, the failure of his argument. He feigned impatience with the traffic, blasted his horn, cursed under his breath at other motorists, wishing all the while that Donna would disappear from his sight. He was shocked, even angered, at how violently he craved her respect, her adulation. He wanted, in light of her experiences with corrupt, dissolute men, to be seen as the perfect husband and father, the very salt of manhood; he wanted to punish her, to crush her with the goodness of his life.

The traffic on the expressway flowed like liquid silver. Mickey tried to make sense of his clash of feelings. At bottom, he supposed, he was in a kind of secret agony over the state of affairs at home (would Emi even remember their date in the garden today?), an agony complicated by Donna's total innocence of it. Truth be told, he had no goodness with which to crush her; he was impoverished in his own way, and resented Donna for making him feel, by mere virtue of her material want, that he ought to be a better man than he was.

But there was something else as well, some other issue that he couldn't quite put a finger on; and as he exited the expressway, with Donna gazing out her window, he was overcome with an urgent, almost panic-stricken desire to get home to his wife—a desire which, as they passed the Lyric Opera House, the hipster shops of Read Street, the old Alcazar Ballroom and the grassy western square of a cobblestone-bordered Mount Vernon Place, sharpened itself to such a needlelike intensity that minutes later, driving back to the expressway, Mickey could hardly recall having stopped in front of Donna's workplace, or her thanking him and getting out of the car with a clank of jewelry ("Now don't tell Nelson we talked; he'll just think I'm getting in his business!"), or his own sense of helplessness in having failed to accomplish a damn thing with regard to Ben; no: all Mickey could see, all he allowed himself to see, was the road home, the route leading to the garden, to Emi, to the life he wanted so desperately to put in order.

By the time Mickey arrived, Emi was already out back, kneeling by one of the flower beds, shears snipping at the hibiscus that Mickey had bought at a nursery in Timonium. He watched from the bedroom window as she attacked the stems: Lord and Lady Baltimores, they were called; the Lords were yellow and the Ladies were pink. Mickey'd thought Emi would get a kick out of the idea—an aristocratic couple in bloom. Now he winced as she beheaded them.

He removed his shirt and tie and changed into his work trousers and tennis shoes, wondering if he should tell Emi about his busy morning. She knew little about Ben's friendship with Nelson, and even less of the history—the strange, shared destiny—that seemed to exist between the two families. Mickey felt protective of these dubious items: they were his secrets, his ugly little pets.

He went downstairs and out the kitchen door. The temperature was above seventy: Indian summer. Mickey grabbed his clippers from the closet-size shed attached to the back of the house and joined his wife in the dirt. "Some day, huh?" he said. He crouched down: his joints crackled like split wood.

"Too hot," said Emi. She wiped her forehead with the sleeve of her gray sweatshirt. She was panting softly.

"It'll be cold soon enough," said Mickey. He saw, through her slightly graying hair, a pinkish grid of scalp. "Reminds me, we should get the parsnips in before the first frost—they'll be sweeter that way, growing in the frozen ground all winter." In the daylight he noticed that her hair, like her body, seemed to have thinned a good deal over the past few months, and there were lines on her face that he was sure hadn't been there before she left for New York. She was working too hard, worrying too much.

She said, "Where were you?"

"This morning?" Mickey's voice barely modulated. "I took the car down to Gordy's. There's been this noise when I start it up." He poked the soil with his forefinger. "A choking sound." It was a small, merciful evasion, of the sort he'd made a hundred times before (an evasion, not a lie: there really *was* a problem with the starter), a means of sparing the both of them a heated argument over Ben ("What's wrong with his being friendly with a black boy?" she would say accusingly, missing the point); but as soon as Mickey uttered the words "I took the car down to Gordy's," he felt he had crossed a dangerous line, had committed the first of a new kind of deception. He said, "Gordy told me to bring the car in next week," and made a mental note to see Gordy later in the day.

Emi nodded; she didn't seem the least bit suspicious. Mickey felt a small disappointment.

"So," said Emi, and Mickey knew from her tone that she was choosing her words: "Where's Ben today?"

Mickey took a breath. "He's at the bakery," he said, furious that Emi would dare to touch on that controversy during what little time they'd set aside for each other. "He's helping me out so we can spend the day together."

"I see."

She'd wanted to push Ben to go to school in the fall—he'd been accepted to two or three lesser area colleges (his grades in high school had been awful)—and Mickey had said no, let him wait a year, let him think about what he wants to do. Benjie, meanwhile, didn't seem to have an opinion either way.

Emi said, "He's been helping out a lot lately."

"How would you know?" Mickey said. She wanted a fight, he'd give her war. "It's a wonder you even remember his name."

There was a silence. Mickey was surprised: normally Emi defended her spates of absence by equating them with the kid's braces, his basketball camp, his computer, his investments; but now she looked abstracted, troubled, as if realizing for the first time that her son had grown up without her.

Mickey relented some. "Anyhow," he said, "I don't see the harm in it. The bakery is a good experience. Teaches him some responsibility." Still, he knew what Emi meant. She was afraid the kid would end up working there permanently, just like his father, and Mickey was forced to behave as though her fears were unwarranted. There were several levels of degradation to this, Mickey perceived.

"I just don't think you should push him into anything," Emi said.

"I'm not pushing. But if he wasn't at the bakery, he'd be out playing ball, or else sitting in his room all day with the damned computer."

"Maybe he's learning something on the computer."

"He plays games."

"And what's he doing now? Standing behind a counter? Bagging bread?"

Mickey drove the clippers into the ground; the wooden handles shivered. "Okay," he said. "It's my fault. You happy? It's my fault he's not a genius." He gripped the handles. "Maybe if you'd been around—" He stopped himself: to blame her for not being there to nurture Benjie would be to open himself to charges of genetic failure. *What would it matter if I was around?* she could say. *He's naturally limited.*

Of course she would never actually say it. But she wouldn't have to.

She was quiet again, began snipping the lilies with fierce little bites. She was surrounded by lopped-off heads, stems, the wilt and wither of old, strewn bouquets; for a brief moment she resembled a faded performer collapsed on the stage of some long-ago triumph.

Mickey suddenly felt penitent. Their garden time was too precious to be spoiled by arguments, and in any case he couldn't afford to drive her to the edge of her anger. What would he do if she ever left him?

He lifted his hand and placed it gently on the back of her neck. She barely quaked in his palm, and touched his hand with her own. She hadn't the strength to fight.

She said, "We should add the compost."

"Another week," said Mickey. "We'll have to pick up that gypsum, too. I figure six bushels of compost."

He smiled. When he first met her, she hardly knew mulch from mud; she was a city girl—Paris, New York—and he'd taught her most everything she knew. The garden was the one place he felt in command, and sometimes he was moved to draw comparisons between their fields of expertise, not so much to raise himself in her estimation, he thought, as to try and mingle their fortunes.

"Thought hit me the other day," he said, "how the garden is like a symphony. A concert. The colors, the plotting; but especially the timing. Planning it so that when one group of flowers fades, the other is coming up. New combinations, new moods. The string section, the brass, the woodwinds." He picked up a stem and made like a conductor, pointing at the various plots of shorn flowers as though summoning them to blossom. "It really is like a symphony," he said, but then stopped himself upon hearing something too passionate in his voice.

Emi laughed. "And now we have the requiem." She scooped up a bunch of dead flowers and brought them to her nose, so that her entire face was covered. For some reason, Mickey thought she might be crying.

"Are you okay?" he said.

She tossed away the flowers. She wasn't crying, but there was distance in her eyes. "Just tired."

Mickey dropped the stem. "Too much practicing."

"I guess it's like training for a fight," Emi said. She turned to him. "*You* know."

"Yeah," Mickey said. "No screwing."

Emi said nothing.

"If you ate some food," Mickey said, "I think we'd both feel a lot better. How about we get showered and dressed and I'll take you out. Anywhere you want, you name it, we'll—"

"I can't," she said, in a tone imploring him to understand, to *see*. "Not until—after these concerts."

Mickey sighed. "Then how about some salad?" he said. "I've got a whole salad in the refrigerator." He uprooted his clippers, flexed them to clean the blades. "You'd starve to death if it wasn't for me," he said, with a note of righteous accusation aimed at others, at the musicians who took so much of her time. "You work so hard you forget to eat."

"I eat plenty."

"Then maybe," Mickey said, "you've got some kind of bug."

Emi laughed. "How did you guess?"

"You do?"

"Yes." She blew a strand of hair from her lips. "David Shaw."

Mickey's skin tingled at the sound of the great pianist's name. Emi rarely shared the details of her professional life (she probably thought it too boring), and though Mickey often imagined that the grandeur of her world might somehow be tarnished by his access to it, he was always grateful for any small crumbs. "What do you mean?" he said.

"He's driving me crazy," she said. "His quirks, his ego. He resents the fact that I've been getting more attention."

"So let him resent it."

"But he's the pianist. He's my safety net."

"You don't trust him?"

"He's been erratic at rehearsals. Memory lapses." She paused. "I think after this I'm going to take a long break."

"You? A break?" Mickey laughed, shook his head. There'd been a time when he would have encouraged her to keep on, a time when it was just as well for her to be away, when he feared what might happen if she spent too much time with him. Now he'd happily risk boring her: it was becoming more and more difficult to be alone.

Emi shrugged one shoulder. "Sometimes I feel like I'm missing something."

"Like what?"

"I don't know. Everything." She closed her eyes. "God, what's happened to me?"

Mickey scratched his ear. He didn't want to hear this. He'd always thought her so lucky to have an obsession, a passion, hell, he'd give almost anything to find one for himself. How could she complain, now, so late in the game? Mickey had always invested a certain amount of his own longings in her love for what she did—it helped him get through her absences—and it shook him to think that it was all a heap of regrets.

"Come on now," he said.

Emi put her hands over her face.

Mickey looked around nervously at the neighbors' yards. It wasn't normal for her to break down like this.

"It'll be fine," Mickey said. He couldn't help but wonder if there was something else bothering her. He kissed her head and rubbed her back; her entire skeleton seemed available to his fingers. "It'll be fine," he said. "Don't worry." She winced, as though his touch were painful.

Mickey tried to think of a way to amuse her, to bring her around. "Here," he said, remembering an old trick that used to make her giggle. "Look." He took up a spade and unearthed one of the tulip bulbs they'd planted two or three years ago. Clods of dirt fell from the tangled roots. He carefully brushed the dirt from the white globe, a whiteness thrown into bone-colored relief by the dark soil, and pointed out the small cloves that adhered to the roundness like sucklings. "See?" he said. "Little baby bulbs."

Emi smiled, but it was more for the past, for the times when they'd give the babies silly names. She pulled away from him and stood up, brushed the dirt from her jeans. "We need some bags for this," she said, waving a hand at the cuttings. A red maple leaf from the Finkles's tree floated down and landed near her feet.

"Great," said Mickey, looking up at the tree. He stood, wobbled a moment. "More mess to clean up." He picked up the leaf and dropped it over the fence.

"I think they're pretty," Emi said.

Mickey ignored that. Suddenly he thought of Ben; he should probably call the bakery, see how things were going.

"Mookie."

Mickey turned at the sound of his pet name, his bedroom name.

Emi pulled off her gloves. "Come downstairs tonight at ten o'clock," she said. "I'll move my music stand."

Mickey raised an eyebrow. It had been quite a while since he'd stood before her like that, buttocks tensed, his pants at his knees; and even longer since he'd knelt before her, his face wedged between her thighs as she sliced the strings with her bow.

Looking up at her at that angle—he remembered—it appeared that she was severing her own neck.

"Okay," he said, his blood pumping. "Ten o'clock."

3

The hour could not have arrived soon enough. Emi was down in the basement the rest of the afternoon, starting, stopping, cursing aloud when she missed a note. Around dinnertime Mickey prepared a bowl of salad and a slice of bread and took it downstairs, but instead of interrupting her in the middle of a long, tricky passage and demanding she put down the goddamned bow and *eat*, for Christ's sake, he left the food on the bottom step and tiptoed back up, lest he give her any reason to deny him what she had promised.

As for himself, he decided to order carryout from Chen's Garden. He phoned in his order, then drove to the bakery to check on Ben.

He entered the parking lot that served the dozen or so stores that made up the shopping center in which the Lerner Bakery—the "new" Lerner Bakery, flanked at the moment by a hair salon and a drugstore (neighboring businesses came and went: only the Lerner Bakery was a constant)—had stood for nearly thirty years. The delivery van was parked at the far end of the lot, which meant that Nelson had finished his deliveries, had taken the bus back home. Through the bakery window Mickey could see Benjie and Morris behind the counter, handling a line of customers. He watched his son for several minutes—the

bagging of goods, the explanations to cranky customers—and lapsed
for a moment into memories of his own first days on the job under
Morris's frowning eye. In a certain way, the world hadn't really
changed at all.

Satisfied that things were okay, Mickey headed over to Chen's Garden. He'd been going there forever, it seemed; the Garden was an
institution. Mickey sometimes mused that he and his friends could
have kept the place in business by themselves; between them, they'd
consumed enough noodles and duck and wonton soup to feed a starv-
ing country, and Benjie had practically cut his teeth on the spareribs.
But it had been a long while since he'd gone there to dine socially;
Emi had never been too crazy about the fellas—Joe, Marv, Buddy
Grossman—and somewhere along the way Mickey had reluctantly
withdrawn himself from the group, as if to prove to Emi that she'd
been right about him, that he *was* different, more enlightened, more
visionary than the crowd with whom he'd grown up.

Mickey parked in front and went in. Ah, that warm, greasy smell.
He took a seat on one of the red-cushioned benches, where several
black customers were awaiting their food with bored expressions.
Back in the dining room, which could be glimpsed through an en-
tranceway festooned with garish Oriental tinsel, potted plants and
long, contorted plaster dragons (their mouths open as if to attack, a
strange welcome), Mickey could hear the din of voices, of forks, of
the hot metal vessels that concealed, under hot domelike lids, a florid
hodgepodge of ingredients, bright and gleaming, the ungodly combination of things, the fabulous perversions of the wok.

He then heard, from the depths of the restaurant, a familiar laugh.
Joe? Mickey stood and walked to the threshold of the dining room, at
the back of which he saw, sure enough, Joe Blank, seated at a table
decorated with steaming platters of food. Joining Joe were Buddy
Grossman, Marv Kandel, Marv's lady friend Bernice Stein and another
woman whom Mickey didn't recognize. Mickey felt a start of excitement, and then, almost immediately, a sinking despair. He wanted to
be with them, to share in their crude gossip, their dirty jokes. He felt
lonely, weak. The past beckoned, just as it had this morning; it was as
though he were on the verge of a dramatic life change—a move, an
affair—and in his fear had gone rushing back to what he knew best.
But what change? What fear? Granted, things weren't great at home,
but in a world of failed marriages, of estrangements and broken ties,
he could hardly be said to be miserable. Still, there was a definite sense
of crisis, and for the second time that day—it had happened this

morning, driving Donna Childs down to Cathedral Street—Mickey found himself in something of a panic, wanting more than anything to get home to his wife.

He returned to the red benches, wondering if he ought to forget the food and just hightail it home, but before he could make up his mind he heard his name, and a moment later Joe was standing over him, fingering a stained handkerchief.

"Didn't you see us back there? Jesus, you look like hell."

"Joe."

"Christ, what's it been, a month? Two months?"

"Something like it."

"You used to look like a Greek god," Joe said. "Now you look like a goddamned Greek."

Mickey laughed; it was an old joke between them.

"Come on back to the table, we got dragon turds and pigeon chow mein."

Mickey stood up, surprised at how glad he was to see his childhood friend. "Thanks," he said, "but I'm waiting for some carryout."

"You okay?" said Joe, studying Mickey with his small black eyes. He had a horseshoe of dark hair left on his head and a small, graying mustache. He'd been a handsome kid, tough and wiry, a good athlete. Coaches called him scrappy, a competitor. Now his forehead shone with the pent-up anger of a man beaten down to spousal obedience, a man who could be spotted at the grocery store, the mall, standing by in dark sunglasses while his wife talked on and on to one of her many friends, some of whom smiled at Joe with luridly painted mouths. Across his brow, a long vein raged like lightning.

"I'm fine. Just a little tired. Trying to get the store ready for the holidays."

"How's everyone? Morris?"

"They're fine. Emi's going to Paris next month." Despite his age-old resentment over Emi's travels—the names of cities were like the names of other men—Mickey took a secret pleasure in describing her itinerary to friends and customers, most of whom responded eagerly to the sounds of distant places, and tended to lavish their awe on the speaker.

"Paris, huh?" said Joe, trying hard not to betray his wonder. He looked straight into Mickey's eyes, as if challenging him to draw comparisons between their wives. "Well," he said, softening his features into a picture of sad resignation, of surrender, "must be nice, having a wife who's gone half the time." He laughed, as if at his own comic

misery—the endless nagging, the motherly reminders ("Put a hat on,
you'll catch a cold!"), the inevitable heap of flesh snoring and farting
beside him in bed each and every morning—but Mickey heard, beneath the surface of this, a distinct pity, the slow shake of the head for
the emptiness in Mickey's life, an emptiness that should have been
filled, as Joe's was filled, with the homely pleasures of one's autumn
years: breakfast on Sunday, the groceries carried in; pleasures within
whose small, simple core lay the very seed of happiness.

Mickey scoffed inwardly at this notion; the litany of workaday
blessings struck him as bleakly conventional, a bore. Yet he submitted,
nodding in agreement like a defeated man ("Yes, it's true," he seemed
to be saying, "your life *is* better than mine"), not so much to gratify his
friend as to enjoy the spectacle of his delusions. Poor Joe. Time and
again, and in so many carefully chosen words, he'd denounced Emi as
a subversive, an elitist, the original duplicitous woman; and the only
thing that stopped Mickey from defending her—aside from his sense
that Joe was trying to provoke him into exactly the sort of inelegant
response (a punch in the mouth?) to which his marriage purported
him superior—was his even greater sense that Joe, in some dark, ail-
ing region of his heart, was and always had been painfully in love with
her. And why not? Her talent, her European bearing, her small, delicious fame; but of course. It was obvious.

"You going with her?" Joe said, his tone intimate, concerned, nudg-
ing gently at the idea of Emi's infidelity. "To Paris?"

Mickey laughed: Joe had him there. Mickey Lerner never went anywhere; the bakery couldn't run without him, at least not for any extended period of time. He was needed here; he had a business to run.
"Maybe next time," he said, and shrugged carelessly to demonstrate an
unshakable trust in his wife.

Joe looked askance. "So how you been?" he said.

"Good," said Mickey. He felt like talking. "Well, maybe not so good.
This is always a crazy time of year. After the garden dries up, I hardly
know what to do with my hands." He became aware of those hands—
stupid, useless things! He put them in his pockets. "It's strange. I don't
know."

"Take up smoking," Joe said.

"Maybe I will."

Joe laughed. "Think I'll step out for one now." He pulled a pack of
Kents from his shirt pocket. "Join me?"

They went outside and stood under the red neon sign, gazing at the traffic, the stars, the lights of service stations and fast-food huts. Then came a sound of sirens approaching from the east, the sources of which sped past in a shriek of metal—one, two, three squad cars—and diminished into tiny lights shooting off in the wide sea of road. The men turned their heads in unison, watched until the cars were out of sight.

Mickey said, "Guess where I went this morning?"

Joe put a cigarette in his mouth, cupped the lighter around his hands. There was a click, a spark; smoke leaked from between his fingers. "Where?"

"Down Percy Street."

Joe blew smoke from the side of his mouth. "What the hell for?"

"Had some business to take care of."

"Selling crack?"

"How'd you guess?"

"That's the only business they got down there."

Mickey laughed. "I wouldn't go that far," he said. It was an old conversation, one for which Mickey was often grateful: if ever he felt himself lapsing into the popular attitudes to which he'd always believed himself immune—the fear and hatred of the blacks—he had only to chat with Joe to regain his footing. "They're not all teenage mothers and criminals," he said, referring to Joe's favorite depictions. "Some of them actually have jobs."

"Hold on now," said Joe. "Remember who you're talking to. I had shvartzes working for me thirty years ago, long before you did."

"Sure, thirty years ago. What about now?"

"Now? You kidding?" Joe shook his head. "These shvartzes today— once you hire one, you're stuck, for better or worse. Mostly worse. *You* know how it is. Don't you got one driving the van? Young fella?"

"Know how *what* is?" Mickey said.

"You know—telling 'em what to do. Being their goddamned boss." Joe examined the bright tip of his cigarette. "They all got a chip on their shoulder, you know that as well as I do. You can't even make a criticism without the NAACP jumping in." He rubbed his temple. "And God forbid you should fire one of these characters—it could mean your life."

There was a silence, in which Mickey tried to imagine what might happen if he did in fact fire Nelson. He could hardly picture it; he'd never fired anyone in his life.

"Remember that fella from the Quickee Mart?" Joe said. "The manager, white fella? And how the bastard he fired came back the next morning and shot him in the head, right in front of his three-year-old kid? Remember?"

"Things happen," Mickey said. "What can you do?"

"They'll shoot you for nothing," said Joe. "In a heartbeat they'll shoot." The vein in his head was pulsing, lighting up; he sipped his cigarette, seeking relief, then watched calmly as the wisdom of his smoke was torn apart by the chill night air. "So," he said. "What exactly were you doing down on Percy? What kind of business?"

"Business?" Mickey rubbed his chin. Joe wasn't too familiar with Nelson, with Donna; nor did he know the details about the match with Thomas Childs: he'd been away that summer, working for his uncle in Jersey, and by the time he returned, Mickey was firmly entrenched at the Lerner Bakery (he'd taken over for his father, who'd died of a heart attack just a day before the fight), and was trying his best—it wasn't easy—to put the memory of the fight behind him. It was, Mickey now decided, too long a story: Tommy Childs, Donna, the situation with Nelson and Ben; he wouldn't have even known where to start. He said, "Well, not business, exactly. I just—I don't know. I just wanted to go down there, see what it was like. It's been years. I mean, that's where I grew up—where we all grew up. Lot of memories there."

"Memories?" Joe drew smoke, blew two angry tusks through his nostrils. "Those days are gone. Let 'em go, is what I say. We got what, ten good years left, fifteen if we're lucky? Who's got time for memories? Christ, the doctor could stick his finger up my ass next week and tell me it's all over. You been checked lately?"

"Last month."

"Listen, forget Percy Street," said Joe. He dropped his cigarette to the ground, crushed it with his shoe. "We've got enough problems here already. I can't even walk out of my own house anymore."

"I walk out of mine every day."

"Sure. At your own risk."

"You can't live in fear," Mickey said.

Joe looked at Mickey, narrowed his eyes. "I used to think you just had your head in the clouds," he said. "But now I'm not so sure."

"No?"

"I think you're afraid to admit your true feelings," Joe said. "Scared to. What do you think of that?"

"What do *you* think?"

"Me?" Joe spat on the pavement. "I think there's nothing wrong with being pissed off. You go to work, you bust your ass, you pay your taxes. You didn't ask for this. All this crap going on. You go about your life in an honest way, and the next thing you know, some shvartze jumps from behind a car, puts a gun to your head and pulls the trigger. This is unheard of in other countries."

"I think my order's ready," Mickey said.

"Know what I did last week? Applied for a gun license."

"A gun?"

"Goddamned right."

"Well, it's a constitutional privilege."

"Ever thought about it?"

Mickey laughed. "Your food's getting cold."

"Have you?"

"Sure. Every day."

"You never learn."

"I've learned plenty."

They went into the restaurant. A big brown bag with a receipt stapled to it lay on the carryout counter.

"Come back and say hello," Joe said.

"That's okay," said Mickey. "I'd better get home."

Joe nodded his understanding. "Well. If you ever wanna mix with us 'common people,' you know where to find us."

"Ha, ha."

"So long," Joe said. He turned and headed back to his table.

Mickey paid for his food. Expensive. Had prices gone up? He received his change, refusing to glance back at Joe's table. The bag was heavy, warm. He could hear their laughter.

He clutched the bag to his chest and inhaled.

Back home, he removed the contents of the bag and dumped them onto a plate, thinking that if Joe's attempt to seduce him into some sort of outburst against the blacks was any indication of what he'd have had to endure had he joined the whole crowd back at their table, he was sure glad to be in his own house, even if it meant dining alone, even if it meant—and it wasn't too harsh a word, for he hated dining alone—being miserable. And wasn't that proof enough of where he stood on the race question, that he'd sooner be miserable than listen to a bunch of loudmouths?

Still, he wished he'd have defended his position more strongly. But to what end? People like Joe, they never changed. No: they bought guns. They moved to the wilderness. Mickey concluded that it would have been a waste of breath.

He was almost finished eating when Ben came through the kitchen door. Mickey sat up.

"How'd it go?" he said.

"Fine," said Ben.

"No problems?"

"No."

"Everything go okay with Nelson? He get all his deliveries done okay?"

"As far as I know."

"Good." In the wake of Joe's rantings, Mickey felt inclined to be more generous with regard to Nelson. "Good," he said again. He decided not to press for any more details—it was enough that no emergencies had cropped up, no disasters. And best of all, Benjie didn't even seem resentful; you'd even have thought, by looking at him, that he'd actually enjoyed his day at work, had actually taken a little pride in what he'd done.

"G'night," said Ben. He walked out of the kitchen.

Mickey listened to the kid's footfalls on the stairs, the closing of his door. In a moment, he figured, the computer would go on, and Ben would lose himself in the druggy depths of the screen.

By 9:45, Mickey was champing at the bit. The dishes were washed, the newspaper was in pieces. He couldn't wait much longer. Emi's playing seemed to be winding down; she always ended her sessions with exercises, and Mickey could recognize one of them now. He opened the basement door.

The music stopped. She had heard him coming. When he arrived at the bottom step, he found that the salad bowl he'd set out earlier was empty.

"All gone," Emi said.

Mickey looked at her. She was seated in her chair, luminous with the hours she'd put in. He could tell that it had been a good session.

She smiled at him. "You're early," she said.

"Am I?"

"What did you do?"

"Not much. Got some carryout from the Garden." He approached her. "Benjie's home."

"What did you have?"

"The usual."

Emi put down her bow and pushed the music stand away.

"You sure about this?" Mickey said. "I mean, we could go upstairs."

"Hush."

Mickey laughed. He stood in front of her, watched as her fingers unbuckled his belt. This would be good, he thought, just what the doctor ordered. She unbuttoned his trousers, pulled on the zipper. He closed his eyes and felt her reach in. He placed his hands on her shoulders, then removed them without knowing why. It was to be a balancing act: no hands, just him floating there; a new sensation. He heard her spit into her palms and rub them together. Those hands: such valuable things, reduced to this! The idea thrilled him: instantly he was hard.

"Hey," she said. "Ve-ry nice."

She gripped him, slid her hands along his length. With her tongue she teased the tip.

"Jesus," Mickey said. His mind scrambled for a fantasy image, a woman, someone he'd seen, someone he'd thought of once, a celebrity, a customer, but before he could think of anyone there came a noise from the top of the stairs.

"Shit!" Mickey whispered. He turned away and struggled with his prick as the footsteps came closer.

"Mom?" came Ben's voice. "Can I come down?" He had stopped on the middle of the stairs; he could see nothing.

"Benjie!" Emi said. "Have you heard of knocking?"

"I did. Nobody answered."

Emi sighed.

"Is Dad down there too?"

"What is it?" Mickey called, buttoning his pants. His prick had shrunk to nothing. Goddamned kid. Like a dog, he'd sensed something, a food, a danger, had intruded without fully knowing why. "Benjie?"

"Can I come down?" said Ben, his voice betraying, to Mickey's surprise, a respectful caution, a new awareness of things. In a flash, Mickey considered that the kid maybe had a girlfriend, was balling her during the day, right here in the house, or no, in *her* house—God forbid!—without a rubber, and with her parents—decent, respectable people—pulling up in the driveway, home early, unexpectedly.

"What is it?" Mickey said.

Ben seemed to take this as an invitation to enter the room, and Mickey did his best to look like a man in the midst of a serious discussion with his wife, who, for her part, pulled the music stand back to its original space and made a small production out of turning the pages.

"Yes?" said Mickey.

Ben stood at the bottom of the stairs, looking at his parents, at the room, as if for evidence of sexual conspiracy. He said, "I meant to tell you—I had to throw away all the onion bread. Mold all over the bottom. Luckily, no customers saw it."

It was, Mickey knew, a jab. He tended to go a little too far sometimes in stretching a product's shelf life, and while he was happy to find that Ben was taking at least *some* interest in the bakery, the timing for this announcement could not have been worse.

"Thanks," Mickey said, feeling a soft pearl roll down his hairy, trembling leg. "Now if you don't mind, your mother and I are having a conversation."

"Okay," Ben said, and lingered a moment before walking over to Emi and bending to kiss her cheek.

This was notable, Mickey thought: aside from being at an age where displays of affection toward one's parents are virtually taboo, Ben had always been shy with Emi, and even as a child had never been one to jump into her arms. But what was even more unusual about the whole thing was Emi's reaction: she received the kiss without a hint of surprise, almost imperially, like an ancestress immobile in her chair; as if—and here Mickey allowed for something of the mystical— as if she had somehow drawn him to her, or as if Ben, alert, had intuited in her some obscure pulse of urgency. They were, after all, mother and child, filled with their own biological intrigues, and Mickey, his loins moaning, his entire body anticipating the moment when Ben would go, disappear, be gone, could only stand there dumbstruck as Emi, watching as Ben moved toward the stairs, called out to him in a voice tense with purpose.

"Benjie," she said. "Your computer. Didn't you tell me you had a new program, a game?"

Ben turned to her. "Yeah," he said. "It's called *Empire.*" He seemed baffled by her interest, excited by it. "Why? You want to play?"

"Well—"

"It's fun," Ben said, and as he began to describe the game in a rapid, rambling speech, as though Emi's attention were a scrap of paper that must be weighted down with words, with detail, and went on about the nations he had conquered, the provisions he had made, Mickey, his fists in his pockets, faded back into shadow, watching as Emi lav-

ished the kid with a steady, prodding gaze and quick nods of understanding, eliciting wave upon wave of information.

It was like a crime, an act of violence Mickey was helpless to stop.
He'd taken Emi to task enough times about her lack of involvement
in Ben's life—he'd alluded to it just this morning in the garden—and
now he could do nothing. It was clear: she meant to avoid him at all
costs. She was wriggling out of their date, and using Benjie to do it.

Finally, Ben exhausted himself and went upstairs, but not before se-
curing a promise from Emi to come up in a few minutes and see his
game. Mickey noticed that Ben didn't even acknowledge him as he
left the room.

He turned to Emi, who looked up at him as if wanting to be praised
for her good works.

She said, "I told you. He's learning a lot with the computer. You
make it sound like such a toy."

"Cut the bullshit," Mickey said.

"What bullshit?"

"Cut it!" Mickey caught himself, lowered his voice. "What was that
all about? All that nodding and phony interest?"

"Phony? How can you say that?"

"You could give a crap, and now, all of a sudden—"

"That's not fair."

"Forget what's fair. You're avoiding me. Why?"

"How am I avoiding you?" said Emi. "I'm right here."

"Are you?"

"I promised him I'd look at his game. What am I supposed to do?"

"Nothing. You're absolutely right. Go. Go up now."

"Mickey."

"Go ahead, he's waiting. Been waiting all his life."

"You're being unreasonable."

"Oh. I see," said Mickey. "*I'm* the unreasonable one."

"You're being absolutely selfish."

Mickey laughed, a wretched, maniacal laugh. Selfish! Who was she
kidding? He felt insane with laughter; he was dealing with a mad-
woman, and she was making him crazy too.

Emi picked up her violin, began turning pages. "I think," she said,
"that you'd better go."

Mickey stopped laughing. He was not about to be ordered from a
room in his own house. "Tell me," he said.

"Tell you what?"

Mickey felt himself shaking. "Who. Tell me who you're screwing."

"Mickey."

"Who!"

"Calm down."

"So it's true?"

"You're not calm."

Mickey touched his head. "I don't believe this." He felt sick, weak; he thought he might fall to his knees.

"I told you this morning," Emi said. "I told you what was wrong. Or weren't you listening?"

"What," said Mickey. "The concerts? David Shaw? That's the cause of all this? I'm supposed to believe that?"

Emi said nothing.

"Why can't I touch you?" said Mickey. "Why? Why don't you want me?"

He watched her, sitting there, tight-lipped as a frightened little girl. He knew. She was bored, she was dissatisfied, she was fifty-two years old and in need of new validation, however temporary. Or maybe she had fallen in love—"one of those things," no one to blame; or had fallen out of it, again no one's fault. These were the potential hazards Mickey had lived with all his married life. Why, then, should it come as such a shock?

He hung his head. She was his chief accomplishment in life; her love had distinguished him. He was headed for loneliness, oblivion, and already he could hear the talk, the whispers around the table at Chen's Garden.

"It's not what you think," Emi said.

Mickey looked at her: her face was in her hands, the violin on her lap.

"What do I think?" Mickey said.

"I'm not," Emi said, "in love. That's ridiculous."

"You don't have to be in love."

"There's no one else. I'm just not happy with myself right now. My playing. It's shit. And I can't do anything until I fix it."

Mickey considered this. There had, he conceded, been times over the years when she'd become so frustrated—a flaw in her technique, her intonation—that she began to see herself as physically repulsive, a filthy, diseased creature unworthy of affection. But in those cases, the frigidity, if that's what it was, had lasted for no more than a few days; she'd always recover herself quickly.

"I want the truth," Mickey said. "You owe me that much."

Emi closed her eyes. "I owe you everything," she said, without irony; and then, as if in finality: "I'm tired."

Mickey nodded. In a certain way, the details didn't matter. She was—she'd just said it—tired. Of him, of everything. Oh, there was probably someone else; these things were always brought on by others. Mickey considered that her resistance to him was rooted less in a lack of desire than in a fear that, in bed, she'd give herself away, reveal with her body what she didn't want him to know. And in her sudden interest in Ben, which she claimed was sincere, Mickey saw more than just a way for her to avoid her husband: it seemed to confirm beyond a doubt that she was planning to leave, to go away forever.

Mickey felt a sickness heaving upward from his bowels. "Goddamn you!" he shouted. His fists were clenched so tight at his sides that the fingernails had dug into the palms. "Goddamn you!"

Emi began to weep softly into her hands, as though in confession of her sins. Mickey awaited her defense, but none came: there was nothing more to say. Mickey couldn't bear to look at her. He turned and ran upstairs, propelled himself through the rooms to the back door and out into the cold, starry night, under whose faint light he began to cry, kneeling by the stems whose heads had been cut off, his mind reeling, spiraling backward to the day he met her, a day that he now cursed, even as he cherished it as the sweetest in all his years.

She had come into the bakery wearing a brown scarf around her forehead, a large silver hoop in one ear, a zebra-striped dress (short, tight, and probably not much help against the March wind that blew cigarette butts and gum wrappers across North Avenue) and black boots to her knees. With the stripes and the high boots and the long dark hair, she was insistently vertical, and appeared taller than she really was. Mickey watched her, not too critically. The Lerner Bakery normally didn't attract her type—hipsters, mods, or whatever they called them—but Mickey had learned from his father that when someone walked through that door, all the things that tended to set people apart remained outside in the street: that person was no longer Jew or Gentile, black or white, this or that. He was a customer. A friend.

"May I please have six poppy-seed rolls?" the young woman said. Something in her voice told Mickey she wasn't from around here; there was a hint of accent, he thought, foreign, something she was losing, or else taking up, affecting. She couldn't have been more than twenty-five.

"Where are you from?" Mickey said. His back was to her as he bagged the rolls.

"France," she said.

"France." Now that was something. A French girl in the Lerner Bakery. This was an event, a first. Mickey wished he had something to add to the idea—an anecdote about France, a little fact that would demonstrate his knowledge—but he'd never been to her country and had no real impressions of it, though certainly he was aware—acutely aware, now—of the reputation of Paris as a world capital of baking. He welcomed the challenge. "So," he said. "What are you doing here in Baltimore?" He pronounced it in the local, folksy way—*Bawlmer;* in the face of her worldliness it seemed he could do nothing but play the cheerful yokel. "Don't you know they call this place Nickel Town? Mob Town?" He felt loose, proud, full of pluck and good humor. "Sure you didn't take a wrong turn somewhere?"

"I'm here to study music," she said. "The Wurther Conservatory?"

"Ah." Mickey nodded. The Wurther. That explained it. The Wurther was one of the city's jewels, drawing people from all corners of the globe. "What instrument?" he said, turning to place the bag on the glass counter. "Wait, don't tell me." He set his elbows on the glass and pretended to appraise her. "Let's see. The violin?"

She flashed a look of surprise, delight. "Yes," she said. "How did you know?"

"How?" Mickey stood up straight; he was now a man of subtlety, of keen observation. "You just—look like it," he said, and though he didn't quite know how to explain himself (what did a violinist really look like, after all?) he could nevertheless picture her in a chair, her feet planted aggressively in a kind of musical stride, her back arched like that of a dancer. He noted her small hands (too small, it seemed, to command a keyboard) and the strange exposed quality—the eye was drawn to it—of her long white neck, with its faint veins branching up to the tiny fruit of her chin, her nose, her red mouth. Her face was round as a moon and she had shiny, silvery coins for eyes; you could almost hear them jingle when she smiled.

"I *look* like it?" she said. "Why?"

"You just do."

"Looks cannot always be trusted," she said. She reached out and took one of his hands in her own, his right hand, examined it as though it were apart from him. Mickey dared not move, and hoped to

God that none of his regular customers came in. No telling what they'd make of it. "These," she said. "The hands. They tell the real story, I think. You have a very interesting hand."

Mickey got the picture. The hoop earring, the schmatte around the head; she was a palm reader. "Interesting?" Mickey said. He thought his hands downright ugly, a regular road map of bumps and calluses and scars from oven burns. Hers meanwhile looked smooth, intelligent, skilled, and bore no rings at all. At twenty-eight, Mickey had made it his business to notice rings.

"Yes," she said. "Interesting. And beautiful. All hands are beautiful; hands are the most beautiful part of the body. They make everything possible." She let his hand fall on the counter. "The hands tell about a person's life. More than the face or the eyes. You have honest hands. A workman's hands."

Mickey wasn't sure how to take that. "I guess I could never be a musician with these jobs," he said. He displayed his fingers, his fat knuckles. "Fact is," he said, "I messed them up pretty good from boxing."

"Boxing?"

"You know, like these fellas." He hooked his thumb behind him to indicate the framed pictures of the old-time fighters on the wall: Jackie Fields, Maxie Rosenbloom, Barney Ross. And of course Benny Leonard. Many of his customers got a big kick out of the pictures—those fighters had been their boyhood heroes: they could remember a time when Jewish fighters dominated the sport. From the beginning of the century until the dawn of World War II there was a Jewish champion just about every year, and in some years two or three champions. Nowadays, though, you'd be hard-pressed to find a single Jewish amateur; there were other, better ways to battle the goyim.

"You see?" she said. "Looks are deceptive. You don't have a face like a fighter."

Mickey laughed: it was true: his nose was on straight as a light switch. "I haven't fought in years," he said. "I trained a lot, but I quit after one fight."

"Why?" she said. "Were you hurt?"

Mickey shrugged one shoulder. "A little."

"And your opponent?"

"My opponent," said Mickey. He grinned. "Ah, my opponent." The ghost of sexual possibility—more than ghost: a fragrance, a pollen—had stirred the braggart in him, and he regretted his words even as he spoke them. "Ever seen a hamburger before it's cooked?" he said, despising his arrogance, sinking into it like a drunk in his own joyous mess. "That's what my opponent's face looked like by the end of the fight. Meat. Raw, ground beef."

"Aw nooo," she said.

"Aw yes," said Mickey. He smacked a fist into his hand to demonstrate the lightning of his attack. "Knocked him into another world." Forgive me, Tommy, he thought, I'm half-cocked from her perfume. It was as if the finest lavender were boiling softly under her skin.

"If you were so good," she said, "then why did you quit?"

"Ah." Mickey had a feeling she didn't believe him; probably she figured he'd been beaten, bloodied, frightened out of the game. Good, he thought. Maybe that absolved him somehow. He said, "Quit, why did I quit? Hmm. Well, there's a few reasons."

"Tell me."

"It's boring."

"I want to hear," she said.

Mickey felt his nerves clanging. He wasn't used to this kind of attention. He gathered himself. "For one thing," he said, "my father died. A day before my fight, believe it or not." It must have sounded utterly contrived, this untimely death, but Mickey was the kind of person who was entirely believable, not so much for his having practiced honesty all his life as for the sense, among those who knew him, that he simply lacked the wit to lie successfully. Mickey was aware of this opinion, but never exploited the interesting opportunities that it afforded him; it was enough to know that he could, at any time he wished, bring off an absolute whopper. "I should have never fought that day," he said, and ten years after the fact he could not be sure which guilt weighed more heavily upon him—the guilt over his father, or the guilt over what happened in the ring. "I thought I was being brave, I guess. But if I could do it over . . ." He gazed out the store window at the cars passing on North Avenue.

The young woman looked up at him. "I'm sorry," she said, as if she understood everything, even the things he had yet to tell her. "But you know, you cannot change the past."

Mickey met her eyes. Her sympathy seemed so pure, so rich with the promise of consolation that Mickey had a mind to tell her everything. Despite himself (he hated to add to the gloom, already he missed her smile) he went on, in hopes of drawing her further into his history. "He started this bakery twenty-five years ago," he said. "From nothing. My father was a self-made man. That phrase is used a lot, I know, but in my father's case it was true. He made himself. He opened

a business and earned a living. It was his dream to pass the business on
to me, and for me to pass it on to my children. And so when he died
I had to choose right then and there. To keep the business or sell it.
Boxing or baking." He shrugged. "I couldn't sell it. And so here I am."

He could hardly believe that he'd just given his life story to a total
stranger, but then maybe that's what a yokel shopkeeper was supposed to do.

"And your children?" she said. "You will pass it to them?"

"That's a little ways down the road yet," said Mickey. "I'm not even
married."

"No?" The young woman tilted her head slightly, as if to find the
flaw in him, the clue. "And why is that?"

"Circumstances," Mickey said. But why go into it? It had always
stung him that the women he'd longed for in high school—the tennis
princesses, the college-bound bobby-soxers—had written him off as a
baker's son, a hunk, unmarriageable; and Mickey, who for years had
watched these girls from the lesser corners of diner parking lots and
gymnasium dance floors, was relieved to find, when one of them came
into his store, that what had attracted him most at sixteen—their
tanned, lean bodies, their laughter, the leggy confidence with which
they strode onto athletic fields in their jouncy, light-blue uniforms—
had now, ten and twelve years later, all but vanished into the creases
and folds of a too-early motherhood; they'd become worn, bereft of
that youthful spark. How they flirted with him, now!

"Circumstances, you say?" said the young woman. "Perhaps it is just
bad luck?"

"Perhaps. How about you?"

"Me?" She averted her eyes. "Oh, very bad luck. I was with a man
very crazy. One reason I am here: to get away. You cannot change the
past, but that does not mean you must be a slave to it. I do not look
back; only forward."

"You mean you ran away from home?"

"What home? I do not believe in this idea of home. Home is something inside of you." All at once she seemed young, scared. "A home,"
she said, "can be anywhere."

"Do your parents know where you are?"

"I do not have parents," she said, and sighed, as if reluctant to go further but feeling obligated to meet his candor with her own. "My
mother died when I was a young girl," she began, "and my father—"
she raised her eyebrows and blew air from her lower lip—"my father
does not exist for me." She shrugged. "And so."

"Why?" Mickey said. "Why doesn't he exist?"

"You are a curious one. Do you always ask so many questions?"

"Did he . . . hurt you?"

"He hurt many people. During the war he was with the police. He did many bad things."

Mickey nodded; he had a fuzzy idea of what she meant, but didn't want to expose his ignorance by asking. "Well," he said. "You're here now."

"Yes."

Mickey felt his heart beating. He wanted to tell her more, tell her about his mother's illness and death, his father's heart attack, but in light of her foreign dramas his own life seemed small, his losses petty. Still, their exchange of histories thrilled him; it was like a commitment to some deeper involvement.

"So," he said, hoping to brighten things up. "I never got your name."

"My name? It's Emilie. People call me Emi."

"Emi. That's nice."

"And you?"

"People call me Mickey."

"Mickey?"

"Ya know. Like Mickey Mantle."

She wrinkled her brow.

Mickey scratched his head. "How about Mickey Mouse?" He grabbed two round pumpernickel loaves and held them to his ears.

Emi put her hand over her mouth and laughed like a child. Mickey felt his confidence rise. He wished he had one of those long French breads—a baguette—so that he could grip it like a Louisville Slugger and explain Mickey Mantle. He set down the loaves. "If you ever go to New York," he said, "that's where Mantle is. Plays for the Yankees."

"I love New York. I was just there."

"Hell of a town," said Mickey. He declined to mention that he'd never been there.

"There was a big manifestation," said Emi.

"A what?"

"You know—many people coming together. To protest."

"A demonstration."

"Yes, a demonstration. Against the war. I thought maybe this is the reason you are not in Vietnam—because in your boxing match, you were hurt. Perhaps you suffer from something of the brain, I don't know what. But something. And so you cannot go."

Mickey laughed. "Well, that's an interesting idea. But the truth is, I'm too old."

"Old?"

"I'm almost thirty."

"Thirty? You look younger."

"Like you said. Looks are deceptive."

"You see, it's true. Do you support the war?"

Mickey laughed, he wasn't sure why. "I can't believe how well you speak English," he said. "You speak better than a lot of Americans I know."

"This is not an answer."

"I love my country," Mickey said. "How's that?"

Emi smiled. "But you can love something and disagree with it at the same time, yes?"

"I guess you're right," said Mickey. The last thing he wanted was to get involved in a political discussion; he wasn't equipped, and he knew she sensed it. "So where did you learn such good English?" he said.

"Oh, it's not so good. But I spent some years in England."

"I can't imagine. To speak a whole other language."

"I prefer to speak with music."

"Music is a language too, as far as I'm concerned."

"Would you like to hear me play?"

Mickey felt a chill. "You mean—the violin?"

"This Sunday, at eight in the evening. I'm playing in a concert at Lubin Hall, at the Wurther. Do you know it?"

"Sure," said Mickey. He didn't, but he'd find out. "Lubin Hall."

"Would you like to come?"

Mickey scratched his head. "Sure." He'd never attended a symphony concert, though he'd seen a few programs on television—the Boston Pops, he believed it was, and some performances with Victor Borge, whom he thought was terrific. He also owned a few LPs—The Tijuana Brass, Brazil '66, Bobby Darin—and could appreciate a good dance number. As for modern rock music, he was in accord with Uncle Morris, who often complained that you couldn't walk down the street these days without passing some long-haired kid blaring his (or her, you couldn't be too sure) transistor radio. "Sure," he said again.

"Then I will see you," said Emi. "For the moment I must go."

Mickey swallowed. "Okay," he said, turning on a friendly smile. "Aul revere."

"*Au revoir.* How much do I pay?"

"It's on the house," Mickey said.

"The house?"

"A gift. Free. Go ahead." Mickey handed her the bag of rolls, and was stunned by her reaction; she smiled and turned three shades of red, and damned if her eyes didn't get a little watery. It's just bread, he wanted to tell her, not flowers. Mickey figured she wasn't used to people being nice.

"Thank you very much," she said. She gave a slight bow, then walked out.

Mickey watched her go to the curb and put out her thumb. Within seconds she had a ride.

He thought of her for the rest of the afternoon, forgetting customers' names, screwing up their change, losing track, so that by day's end the register was off by three or four dollars.

He arrived at the concert hall a good twenty minutes before show-time, wearing his best suit, the one he'd bought at Hutzler's three years ago for Joe Blank's wedding. People had told him he looked like a million bucks in it, and Mickey was satisfied that it struck just the right note for the Wurther.

It was an old building, full of marble columns and stairwells, frescoes of harp-plucking cherubs, narrow academic corridors and crumbling statuary. Lubin Hall was on the main floor. Despite his fine clothes, Mickey was a little nervous about what to do with himself around all these highbrow types, not wanting to make a *faux pas*, such as betraying shock when told the price of the tickets, or doing something foolish with an hors d'oeuvre during intermission. As it turned out, the tickets weren't that outrageous—no more than he'd pay to sit on the fifty-yard line and watch the Colts. He entered Lubin Hall, a small, intimate space that reminded him of an old-time movie theater, and took a seat toward the back.

The place filled up. Mickey estimated two hundred people.

The house lights went down. There was a grand piano in the middle of the stage. Nearby was a single music stand and a chair. Mickey checked the program that the usher had handed him. Brahms, the Three Violin Sonatas. Emilie Lutter, violin. David Shaw, piano.

It got quiet. The musicians entered: first came Shaw, a young, handsome, light-skinned Negro. He had a tall, swaying Afro and long sideburns; if he hadn't been dressed in a black tuxedo, Mickey thought, a few people in the audience might have run for cover. Maybe looks were deceptive—Emi did have a point there—but this Shaw was a dead ringer for one of those bold, assertive young blacks you saw on the news, waving weapons out the window of an occupied building on some godforsaken campus. Not that Mickey had anything against the colored asserting themselves. They had legitimate grievances. But still, the way they looked; they *wanted* you to be afraid of them. But he couldn't believe that of Shaw, who was now bowing deeply to the enthusiastic applause of the audience. Shaw had won respect the hard way. Bravo for him!

As Shaw took his place at the piano, Emi appeared, wearing a long black gown and a black scarf around her head. She carried a violin in one hand, a bow in the other. The applause was measurably louder for her. Mickey clapped as hard as he could, wanting her to hear him. She acknowledged the cheers with a nod. Could she see him? No; she was smiling into her own personal distance. Mickey felt a vague dread. She had changed, he realized. This wasn't the same girl who had come into the bakery. He didn't know this woman at all. She belonged to the world. She would have already forgotten him. And yet she had invited him here, she had touched his hand; she revealed things about herself and had nearly cried when he'd given her the bread.

The applause faded as she took her seat.

The music started. Mickey'd never heard anything like it. The violin sang a slow, persuasive song, plaintive but urgent, an idea excited by its own beauty. It seemed to be waging an argument against the hesitant, cautious nods from the piano; it coaxed the piano, lured it, really, bringing it to a unison passage that was like a sexual coupling; by the end, the piano was in full support, a convert, a strident believer, allowing the violin to conclude on a short but confident burst of notes, then two decisive strokes—one, two!—before an electric charge of silence. Mickey had been waiting for that moment—the music building inside him, and his sense of Emi's beauty, so confirmed by the music, also building—waiting so that he could be the first to spring from his seat and applaud with all his heart; and at the very instant Emi rested her bow, his hands flew out from him and clapped briskly together, with such force that it took several seconds for him to realize that his was the only clapping to be heard. He stopped as though he'd been struck with an arrow. Faces turned to him. He froze, horrified, then melted under the heat of his shame, slumping down in his seat.

Later, he would understand that he had applauded between movements, a mistake he would see others make in the years to come. At the moment, though, he was aware only that he had broken some sa-

cred law. He gripped his armrests. Faces turned back to the performers, who appeared unruffled. When the music resumed, Mickey
bowed his head. He dared not applaud again until everyone else applauded, and even then he clapped delicately.

But as the program went on, another thought occurred to him. Was
it possible that Emi and Shaw were a couple? On the face of it,
Mickey'd have thought not—you just didn't see that sort of thing
around here—but then you could never be sure with the French. They
had a certain reputation, Mickey seemed to recall hearing. The colored, too, were known for a brand of sexual license. But it was the way
they were playing together, these two musicians, that got Mickey
thinking. There was real passion there, a communication. They looked
at each other, nodded, cocked their heads to listen and responded
with flourishes of sound. They smiled, frowned, closed their eyes.
They were, Mickey saw, making love.

He sank into a mix of anger, jealousy, self-pity. Shaw, of all people!
What kind of woman carried on like that? Flirting, inviting him to her
concert, inducing him to stand for an hour in front of the mirror, fuss-
ing with his clothes; and then to be carrying on with this character. Not
that Mickey had anything against the races mixing; he believed in live
and let live, and equal rights for all. But somehow he'd been misled.

When it was over, bouquets of roses were launched from the first
few rows and landed at Emi's feet. She beamed, a basking diva.
Mickey was glad he forgot to buy flowers. He watched to see if she
and David Shaw would join hands as they took their bows. They
didn't. Was that a sign?

Heartened, Mickey rushed up the aisle and went outside. He loitered on the sidewalk, watching all the fancy people walk arm in arm
to their cars. If they only knew who he was—a personal guest of the
violinist! But the idea depressed him. How many others were here on
the same account—people whom she'd met during her day, talked
with, invited along? He felt like a fool. It was bad enough to have
clapped in the wrong place; now he was waiting for her, as if it were
possible that she'd come looking for him. He was prepared to be punished for his expectations, and already he could picture it: Emi and
Shaw, coming out together, hand in hand.

He then felt a tap on his shoulder: he turned: it was Emi, standing
there alone, wearing a long black coat. The scarf was gone, revealing a
broad, clear forehead that seemed obscene at first glance, like the chin
of a formerly bearded man. In her hand was a violin case. She smiled
at him. "So," she said. "Did you enjoy?"

Mickey felt his throat tighten up.

"Yes?" said Emi. "No?"

"You were terrific," Mickey said. He could hardly believe she was speaking to him; she was practically famous. "I liked it very much."

"Thanks," she said. "But it is Brahms who deserves more credit." She looked over at the stream of people heading toward their cars. "And my pianist as well."

Mickey tried to ignore that. The pianist was nowhere in sight; it was only them. But that could change. "You want to go get a drink maybe?" Mickey said, his voice rising like an adolescent's. "Or eat?"

Emi looked at him. "Eat," she said. "Yes. But maybe it is too late for the restaurants?"

Mickey looked at his watch. It was almost ten. They might be able to get a table at DeNitti's.

"Maybe," Emi said, "we could go to your bakery and have some cake. Can you have a coffee there?"

Mickey laughed. "No coffee, but I got cake, I got bread, I—hey, that reminds me. Did you ever get around to those rolls I gave you the other day?"

"Rules?"

"The rolls, the rolls. The bread. From the other—"

"Oh, yes, yes," she said, excited by her comprehension. She grabbed his arm. "The rolls. I am sorry. Yes. They were wonderful!"

"Really?"

"Yes. Because they came from you."

Mickey scratched his head. The language barrier allowed her to speak directly, without embarrassment; maybe she didn't even know what she was saying.

"Well, any time you're hungry, you should just drop by the Lerner Bakery."

"I'm hungry now."

"Well then," Mickey said. He led her to his car.

Emi did most of the talking. She'd just met David Shaw, she said; they'd rehearsed only a few times. He was an extremely intelligent and interesting man, she found, but also conceited and a bit of a snob. He longed for Europe and didn't seem to identify very much with current liberation movements.

"Good for him," Mickey said.

"Why good?"

"He's a free man."

"No," said Emi. "He only thinks he is."

"You can't tell a man what to believe," said Mickey. He was happy to encourage any wedge between Emi and Shaw, but there was a trick to doing it without antagonizing her. Mickey wasn't too sure he could bring it off. He said, "Lutter, huh?"

"Yes," she said. "But it is pronounced Loo-*tay*. It is a French word."

"Right." Mickey sighed, kept his eye on the road.

The bakery was pitch-black. Mickey parked in front. "Here we are," he said. He felt more at ease, being on his home turf.

They walked to the bakery door, which Mickey unlocked with a showy jingle of his keys. Did David Shaw, for all his brains and dash, have his very own business? Mickey thought not. He turned on the lights.

Emi smiled and took his hand in hers, running a finger over his calluses. "Where did you get these?" she said.

"From the rolling pin." He nodded at the worktable. "You know. The wood."

"They're nice."

The next thing he knew he was kissing her. Or rather, she was kissing him. And some kisser! She used her tongue, her teeth; it was all Mickey could do to keep up.

They licked and bit. Her gown was damp. She slipped her hands under his shirt and shuddered at the wall of muscle. He tensed his abdominals and arched his back, feeling strangely feminine in his movements, his seductiveness. He unbuttoned his shirt and threw it off. She pulled off his T-shirt and placed her hands on his pectorals, feeling their shape as though they were faces.

Somehow they ended up on the worktable, which was covered with a fine dusting of flour that always reminded Mickey of the rosin in the gym. Within moments they were white with it. Mickey raised Emi's gown and yanked off her underpants, oddly aware that he was responding to certain unspoken expectations of animal force, but wanting, at the same time, to surpass these expectations, to surprise her with other gifts, like the brute puncher who shows he can dance, run. With gardener's fingers he parted her skin and slowly lowered his tongue to a moisture that had gathered to itself countless particles of fugitive dust, the yeast of the air, catching and holding it like a sticky carnivorous plant, in whose secret warmth—Mickey could taste it— rose new life, a tangy culture nourished by a high cream of tidewater, the salt, it seemed, of her very soul. He licked incessantly, his hair in her fists, and when he'd summoned her hips from the table he straightened his back and let her unzip his pants. Dust flew to him.

She murmured in other languages; she cried his name. Mickey closed his eyes and concentrated. He would wait for her.

Afterwards, they beat clouds from each other.

Emi asked him to call a taxi to take her back to her "room." Mickey was too bewildered to protest—never had he made love so thoroughly, or climaxed with such violence—though certainly he would have been glad to drive her home. But something in her manner—the hint of a secret ruthlessness, evident in the slow movements of her hands as she pulled up her panties and brushed off her gown—humbled him; he felt a passionate loyalty growing in his heart, an exuberance of subordination. Maybe she had a man at home, Mickey thought, Shaw or someone else, and didn't want to chance an encounter. Mickey attempted to relish the role (his release seemed to have temporarily cured him of his jealousy), imagining himself a man of liaisons on an international scale. Surely it was better to be the lover than the sap. He zipped up his pants, tucked in his shirt and called a cab.

They returned to the front of the bakery, where Mickey fixed them some cake. They ate in a silence that was like the quiet between sonata movements; civilized, respectful, but tense with both the echoes of the moment before and the anticipation of what was to come.

When the taxi arrived, Emi kissed Mickey on the cheek. "I'll call you soon," she said. But when she walked out, Mickey had a feeling that he'd never hear from her again.

A day went by, two days, a week. Mickey fell into a state of depression. What had he been thinking? She had her life. He'd been an amusement, a local amusement. To relieve himself of his anguish he met Joe Blank for beer and crab cakes over at Bo Brooks and told him all that had happened, going so far as to say that even if she did call him, he'd turn her away as a matter of principle. "She's a French whore," Joe said, crushing a can of National on the table, and Mickey added some choice words of his own.

The very next day, Emi called. Right away she explained that she'd been up in Philadelphia for musical reasons, but Mickey knew that he would have forgiven her anyway. He'd never been so happy to hear a voice in all his life. Arrangements were made to meet for dinner in Little Italy that very evening. Mickey kept this new development to himself; he didn't need to hear any flak from Joe. Joe and Emi should be separated at all costs, Mickey thought; the two ideas were not compatible, and it even crossed his mind that Joe might somehow become a liability, should things get serious. But that was thinking too far

ahead; he had to prepare for his date. Emi, Emi. He sang the word as
he dressed. A spot of Brylcreem, a spritz of deodorant, a cool splash of
aftershave—*Em-i-lee!* On the way to the restaurant he bought a single
red rose, intent on covering their previous night of passion with the
muslin of courtship: dinner, conversation, a brief goodnight kiss. He
wanted her to feel he respected her, though he knew, too, that she
probably had little trouble—the French being what they were—with
making love to a complete stranger; and perhaps it was this alarming
fact that led him to pour out his life to her over wine and mussels and
crumbs of Italian bread, that he might somehow emerge from the fabric of so many names and faces.

But he would not have spoken so much had she not seemed so interested; she questioned him, sometimes like a reporter, sometimes
like a child, and listened carefully as he explored the limits of his
knowledge. At times he felt as though she saw him as a kind of representative sample, an authentic product of the region, the answer to
some romantic class fantasy at whose center lay a terrible guilt of privilege. Clearly she'd enjoyed the finer things in life, and Mickey knew
better than to try to impress her. She was easily fascinated, and despite
himself he offered what he knew she wanted: anecdotes of childhood,
of the boxing gym, of incidents at the bakery and the stories of certain
colorful customers he'd known, all spoken in a local dialect which
he'd never really heard in his speech until now.

She, on the other hand, was less forthcoming; if he asked her a
question about her past she'd turn it around—I am here to make a
new life, she'd say—and the next thing Mickey knew they were driving past the Percy Street row house where he grew up, with him
pointing out familiar addresses, the faded paint on brick façades, the
boundaries of football games waged in traffic, the fire hydrants whose
mouths had been opened to the heat of summers, their white jets
flooding the order of life, sending the debris of afternoons rushing
down the gutters.

The next month was grand. They were like young sweethearts—
they went to the movies (*Bonnie and Clyde* at the Westview—what
a picture!), established a table at DeNitti's. They held hands, took
walks in the woods. Mickey pointed out trees, flowers; Emi practiced
the names. They drove across the Chesapeake Bay to the Eastern
Shore, ate cherrystone clams in tiny colonial-style inns as late winter
storms whipped up in the distance. Emi had suggested taking him to
New York for a few days ("I'll show you the city," she said, "I have

friends in Greenwich Village")—an offer that signaled to Mickey, among other things, her intent, her desire, to sleep with him again. But Mickey wasn't able to juggle his schedule at the bakery, and besides, the idea made him nervous: the hotel room, the unfamiliar surroundings, her friends, would all have amounted to a test that he wasn't sure he was ready to pass, physically or intellectually. And while it pleased him to cite his important business doings as an excuse—he fed a community, after all, he couldn't just up and go—he was even more delighted to submit her idea to the future ("Maybe during the holidays," he told her, "in April"), to draw parentheses around days on a future page of the calendar. Yes, in April, during Passover; the bakery would be closed. They would go to New York, share a room, a bed. They shouldn't wait much longer than that. April would make a month since their episode on the bakery table; a whole month. That was enough, Mickey thought. They'd started over and done it right. The next time would be like the first time. Their restraint would be rewarded.

It was a Thursday afternoon in early April. Mickey was standing behind the counter, sleeves rolled to his elbows. Mrs. Applebaum was looking across at him.

"I'm sorry you find the crust too hard on your teeth, Mrs. Applebaum," Mickey said. "But people like a hard crust."

"People! What sort of people?"

The shop door opened. It was Emi.

Mickey lit up: this was a surprise. Maybe she'd come to tell him that she'd set things up for New York; they'd been planning to go the following week. "Excuse me, Mrs. Applebaum," Mickey said. "Morris'll take care of you."

Mickey walked around the counter and joined Emi at the door. They were out of earshot, but Mickey knew that his uncle was watching with a critical, mischievous eye. Morris had yet to be introduced.

"Mickey," Emi said. "I must speak with you." She was all business. Had something happened? A change of heart?

"What is it? How did you get here?"

"I took the bus."

Someone knocked at the window. It was Joe Blank. His white Rambler was double parked.

Mickey placed his hand on Emi's shoulder. "Excuse me a minute," he said. He'd known Joe since they were little kids, sneaking into The

Cluster to watch the westerns, and maybe only two or three times had he seen such an expression on Joe's dark, intense face. Always for a death.

Mickey went outside. "What is it?" he said, thinking that maybe something had happened to Joe's wife or kid.

"Didn't you hear?" said Joe, narrowing his small eyes.

"Hear what?"

Joe looked up and down the street. "You'd better close up the store and get the hell home," he said. "There's gonna be trouble."

"What is it?" said Mickey.

Joe lit a cigarette. "It's all over the radio," he said. "Somebody shot Martin Luther King. Killed him. The colored fellas down my place says it's gonna be murder around here."

"Jesus," said Mickey. No wonder Emi looked so upset, he thought. "Where did it happen? A white fella did it?"

"Bet on it," said Joe.

Mickey shook his head. "Son of a gun."

"I gotta go," said Joe. "I'll talk to you later." He hurried off to his car.

Mickey looked across the street. Where Klein's Shoes used to be, a group of six or seven Negroes stood around, drinking, carrying on as usual. The sky was a deep, day-ripened blue. A soft breeze picked up. Mickey inhaled: in spite of Joe's bad news, the air smelled sweetly of raw pavement, of sea spice from a crab house two blocks away, of spring and of new love.

He then heard a police siren, coming closer, screaming.

Joe's Rambler sped off.

Mickey went back into the bakery and made an announcement: "We're closing a little early tonight. Everybody out." Better safe, he thought.

"Everybody out?" said Mrs. Applebaum. "Is that any way to treat your customers?"

"I'm sorry, Mrs. A.," Mickey said. "It's nothing personal." He glanced at Emi, but she was looking out the window. "Everyone to the register."

"Your father, God keep him, should hear the way you speak. There was a man who knew from polite. Oy, how he used to walk the older ladies to the streetcar. A gentleman!"

Mickey hopped over the counter.

"What is it?" said Morris.

Another customer, a colored woman, looked at him.

"Take," Mickey said abruptly. "Everybody take what you want." He began grabbing bread from the shelves and stuffing it into bags; with Passover coming up, all this leavened bread would end up in the garbage anyhow, assuming he kept the store closed tomorrow.

Morris said, "What the hell's going on?"

Mickey looked at the colored woman, but could not meet her eyes. He pushed a bag into her arms. Without a word, she turned and walked out.

"What's the idea?" said Morris.

"Just take the money out of the register and the safe." He pushed more bags into the arms of the other customers.

"What do I need all this bread?" said Mrs. Applebaum. "It's going to be holiday already."

"So feed it to the birds," said Mickey.

There was a babble of questions and protests, but Mickey managed to herd everyone through the door. He felt a little foolish, acting on advice from Joe Blank, but it was too late now. "Sorry to inconvenience everyone," he said. He locked the door and displayed the CLOSED sign.

"Mickey, what is it?" said Emi.

"That's what I'd like to know," said Morris, dumping the register drawer into a money bag.

Mickey scratched his head. "Martin Luther King was—killed." He shrugged. "It could mean trouble."

Emi placed her hand over her mouth. Apparently this was the first she'd heard of it.

"I'll be damned," said Morris. "What's it going to be next?"

They left through the back way; Mickey's white Buick was parked there.

The balmy air had a cool underside to it, like the feeling you get when you remove a bandage.

Emi insisted that Morris sit in front.

"You'll come home with me," Mickey told her. He hadn't planned on bringing her to his house, not yet, but the situation seemed to demand it. The world had gone topsy-turvy. It was like being in a storm, a hurricane, like hearing word of approaching missiles. He wanted to hold her. This was life. There was fear, invigoration. He didn't want to be alone.

Morris turned around in his seat and held out his hand. "I'm Morris, by the way," he said. "The uncle."

"I'm Emilie."

Mickey started the engine.

"Where are you from?" Morris said.

"Many places. Mostly I am from France."

"Is that right?"

Morris had no use for the French—poodles to the Germans, he called them. He said, "I knew some fellas personally that landed on Normandy—one died in the water. They kept me back, though, on account of my eyesight. I helped build ships down there in the harbor. Ever heard of the *John W. Brown*?"

"She doesn't want to hear your life story, Morris."

"You think war is hell? You should spend an eighteen-hour day in a shipyard in the middle of January."

"Don't tell that to Sy Berman," said Mickey. Berman was a regular customer whose pecker was blown off in North Africa.

Morris turned on the radio. A voice said: ". . . had been in Memphis to lead protests on behalf of striking sanitation workers. President Johnson has—"

Mickey switched it off. "Not now," he said. He could be jealous of this news, he realized, jealous of its power over the emotions. He wanted Emi to himself.

"So, this is it," said Emi as they walked up the front steps. "Your *château*." They had just dropped Morris off at his house near the racetrack.

"Yup," said Mickey. "Ten years ago, when my father died, I had a choice. Sell it or keep it."

She said, "I love the look of bricks."

Mickey laughed. "I could show you some houses." He imagined leading her on a little tour of the city—all those Victorian row houses of brick and stone, the church steeples and cupolas and conical turrets of corner houses blackened like witches' hats against the orange sunset; he'd tell her that the word Baltimore was Gaelic for "place of the great house" (he remembered that tidbit from high school), and then show her his favorite neighborhoods.

He opened the door. He supposed he ought to be a nervous wreck—it wasn't often that he brought home a woman of this caliber (or any woman at all, for that matter)—but the news of the day had rescued him, had colored the afternoon with larger meaning. Once inside, he went straight to the bay window and opened the curtains. "Ever grow African violets?"

"No," said Emi. "I don't keep plants. They would die."

"You think?"

"In Paris I had a cat, but it ran away. It was three days until I realized it was gone."

"Too busy, is that it?"

"No," she said. "It is not a problem of too busy. No: I think it is a gift, to be able to nurture something. Do you understand, a gift? Like a talent. I admire this talent in others. For myself, I don't have it."

"Sure you do," said Mickey. "Everyone does." He looked at his plants. Damned things. A bunch of happy green leaves. They could care less if they flowered, and here it would have been nice to have had some blossoms on display for Emi.

"They say they're the easiest plants in the world, but mine are stubborn as hell." Mickey shrugged. "Can I get you anything? Coffee?"

"No, thank you. I'd like to listen to the reportage. Is there a radio?"

"Right," Mickey said. "Upstairs, there's a radio. Or you can watch the television." He pointed to it: a brand-new Zenith from Diamond Electric, with big fat dials and antennae stretched to a giant *V.* Jack Diamond had given him a hell of a deal.

"Upstairs? Is there a bed? I would like to lie down."

"Are you okay?"

"Just tired," she said. She seemed distracted, as if there were something else.

Mickey led her upstairs. He was glad he'd made his bed that morning. Usually he didn't.

She entered his room without hesitation and sat on the edge of the bed. "This was your parents' room?" she said, eyeing the relics that the elder Lerners had left: the antique hat tree in the corner (several of his father's hats still hung there), and the curved vanity table against the wall, where Rose Lerner would brush her wavy red hair in front of the mirror. Her gold-plated brush was still there, hairs and all, along with the tiny glass figurines—elephants, giraffes, camels—that she had collected and fondled with the simple amusement of a queen.

"Yes," said Mickey. "This was my parents' room." He went to the cedar chest of drawers, upon which stood his parents' wedding portrait: the bride in a chair, bouquet spilling over her knees, barely smiling; the groom standing by, hand on the back of the chair, his casual stateliness seeming to have been strenuously arrived at under the photographer's fussy direction. "This isn't a great picture of them, but—"

"Mickey?"

Mickey closed his eyes. There was something in her tone.

"Mickey," she said. "I'm pregnant."

Mickey placed his hand on his belly. *Pregnant*. The very sound of the word! Worse than *cancer*—those ugly medical syllables, so much like "malignant," or "stagnant"—and Emi, protected by the armor of a half-learned language, pronounced it gamely, managing to draw up from the roots all its stigmatic horror.

"Jesus," Mickey said, and then it hit him like a shot: it wasn't his child, but someone else's. Shaw's, he thought. The pianist. Maybe Shaw had seduced her, or worse—

"Mickey—what should we do?"

It took a moment for him to understand. "Christ Almighty," he said. The room seemed to tilt under his weight, and everything he had thought a moment ago shifted the other way. "Are you sure?" he said. "From one night?"

"I'm sure."

He dared not suggest that she may have been with someone else; what good would it do, anyway? She'd just angrily deny it, turn against him entirely, maybe even resort to something desperate. He saw scandal, threats—

"Mickey."

He couldn't look at her. "Just give me a second," he said, holding up his hand. He thought back to their night of passion, now a fateful night. And hadn't he known it, really, even then? Hadn't his climax come with a certain shrewd eye toward the future? And hadn't her passion also been colored by a vague sort of ambition? Was this really such a shock?

He walked over and kissed her forehead, not quite sure what he was doing, trying his best to follow his instincts. He sat and put his hand on her shoulder, gently brought her head to his chest. He could feel, in the way she yielded, a kind of pity for his awkwardness, and so found himself trapped in the embrace, holding her head as though it were an incriminating object that someone had thrust into his hands in a crowd.

He stood up, making the withdrawal seem natural by going straight to the chest of drawers and straightening the wedding portrait. The faces there were too young to reprove or advise; it was their innocence that stung the eye, their simple propriety.

"Mickey. Are you angry?" She was now curled up on the bed, her head propped up on one hand.

He turned to her. "No, no," he said. "I want you to be happy." He felt a surge of tenderness—a measure of his need for an ally, he supposed. "I'll do anything you want."

"What's there to do?"

"I don't know. What do people do in this situation? Get married?" He tried a laugh. "See one of those doctors?"

Emi said nothing, only smoothed her hand over the blanket. Mickey remembered how she had gotten dressed that night at the bakery, those slow, deliberate movements that suggested poise after a narrow escape.

Mickey sat down next to her on the bed, moved a strand of hair from her face. She smiled weakly.

He said, "We have options."

She took his hand in her own and closed her eyes. "I think I'm afraid," she said.

"Don't be. Everything's going to be fine." He felt her relax.

The wet, metallic smell of the window screens mixed with the scent of the twin fir trees that flanked the front of the house; soon the azaleas would explode all pink and red and white in the flower bed, insects would crawl, mists of pollen and drizzle would glaze the windowsills.

Mickey said, "I'll let you get some sleep."

That night there came a knock at the back door. It was Joe. He had a six-pack of National, which meant they'd be discussing his marriage. "You got a few minutes?" he said.

Mickey shrugged as Joe entered. "Sure."

Joe set the beer on the kitchen table and plopped down in a chair. "Barbara wants me home in an hour," he said. "Laurie's got the chicken pox. You could play connect the dots." With a wave of the hand he dismissed the whole trifling matter of disease in children. "Don't have kids," he said, and opened a beer.

Mickey joined him at the table. "Christ, I saw you today, you were gone like a bat outta hell."

"That's what I came to talk to you about. I wasn't just blowing air out of my asshole when I said there was gonna be trouble. Did you look at the news tonight? All the politicians in the country are calling for calm. They know what's gonna happen—Detroit all over again. You got a whole population ready to explode." He shook his head, sighed. "Christ, I shoulda moved the store out of the city years ago. You too. And Howard and Buddy and Marv and the whole bunch of us. Now we're stuck down there. Sitting ducks."

"Well, look, Joe, nothing's happened yet."

"Ducks on the pond."

"This could blow over. And besides, if worse comes to worse, insurance'll cover you."

"What, for theft? Big deal! Theft. They can take all the parts and tires they want."

"So what are you worried about?"

Joe looked at him. "*Fire*, for Chrissake. Getting burned to the ground. That's what I'm worried about." He slurped his beer and set the bottle down hard. "We both took out the same policy, right? Well, I talked to a fella today. 'Damage incurred in a civil disturbance isn't covered,' he says. Meanwhile, they want an arm and a leg."

Mickey tapped his fingers on the tablecloth. "I think you're getting yourself worked up over nothing. As much as the area's changed, have you ever had a problem?"

"But this is different. This is Martin Luther King we're talking about."

"That's right, and his way was always the peaceful way. Nonviolence. He always told the colored: nonviolence."

Joe snorted. "You think every black in the city is lining up at a church right now?"

"How should I know?"

"That's the problem with you, Mick. You have too much faith in people. You're gonna get screwed."

"Look, I know how rough it is. I see the same things you do. But personally I've never had any problems, and the colored who come into my store are always as polite as anybody else. Better, in fact. You never hear a complaint."

"So you feel secure then, is that it? Invincible?"

"A meteor could come down. Who knows what might happen? Look, if there was an affordable way to protect against this sort of thing, whether it's a meteor, a riot or a tornado, I'd be the first one in line."

"That's my point," Joe said. "That's what I'm trying to tell you." He took a handkerchief from his pocket and blew his nose. "I'm trying to help you out here."

"Uh-huh." Joe was always trying to "help out," Mickey reflected, and it always amounted to some wild scheme.

Joe folded the handkerchief and stuffed it back in his pocket. "You know I've got two colored fellas down my place," he said. "You've seen 'em. Big sons of bitches. Linebacker types."

"So they're big."

"Not only are they big. These fellas are very well-connected in the shvartze community. You know blacks—everybody has a cousin who knows this one who knows that one. So today my fellas take me aside and say, 'Baby, we just want you to know, if trouble breaks out, we got you covered.' Just like that. No discussion. 'We got you covered.' Loyalty, right? Then they says to me, 'Do you have any friends who need protection?' Not exactly in those words, but that was the gist. So of course I think of you, and Buddy, and Marv, okay, fine. I says, 'Yeah, I might know some people.' They says, 'We've got plenty of people. For a reasonable price, we can keep the *bruvvahs* away.' "

Mickey clucked his tongue. "You get a commission?"

"I'm goddamned serious, Mick. These fellas seem to know what's what. They know all the top shvartzes in the streets."

"Well, as long as you got your fellas, you're safe, right?"

"What about you?"

"Look, I got nothing but bread in there. I was thinking to myself after I closed the place up today: a person wants to break a window and take, what are they gonna bother with bread? Clothes, jewelry, okay, sure. But pumpernickel? Rye?"

Joe rubbed his nose with the sleeve of his white windbreaker. "When a shvartze is on a rampage," he said, "the stealing becomes indiscriminate. They see a window, they'll break it and take whatever's there. Men running with lingerie in their hands. Brassieres. And then for good measure they'll spritz some gasoline and toss a match." He sat back and folded his arms. "Ask my cousin Barry in Newark, he'll tell you."

Yes, Newark. Joe had never been the same since Newark. Barry was beaten unconscious, and Barry's father, Max, had taken a whack across the knees with a pipe, all this in the back of Max's dry-cleaning shop. But that was no reason for Joe to make blanket statements. Did he forget that it was a colored nurse who was caring for his grandmother? A colored woman who looked after his kid?

There came the sound of footsteps; before Mickey could say anything, Emi came into the kitchen wearing Mickey's striped pajamas. "Excuse me," she said.

Joe's eyebrows arched.

Emi went to the sink and poured herself a glass of water.

Mickey watched, speechless, as Joe stared at her. Instantly he regretted not having told him that she'd come back.

Emi sipped from the glass. The pajama bottoms covered her feet. Walking out, she trailed a fresh soapy smell from the bath she had helped herself to earlier. Mickey looked down at the tablecloth.

"Well," said Joe. "That explains a thing or two."

Mickey looked up at him. "What do you mean?"

"Naturally you're not thinking about the bakery. You've got other things."

"I've been meaning to tell you. Remember the violinist—"

"You mean the French whore."

"Now wait a minute," said Mickey.

"Take it easy. I'm just joking."

"You'd better be. That's exactly why I didn't want to say anything—I knew you'd give me hell."

"Who, me?" Joe crossed his legs, attempting to appear blasé, but Mickey could see that he was hurt. "Yeah, I remember. You made her out to be Brigitte Bardot."

"I only said she came from France."

"Same difference."

"Well," Mickey said, "it just so happens I'm going to marry her." It came out like an attack on Joe.

"What?" Joe said.

Mickey squeezed his hands together. "It all just happened. She doesn't even know yet." He put a fist to his mouth as if to stifle a cough.

"Wait a minute—hoo boy, Mickey. Don't tell me you knocked her up."

Mickey said nothing.

Joe opened another beer and slid it across the table. "Hoo boy." He whistled like a bomb. "Hoo boy oh boy."

"Cut it out."

"Tell me," Joe said, and he fixed his eyes on Mickey and lowered his voice. "Is she white or rye?"

Mickey shrugged. "I haven't asked."

Joe leaned forward on his elbows. "You mean you don't know?" They might have been boys again, huddling around their discovery of some forbidden adult knowledge. "Hoo boy." There was awe in Joe's voice—no one in their circles had ever been with a Gentile—but also a hint of rebuke: Mickey would be breaking with tradition, putting himself outside the community.

"The truth is," said Mickey, with an edge of defiance, "I could care less if she was a Martian."

Joe shook his head. "Does Morris know about this?"

Mickey touched the cold brown bottle. "He doesn't know she's—no. He doesn't know anything. And we can keep it that way."

"Sure, sure. But will he approve? I know he likes to put his two cents in."

"At this point," Mickey said, "I think he'll just be happy I didn't go in for pumpernickel."

Joe laughed at that one. "I'll be damned," he said. "Boy, some day this has been." He drank to that. "So," he said. "You mean to say that I'm looking at a soon-to-be husband and father?"

"In that order."

"And you know for a fact that you're the one? I mean, Mick, with all due respect."

"That's a hell of a thing to say about her, Joe. A hell of a goddamned thing. Take it back."

"Looks like I struck a nerve."

Mickey banged his fist down on the table. "Take it back."

"Okay," said Joe. "Okay. Just looking out for you, that's all." He checked his watch. "Of course, the important thing is that you—love her."

Mickey gripped his bottle. "I do," he said softly. His head bobbed slowly at the phrase, and he could hear a pulse beating in his ears. "I do."

The next day, Friday, Mickey decided to open the bakery. So far, there had been no signs of violence or unrest. Besides, Fridays were his busiest days; it would take nothing short of Armageddon to keep him from opening. Let Joe Blank eat a day's worth of business.

Most of the regulars came in for their Sabbath bread. In fact, the King assassination took a temporary backseat to the news, spread proudly by Morris, that Mickey was "involved" with a "French woman," though of course he did not yet know to what extent, didn't know that she'd woken up this morning in Mickey's bed, and that he'd made repeated athletic love to her the night before, as though hoping to influence the development in her womb, to coat or inject it with his own substance, to sway the biology toward himself. Joe had planted the seed of doubt, no question.

Mickey went home an hour earlier than usual, anxious to see Emi. As he entered the house he caught a whiff of his favorite aroma in the world: the salty, hot, mustard-colored seasoning marketed under the name "Old Bay," used in the steaming of crabs and shrimp—a summer smell, a holiday smell. What was Emi up to?

He went back to the kitchen: there was Emi, clad only in one of Mickey's flannel shirts, washing dishes. On the table was a large brown bag, its bottom wet and heavy with juices and clumps of seasoning, tiny pink claws poking out here and there. Mickey's throat went dry with wonder and gratitude, and for a moment he couldn't speak.

Emi looked up at him. "Are you hungry?" she said, as though he had just walked through the door for the thousandth time. It was strange: the suggestion of familiarity gave birth to an instant history. Mickey perceived a hazy tradition of comings and goings, of aromas in the yard and the clink of pots and spoons. He went over and kissed her softly on the cheek.

"Crabs," he said.

"You said they were your favorite food."

"Where did you get them?"

"Oh, I captured them myself. Didn't you know, I am also an expert of fishing? Oh yes—I also took a taxi to my flat and brought back some things."

"What things?"

"Just my violin. And some sheet music. Don't worry."

"No, no," said Mickey. "I'm not worried." She must have gone to her place and hit Bo Brooks on the way back; he'd pointed it out to her one time, saying how they had the best crabs in town. She herself had never eaten crabs. "Bring everything you want. I've got plenty of room." He could hardly believe his words, but he really meant it. "I'll get some newspapers."

He spread some old newspapers out on the table. He saved papers for this very purpose, though it had been a while since he'd utilized them. He laid out two wooden mallets and two knives, and grabbed one of the bottles of National that Joe had left the night before. Then he ripped the bag down the sides, revealing a heap of red shell-plates covered in muddy spices and curds of fat that had oozed out from the bodies during steaming. He picked one up by its pincer, causing Emi to jump back. There it was: eight little legs like folding knives, two long arms, the pincers carefully toothed; hell, Mickey told her, these weren't even biggies, it wasn't even crab season yet. You ought to see them late in the summer.

When they were through—the debris and papers thrown out, the legs bagged and refrigerated, hands washed—Emi went upstairs. As Mickey rinsed the mallets and knives in the sink, he heard, for the first time in the house, the squeal of her violin—so much like a voice in distress that he froze momentarily in perfect fear.

It was then that he realized he couldn't wait. The moment had arrived. The sound of urgency filled the house. Tomorrow, first thing, he would do it.

He awoke in the guest room, which was his old bedroom; he had fallen asleep there waiting for Emi to finish with her practicing. Rubbing his eyes, he saw a frost on the windows. He liked an April frost, just so long as it came in early April, and not after he'd done the bulk of his planting. He threw off the blankets and dropped his feet on the cold wood floor, then straightened his pants and his shirt and went to the closet.

There was an old El Producto cigar box on the top shelf. He took it down and opened it. Inside was a smaller box that contained the diamond ring his grandmother had given him years earlier. Just days before her death, she had summoned him to her bedside at the nursing home and motioned for him to lower his ear to her lips.

"Take," she said. It was her favorite English word.

"Take what, Nanna?" Through the net of white hair he could see the brown and reddish spots on her scalp.

"Take," she said, the voice a small croak.

Her closed hand rose from the bed. Mickey caught it and pulled gently at her fingers, as he used to when it was meant as a game, when the prize was a butterscotch candy. But the old woman was resisting: she would have no help. He let go, and the fist opened slowly, like balled-up plastic. He cupped his hand under hers, and something hard fell into his palm. He was afraid to look; it was as if her gradually departing spirit had passed a tiny nugget, a sudden morsel of her being.

"Nanna," he said. He felt her hand on his, coaxing his fist closed. She gave a squeeze.

"It belonged to my mother," she said with some effort. "Your great-grandmother. I always thought I'd see the day when you would walk down the aisle. But you take your time. You're my grandson." She blinked her eyes, and a drop rolled down a cheek whose skin was delicate as tissue paper, leaving a dark stripe.

That had been a dozen years earlier. Now, with the small box in his hand, Mickey walked out into the hall. He could hardly believe the moment was upon him, that he was about to approach a woman with Nanna's ring—albeit under considerably different circumstances than Nanna would have preferred, or that he himself would have imagined. Still, he felt there was much at stake: what other chance in life would he get to marry so high up? To marry at all? There were no other candidates, and here he was almost thirty. This was a chance he couldn't afford to blow. And hell, it wasn't as if he brought nothing to the table; he could offer a house, a yard. Tenderness and loyalty. He wasn't rich, but the cupboards were never empty. And he had a respectable business. Emi was smart enough to see the advantages; he saw her seeing them when she first walked in the house. The way she moved from room to room, wearing his clothes. The way she looked things over.

He stopped at the closed door of the master bedroom. Was she still asleep? Should he wake her softly, or come back later? He felt a jitter in his knees. He was no good at presentations, at speeches. He opened the box and peered in at its contents. What should he say?

The doorknob turned: there she was, cloaked in a bedsheet like a little girl playing at Gypsies. Mickey stepped back, and the box fell from his hand. The ring spilled out onto the gray carpet.

Mickey stared in horror at the twinkling band, aware that Emi was looking at it too. Another man might be able to make a joke and move on, even make the dropping of the ring seem like part of the proposal, and not feel, as Mickey did, that he'd been caught red-handed in a theft. There was no escape: Mickey could not pick up the ring without appearing clumsy or absurd, nor could he flee the house and never return; all he could do was stand there as his mind scrambled to find a clever remark, hoping against hope that Emi would take action and rescue them, but of course she wouldn't, her silence was like a punishment, a lesson for a careless little boy.

The phone rang. It was pure deliverance for Mickey—suddenly he was the man of the house, the one who answered the phone, and in a small way he hoped for a crisis on the other line, that the dropped ring might be forgotten and his authority brought to the fore. He walked past Emi and entered the room with an air of importance, a man of affairs about to receive breaking news. He stood before the night table and let the phone ring again, affording Emi a glimpse of his masculine restraint. Then he picked up.

"Hello?"

"Mick. It's me."

"Joe."

"Listen, I'm down here at the store. The fellas told me there's gonna be trouble tonight for sure."

"We already had this conversation."

"Mick, I'm trying to tell you something."

"This isn't Detroit, for Christ's sake." Mickey knew he was performing for Emi on the one hand, but he also knew that he was responding in earnest, and this merging of the image he wished to project and the man he actually was gave him increased confidence in his argument. "The worst thing we can do," he said, glancing at Emi, "is panic."

"Did you see the headlines this morning? 'NINE KILLED IN D.C., CHICAGO RIOTS.' *Washington*, Mick."

"Washington is Washington. Besides, it's too damn cold out for a riot."

"You know of an Abe's Grocery, on Druid Hill Avenue? Someone tossed a Molotov cocktail last night."

"Thanks for the update, but I think I'll take my chances." He hung up.

Emi entered the room; the sheet had fallen from her, revealing a nakedness of circles: the small breasts, the belly, the dark patch of hair; it was as though she were making herself equal to him, baring herself, reducing herself, but her obvious self-possession (for what was nudity, after all, to a European?) seemed to undermine her intent, turning the gesture into a kind of musky cultural challenge.

The ring was in her hand.

She said, "Is everything okay?" The concern in her voice was like a reward, an opportunity.

Mickey smiled and nodded, allowing for some tension at the corners of his mouth, hints of heroic reserve under a great and secret pressure. "So," he said, winking at the box in her hand as though it were something she had retrieved, maybe a little earlier than she should have, from under a Christmas tree. "How do you like it?"

"Mickey. This is a—ring."

Mickey felt the hero in him buckle, but he managed to keep his shoulders square and his chin up. "Yes. That's what it is."

Emi stared at it.

"You don't have to accept it," Mickey said.

"No." She shook her head slowly. "Fate has put us together, I think. I'm not afraid of that."

Mickey folded his arms and nodded, wanting to match her professed fearlessness with a courage of his own, though clearly she was the one who, for whatever reasons, had nothing to lose, the one whose circumstances had left her so meekly philosophical, invoking Fate.

"Mickey," she said, looking at him, "you don't have to do this."

"Don't talk nonsense," he said, and it occurred to him that by acknowledging mystical influences—Fate—she had eclipsed the primacy of the will, *his* will; indeed, she had stripped his decisions, his attempts to do the brave and correct thing, to shoulder responsibility for a single reckless night, of any meaning whatever. And yet the notion of Fate did have its allure: it justified nearly anything, and to a degree pardoned him for acts and consequences that would no doubt be judged harshly, would shame the memory of his parents and destroy the sanctity of Nanna's deathbed gesture. This idea now seemed far more appealing than the grimaces of a proud man bearing awful burdens; it was an opening, and Mickey pounced on it: "You're right," he said. "Fate has put us together." He stepped toward her and put his hand on her shoulder. Even in a world where events are predestined there had to be someone to step forward and make sense of things; and Mickey was resolved, in this relationship, to be that person. But what bold, authoritative thing could he say? How best to gain some sort of foothold?

Emi looked into his eyes, as if seeing there his effort to master her. "Mickey."

"I love you," Mickey said hoarsely. He regretted this the moment it crawled up from his throat. Not that it wasn't true; he was certain that he had very significant feelings for her. But he hated appearing so predictable, so flatly unoriginal; he could feel her intelligence bearing down on him, making even his most innocent and honest remarks shiver with uncertainty.

Emi looked down again at the open box. "It's a beautiful ring."

Mickey removed his hand from her shoulder and scratched his forehead. "My grandmother gave it to me," he said readily. "It's been in my family for quite a long time." He looked at it with her.

"I should tell you something," she said. "You'll laugh at me, probably."

Mickey put his hands in his pockets, hoping to recapture some of the quiet strength that had marked his advance to the telephone. "Tell me."

"I've never worn a ring in my life."

"Never?"

"Well, maybe when I was a little girl. But when I started playing the violin, I got rid of them. I don't even wear a watch."

"Well then." Here it is, Mickey thought, the first humiliation: the ring wasn't good enough. What the hell did she expect—the Hope diamond?

"Don't be angry."

Mickey scratched his head. "Listen, I wouldn't wear a ring in my

line of work either. It could fall in the dough and end up in someone's
loaf of bread."

Emi laughed. Mickey laughed too, telling himself that maybe it was
all for the best, that Nanna's ring, so sacred, would now be spared the
finger of a pregnant woman of shadowy origin—which was how
Nanna herself would view it. "But we still have to have some kind of
wedding ceremony," he said, taking a childlike joy in discussing so
grave a matter. It was like a game of make-believe. "And if we end up
not liking each other, we can get a divorce."

"Yes, a divorce!" said Emi, rising to his mirth. "We are free to do as
we want." It was becoming clear to Mickey that they were striking a
bargain of convenience, but Mickey sensed a real romantic love gal-
loping alongside their practical needs, keeping up, determined to
make their union legitimate.

"But a small ceremony," he said. Discretion would be best, he
thought; none of the pomp and circumstance—announcements in the
paper, overflowing banquet hall, eight-piece band, multitiered cake—
that attended Joe's wedding three years ago.

"And nothing religious," said Emi.

Mickey thought about that for a moment. She had a point. Why
bring religion into it? Aside from attending shul with Morris on the
High Holidays, and loathing every minute of it, Mickey hadn't a single religious bone in his body. But still he wondered about Emi. "What
are you?" he said. "I mean, religion-wise?"

"Nothing," she said. "Unless Marxism is a religion, but I don't think
it is."

"Marxism?" said Mickey. "You mean communism?" The word gave
him a thrill of international peril; for a moment he was Sean Connery
in a hotel room. "Very interesting." He scratched his head. Morris and
Joe would have a few things to say about this.

"Do you know it?" said Emi.

"Sure," said Mickey, though in truth he had no real concept of communism, save for its being the Number One threat to world peace—
you had Castro, and Ho Chi Minh, you had the Russians and Mao and
a few million American longhairs running wild at the colleges—but
for some reason the idea didn't really bother him that much. In fact,
he felt a tiny stir of excitement at the prospect of shocking his peers.

"You're disgusted," said Emi. She frowned, then reached into the
crumple of blankets and pulled up a white nightshirt. She put it on.
"You think I am the evil one."

"Who, me? Not at all," Mickey said. He rubbed his eye. "Though maybe you think *I* am."

"No. You are not my idea of a capitalist."

Mickey wasn't sure if he should feel insulted. "No?" he said. "Then who is?"

"My father, for one."

Mickey had forgotten that she had a family. "What does he do?"

"He was in textiles. He had a factory in the suburbs."

"Is he alive?"

"Alive, dead, what is the difference? I have not spoken with him in two years. Anyway, it does not matter."

"Sure it does. You've got these feelings. You can't keep them all inside. You have to talk."

"This is not my method. Perhaps you do not understand what it is to make a new life. Sometimes you must cut off the past in order to go on. I am hiding nothing. It is just a philosophy. I prefer to go forward. Life is very short, you know. We can spend half of it remembering. But really, we must live."

"Okay," said Mickey. "Okay."

"When I was young," Emi said, "he tried to break my hands. It was after my mother died. He thought I wasn't his child. An old story. Perhaps he was right. This was a violent, unhappy man."

Mickey was at a loss. "I'm sorry," he said. He sat on the bed and smoothed out the robe over his knees, remembering a promise that he had made to himself after his father's death: that he'd marry a girl from a large and loving family, so as to provide their children—and Mickey himself—with the tribal joy and abundance that he had longed for even as a child.

Emi sat down beside him, took his hand in hers. Mickey put his arm around her and held her close.

"I'm cold," she said. Her teeth chattered.

Mickey pulled back the blankets, and without a word they maneuvered their bodies underneath and covered up.

Emi said, "I like you very much."

"Yes," Mickey said. He held her tight.

"But I am afraid," she said. She was crying softly. "I'm not ready to be a mother."

"It's okay."

"A baby. Especially if it is a boy. I am afraid it will remind me of . . . him. It is bad blood. I should not have a child." And she broke into breathless sobs.

Mickey wasn't sure what to make of her words. He held her, stroked her, kissed her head. She seemed to be referring to her father, but Mickey couldn't help but think that she was really talking about *him*. Bad blood? No: common blood! That's what she meant. She is charmed by me, he thought, maybe she is even in love, but in the end I am still in her eyes a peasant, hardly an adequate father. "Don't worry," he whispered. "Everything will be okay." An abortion, he now decided, was out of the question; it would be a hateful act, a crime against his own biology. To kill the fetus would be to kill the man. He mustn't allow it.

But what if the child wasn't his? Wasn't that an argument to abort—the possibility that he wasn't the father? How would he ever know for sure, how would he ever be able to tell?

It was amid these thoughts that Mickey fell asleep. Emi slept too; the afternoon covered them in its shadows.

The phone rang. Mickey, awakened, reached across Emi and picked it up.

"Hello?"

"Mickey! It's starting, Mickey! I told you! I goddamn told you!"

Mickey sat up. "Joe, what's going on?" There was noise in the background. "Where are you?"

"I'm in a phone booth. I was in the store, boarding up my windows, and I heard glass smashing in the street. I ran out, and a whole gang was in front of Marv's place. Listen! Can you hear?"

There were shouts and ringing alarms and explosions of glass.

"What the hell's going on? Joe!" The line crackled, went dead.

Emi opened her eyes.

"Joe? Joe!" Mickey slammed down the receiver. "Son of a bitch!" He hopped out of bed and began dressing.

"What is it?" Emi said. She yawned.

"Something happened," Mickey said. "Down at my friend's store. Looks like there's a riot going on."

"A what?" Emi sat up. "Where are you going?"

"I'll be back," he said. He was hardly thinking, but he savored the kiss he planted on Emi's head, savored the look in her eyes that told him she was worried for him.

"Mickey!"

"Stay here," Mickey said. He felt a strange lightness as he skipped down the stairs, a weightlessness, as of a balloon let go.

He took Reistertown Road all the way to Pennsylvania Avenue, but instead of turning left on North Avenue to head toward Joe's place, he turned right on a sudden impulse, heading west. It would just take a minute, but he had to do it, had to check on the bakery, it was just a few short blocks away, just beyond the corridor of dilapidated row houses through which he now passed, to say nothing of the sporadic places of business—Lake Trout, Package Goods, Checks Cashed Here, Afro Cut, Wash and Dry, Sister Eunice Palm Reading and Psychic Consultation—which reflected the "changes" that certain of his customers would grumble about as Mickey rang up their purchases. Mickey noticed that on several windows of the colored businesses the words "Soul Brother" had been spray-painted in large white letters— the only evidence of what might be called vandalism that Mickey had yet seen.

It was strange: the west side was surprisingly quiet under the cold night sky; the Negroes on the sidewalks moved about in their usual slow, graceful, truculent way, wool caps pulled down tight over their dark heads, eyes flashing. There was a distinct sadness in the air, perhaps an anger, but not a violence; it was hard to believe that just a couple of miles away, Joe Blank was under siege.

There was the Lerner Bakery, sitting anonymously in its strip of stores. There were no people around at all, nor had his windows been defaced with painted slogans.

Satisfied, Mickey made a U-turn and sped east. He turned on the radio, and heard a bulletin ordering motorists to avoid the very area to which he was headed, due to "disturbances."

Mickey was astonished by the change that had come over him. The Mickey of old, he considered, would not have thought twice about heeding such a report, and with fear in his heart would have done his citizen's best to cooperate; whereas the new Mickey, the one who was about to marry a Communist and have a kid, the new Mickey kept driving, determined as hell to reach Joe in his critical hour. The new Mickey understood the meaning of loyalty to one's friends; he didn't think of the costs. Why else would he be speeding across town, heading into a zone fraught with danger? What else could this be, if not fierce brotherly devotion, a call to arms in the name of friendship? And yet there was this nagging sense, as he crossed Charles Street to the east side, his knuckles marbled yellow and white on the steering wheel, that he wasn't so much running toward something as he was being chased, pursued by phantoms into the fires that he could begin to make out ahead: dim flickers beyond rooftops, suggesting furnaces, steel. But it was of course the very opposite of industry.

He remembered how he felt that morning, when Nanna's ring fell from his hand to the floor—how he wanted to jump into his car and drive forever, into oblivion.

Ahead he could see police activity: the intersection at Greenmount Avenue was blocked off by several squad cars, lights awhirl. Mickey could see trash cans burning along the curbs, and on the sidewalk was an overturned car: it lay like a senselessly murdered animal. Scores of Negroes massed in the street, sizing up the meager police presence. The spinning lights of the squad cars suggested a kind of apocalyptic dance floor; the Negroes warmed themselves to it.

Mickey cursed aloud and backed up to the next street, more angry than afraid: it was crazy, everything was crazy, all was madness and destruction and senseless action. In every burning tire or smashed window he found a metaphor; for a moment he even felt a kinship with chaos itself, recognizing in it the roar of rebellion, the struggle toward freedom—and saw, too, the gunfire of his own being flash into the darkness of Emi's womb, kindling fires there, lighting the way to a different life, it didn't matter what sort, so long as it was different from the one he'd been leading, or rather following, for nearly thirty goddamned years.

"Revolution is possible only through violence," Joe had once read aloud, his eyes burning into the newspaper from which he was quoting some campus rabble-rouser who was paraphrasing Marx. It was intended to get Mickey to understand the importance of obliterating the Marxist enemy everywhere on the globe, and now the phrase came back to him with the eloquence of a homespun truth.

He drove south two blocks and turned left. A dozen or more Negroes came tearing around the corner on foot; some ran over the tops of cars, and Mickey froze as they passed: they shouted and shrieked, toppling cans, smashing the windshields of parked cars with pipes and sticks. A moment later, several policemen in riot gear came lumbering round the same corner, hurdling the rolling cans in a hideous ballet, clubs raised, boots clacking with their gasping, ponderous strides.

They were all coming from Joe's block. "Jesus," Mickey heard himself say. "Jesus God." He backed out of the street and continued south, his thoughts and prayers so feverishly with Joe that he no longer doubted the reasons for his arrival here.

He drove around the block and stopped at the corner. He looked to the right, and could hardly believe what he saw: two cars were parked on the sidewalk in front of Joe's store—not pushed there by an angry mob, or abandoned by terrorized motorists, but arranged defensively.

In front of this fortress and atop it stood several large Negroes, all holding baseball bats. The words SOUL BROTHER had been painted in white on the store windows.

Mickey recalled the old Passover story, the one in which the Angel of Death passes over the land and slays every male child, sparing only the ones whose homes are marked.

Across the street, a few youths were picking over some ladies' discount apparel that had been dragged through the broken windows of Marv Kandel's.

Mickey pulled up in front of Joe's store. The "guards" were stone-faced. Mickey rolled down his window. "Excuse me," he said to the man closest to him. "I'm a friend of Joe Blank's. Is he okay? Where is he?"

The guard waved him along. Mickey turned his head: the youths in front of Marv Kandel's were taking a break from their looting to have a look at him.

"Drive!" said the guard.

Another of Joe's men kicked the back of the car. "Joe Blank home," he said. "Now get the fuck outta here!"

Mickey stepped on the gas and screeched down the street. Something crashed against his back window; a stone: it left a small seashell impression in the glass.

Mickey drove faster. Was Joe really home? Mickey wasn't sure what to make of it.

Up and down every street small fires burned; fire trucks kept coming toward him, and as they passed he felt the odd sensation of leaving the scene of his own misdoings.

When he returned home he heard laughter in the kitchen.

"Germapelle Morris," came a voice.

"No, no, no. *Jzuh.*"

"Juh."

"Je m'appelle Morris."

"Germapelle Morris."

Mickey walked back, cleared his throat.

"Is that you, Mickey?" Morris called.

"Who else would it be?"

"Well, according to the news reports, you could be a big colored fella coming to loot the icebox."

Mickey entered the kitchen, where Emi and Morris were seated at the table, drinking coffee. There was a fresh pot on the stove. "Don't laugh," Mickey said. "I just saw it for myself, down near North and Greenmount. They're setting fires everywhere." Emi, he saw, was wearing a pair of his pajamas; he couldn't meet her eyes. "To tell you the truth, I'm worried about the bakery." He took off his overcoat and draped it over the back of a chair.

Morris waved his hand. "Don't worry. Our genius governor is calling in the militia. The first smart thing he's ever done."

"Good." Mickey felt some relief; he had thought of going back to the bakery with a can of spray paint to write SOUL BROTHER on the windows, but was stopped by an unhappy vision of being caught in the act by passersby. Now there'd be no need; the troops were coming.

"We even got a curfew," said Morris. "Eleven tonight to six in the morning. I can't ever remember such a thing."

Emi spoke up. "Mickey. What did you see?"

Mickey didn't look at her. "Fires," he said. "And glass." He felt a chill. "Glass all over the street."

"Why the hell were you out in such a mess?" said Morris.

Mickey had to think for a moment. "I went down to check on Joe Blank—he called, and it sounded—"

"Joe Blank. He called while you were gone."

"He did? What did he say? Where is he?"

"He's home," Morris said. "Wanted to know if we still didn't want to hire anyone to look after the store. I says to him, 'That's what we got federal troops for.' 'Suit yourself,' he says. I says, 'You'd have me pay money to have the foxes guard the henhouse.' "

Mickey sat down at the table. Emi got up and went to the stove.

"Money," Mickey muttered to himself. Even if he wanted to, he couldn't afford to pay for any protection—not with the slew of expenses that would be visited upon him in eight short months. He said, "Sid Kandel's place got hit pretty bad."

Morris looked up. "Was Sid or Marv in the store?"

"No. It was closed already."

"And I suppose Joe Blank's place was as safe as Fort Knox."

"Just about," said Mickey. Emi returned with a hot cup of coffee and set it in front of him. Their eyes met: Mickey detected a kind of nurselike admiration there, as if for his valor, and he did his best to look like a soldier in gloomy recovery who could still manage a little smile.

She kissed him lightly on the head.

Mickey shivered with comfort, then looked down into his steaming mug. He saw a ghost of his image there, quivering in the black liquid; he blew lightly onto the surface.

Emi took Morris's empty cup. *"Encore du café, monsieur?"*

"What's that?"

"More coffee?"

"Wee. Anker doo k'fay."

"Très bien, Morris. À bientôt."

"Al Biento," said Morris. He took Emi's hand and held it a moment too long. "Means 'See ya soon,' right?"

"Très bien, Morris."

"Ya hear that, Mickey? Al Biento."

Emi smiled at no one in particular and went back to pour more coffee. Morris leaned over and spoke into Mickey's ear. "Marry this one," he said, with the same hint of illicit knowledge he used when telling others which horse to bet on at the racetrack. But Mickey could tell that his uncle was still reeling from his French lesson, still drunk from the scent of a woman's perfume; poor man, it had been a good fifteen years since his wife left him because he couldn't give her a child.

The next day, Mickey took Emi to a place a little ways down the road where you could get pancakes made in any style you could imagine, even the French style. On the parking lot of a nearby shopping center less than half a mile from the house soldiers with fixed bayonets stood at fifty-yard intervals. It was a sunny day, cool, almost a plea from Nature for calm. Through the window of the restaurant, Mickey watched a convoy of military vehicles pass, their headlights shining.

Strange, he thought, that they were all the way out here, on the edge of the city. Had the rioting spread, or was this a precaution? It seemed unlikely that there should be something other than peace on this Sunday morning; the troops were here with their rifles, their tear gas, and didn't most colored go to church?

He looked at Emi, who was examining color photos of the world's pancakes on the laminated menu, seemingly oblivious to the drama unfolding in the streets. He remembered what Joe had said—how the Communists would be the first to cheer the violence. He had even read a brief article in the paper that morning, saying how Mao over in China was publicly encouraging blacks to "fight on" to victory against the imperialist enemy. Evidently, the Chinese leader considered King a lackey of the U.S. government who had done nothing but suppress the revolution. The statements out of Peking expressed no regret over what happened in Memphis, and Mickey could only wonder if Emi shared those heartless views.

"Mickey? Is something wrong?"

"No." He looked down at his plate. There was something else bothering him; something Joe had said that had nothing to do with politics. "I was wondering."

"Yes?"

He thought it wise to bring the subject up in a public place, where she was less apt to have an outburst. "Is it crazy," he said, "for me to wonder if I'm the actual father of—"

"Yes," she said firmly. "Of course it's crazy."

She had been ready for this question; her quick response betrayed a keen knowledge of Mickey's heart. Or maybe it was just the male heart, the dumb, jealous, suspicious male heart. Mickey let out a self-effacing laugh and shook his head.

Emi softened and touched his hand. "I understand why you ask," she said, almost contrite, as though he had done a brave and respectable thing in asking, as though most men wouldn't have asked, but demanded, and then only between blows. "But there hasn't been anyone for me for a long time."

Mickey nodded. She sounded sincere as hell, and meanwhile Joe Blank had never been right about anything in his life, save maybe for the riots. Screw Joe Blank.

A middle-aged waitress with gold hair bundled a foot high, a pincushion for pencils, came by and said, "Don't mean to rush you folks, but we're closin' up early. Curfew's at four o'clock, 'cordin' to the radio, and the fella does dishes has to get a bus all the way down Cherry Hill."

Mickey checked his watch: it was already after one. Truth be told, he wasn't even hungry, and could tell by the way Emi was looking at the menu that she wasn't very impressed with the selection. The French crepes and the Belgian waffles she'd probably had in France and Belgium. She ordered only orange juice, and Mickey did the same.

"My nephew's in the Guard," said the waitress as she set down their glasses. "Got me worried sick." She lowered her voice and said confidentially, "I heard the coloreds were shootin' at the firemen last night. From rooftops." She held up her chin to express a certain moral outrage, then sauntered off to wait on another table.

Outside, it had gotten warmer. Mickey breathed in deep: through

the exhaust fumes from passing cars he thought he could smell hon-
eysuckle, and behind a fence at the back of the restaurant he saw the
first bright yellow shocks of forsythia. The trees across the street were
touched with a baby-green mist, a pea fluorescence, whereas the day
before they had been brown and bare. These were hopeful signs, he
felt; the push of life. Still, he was concerned. He turned to Emi and
said, "I think I'll drop you at the house and then go down and have a
look at the bakery."

"The bakery?" Her eyes picked up the green of the trees like a musical idea. "I want to go with you."

Mickey hesitated. Should he smile and shake his head at her
charming naïveté, put his hand on her shoulder and tell her that as
much as he'd like the company, he'd better go it alone, that it could
be dangerous? But it was impossible: Emi wasn't charmingly naïve,
nor was she like other women he had known, women who, far from
asking if they could join him, would have pleaded—no, insisted, even
demanded—that he not go, that it was too dangerous (even in broad
daylight, with goddamned soldiers everywhere), and that if he even
thought of driving down to North Avenue he'd be sleeping on the sofa
for the rest of the week; and, like his father before him, he'd have
bowed his head in compliance. No: Emi presented different problems.

"Okay," Mickey said. "But I'm sure everything's fine."

"May I drive?"

He looked at her like he hadn't heard right.

"I drove in Europe all the time. I'm good." She ran her hand
through her hair, as if this gesture alone demonstrated her competence.

Mickey wondered what she was up to. Did she think that maybe he
was too nervous to drive? That with his mind on the bakery he
wouldn't pay close enough attention to the road? Or was she just
plain adventurous?

"Don't you trust me?"

Mickey shrugged one shoulder and made an ambiguous twisting
motion with his hand, hoping to distract her with the many possible
meanings of this while he thought of something definitive. He could
refuse on the grounds that she didn't have a license, but that seemed
a silly argument in the face of a general insurrection. He'd have to
yield, but deftly; the important thing was to make his concessions
seem like gifts as opposed to abject surrender, to appear to deal from
a position of strength.

He flashed a devilish smile, letting on that he was okaying this little no-no, but as she took the keys from his hesitant fingers he saw that
she hadn't even noticed.

They had driven less than a mile when they found themselves surrounded by the cry of store alarms, shrill and loud as the song of the
cicadas that had come fifteen years earlier: Mickey could remember
the sky darkening with them, and his mother holding her ears as his
father drove them out to Bryce's Farm to get ice cream. And afterwards how their shells were everywhere, clinging to tree trunks, to
brick walls. The shells were perfect casts of their bodies, completely
intact, and Mickey could never figure out how they could leave their
own skins without breaking them.

Now he saw a broken window at Caplan's Meats. Further down, a
man was being held down by troopers in front of a ten-cent store. It
was not clear if he had been wounded.

Emi pointed to a building on the next block. White smoke poured
from a second-story window. Funnel clouds of smoke appeared on the
horizon.

"Jesus," Mickey said. "Jesus God. Spare my store."

There was a soldier on nearly every corner. Carloads of Negroes
sped past, blaring their horns. Black rags, like the ones they wore on
their heads—"do-rags," they called them—flew from the aerials.

On Pennsylvania Avenue a gang of youths attacked a car at a red
light: they beat on the hood with their fists before the white motorist
charged through the intersection. The gang chased the car around the
corner, hurling stones.

Emi remained calm.

"Turn right at the second light," said Mickey. "Even if it's red."

The military presence was heavier on North Avenue. There were
groups of soldiers on the corners of larger intersections, their bayonets
pointing up like spires.

Mickey could see that the smoke was beyond his store by two or
three blocks, and as his own block came into view he averted his eyes.

"Slow down," he said. "Stop."

Emi pulled over to the curb. "Is this the place?" she said.

Mickey forced himself to look, and at first felt a jolt of relief, for he
did not recognize the block, and thought at once that they must have
driven past it; and even as he realized that chief among the burned-
out units on the strip was his own bakery, the relief held stubbornly
on in his brain, so that as he stared through the empty store window

at the blackened guts of his business, he could wonder what sort of pain he was about to feel.

"Go forward a little bit," he heard himself say. The car rolled forward and stopped.

The LERNER BAKERY sign above the entrance had been scorched down, not inappropriately, to T AKE, the T formed by the surviving lines of the second ER. Mickey could make out the counter at the back, but that was it. Even the pictures on the wall were gone. Hideous black shapes hung down from the ceiling, and the floor was covered with the bread he hadn't gotten rid of for Passover—most of it black, but some of it merely charred, or even white, like the hands and feet of burned bodies.

The sidewalk in front winked in the sunlight; Mickey tried to imagine fitting all the tiny pieces of glass back together, but it seemed impossible that they would equal so large a window as the one that had been there the night before, and for so many years before that.

Two soldiers patrolled the block, even though there wasn't much left to defend. One of the soldiers entertained himself by using the end of his gun to knock off fangs of glass from the top of the window frame.

Mickey clutched his stomach and rested his head on the dashboard. He was soon to be a husband and father, and because he was not yet aware of the government loans that would be made available to him to rebuild his business, he believed himself ruined, and at once saw an abortion not only as an immediate way to relieve his financial burden, but as a kind of retaliation—against whom, he couldn't be sure—for the murder of his own child; for the bakery was—had been—his baby.

But mostly he thought of his father, who had started the business thirty years before, a business that had allowed him, after his death, to live on in small but poignant ways, be it in the smile of a child eating an éclair, or in the prayers over the bread in pious homes. Now it was all gone.

"Mickey."

At her voice, the alarms and sirens came back to him, and he could hear the grit of glass beneath the soldiers' boots.

He felt her hand on the back of his neck, warm, knowing, and at once his pain began to melt; there was an influence in her touch, a strength, all of it too effortless and unexpected to have stemmed from his imagination; there was nothing about her that he could have invented, and herein lay the terrible truth that he had yet to completely face: he would never possess her the way a man was supposed to possess a woman. And yet at the moment he was thankful for this very fact, for nothing that was fit for his possession could ever be of such comfort to him, nor could anything so easily construed that he might master it ever make as much sense to him as that warm hand on his skin.

"Bastards," he said. "Goddamned bastards."

Emi squeezed his neck. "Yes," she said. "You have a right to be angry. But please. Do not hate because of this."

Mickey turned to her. "Are you crazy?" he said. "I'm ruined. Understand? Not insured. I've lost everything!"

"Yes," she said. "I understand."

"Do you?"

"Yes. But you must understand too."

"Understand what? Whose side are you on?"

"Don't you see? We are all on the same side. You, the people who did this—both are victims."

"Oh yeah?" said Mickey. He kicked open his door. "Go to hell!" He got out of the car and ran toward the rubble.

"Mickey!"

"God Almighty." Mickey saw, on the blackened counter, the bread slicer, the register. "How could they do this to me?" he called out from the blindness of his rage. "Why? What did I do?" He stumbled forth, drunk with anguish. "Ashes! It's all ashes!"

"Hey!" said a voice. "Get back!" A soldier grabbed Mickey by the arm. "Where do you think you're going?"

"How could someone do this? Why?"

"Look, mister. This area is off-limits."

"This was mine. Look what they did! Look!" He closed his eyes; his body went slack. "Bastards!"

"Hey, lady—ma'am—you with him?"

"Yes," came Emi's voice. Mickey felt himself being transferred from the soldier's grip to Emi's. "I will take him home."

"No," said Mickey. He swung his arm free, wanting to take a swing at her, at someone, anyone; he stood there, fists clenched, trembling, and then, the sun in his face, his vision shattered by the glare of metal, of glass, he fell to his knees. The world had slipped from him; he had lost control and was falling. "I'm sorry," he whispered. He was lost, and was ashamed. "I'm sorry."

Emi held him. "Mickey."

He crumbled in her arms. "Don't leave me," he said. "Please, don't leave."

"I won't," she said. "I won't."

⁓⁓⁓⁓⁓⁓

Mickey wondered how long he'd been sitting there in the garden. An hour? Two hours? It had gotten colder; his tears were nearly frozen on his cheeks. He closed his eyes, and his memory took him through the events following the fire: the brief pagan ceremony at City Hall (Joe and Morris in attendance, Emi in her mod outfit, the mood desperately casual, wisecracks flying self-consciously as though it were the overdue funeral of a long-suffering relation), the abortion a week later arranged in secrecy through Mickey's doctor (they'd agreed to tell everyone it was a miscarriage), and then, a dozen years after that, the surprise arrival of Benjie, the light from whose bedroom window was now shining through the branches of the cherry tree and into Mickey's damp, stinging eyes.

Mickey stood under the wide night sky and regarded his house. It might have been in another lifetime that he'd brought Emi home, another lifetime that they'd driven down to North Avenue and made their awful discovery. And yet the memories were so immediate, so vivid; in a certain way, it was as if no time had passed at all. Emi had gotten him through his ordeal; she'd held him, counseled him, made sure he kept his head, supported his effort to open a new store. A fine contrast with his behavior tonight! She'd asked him to bear with her, but all he could do was think about his own needs. Sure, it was frustrating. Of course it was. But that was no reason for him to have blown up like he did. They were adults. He had to trust her. He had to give her the benefit of the doubt. For better or worse, she was his wife, the only woman he had ever loved. He owed her a better effort.

Exhausted, penitent, he went inside. Emi had begun practicing again.

Mickey opened the basement door and went down. Emi looked up at him. "Are you back for round two?" she said, lowering her instrument. "Because this really isn't the best time."

"I'm sorry, baby," Mickey said. "That's all I wanted to say. Okay?"

Emi wilted visibly under his apology. "Okay," she said. There was a softness in her voice; she raised her eyebrows, bit her lower lip.

Mickey had a mind to go over to her, hug her, bury his nose in her neck and tell her how much he loved her, but he knew the rules, and it even pleased him to hold back for her, to demonstrate his undying respect for her art.

"See you upstairs?" he said.

"Soon," she said. "I haven't even gotten the chance to see Ben. This page has been giving me fits."

"Don't worry," Mickey said. "I'll tell him you're busy. He'll just have to understand."

Emi sighed.

"Well," Mickey said, "good luck with that page."

"Oh," said Emi. "There's something I meant to tell you."

Mickey bounced on his toes. "I'm all ears," he said, knowing that she was about to make amends, or try to. Usually it was a bit of cheery financial news—a check she was expecting, a job she'd been offered; she saved these tidbits up, it seemed, to cover her debts in their arguments, and Mickey wondered if he didn't provoke her sometimes just to get at the reward at the end.

She raised her violin. "Tomorrow night," she said, "if you're not too tired, there's a party at David Shaw's."

4

"Next time," said Nelson, one hand on the wheel, "I'll shut you down. Dunk on y'ass all day."

"Shit," said Ben. "You couldn't dunk with a ladder."

Nelson winced. "You couldn't dunk if you was on coke."

Ben laughed. "You couldn't dunk if you was wearin' your mama's high heels."

"Yo. Don't talk about my mother."

"Your *grand*mother's high heels."

"A'ight then, Breadcrumb." Nelson popped a stick of Wrigley's in his mouth. "A'ight then." He had one of those dark, bald heads on which you could see every muscle move when he chewed gum. Temples popping. Tiny pointed ears that stuck almost straight out, wiggling. "Nex' time, we put money on it." When he smiled, it was always out of the side of his mouth: cautious, tough. Like he *knew*.

"A'ight," said Ben. "Fifty bucks."

Nelson laughed. "Better get a job, boy."

Ben remembered when he was twelve, thirteen years old, playing ball on the outdoor courts at school (the only courts around for miles that had nets) with a bunch of serious homeboys, for whom the phenomenon of actual netting hanging from a hoop was enough to draw them up from the city in carloads. All Ben had back then was a love for the game. Couldn't shoot, couldn't dribble. His shots rattled the wooden backboard or sailed enthusiastically over it. No control. To compensate he played a pesky, epileptic defense, flailing his arms, batting his hands, going for the ball at all costs and occasionally succeeding in knocking it away from his opponent. Niggas called him Ichabod.

In time, the nets were removed by the Recreation and Parks people at the request of concerned neighbors—the same ones who used to play tennis on the adjoining courts, and now jogged around the track that circled the football field—who could remember a time when the only shvartzes you ever saw out your window were the garbage collectors. But even without the nets they came: shirtless, muscular blacks, running, shouting, jumping up and hanging onto the rim, legs twisted in midair in a crushing ballet whose music—pounding rap, clinking forties—could be heard clear across the baseball diamonds behind the school. The nets hadn't been the main attraction after all: it was more the green grass of the ballfields, the elms and oaks, the pretty houses.

Without the nets Ben was forced to zero in. His eye became sharper, his touch more assured. He watched the other guys, picked up on their moves, their form. Later, when he played with nets in the school gymnasium, the hoop seemed twice as big. His shots began to fall.

Come summer, more blacks outside. Hot, angry games. Niggas chin to chin. The community newspaper reported an increase in break-ins, stolen cars, robberies, even shootings.

Petitions circulated. Local politicians got involved. Something had to be done. And so finally the hoops themselves were removed.

Now it was just these blank white boards.

Ben and Nelson had to go elsewhere to play. Whenever Ben accompanied Nelson on deliveries, they tried to squeeze in a game or two, weather permitting. And what games! Nelson, like a lot of the black guys Ben had played with, refused to concede defeat. Disputed everything. Hurled accusations. Cried foul every time he missed an easy lay-up, saw conspiracies in every point scored against him. Would literally walk off the court if he didn't get his way.

And when he buried one from outside? Shot out his arm and pointed a long, ruthless finger at his opponent. Strutted. Scowled.

Claimed he got scouted in high school by Maryland, Georgetown, Florida.

"They all was watchin' me," he'd say. "Then I got hurt." And he'd look the other way, rubbing his chin as the undisclosed injury rose up in a mysterious bandage-colored cloud.

His lies were too big to be challenged; their size astonished, overwhelmed. Sometimes they instilled fear. Left alone, they settled and formed their own semblance of legend.

The van went over some potholes. The metal walls rattled, and the boxes in the back, filled with rolls and pastries, slid across the floor.

Despite everything, Ben felt lucky to have Nelson as a friend. At school he'd hung around mostly with his teammates, but they'd never really accepted him. It wasn't just a question of race; had he been a star, they'd've probably let him hang. As it was, he stayed quiet: poured drinks alone at parties as the guys laughed and cornered girls; raised his glass to them as they disappeared down dark hallways.

He himself had never actually gotten laid—he was shy, unconfident, cowed by both the professed virility of his peers and gigantic visions of his own sexual failure—but Nelson was under a slightly different impression. Ben felt entitled to his own lies, and of course there was no one around to catch him out: the teammates with whom he'd graduated had all moved on, and as for the guys still at school, well, they'd have nothing to do with him now: he was an old man, a nobody; he'd failed to leave a mark.

"What's wrong, Crumb? You all quiet."

"Nothing," said Ben. They passed a shopping center, a car dealership.

"You sure?" said Nelson.

Ben sighed. "I've got to do something."

Nelson cracked his gum. "You mean get a job?"

"Maybe."

"Come on now," said Nelson. "You got it made. Last week—remember?—last week you was runnin' the show. King for a Day 'n' shit." It seemed he was forcing his optimism. "Bread be gettin' you ready," he said, using his favorite nickname for Mickey. "Bread preparin' your ass."

"For what? The bakery?"

"Hell, yeah."

Ben laughed. "Shit. I'm gonna be a shopkeeper the rest of my life?"

"Ain't no shopkeeper," said Nelson, staring straight ahead at the road. "*Business*man."

"Shit." Ben could sense, behind Nelson's grave and reverent verdict, a jealousy, a resentment, and so waved off the idea, as though being groomed for a lofty position were beneath him, something for punks, for white boys who had everything handed to them on a platter. Still, the notion of a powerful Lerner legacy was appealing, and Ben was careful not to deny to Nelson the existence of a possible nepotism. What Nelson didn't know, and would never believe, was that the only reason Mickey was encouraging Ben toward the bakery—"preparing" him, as Nelson put it—was because he wanted someone around who could afford him an occasional day off. Certainly he had no aim toward installing his son permanently, and Ben, who by his own admission had never stirred in his father a great confidence in his ability, be it in the classroom or on the court, knew better than to expect any rewards. Still, he wished it would happen, wished Mickey would retire a few years early and hand him the reins. A *business*man. He liked the ring of that.

Sometimes he imagined Mickey taking ill and himself stepping in heroically to keep the business aloft and, in distinguishing himself, somehow inspiring Mickey to recovery. But such a scenario was about as unlikely as an early retirement: Mickey was healthy as a man half his age, and showed little sign of slowing down. And so Ben was reduced to baser fantasies, schemes to disable his father, injure him, put him on the sidelines long enough to establish himself behind the counter. A gardening accident, maybe? A fall down the steps? Ben assuaged his guilt over these thoughts—and they were, really, just harmless thoughts—by reminding himself that the whole idea was to make his father proud of him. Surely, he thought, Mickey would trade a few months on his back for a chance to see his son make good.

"I'm tellin' you, Crumb," Nelson was saying. "Your father gonna take care of you."

Ben knew Nelson was saying this not only out of his own worst fears—Ben getting ahead, leaving him behind—but in hopes that, by prophesying so bright a future for Ben, he might bring about a jinx; and yet it was the very hint of fear in Nelson's voice that gave Ben even the remotest faith that such a miracle as Mickey "taking care" of him could happen: a faith so fragile that he felt a panic, a need to change the subject before the hope faded and disappeared. "Forget about me," he said. "What about *you*?"

"What about me?"

"What do you want to do? Drive the van the rest of your life?"

"Hell, no," said Nelson. "You crazy?"

Ben said nothing. Sometimes he wished Nelson were out of the picture so that he himself could drive the van and prove himself to Mickey on a simpler level. But Mickey didn't seem to want him to drive the van.

"You wouldn't understand," said Nelson. "You got a mentality of money. I know you, Crumb. See now, with me, it's different. I'm not stuck on material things. I just want my own little piece. Grow my own food. Live off the soil."

"My mother used to talk like that—how everybody should just be satisfied with their own little piece." He recalled how Emi had failed to come upstairs to see his game last night, when she'd said she would. "She wanted to overthrow the government in France."

"How?"

"I don't know," said Ben. "I guess the idea was to assemble a people's army. Just regular people with guns. Working people. I don't know." He didn't want to talk about his mother.

"Guns?" said Nelson. "You mean like this?" He reached down into the pocket of his sweatshirt and pulled out what appeared to be a real handgun.

Ben tried to be calm. "Nice," he said, but his blood was racing.

"Go ahead. Hold it."

Ben felt a rush of fear and fascination, a kind of juvenile sexual dread. He'd never seen a real handgun before.

Ben took it in his hand. Small, meaningful weight; the very weight, it seemed, of a human life. "Where'd you get it?"

Nelson smirked, shook his head.

Ben pointed the gun at the windshield.

"Keep that shit down," said Nelson. "And don't say nothin' to Bread."

Ben lowered the gun. "You really think I would?"

"He's your father."

"Shit."

Nelson laughed. Ben laughed too: he knew Nelson trusted him. It felt good to be trusted. Sometimes it seemed like it was him and Nelson against the whole world.

"Is it loaded?" Ben said.

Nelson laughed. "About as loaded as you are, Crumb." He held out his hand.

Ben gave it back. For a moment he thought about what it might be like to go on a cross-country crime spree in the van. Him and Nelson.

Robbing stores, getting rich. Like a movie. He could feel the gun's warm weight lingering in his hand.

The van entered a narrow, hilly road. Ben looked out the window—fluffy clouds coming apart like bread, robins falling across the white rind of sky. The trees that lined the road were speckled and feathered with gold, red, pumpkin-orange. The doors of houses were decorated with cardboard skeletons, ghosts.

They passed through the gates of the Seven Pines Country Club.

Ben recalled that his mother had given a concert there once. It had all come out of Mickey's connection to Jay Rattner, the banquet manager. Emi hadn't wanted to do it—she had her opinions about country clubs and their members—but finally she gave in (the pay must have been pretty good), and performed the Paganini Caprices. Of all the composers that Ben had been exposed to over the years, it was Paganini ("Pags," Mickey called him, like he was a ballplayer or something)—the great Niccolò Paganini—who made the greatest impression. The diabolical speed of the notes was exciting enough, but when you considered that Paganini (he even had the word "pagan" in his name) was suspected in his time of being in league with Satan (and listening to his music you could understand why) it colored your pleasure with a touch of evil. The club members, Emi recalled with a smile afterwards, had been a little shaken up.

Nelson drove through the low valley of the soft green hills of the golf course toward the back of the main dining hall, where there were garbage bins and disabled golf carts and foul milky smells.

"Can I take in the rolls?" Ben said.

Nelson looked at him. "Why?"

Ben shrugged. "I'm bored."

"Naw," said Nelson. He turned off the engine. "That's *my* job." He hopped out of the van, took out the large box of rolls from the back and strode proudly to the doors, an employed man.

"Shit," Ben said.

The keys were still in the ignition. Ben slid over to Nelson's seat. The cushion was warm. He placed his hands on the wheel and gazed straight ahead, imagining that he was going a hundred miles an hour on a highway, a gun between his legs. He could feel the speed in his nostrils, his skull. No one could catch him.

When Nelson came back out, Ben smiled through the window and tooted the horn.

But Nelson didn't look happy; he was shaking his head as he

opened the van door. "Jay Rattner out of line," he said. "Talkin' 'bout how the rolls ain't fresh. Like it's my fault and shit."

"Fuck him," said Ben. "Smoke the motherfucker."

"Wish I could," said Nelson. "Come on, move your bony ass."

Ben slid over to the passenger seat, but the thrill of the steering wheel, like that of the gun, remained hot in his palms, a new and important toy that had been wrested from him.

5

Mickey sat at the desk of his enclosed office and stared through the glass window at the large kitchen of his bakery, trying to take his mind off the alarming prospect of David Shaw's party. What would be expected of him? He hadn't been to one of Shaw's functions in years, and though he'd been delighted by Emi's invitation, he was beginning to perspire at the very thought of having to make conversation. What would they ask him? What were the current topics?

Mickey stared harder, as if hoping to find inspiration in the massive equipment by which he earned his living. The oven and mixers were silent now; they would not heave to life until ten, when his nocturnal staff of bakers would carry out their tasks under the sleepy eye of Lazarus, who was paid to observe, to make sure everything was being done in compliance with religious guidelines that Mickey himself could never understand. It cost some money to keep Lazarus around, and the product line was somewhat limited by the restrictions on milk and butter, but Mickey had no choice—his clientele demanded it.

Sometimes it made him a little uneasy to think that Lazarus and the bakers were working here while he and the rest of the world were asleep. Not that he didn't trust them; he did. Maybe it was just that old sense of things going on without him, behind his back.

He was about to begin putting his desk in order when Morris poked his head in the door.

"It's a stampede," Morris said. His glasses were crooked on his nose.

Mickey sighed. "I'll be there in a second."

He stood up and straightened his shirt. The truth was, he sort of reveled in these moments; he liked the idea of making an appearance, enjoyed the image of the owner emerging from the mysterious importance of the back of the store to lend a hand, to set things right.

But as soon as he arrived behind the counter, the fantasy died. Mickey watched as a dozen frail, bundled gremlins created their usual havoc, touching and squeezing the breads and squawking their expert opinions (retired, they had time to become experts on everything) on matters of size, shape and texture. Such tumult and aggravation made Mickey's own eventual retirement seem less like a death sentence, as he had recently begun considering it (witness these customers), and more like the sweet afterlife of jogging, gardening and cards that he had imagined thirty, forty years ago, when he was too young to believe the moment would ever really come, and so saw in it only bliss.

He shook his head as the small mob shouted at him, at each other, waved their money, and rummaged through the boxes like a peasantry whose government has just collapsed. "Nobody is getting served until we have a little order," he said. "Is that clear?"

No one paid attention. Tugging wars broke out over the few remaining loaves; there hung over the scene an eerie suggestion of hip injuries and lawsuits.

"That's it!" said a shriveled man in a long black coat who seemed to be sinking into his crinkled white beard. "No more challah!"

All eyes turned to Mickey.

"What, Mr. Siegel?" Mickey said carefully. "You can't make do with a pumpernickel this week?"

"Pumpernickel? I should say the blessing over a pumpernickel?"

"It's fresh."

A hush fell over the place.

"Fresh?" said Mr. Siegel. A moral tension filled the air.

Mickey said, "Baked this morning—and half-price for your trouble, how's that?"

Mr. Siegel pulled out his wallet. "Gimme two," he said discreetly, and there followed behind him a loud chorus of gimmes. Siegel looked over his shoulder with contempt.

Morris, who had been witnessing all this from beside the bread slicer, braced himself as Mickey lifted a box onto the counter. One molasses-colored loaf after the next was dispensed, and a well-behaved line formed at the register. Those who had swiped the last challahs were now obliged to maintain an air of dignity; they held their braided bread close to their breasts, frowning upon those who would compromise the Sabbath.

Morris performed his job slowly: he'd place the loaf on the slicer, slide the finished product into the plastic bag he had opened with a swipe of his moistened forefinger, tie the excess plastic at the opening into a tight knot, and place the completed order on the counter by the register. At times it appeared that the tempo of his performance was dictated by the looks of the customer he was assisting: he became noticeably slower—"milking the moment," Mickey called it—while waiting on buxom women, though Morris claimed it was only timely arthritis. In any case, he found that the more attractive the woman, the more impatient she turned out to be. "In a big hurry to get to her next beauty appointment," he would say into the lingering fog of perfume. Then he would scratch the thick, wild, sea-salt colored hair that some ladies felt gave him an air of laboratory genius.

"These people want to get home, Morris," Mickey said, operating the register, "and so do I. I could get things done faster myself."

"That's your uncle you're talking to," said Bunny Kirsch, who, despite having recently become eligible for her senior-citizen discount at Lerner's, was wearing a form-fitting pink jogging suit with gold trim and the name of some French designer emblazoned across the chest. "*You* should live as long as he has," she said, "and be *half* as spry."

There was a victorious twinkle in Morris's eye, which Mickey caught. "If you can't move faster, Morris, then stay home," Mickey said with a shrug. "You're not doing me any favors by being here."

"If I thought I was doing you any favors, I *wouldn't* be here," said Morris, blinking behind his glasses at Bunny's sagging, lopsided breasts. Old age had become a shield from behind which he could fire his shots.

Mickey shook his head. There was nothing to do about Morris: he was royalty around here. No matter that he, Mickey, kept track of the books, organized the schedules, the shipments, the stock; no matter that his father had started the business single-handedly before Morris—a skeptic and doomsayer until his own private venture in off-track betting was found to carry risks of imprisonment—climbed aboard with all sorts of ideas and enthusiasm; no matter that it was now Mickey's signature on the lease, on the accounts, on the insurance policy; no matter: the soul of the bakery was Morris.

Sometimes Mickey couldn't help but think of the not-too-distant future, when Morris would no longer be around. Would the bakery lose its appeal somehow, its charm? And again, what of his own retirement? Mickey knew he wouldn't be around long enough to become some sort of elder statesman like Morris. Should he then sell the place? Close it altogether?

He cautioned himself against getting too excited about the chances of the store remaining in family hands. Ben was slowly learning, and it was probably no secret to anyone that Mickey's hopes for his son's education were at odds with his desire to preserve an institution founded by his own father nearly fifty years before. Sure, Emi had her ideas for the kid's future, but these seemed to have little to do with reality. Benjie was Benjie, and it didn't take a genius to see as how his track record in the classroom would, in a couple of years, land him squarely behind the counter of this venerable store.

The place looked as though it had been picked over by a hundred birds. There was only one customer left—Shirley Finkle, Mickey's next-door neighbor of thirty-odd years. Mickey hadn't seen her come in; he wondered how long she had been there.

She put her loaf of rye on the counter and set out exact change.

"The way your customers carried on," she said, moving her hands in her purse, "you'd think there was a blizzard in the forecast." Her cheeks had been hastily smudged: pink here, orange there, green about the eyes. Nor had she been judicious with her perfume. "That reminds me, I have to call the realtor down in Florida."

"Another realtor? Where?"

"Oh, Boca Raton." She tried to put a little Latin twist on the pronunciation, but it came off badly. "So how is everyone, Mickey? How's Ben?"

"Ben? Oh, getting by." Mickey scratched his head.

"And Emi?"

"Busy as usual. Just got back from New York."

"New York, New York," said Shirley. "So nice, they named it twice."

Mickey fingered some crumbs on the counter. "Yup."

"I remember taking the train up to New York to visit my grandparents," said Shirley. "My grandmother would take me to the market and blow the feathers on the chicken to make sure the tuchis was a nice yellow." She laughed musingly, then broke off, as though having forgotten what she intended to say. She turned her head to the window. "I saw in the paper that Emi is heading to Gay Pa-ree. Oh, look, it's dark out already."

"To be truthful," said Mickey, "I've never been crazy about these junkets of hers. But what do they say? Absence makes the heart grow fonder."

"Oh?" Shirley made some adjustments to her coat buttons. "Well, that's the right attitude. People need a break from one another now and then."

Morris, wiping down the bread slicer, cleared his throat pointedly.

"Well," said Shirley, "I don't want to keep you fellas here all night." She patted Mickey's hand; the material of her glove felt unworldly, reptilian. "I just wanted to let you know that I'm having some people over tonight, if you're not busy."

"Yeah?" said Mickey. He couldn't remember the last time he'd had two invitations for an evening.

"If I had the energy," Shirley said, "I'd throw a big masquerade party. I tell ya, I must really be getting old."

Mickey made a face. "Old? What are you, thirty-two?"

She squeezed his arm and winked at Morris. "You taught him good, Morris—you taught him good!"

Mickey said, "Don't flatter him."

"Shirley, what's got six balls and screws you once a week?"

"Oy! Morris. Should I ask?"

"The lottery."

Shirley giggled in a way that made Mickey wonder if she hadn't started in a little early with the whiskey sours, or whatever mixed drink it was that Shirley sometimes claimed she could sure use.

"Well," said Shirley, patting her chest, "I'd better go get the house in shape. Do you and Emi have plans?"

"No," said Mickey. "She went to some get-together or another." He stopped short of explaining that it was David Shaw's party, lest Shirley begin to tingle over the celebrity possibilities and ask him twenty questions. "I was planning to join her, or maybe I'll stay home with Benjie."

"Benjie? Doesn't he have anywhere to go? A party?"

Mickey shrugged. Was it that unusual for a grown kid to stay home on Halloween?

"Well, you can bring him over if you want," said Shirley. "I've got plenty of food." She squinted. "Doesn't he have any friends?"

"Sure," said Mickey, but no names came to mind.

Shirley took her bread. "Well, Mickey, maybe I'll see you outside this weekend. Gilbert has a bad back, so I'll be the one raking the leaves." She patted the counter. "G'night Morris. The lottery, huh?" Smiling, she moved toward the door.

Mickey watched through the glass as Shirley crossed the parking lot.

"A tuchis on her," said Morris, shaking his head.

A pair of beams appeared on the lot, coming closer, brighter. Mickey saw that it was the van; the sight of Ben in the passenger's seat filled him with a sudden and unexpected joy that faded as soon as the van stopped. Ben emerged while the headlights still shone. Then the beams switched off, and Nelson got out and opened the rear doors.

As Ben entered the store, Mickey came out from behind the counter. Ben appeared rangier, more shifty than usual; his hands were deep in the pockets of his jacket, and he seemed to be shuffling at an angle. He stopped two feet in front of Mickey. "Trick or treat," he said.

Mickey did not meet his son's eager gaze. "Everything go okay?" he said.

"No," said Ben. "Nelson crashed the van and all the bread fell out the back into the middle of the road and got run over."

Mickey sighed. He'd play along—for a moment. "Well, that sounds like a busy day. Anything else?"

Ben shrugged. "Not really."

"Do you think," said Mickey, "that you accomplished more by driving around in the van with Nelson than you did the other day when you ran the bakery all by yourself?"

"I think I'd get more accomplished if I drove the van," Ben said. "I bet I could make twice the deliveries in half the time."

Mickey ground his teeth. "That's Nelson's job."

"I'll drive for half the pay," said Ben. He looked over his shoulder at Nelson, who was unloading a box outside. "You can get rid of Nelson and save a lot of money."

Mickey scratched his head. The same idea had crossed his own mind once or twice, and it did please him to think that the kid was maybe developing some good business sense. "That's fine and well," Mickey said, "but we've already discussed the van a hundred times. Didn't you enjoy it the other day, running the store on your own?"

Ben shrugged.

Mickey saw some hope there: the kid didn't say no. "You did a good job," Mickey said. "I meant to tell you."

Ben looked down at his shoes.

Mickey wondered if this were the time and place to make the formal announcement, to proudly proclaim that Benjamin Lerner, the founder's grandson and namesake, was to someday assume stewardship over the Lerner Bakery. But what if it backfired? There had never been any sure signs from Ben that he would embrace the idea, and indeed, Mickey had often supposed that the kid might laugh in his face. The bakery—and Mickey harbored no illusions about it— was not exactly the most glamorous place in the world ("It ain't the Bread 'n' Basket," he would say with a certain pride, referring to those trendy new chain bakeries that were sprouting up in shopping malls, with their espresso machines and three-dollar croissants), and he himself, in all likelihood, did not blaze in the kid's imagination as the picture of success. And so he was left to dance around the topic, hoping to somehow lure the kid in without revealing his intentions.

He squeezed his hands together. He knew Ben was getting fed up with the uncertainty of his role here, knew he probably hated working at the bakery the way he'd hated doing homework. But what else was he qualified to do? What kind of future could he expect? The bakery was his best chance in life. Maybe his only chance.

Nelson's entrance saved Mickey, momentarily at least, from making any clumsy announcements regarding Ben's future. Nelson dropped a tall stack of empty boxes to the floor and handed Mickey the clipboard, on which he'd recorded the day's transactions. "Jay Rattner said the rolls haven't been fresh," he said. "Told me the members been complaining."

Mickey turned his attention to his delivery man. "Can you imagine?" he said. "These people play golf and tennis and bridge all day, and all they can do is complain." He shook his head and looked over Nelson's figures.

"Well, they *are* paying a lot of money," said Ben. "I'd want things to be right too."

Mickey ignored that. "The numbers look good," he said. He set the clipboard on the counter, then went over to a basket by the window and came up with a nice raisin bread. He held it out to Nelson, hoping, out of a vague desire to communicate something—a "hello," really, nothing more—that he'd take it home to his mother.

"No, thank you," said Nelson, putting up his hands. "We got enough at home."

Mickey assumed Nelson was only being polite, but something

about the refusal gave him pause. He hoped he wasn't coming across as charitable.

He wiped some perspiration from his forehead. "Morris? You want a loaf?"

"Raisins I can't eat."

Mickey felt stupid as hell all of a sudden, holding the loaf of bread. He set it next to the clipboard. "Want a lift, Nelson?" he said, thinking it might be helpful to drive through the old neighborhood, gather up his full history before going to Shaw's. "I'm heading downtown, so it's not too out of the way." He held out his hand.

Nelson gave him the van keys. Mickey pocketed them.

"I got the bus," said Nelson.

"You sure?"

"Yeah," said Nelson. "Thanks." He put his hands in his pockets and looked askance.

Mickey sighed, smiled, tried to think of something to do. "Hey! Watch your guard!" He feigned a punch to Nelson's head.

Nelson reacted quickly, ducking. His face lit up like a child's. "Almost got me that time," he said.

"Remember what I showed you," said Mickey. He demonstrated. "Hands up. Lead with the left." He felt a strain in his rib cage. "See that?"

Nelson mirrored him, smiling shyly. "A'ight then. Next time, I'll be ready."

Mickey was aware of Ben on the perimeter of their make-believe ring, watching them. Sometimes he seemed to feel left out, sulky, but hell, Mickey thought, it was like Donna said: Nelson grew up his whole life without a father. He needed some special attention.

"If you want," said Ben, "I can close up."

Mickey turned to his son. Had he heard right? It seemed a little fishy, Ben volunteering to help out. And why wasn't Nelson leaving for the bus stop?

"Sounds like a good idea," said Morris, who had already put on his coat and hat. Mickey's coat was over his arm. "I'm tired, Mickey," he said. "Leave Benjie to close up so you can take me home."

"What do you think we're going to do?" said Ben. "Burn the place down?"

Mickey looked to Morris for help, but the old man was already outside, waiting by the car.

Ben took up the broom.

"Don't be a wiseguy," said Mickey. "And don't forget the locks."

"Okay," said Ben.

Mickey took a step back. "I'll see you later," he said. "So long, Nelson."

"So long," Nelson said.

Mickey turned and walked to the door, feeling their eyes on his back like nails.

David Shaw lived alone in a renovated Victorian row house in an area frequented by artists and homosexuals. Mickey didn't mind the area—the gays certainly kept the neighborhood up, you had to give them that—but he wasn't so sure he'd want to be caught walking around here in broad daylight. He approached the house, swiping at his hair, patting it, straightening his collar. Shaw's windows were aglow, and faint shadows of bodies could be seen passing, some of which appeared wildly distorted, as though decked with tall hats, wings. Was it a costume party? Emi hadn't said anything about costumes.

Mickey pushed the doorbell with a cold nervous finger and waited. He could hear the jangle of a piano—Shaw or Keskov, probably—and the distinctive belly laugh of Gonzalez. Mickey hadn't seen these notables since the reception after Emi's performance in Washington, over a year ago. He rang the bell again, and the door was opened by a huge man who stood before Mickey like one of the Japanese stone gods that were arranged on the floor of the vestibule. Gonzalez.

"Yes?" said Gonzalez, dabbing his forehead with a white hand towel. Mickey guessed that the famous tenor, wearing only a cream-colored robe, was masquerading as the high priest of some gluttonous Eastern sect, though of course there were other possibilities, as was often the case at Shaw's.

"Trick or treat," said Mickey, certain that Gonzalez would recognize him in a moment. When Gonzalez only stared, Mickey cleared his throat and said, "Mickey Lerner. Emi's husband."

"Yes, of course," said Gonzalez. "Welcome. I'll take your coat."

The house was just as Mickey remembered it from the New Year's Eve party that Shaw had thrown five or six years ago: the bamboo curtains, the rag-weave-covered cushions on the floor, the chandelier hanging like a giant icicle-covered claw, the cherrywood bookcases, the carved marble mantle, upon which stood a collection of stone obelisks, and the "modern" paintings done in a style Mickey was certain he could duplicate blindfolded.

Most of the guests were in costume: Sue Wang, the cellist, had penciled in some whiskers and freckles, and host Shaw, in flowing black, was a merry Grim Reaper, refreshing everyone's drinks and spreading gossip. His face was powdered white, and his reaper, made of tinfoil, was taped over his shoulder so he wouldn't have to carry it. He spotted Mickey and beckoned him with a black-gloved hand.

Mickey felt naked without a costume, too easily singled out; and yet to have donned one would have somehow been presumptuous, as if he were making himself one of them. But as he approached David Shaw, Mickey felt himself brighten; he could forget all about the customers at the bakery, about Shirley Finkle, Nelson, Morris, the gang at Chen's Garden. These people assembled before him, these brilliant artists; these were the people who mattered. These were the culture bearers, the world travelers, and damn if they didn't know him by name.

Mickey noticed the spread at the back: wooden bowls of chopped liver, sour cream, chickpea dip; fingers of carrot, celery, zucchini; wheat and sesame crackers; wooden boards holding hunks and drifts of imported cheeses; and, on a long silver platter, a golden, honey-basted turkey from whose eroded breast rolled pinkish shavings, curled, fluted, to be placed atop thick slices of the rye and pumpernickel loaves—his loaves—that rose in tanned hills at the far end of the table. Pumpkins and twisted bumpy gourds rounded out the display, which Mickey could admire even more than the music coming from the white Baldwin grand in the next room. A crowd was gathered there, and Keskov, dressed in a tuxedo and a barrister's wig, was hunched impishly over the keyboard.

Mickey spotted his wife standing by a fireplace whose flames were beginning to smolder. She was radiant in that failing light. Three young men, possibly students, vied for her attention. Mickey walked over.

Emi looked up at him without surprise. "You made it," she said. She seemed pleased.

"Yup," said Mickey. "Where's your costume?"

She extended her hand. "David didn't tell me it was a costume party," she said.

Mickey lifted her wrist and kissed each finger.

"Mickey. I'd like to introduce you."

Mickey nodded at her three young gentlemen friends, all cigars and glasses and phony noses, working their eyebrows. He disliked them instantly.

"Friends," said Emi, "this is my husband, Mickey Lerner."

The men exchanged quick glances.

"Good to meet you," said Mickey. He shook each of their hands, not too firmly, but with the calm knowledge that he could easily squeeze their bones to dust and end their careers.

No, he wasn't the type to fly into a jealous rage and hurt anyone. Emi had her life, he had his. He'd be a fool to think there hadn't been a few encounters with other men over the years, but then he'd also be a fool to insist on believing there had. It was precedence that mattered, and the fact remained that whatever trespasses she may have committed, say, during her travels abroad, or even at some party such as this (what if he hadn't shown up?), she always returned, didn't she, to the semidetached brick house at the edge of the city, with its gardens in back and the wide alley beyond, the golden porch light in front, the cement steps, the iron falcon with the house number on its wing protruding from the tiny grassy hill; always she would open the door, ascend the carpeted stairs, and curl up in bed next to her supine husband, his arms at his sides, so that, lying together, they neatly resembled the word *Is*.

"Did you come straight from work?" said Emi, observing her husband's rumpled light-blue shirt with its slightly yellowed collar, and the three men, seeing that Emi's attention had narrowed, now faded away, coattails dragging.

Mickey followed the young musicians with his eyes. "Yes," he said. "Didn't want to be late."

"Just promise," Emi said, "that you'll protect me from David."

Mickey turned to her. "Gladly," he said, though normally he felt it was himself who needed to be protected from the great maestro. "Has he been drinking?"

"No more than usual." Emi touched a finger to her chin. "Is Benjie home tonight?"

Mickey's neck heated up. Why would she bring this up now? "He's closing up the store," Mickey said, almost defiantly, knowing that Emi wouldn't argue in these surroundings. Oddly, he felt he had the upper hand, and was prepared to give her the what-for should she dare to raise the ante. "And tomorrow morning," he said, "maybe he'll *open* the store." He squared his shoulders in challenge, but Emi was looking past him, gathering her features into a reluctant smile.

Mickey felt a finger on his back; he turned to find David Shaw regarding him from the shadows of his black hood.

"Well, if it isn't the King of *Pain*," said Shaw, making the old play on the French word for bread.

"Mr. Shaw," said Mickey. They shook hands.

Shaw threw off the hood, revealing his magnificent copper-colored head. His perfect baldness had become his trademark; the skull was like a carved object, something recovered, polished, sought by dealers. "Tell me," he said, his white makeup flaking, "how is business?"

"Business is good," said Mickey. "Making a lot of dough, ha, ha."

Shaw screwed up his eye as if in confusion, then raised his eyebrows and burst into a laugh that caused several guests at the piano to turn their heads. "Very good, very good," he said, nodding as though in emphatic agreement on some fine point. Shaw was maybe two or three years Mickey's junior, but Mickey always felt like an inexperienced young man in the maestro's presence. It had never bothered him that Shaw seemed to be a little on the "funny" side; Mickey believed in live and let live, and keep your hands to yourself.

"Thank you for the loaves that Emi brought us," Shaw said. "Did you bake them yourself?"

Mickey felt his face go red. No doubt Shaw was picturing him as some sort of jolly, apron-wearing shopkeep, a dab of flour on his nose, forever at war with the resident crumb-hoarding mouse. "No," he said, "I haven't done the baking in years. I'm strictly on the business end of things these days."

"Of course," said Shaw. "You have bakers."

"Six of them," said Mickey. He glanced at Emi: she was looking at him with what he thought might be admiration.

"Baker's men," Shaw said. "I haven't thought of that rhyme in ages." He fell into a drunken singsong: "Pat-a-cake, pat-a-cake baker's man; bake me a cake as fast as you can. One for the . . ."

Mickey found himself growing disappointed in Shaw, who was seeming less and less like a man who had concertized for five presidents and nearly been knighted. Perhaps Mickey was biased by memories of his old jaunts to the conservatory, when, loitering outside Emi's classroom, he'd catch sight of a younger, sharper Shaw, clicking purposefully down the corridor, books in hand, his gait furious with reputation.

"Something, something, cross it with a *T*; put in the oven for baby and me." Shaw turned away to think privately.

At the piano, Keskov switched to Strauss; several couples began to dance. Mickey saw Emi watching Shaw with horror. What if his memory failed on stage? Mickey took his wife's hand and led her to the middle of the floor.

Keskov was rushing the Strauss, but Mickey waltzed his partner leisurely, using techniques he had learned several years back in an adult dance class. He could feel a gravitational pull in her step, but would not allow her to carry them to the pianist's reckless tempo; there was, in the speed, a certain peril that she seemed to be warming to.

"I didn't think I could still do this," Mickey said, nodding at several passing faces that he thought he recognized. He pressed his lips to Emi's forehead, and, to his surprise, developed a partial erection. He held her closer: her body was warm, almost hot. The ideas of fever and passion got confused in his mind; he wanted to extinguish with his prick all the troubles he perceived burning inside her.

"There's Toshiki Sato," said Emi. She nodded at a small Oriental Dracula who was pouring himself a drink on the other side of the room. "He's new in town. I should go over and say hello. Come with me?"

As she led him by the hand, David Shaw intercepted them.

"Mr. Lerner," he said, raising his chin, as if to recall for Mickey a splendor that he feared he may have compromised earlier. "Tell me, how's business?"

"Well," said Mickey. Hadn't they been through this earlier?

He felt Emi's hand fall away.

"Are you much for apple bobbing?" Shaw said. "You know, I've set up a bobbing tank in the kitchen."

Mickey saw that Emi had joined Sato at the punch bowl.

"What you need," said Shaw, "is a costume. Look at me."

Mickey turned. Shaw held a tube of stage blood; he uncapped it and, raising one eyebrow, held it to Mickey's forehead. Mickey closed his eyes, felt himself be anointed.

"Very good," said Shaw, who seemed to be taking inordinate pleasure in transforming Mickey into a severely wounded person. "Emilie once told me you used to box?"

"A little," said Mickey. "And a long time ago." He wondered in what spirit Emi had divulged the information.

"Now," said Shaw, "if we can get you into a pair of baggy trunks, you'll be all set."

"I'd be out for the count with all this blood," said Mickey. He opened his eyes. Shaw was looking at him with a strange expression, critical, concerned.

"You know," said Shaw, with what Mickey thought was more than a hint of homosexual intrigue, "we must talk someday, you and me."

"Talk?"

"Yes." Shaw didn't seem quite as drunk now. "Soon." He glanced around quickly. "You'll please excuse me," he said, and turned and made his way to the piano.

Mickey thought it a good idea to avoid Shaw the rest of the evening. Should he join his wife, then, introduce himself to Sato? He made his way over to the punch bowl, feeling more and more conspicuous. Emi and Sato stood in a corner. Sato, drink held close to his chest, nodded, smiled, nodded some more.

Mickey watched them for a while and then, satisfied that the little vampire was harmless, went to the long table and helped himself to a slice of his own bread.

6

Ben drew hard on the spliff, chased the orange tip halfway to his lips. Skunkweed. No telling where Nelson had gotten it; Ben connected it vaguely with the gun, which Nelson kept twirling on his finger.

He let the smoke curl up from his nose. "I never bought herb in my life," he said. "Too expensive."

"Always thinkin' about money," said Nelson.

They were in the back of the bakery, sitting on one of the worktables. Mickey had left an hour ago for David Shaw's party, and the bakers wouldn't arrive for another two hours. They had the place to themselves.

Ben passed the spliff. It was different, smoking with black guys. They puckered their big purple lips and drew the smoke in a profound way, as though harboring a tropical knowledge of the plant: the smoke tumbling in the mouth, swirling about the nostrils, disappearing with a suck into the lungs, then out like a smooth musical note. White guys meanwhile coughed, talked about existence, got paranoid. Black guys just chilled.

"You nice yet?" said Ben.

"Yeah," said Nelson. His eyes were pink. "I'm nice."

"Hungry?"

"Yeah. For pussy."

Ben giggled, his boyish laughter clumsy with racing hormones. "Me too."

Nelson shook his head. "When I smoke herb? Shit."

"Hell, yeah," said Ben.

In the next moment they were standing in front of the main refrigerator, stuffing their mouths with the chocolate-covered éclairs that had been stored along with the strawberry tarts and apple pies and other items that contained eggs or fruit and therefore needed to be kept cold. The quivering yellow custard was a shock to the tongue: in its sweetness it seemed dangerously alive.

Nelson fell to staring across the room at the oven, which, Ben had to admit, was a dreadful sight—a great mass of bulging steel (an old "carousel" model, with six rotating racks) that took up the entire back wall. Even at rest it seemed full of fire and destruction; and yet it could produce the sweetest delicacies imaginable. The juxtaposition of the monstrous and the desirable, of terror and sugar, was the very stuff of fairy tales, and so it followed that as a child Ben had seen the bakery as a fantastical place, a land of cinnamon smells, of white dust settling and—not least of all—the terrible giant sleeping. Sometimes he saw it that way still.

He turned to the refrigerator, and on a sudden inspiration pulled out a carton of eggs. "Hey," he said. "Look what we've got."

Nelson swallowed a bite of éclair. "Eggs?"

"Let's go to the Valley, fuck with the rich people," Ben said. "A lot of kids from my school live over there."

Nelson looked at the eggs.

Ben tried to catch his friend's eye. "All got cars for their sixteenth birthdays," he said. "Nice cars."

Nelson smiled out of the side of his mouth. "They leave you out, Crumb?"

"Shit," said Ben. He felt his nerves starting up. "I left *them* out." He had imagined that his own ostracism from the school elite on social and economic grounds would have somehow rallied Nelson to his side, but Nelson only watched him dispassionately. "I had lots of friends," Ben went on, but it sounded false, defensive. He looked at the eggs, unable to face Nelson. "When I was little," he said, "I had lots of friends. Every kid had a grandmother who'd buy them Lerner's buns and strudels and éclairs." He recalled how the cafeteria would stir forestlike with the rustle and crinkle of Lerner's monogrammed wax paper. "Kids thought my father was the Candy Man. Trouble was, he didn't make enough money."

"The *Candy* Man," said Nelson. He liked nicknames.

"He could've made more," Ben said. "But he doesn't really know how to manage things. It's like he's built this engine and is just happy to watch it turn. It doesn't even cross his mind that he can make it go faster."

"What about your mother?" Nelson said. "Doesn't she pick up the slack?"

"Not really," said Ben. It pained him to admit this—he preferred Nelson to think the Lerners a covertly powerful clan, and probably there had been moments when, feeling down, he'd hinted obscurely at a secret wealth—but at the same time it pleased him to confess to a certain lack of privilege ("Money was always an issue," he said, nodding soberly), as this made him appear, he hoped, more a product of the streets. "She could've made more," he went on. "She used to teach privately, you know, give lessons. But she didn't have the patience. There's not a lot of money in what she does. It's not like she's Isaac Stern or anything. Basically she gets to travel."

"Damn," said Nelson.

They headed to the front of the store. Ben stopped in Mickey's office to take the spare keys for the van—Mickey never checked for them, he'd probably forgotten they existed—then caught up with Nelson by the counter. He grabbed the locks and turned out the lights. Outside, he set down the eggs and pulled the gate closed.

The lot was nearly empty. The van awaited. Ben picked up the carton. "Hope we have enough gas," he said, thinking of the long, dark roads of the densely wooded Valley.

"S'pose Bread drives by and sees the van's not here?"

"He won't," said Ben. "And if he does, I'll just tell him I gave you a lift home. For helping me out."

That seemed to settle things. Ben stepped into the van and unlocked Nelson's door, wondering if this plot of vandalism was in some way a response to Nelson's gun, a way of keeping pace criminally. He wanted to lead a charge, win some notoriety.

Nelson climbed in. "You sure you know how to drive?" he said. "Sure you not fucked up?"

"No problem," said Ben. And it was true: all he had now was a damn headache.

Nelson laughed. "Little Man."

"Shit." Ben turned the key in the ignition; the engine roared under his foot. "Just hold the eggs," he said, watching as the needle on the fuel gauge barely moved off the E. "Damn. We got about enough gas to get you home." He sighed; he'd had his heart set on showing Nelson the Valley. "Maybe," he said, "we can get some Hats instead." Hats was their name for the Orthodox Jews who often came into Lerner's— they all wore black hats and long black coats, even in summer, and in their own way were just as exclusive as the Valley people, maybe even more so. A lot of them lived right around here.

Nelson stroked his chin. "I don't know," he said. "I don't fuck with no Orthodox. Ain't you ever read the Bible? The Jews always be fuckin' up they enemies."

"Shit," said Ben. He rolled the van off the lot and onto the street. "You believe in that? You believe in God?"

"You don't?"

"Hell, no."

"Don't say that shit while you drivin'."

"Why not?" said Ben. He sped up a little then slammed on the brakes, causing the tires to screech. Nelson jerked forward.

"That shit ain't funny, Little Man," said Nelson. He sat back and buckled his seat belt. "Shit."

Ben laughed. "I'm telling you," he said. "I can drive." He turned onto a dark street that was heavily Orthodox. His own house was just two blocks away. "Look how they keep their yards: don't even cut their grass. All got like ten kids." And on Fridays they would take over the streets: scores of men and boys in black hats, emptying out of their homes on some cue of light. "Hardly ever say 'thank you' when they buy bread. Not all of them, but most." He cut the headlights, rolled down his window. "Give me an egg."

"Take it yourself," said Nelson.

"Shit." Ben couldn't understand it. Surely Nelson had been involved in far worse activity. Was he really this superstitious about God? Or was it that he was embarrassed to participate in so harmless, so silly a prank?

Fearing it might be the latter, Ben reached over and took an egg from the carton with a carelessness that suggested, he hoped, that he viewed this act as a prelude to bigger things. "Just warming up," he said. He then stuck his arm out the window and flicked his wrist as if putting up a shot: the egg sailed, tumbled and fell toward the windshield of an old brown station wagon, where it exploded into a screaming yellow star.

"Yo," said Nelson. "This ain't right."

"You see that shit?" said Ben.

"Yeah," said Nelson. He fidgeted in his seat, stroked his chin. "I seen it."

It was now obvious to Ben that Nelson was indeed scared; and while this pleased Ben's sense of his own daring—*he* wasn't afraid— he felt cheated of the approval he had so desperately craved.

"I got to get home, Crumb," Nelson said.

"Fine," said Ben. Strangest of all, he thought, and most troubling, was his sense of Nelson's moral displeasure; suddenly he felt as though he were on the wrong side of things, that Nelson had tricked him, trapped him, and that it was Nelson, not him, who yet maintained the advantage.

Nelson said, "Oh, *shit*."

Ben looked at Nelson, then at the rearview mirror, which held, like a powerful lens, the twin suns of headlights. Someone was right on their tail—a cop? Ben's entire skin tingled.

"Shit!" he said. "Hide the eggs!"

Nelson slid the carton under his seat. "I told you, Crumb," he said. "I told you."

In the next moment the interior of the van filled with spinning red and blue light. Jesus! Ben pulled over to the side of the road. He was weightless with fear, insensible; all his hopeful swagger—the eggs, the van, the visions of destruction and glory—had been reduced, patheti- cally, to this: his own shivering body, awaiting in sheets of blinding lights its first dreaded encounter.

He then heard Nelson's voice, calm, even, a voice Ben had never heard before, one that seemed as old and wise as the earth: "Just co- operate," it said. "Do exactly what he tells you."

Nelson pulled out his gun and dropped it furtively into the wide, sack- like hood of Ben's jacket (Ben was too scared to feel or notice any- thing, Nelson saw), calculating that this was their best hope in the event of a search; certainly it was a better choice than under the seat (too obvious), or in the deep recesses of his own bulky coat. He hated to put Crumb at risk, but what choice did he have? Anyway, it was Crumb's own fault. Throwing eggs. Hadn't he been warned?

Nelson made himself small as possible as Ben rolled down the win- dow. Funny: of all the ways he figured he might end up in jail (and it was inevitable, he thought: he was constantly getting himself into stu- pid situations), of all the scenarios in which he saw his sorry ass being led away in chains to some animal destiny of cages and barbed wire, he'd never imagined it would go down like this. In some ways, it couldn't be worse: his crew—Hawk, Rob, Chuckie Banks—would laugh him into the ground ("You was with a white boy doin' *what?*"); Mama would be beside herself trying to figure how a model child like Ben Lerner could've gone bad ("Now I *know* that boy didn't have anything to do with guns; must've been my child got him mixed up"); and Bread, who was maybe the last person in the world he'd want to disappoint, Bread would blame him for everything, would curse the day he hired him for as long as he lived.

Then there was Crumb, stiff as a test dummy in the driver's seat. The boy was wired with fear. Might do anything. Blurt confessions. Step on the gas.

The gun lay deep in the hood of the jacket. Nelson prayed that Ben wouldn't notice it.

"Be cool, Crumb," he said. "Do what the man say."

The officer's frame filled up the entire window. He was one of those milk-fed country boys; his hand was on his weapon.

Nelson hunched in shadow.

The officer pulled out a flashlight. "License and registration."

Nelson felt the spinning lights of the car lick at him as the police radio crackled with descriptions of black males, of weapons, streets, cars.

Ben pulled out his license, then reached over to open the glove compartment. The beam of the flashlight lit up his white hand, revealing Nelson in the passenger's seat. Nelson winced as the light stabbed his face.

Ben handed over the license and papers. "Is something wrong?" he said.

The officer turned the flashlight on the license. He said, "You were driving without your beams."

Nelson had to keep himself from exploding. Of all the stupid-ass mistakes!

"I was?" Ben said. He sounded surprised, relieved.

The officer returned the license.

"Sorry," Ben said. "It won't happen again."

The officer didn't seem to hear him; he poked his head in the window, moved the light around the back of the van. Nothing but a few empty boxes.

He slipped the beam under the seats, squinting.

Here we go, Nelson thought.

The officer straightened up. "What are you gentlemen up to this evening?" he said, still moving the light.

"Nothing," said Ben. He sounded less sure of himself.

"Nothing?" said the officer. "Good. Then you'll have time to step out of the vehicle."

"What?" said Ben.

"Step out of the vehicle. Both of you. Let's go."

Nelson said, "Do it, Crumb." He opened his door.

"Hands above your head," said the officer. "Step around to this side. Hands above your head!"

Nelson kept his hands high in the air as he passed in front of the van. Nausea entered him; his fingerprints were all over that gun, and God only knew where Hawk had gotten it, what sort of history it had. He cursed himself for having brought it to work, for having wanted to impress Ben Lerner. Stupid! But now he was stuck with the false self he had created: it was up to him to be the brave one, to get them through this ordeal like the veteran of police run-ins that he'd so often claimed to be.

"What's going on?" said Ben.

"Shut up, Crumb," Nelson said.

"You shut up," said the officer. Then, to Ben: "You too. Out of the vehicle."

Nelson awaited the worst. He knew he might have to draw attention away from Ben, which meant drawing it to himself. Ben held the goods. Nelson cursed under his breath, just loud enough for the officer to hear it.

"You say something, partner?" said the officer.

"Naw," said Nelson. He relaxed his body as the officer positioned him against the side of the van. Angry puppeteer, arranging lifeless arms. It seemed to Nelson that he'd been through this a million times, though in fact this was the first; maybe it came from hanging around Hawk, who'd described his experiences in so much detail, and so often, that Nelson could believe, especially after drinking, that he himself had lived them. But no, this was real; it was happening to him, and his entire future seemed to hang in the balance.

"You too, captain. Up against the vehicle."

"Wait a minute," said Ben. "You can't search me for no reason. I know my rights."

Nelson shook his head.

"Up against the vehicle," said the officer.

Nelson watched with surprise as Ben was thrown against the side of the van, hands plastered to the roof. Though he was being handled roughly—more roughly than Nelson had been—there was a play of a smile on his face; it was as if, in his submission, his helplessness, he felt a childlike comfort, a sense, within his terror, of a final safety, a place where no more bad things could happen.

Or maybe it was the idiot grin of one sinking fearfully into some fuzzy image of himself as a gangster.

Nelson felt the officer behind him. The big white hands explored his body, seeking information. It tickled on the chest and under the arms. The hands reached in pockets, pulling keys, gum, loose bills, change. Pat-pat-pat on the chest, the back.

"Leroy here your drug dealer?"

"No," said Ben.

Crotch, thighs.

"Same Boy Scout troop?"

"No. I was taking him home."

Calves, ankles.

"From where?"

"Work," said Ben. "He works for my father."

"You work, do you?" Back to the pockets.

"Yeah," said Nelson. His pockets filled back up with his things.

The heat lifted.

"You just stay put," said the officer.

Nelson watched as the officer stood behind Ben. The gun was right under his nose, right inside that hood. Surely he could smell it. Nelson knew he might have to do something, anything, to distract the officer. Run? Shout? Collapse?

The officer started in on Ben. Pockets, legs, tap-tap-tap. Like touching a hot pipe. Nelson watched from the corner of his eye. It was, as he had figured, a less-thorough frisk; and yet it seemed impossible that the officer wouldn't think to reach inside the hood. He stooped down and felt around Ben's ankles. Nothing.

The officer straightened up. His face was red. "Get back in the vehicle. Both of you."

Nelson walked around the front of the van, careful not to make any sudden movements. He got in. They might be home free, he thought, so long as Crumb doesn't pull his hood on.

Ben got in, closed the door.

The cop hung his big head in the window. "I'll let you go this time," he said. His face loomed big and terrible as a planet. "Just get where you're going."

"Thank you, sir," Ben said, his voice leaking gratitude, confession. "Have a good night."

Nelson prayed silently.

The officer hesitated, as if catching a whiff of something—his mustache actually twitched—then stepped away and headed back to his car, back to the spinning lights and phantom transmissions.

Ben started the engine, turned on the headlights and drove off with extreme care, one eye on the mirror. He was still jittery.

"Fuckin' redneck," he said, then began rolling his shoulders and uttering tough, inarticulate threats, intimating that the officer had been lucky they didn't fuck him up, take his gun and whatnot.

Nelson wanted to laugh at Ben's stupidity, but he was too mad. Didn't Crumb realize how close he'd come to getting them locked up? Didn't he care? And all this trash talk about jumping the officer—who did he think he was fooling? It sickened Nelson to think it was all for his benefit, that Ben was trying to impress him, or worse, challenge him somehow, provoke him into making similar vows. Like a smug protégé sniffing out something fraudulent in his master, Ben seemed to be daring Nelson to act. Nelson took a long breath, then reached into Ben's hood—the boy was still spewing nonsense—and retrieved the gun unnoticed. He held it up to Ben's face and poured out his anger.

"You see this?" he said. "See this gun, this firearm? I was this mo'-fuckin' close to being caught with it. All because of your mo'fuckin' headlights. See, you didn't care, you weren't paying attention, 'cause it wasn't you who was carryin' *this.*" He waved the gun for emphasis. "A'ight? You hear me, nigga?"

Ben looked terrified; he stopped the van at the next corner, too shaken to drive.

"I had this shit stuck up my sleeve," Nelson said. He shoved the gun in his pocket. "You know what would've happened if I'd been caught? Do you?" He paused, recalling that he'd once claimed to be on five years' probation. He picked up that thread. "They'd've put me away for good," he said, sinking further into the sewage of old lies. He didn't care; he was too filled with disgust—for himself, for Crumb, for the world—to do anything but drown in a kind of diseased self-pity. "I could've lost everything," he said. "You hear me? You *hear* me, white boy?"

Ben stared straight ahead; he looked close to tears.

"Do you?" said Nelson.

"Yes." Ben sniffed. "I'm sorry, okay?"

"Sorry my ass." Nelson relented, satisfied that Ben was sufficiently awed, and that his own dominance had been restored. To soothe his own guilt over the lies, over his maneuvers with the gun, he grabbed the back of Ben's neck and squeezed, secure as ever in his power of touch, his ability to calm another human being, to make things subside. Still, it depressed him to think how much he valued Ben's respect—no, not respect, something bigger, his idolatry—and how far he himself might go, in word or action, to earn it.

He withdrew his hand and stuffed it into his coat pocket. He longed to start over, to change himself. There was more to him than the image he had hoped to build in Ben's eyes—he'd been to college, after all, and was smart enough to realize, when money troubles had forced him out (though Mama would never admit that it was money!), that he could learn what he needed on his own—and he supposed there was more to Ben, too.

"Guess I'm taking you home?" Ben said.

"Guess so." Nelson sighed.

They headed down to Park Heights. With Ben next to him, Nelson became painfully aware of the changing landscape, as though the abrupt switch from trees and lawns to row houses and liquor stores was symbolic of some personal failure on his part, some shameful biological function that he could no longer control.

Three-step stoops. Bottles. Men on the corners. Little kids bouncing off curbs in the dark.

Nelson tried to think of something to say to distract Ben from the sights, but he found himself speechless, as if punishing himself for wanting to renounce it all. But why should he punish himself? He had nothing to do with this. It wasn't his fault that he came from here. And certainly he wasn't going to stay here the rest of his life.

This vow to leave, this denial of any real connection to the run-down houses, the blinking lights, the baggy-clothed gangbangers and young meaty girls whose early ripeness both fascinated and repulsed him relieved Nelson, for the moment, at least, of his shame, and allowed him to submit himself, grudgingly, and not without an easing of conscience, to the fabric of it. Besides, he knew Ben admired the danger of the place, knew too that this setting, for all its horror, flattered his own masculinity; despite himself, he felt tough, a product of some exotic strain of violence.

There were distant drumbeats. Shouts. Sirens. And yet a desolation, a loneliness to the noise; all was subject to a dominant, overpowering silence that seemed to have a weight to it, a weight that pressed on Nelson's bladder.

"Can I stop in and use your bathroom?" said Ben.

Nelson laughed acidly. There'd been a time when he'd have been too ashamed to let Ben see the inside of his house, but now he was inclined to display it like a grotesque mark on his body which he refused, out of hostility, to hide. He said, "You always have to use my bathroom."

Ben shrugged.

Sometimes, Nelson got the feeling that Ben just wanted to be around Mama. For some reason, Mama adored him. Nelson supposed it was because Crumb was the boss's son, but he preferred to give both Mama *and* Crumb more credit than that. There was, he had to admit, a genuine, mutual admiration between the two, a good deal of which, from Mama's perspective, could be traced to the way Crumb acted in her presence: all good-natured and polite and well-spoken ("The meal was delicious, absolutely delicious, thank you so much"), behavior that Nelson would have found offensive, something on the order of a lie, a con, if he hadn't believed that Crumb really was a corny gentleman at heart. And if Nelson was ever tempted, out of jealousy, to blow the boy's chivalrous cover and expose the other side of him—the egg thrower, the shrill, would-be outlaw—he was also aware that "the Lerner child" reflected favorably on him, made him shine just a little brighter in Mama's ever-demanding eyes. Ben Lerner was, to Mama's mind, more than a few notches up from some of the other individuals with whom Nelson was known to travel, and in bringing Ben to his house Nelson always felt like an eager pet dragging in a gift for his hard-to-please owner.

Nelson turned the key in the door and pushed. Ben followed him inside.

What struck one most about the first room was not the frankness of its poverty—the plum-colored carpet, the telephone on the floor, the blank walls with mysterious white blotches that seemed to signal an eternal waiting for men in white overalls, brushes and buckets in hand—but, rather, the almost shrinelike composition of the shelves on the far wall, which were crowded with framed pictures of Nelson: Nelson at one, two, four, six, a smiling, dimpled, big-toothed Nelson, Nelson in a playpen, on a bike, Nelson at ten, twelve, a suddenly different Nelson, this one posed and carefully lit, arranged shirtless on the floor against a white backdrop—a thin, serious boy, slave black, Caribbean black, the beloved subject of a mother with a secondhand Nikon and a fleeting ambition. The images then tapered toward the teen years, more afterthought than study, a click and a flash, pictures increasingly unfocused and ill-composed, ending, finally, atop the uppermost shelf, on the formal and impassive note of the framed high school portrait: Nelson in a tie and jacket, chin lifted, head slightly turned: studious, unsmiling: the face that is reprinted in the papers, held up by relatives screaming for justice, shown to jurors, the face no one can reconcile with the facts.

It was the effect of the contrast of this room, the spareness and spectacle, which had, when Ben first stepped foot in the house four months ago, demolished any expectations of normalcy for the rooms beyond; so that, when he'd walked through the next room, which contained little more than an old stereo system and scattered cassette tapes and compact discs, he was literally shocked—he felt it in his bones, an electrical charge—to come upon the yellow light of a spacious, sunny kitchen, its shelves alive with bottles of oil and spices, its sills clogged with peaches and apricots. There was a small color television screaming with applause set atop a round table covered with coupons and magazines, and the refrigerator, a fairly new model, was adorned with the crayon drawings (an airplane caught between clouds, spaceships battling under stars) of Nelson's little nieces and nephews, and topped with glass containers of grains and herbs and dried berries.

Now, as they moved toward the kitchen, Ben could hear the television, and Donna calling: "Nelson? Is that you?"

"Yeah, it's me."

"Where you been? Why are you home so late?"

"I had to work overtime. I got Ben Lerner with me."

"You what?" The television went silent.

They entered the kitchen, which smelled as though it had just been scrubbed. Ben threw his shoulders forward and felt a strange anticipation of his own importance.

Donna was wearing an Oriental-type robe—a kimono, that was it— and was so pretty and young-looking and full of kindness that Ben always had a hard time understanding how she could possibly have given birth to a gun-toting homeboy like Nelson.

"Well, if it ain't my boy," said Donna, with a playful folksiness that brought out the dimples in her cheeks. She opened her arms, and without thinking Ben smiled and walked into an embrace full of mint oil and powdered cleansers. He couldn't remember the last time he'd been held so close, and in his ecstasy was only dimly aware of Nelson standing by, watching them. In Donna's arms it was impossible to fear her son; in the softness of her flesh Ben was able to locate a secret about Nelson, a certain tender knowledge of the material of which he was made.

Donna stepped back and looked at Ben with concern. "Does your father know where you are?" she said.

Ben wasn't sure what she meant; she'd never asked him that before, she'd always treated him like an adult. He then recalled Mickey's lecture to him the other night—how he wanted him to stay away from Nelson's neighborhood. Did Donna sense Mickey's disapproval? But how was that possible?

"Yes," Ben said. "I told him I was taking Nelson home."

Donna touched one of her braids. "Because I know," she said, "that parents worry when their child is out after dark." She looked at Nelson, who turned the other way. "Yes they do," she said, her eyes still on her son. "Even in the day they worry."

"You can't blame them," Ben said. "The way things are these days. Even if your kid is good and stays out of trouble, it's no guarantee. Parents have it tough." Ben relished the role of the mature, well-bred young man, it came easy to him, he had a feel for just what to say in these situations, knowing, too, that such performances benefited Nelson, made him valuable to Nelson, put Nelson somewhat in his debt.

Donna nodded her head, agreeing with him, expanding his sense of his own worth; they may have been the parents, and Nelson the child.

"Don't you have to use the bathroom, Crumb?"

"I will," said Ben. He understood Nelson's warning.

"You boys hungry?" said Donna. Without waiting for an answer she turned and opened the refrigerator. "How's your parents?" she called, moving items around on the shelves. Ben noticed what looked to be a few Lerner's desserts in there. Tarts. A pie.

"They're doing well," Ben said, wondering if Nelson had taken those goodies from the bakery. "My mother's going to Paris on Thanksgiving. To perform." He glanced at Nelson, who picked up a magazine from the table—either *Time* or *Newsweek*, both of which Donna would bring home from the waiting room where she conducted her practice—and began to read, or pretend to.

"That sounds wonderful," said Donna. "Is your father going too?"

"No. He has a passport, but never goes with her. He almost went somewhere with her a couple of years ago, to Germany, I think. But at the last minute he decided not to." Ben took a step to get a closer look at the contents of the refrigerator. He supposed it was possible that Mickey had given the food to Nelson, but usually it was bread he gave, not the costlier stuff. Yet even that prospect—Mickey giving it away, donating it—disturbed him for some reason, almost more than if Nelson had stolen it.

"This refrigerator needs a cleaning," Donna said. She turned, holding three apples. "Nelson, get me some plates."

"I'm not hungry," said Nelson. "Neither of us are hungry. We already ate. Yo, Crumb. You comin' up or what?" He walked out of the kitchen and up the stairs that led to his room. "Come on!"

Ben felt a chill. Donna was looking at him. "I guess I'd better go up," he said. He felt confused, caught in the middle of things. Above them, Nelson's footsteps could be heard. Ben thanked Donna and walked out.

Nelson's room was to the right of the landing. Ben hesitated at the door.

"Come on in," said Nelson. He was seated by a window, stroking the leaves of several purple-flowered plants that Ben hadn't noticed on his previous visits. But the rest of the room, with its unmade bed, desk, wall map and comic books, was familiar to him.

He eyed the map. Continents grew like algae on blue water. It was hard to equate Nelson with the idea of such expanses, such distances; he seemed so doomed to his very own block.

Nelson watered his plants from a paper cup on the sill.

Ben noticed Nelson's cheap rubber basketball near the foot of the bed. It was strange: there'd been a time, not too long ago, when he'd have been compelled to pick it up, a time when he'd *needed* a ball, needed to hold it, smell it, feel the roundness of it in his big spidery hands. It was a physical need, he'd thought, infantile, as of a toy, a breast; but now, looking at the map, he wondered if the ball hadn't in some way been like a globe, a world. Maybe it had. But for some reason he didn't feel that strongly about it anymore.

"You like my flowers?" said Nelson.

Ben looked at them. "African violets."

"I *know* what they are," said Nelson, but his maternity over the plants took the edge off his defensiveness. "*Saintpaulia ionantha.*"

"My father used to have some in the window," said Ben.

Nelson was eyeing words printed on a small plastic stake in the soil. "Named after some German man," he said. "Name was Saint Paul. Went to Africa. Tanzania. Found these flowers, sent some seeds back to his father in Germany." He stroked more leaves. "They're not real violets, though. Just look like violets."

Ben wondered where Tanzania was. He ought to know, he felt; Africa had come up often in *Empire*. He looked at the map and noticed, for the first time, the physical prominence of Africa—a continent twice the size of the United States, right smack in the middle of the map; a mass of land that resembled—Ben just now noticed it—a fetus: the coastline from Western Sahara down and around to Nigeria describing the tucked head, and the tip of South Africa, Cape Town, to be exact, forming the foot, the little primordial flipper.

"What color were your violets?"

"Pink," said Ben. He looked at Nelson's wildly blooming plants. There were two desk lamps trained on them.

Nelson nodded, pressed his finger in the soil.

"I guess I'd better get going," Ben said. "Better get the van back."

"Don't forget to use the bathroom."

Ben averted his eyes. Did Nelson suspect he had other reasons for wanting to come inside? "I think I'll hold it in."

Nelson nodded. "Guess I'll see you later then."

"Guess so." Ben hesitated; he didn't want to leave on this note.

"And Crumb—make sure you keep those headlights on."

Ben looked at his friend, who flashed him a little smile. Ben smiled back. "Yeah," he said.

"And careful with them eggs."

Ben laughed. He liked to think that their shared adventure—the two of them standing spread-eagled against the van, enduring the same humiliation—constituted some sort of elite and sacred brotherhood. He said, "I'll take them home, cook up an omelette."

"Careful with that fire."

"A'ight," said Ben. He felt better as he walked out and descended the stairs.

Donna was no longer in the kitchen; she must have gone to bed. Ben walked through the barren rooms and let himself out the front door.

Driving back to the bakery, he wondered at the strange perspective of emerging from the ghetto at night. Was this how *they* saw things, coming out here in cars, on buses?

He fixed the bakery in the needle of his vision, pretending it was his target, that he had a gun, a plan. The lights were on. The bakery really was vulnerable, he thought.

He parked the van on the lot in the usual space. His game of make-

believe was over: he didn't have a gun. Still, he considered entering
the store and in some way surprising the bakers and Lazarus. Scaring
them, maybe. He wished he had a mask.

If this was childish, Ben reasoned, then it wasn't his fault. He'd
been reduced to it. Sure, he'd have rather imagined himself walking in
there as the boss ("Good evening, gentlemen, just thought I'd pop in
to see how things were going"), but he didn't dare dwell on that one.
It was too remote. And yet in a certain way it didn't seem far-fetched
at all. He gazed longingly at the lights of the bakery—the only lights,
it seemed, in the entire night. Hell, he could run the place ten times
better than his father.

He walked to his house, rehearsing his excuse should Mickey demand to know where he'd been. It was simple: he'd dropped Nelson
home and stayed for a snack. What could Mickey say to that?

In the alley leading to his house he stomped on crisp leaves, tapped
the tops of the neatly arranged garbage cans with a stick he'd picked
up on the way. He was the only person out.

He entered the house through the back door. No one home.

He fixed himself a bowl of vanilla ice cream with chocolate syrup
and a sliced banana and sat at the kitchen table, hoping to cap off with
gusto what was maybe the most exciting evening of his life. Suppose
Nelson *had* been caught? They'd been damn lucky. The cop had really
cut them some slack. Deep down, Ben felt he owed everything to that
cop, who, in handling him a little forcefully (and it wasn't so bad,
really; in a way it felt good to be grabbed, flung, straightened out), in
shoving him into the side of the van, had perhaps derived the pleasure
or fix he'd needed to let them go, had quenched the small burning in
his solid, belt-packed paunch.

On the table, in a pile of mail and clippings, Ben noticed Emi's air-
line ticket to Paris. Funny that Donna had asked him if Mickey would
go too; often, Ben had the same thought. More a wish, really. To be
left in charge. Somehow, some way, it would have to happen. One way
or another. He was eighteen years old. It was time.

7

Mickey busied himself with the hors d'oeuvres, aware, on his periphery, of Shaw, whom he thought was eyeing him. He looked across the room at Emi. Toshiki Sato said something to her, then set down his drink and disappeared along the hall toward the bathroom. A few seconds later, Emi followed him. Mickey's imagination took off. Could it be? Sato? He sidestepped the approaching Shaw and pursued Emi through the room, stopping her with a hand on her shoulder at the threshold of the hallway.

"Em."

Emi turned. "Oh, there you are. What happened to your head?"

"Your friend Mr. Shaw attacked me with a tube of red stuff."

"Cute."

"You were on your way to look for me?"

Emi tilted her head. "Yes, I thought—are you okay?"

"I'm fine," said Mickey. He peered down the hall at the blade of light under the bathroom door. "Just tired." He waited for her to cheerfully encourage him to go home, sleep.

She said, "I thought you might be lying down in the bedroom."

"How long do you plan on staying?"

"Why? Do you want to go?"

"You can stay," said Mickey. "Just make sure someone walks you to your car."

"You can walk me there."

"When?"

"As soon as you'd like. I really should get some sleep."

"Good," said Mickey, now wondering if she were trying to trick him, throw him off the trail. I'm no idiot, he wanted to tell her, and yet his own suspicion baffled him. Could it be that he *wanted* her to have an affair, so that he himself would be free to pursue another woman? But that was absurd. He was devoted, and besides, there were no other women. He touched her hair. "Let's go home," he said.

They gathered their coats and said good-bye to David Shaw, who was too drunk and joyous to understand that they were leaving. "Isn't it wonderful!" was all he said, looking not at their eyes but a little above them, lost in a fuzzy alcoholic range that seemed to be located on the foreheads of his guests.

Emi did not, Mickey noted, say good-bye to Sato, who must have still been in the bathroom; Mickey joked to himself that it was all part of the deception.

The streets were deserted, silent, the air seasonably cool. Just to the east, George Washington, arm held out before him at belt level in a gallant, commanding gesture, looked out over the city from his perch atop the tall Tuscan column.

"So where are you parked?" he said.

"A couple of blocks over," said Emi. She took his arm.

Mickey thought to ask her some questions about Sato, but wasn't sure how to pull it off without sounding like a jerk. Instead he remarked on the food, and some of the familiar faces he'd seen. Sue Wang was looking well, he said, as was Keskov, but Gonzalez had put on weight.

"There it is," she said, pointing to the darkness of the next block.

"You couldn't get a space closer to Shaw's?"

"I don't mind walking."

"That's not what I meant." They were on the edge of another neighborhood altogether.

Emi pulled out her keys. "Where did you park?"

"I'm over on Calvert Street," said Mickey. He noticed two figures near the next corner, coming toward them in the darkness. They wore identical rubber masks, representative, Mickey supposed, of some horror film maniac, and walked with their hands in their pockets. Mickey said, "Give me your keys." He took them from her.

The car was exactly between them and the two youths—and Mickey could tell they were youths, it was their bodies, their way of walking. Teenagers. They crossed the street abruptly, as though on a signal.

"Why do you want my keys?" Emi said. But there was a slight trill in her voice; she knew what he was thinking: that he could get them out of there faster.

"Let's move it," Mickey said. He placed his hand on Emi's back and hurried them along; they were almost at a trot. He felt ridiculous.

"Mickey," Emi said, "I'm not wearing the right shoes."

They arrived at the car. There was no one around. Mickey jabbed the key into the lock of the door. Wrong key. He tried another. It slid in like a knife.

"Yo, mistuh," came a voice. It was behind them, not ten feet away.

Mickey opened the door.

"Hey, yo."

"Get in," Mickey whispered.

"Yo, wait up."

Mickey stopped, turned. Emi slipped into the passenger's seat.

"Mickey," she hissed. "Get in here. Give me the keys."

Mickey found himself face to face with the two youths. Gloves, dark clothing, sneakers, the grisly masks; all Mickey could see of their humanity was a faint glimpse of their eyes, the whites of them. They may not have been human at all.

"Don't make a move," one of them said. From his pocket he pulled out a small gun. "Yo, lady. Get out the car."

Mickey looked around frantically. There was no one: even the windows of the surrounding row houses were dark.

"Listen," said Mickey, now looking both of the youths dead on, as best as he could. "Take it easy. We'll give you what you want."

"Tell the lady to get out the car."

"Emi?" Mickey said, not turning his back. "Get out of the car." Then, to the youths, "Is that it? You want the car? Emi—did you hear me?"

He felt her behind him. She touched his back.

"Keys and money," said the one with the gun. He came closer.

"Yo, let's cut out," said the second youth.

Headlights from a car appeared from two blocks away.

"Grab the purse then!" said the first. "Gimme that shit!" He grabbed

Emi's bag from her hands—swiped it, fast as a cat—and rifled through it right there on the sidewalk. "Where the keys at?"

"Yo, somebody *comin'*!" said the second youth. He took off running in the direction from which they'd come.

Mickey looked. The headlights had disappeared, but another pair, more distant, had taken their place. He then felt something hit him in the side of the head: it was the bag: it fell to the ground, spilling coins, vitamins. The youth with the gun stumbled back. "You ain't got shit!" He raised his hand, and there was a loud pop, then another.

Mickey froze. What had happened? The youth ran off. Mickey turned. Emi was on the ground.

"Jesus God," Mickey said. He threw himself on his knees beside her.

She'd been hit. Hideous purple flowers grew up from her eyes. Her head lay in a pool of black.

8

Mickey gripped his drink in both hands and gazed into it. Joe Blank and Buddy Grossman and Morris were watching him. If not for the pale dawn light in the windows, this might have been their old Wednesday night card game: the men seated around the kitchen table, waiting for Mickey to fold.

He had called Morris just before he left the police station.

"What?" Morris had said. "Shot?" He'd been asleep—it was three in the morning by then—and Mickey could picture him putting his glasses on to hear better. "Shot? With a gun?"

Morris must have called Joe and Joe must have called Buddy Grossman, because in less than an hour all three were at the back door of Mickey's house, knocking softly on the glass. Mickey wondered how they knew that he'd be in the kitchen. Maybe they'd knocked first at the front door and he hadn't heard them. In any case they'd been careful not to make enough noise to wake Benjie, for which Mickey was grateful; he had no idea how to break the news.

He opened the door, too dazed to acknowledge the pats on the back, the hands gripping his shoulders. How could he speak? He was living in a nightmare, one which continuously repeated itself in front

of his eyes: Emi on the ground. His own ungodly screams. Her head
in his arms (eyes drowned, nose blown away like the smashed
graywacke noses of some Egyptian sculpture in a museum they had
once visited), her blood on his shirt (gone; as soon as he'd arrived
home from the police station, he'd run out to the alley and in half-
madness removed the shirt and undershirt—the dried blood had an
animal stink, it was like an infection, a mark on his own skin, deadly,
a curse—and set it ablaze). Then came the first sirens, with him holding her and filling with a blood-soaked lunatic hope ("They're here,
baby, they're here, don't worry, they're here") as the street erupted in
noise and light, and a half dozen police appeared and pulled him away
("What is your relation to the victim? What happened? What did you
see? Can you describe the assailant or assailants?") while paramedics
gathered round, kneeling before Emi with their instruments, an efficient, well-trained team of mechanics on hand to repair her, to recover
her life from under the blood, the matted, lacquered hair.

Joe had brought a bottle of vodka. "Sit down, Mick. That a boy."

"Tell us what happened," said Morris. "Mickey."

How could he speak? He'd spoken plenty. Even after he'd been
taken away from the scene, after he'd watched, dazed, as the paramedics placed his wife on a gurney and pulled the sheet up over the
blasted face (he'd actually thought, for a long second, that in doing
this they were merely protecting her wounds), even then, having refused medical treatment (for trauma, for the fake gash on his head
that Shaw had put there), he'd composed himself well enough to ride
in a patrol car to police headquarters on East Baltimore Street and
take a seat under the hot lights of Detective Flemke's cramped, paper-
filled office—so much like his own office at the bakery that at once he
felt a kind of desperate kinship with the man—and pledge his coop-
eration and give as good a description of the dirty sons of bitches as
he possibly could. And Christ, the precinct was crawling with them—
young blacks, handcuffed, looking around, a little nervous, maybe, but
not seeming to fully appreciate the seriousness of their condition.
They should be crying out for their mothers, Mickey thought.

As he described the triggerman—a welterweight, slightly pigeon-
toed, long arms, no hips, definitely black from the voice, no, from the
act itself, who was anybody kidding, look at the neighborhood they
were in, look, as Joe might say, at the statistics, the six o'clock news,
you didn't have to be an Einstein to figure it all out—as he identified,
from pages of photos in a thick three-ringed binder, the exact mask
and the approximate style of tennis shoes—and he was amazed at

what he did remember—he felt himself coiling with a desire to kill, to rip the mask off the little beast and pound that worthless face into pizza with his bare goddamned hands. But he knew an arrest was unlikely; those kids had disappeared, they lived undocumented lives, the city was filled with thousands of them. Sure, there'd probably be a reward—Mickey himself would offer one, and no doubt the pot would be fattened by others—and sure, there'd be a lot of press (a couple of news crews had in fact arrived at the scene just as Mickey was leaving), but how could any of it—the money, the community outrage, the broadcast descriptions, the time and resources of, God willing, the entire police force—how could any of it hope to penetrate the faceless ant farm of shvartzes that was Baltimore City?

And he'd even asked the same of Flemke—"What are the chances of finding them?"—as if by losing himself in this fascinating question, one that inquired into all the various sciences by which criminals are captured, he could ignore the real horror, which was that Emi was dead, her body on a slab at the morgue, cut off from life, the face destroyed, the hands as useless as his own, the ringless fingers curled in the attitudes of ten individual deaths.

This image now fired through his brain as he pushed his drink aside and rested his head on the kitchen table. "I should have saved her," he groaned. "I should have done something." He felt more hands on his shoulders, assuring him that there was nothing he could have done, that it wasn't his fault. Finally he subsided.

He listened as the men tried to piece together, from his intermittent grunts and utterances, the story of what had happened. The voices became whispers. What had they been doing in such a neighborhood in the first place? Had they tried to plead with the killer? Was anything taken that might turn up later? And what about Ben? Who would tell him?

"Terrible," said Buddy Grossman. He must have assumed Mickey was out cold. "Can you imagine seeing that. Being right there, and so helpless. Terrible."

"Brazen," said Morris. "They get more brazen by the day."

Mickey could hear the click of a cigarette lighter. His nose twitched at the first threads of Joe's smoke.

"Forget about that," Joe said. "Us sitting around bitching about the state of the world isn't gonna change a damn thing. The question is, what happens now?"

"What happens with what?" said Buddy.

"The arrangements. Mickey can't handle this himself."

"What arrangements?" said Morris.

"A funeral, for one."

"How can you think of a funeral?" said Buddy. "This is a tragedy. Meanwhile, the shvartze that did this is running loose."

"Forget the shvartze," Joe said. "We've got to think of Mickey. The police'll do their job."

Morris took off his glasses, rubbed his eyes. "There won't be a funeral. She wants to be cremated and dumped into the water. She told me once, years ago."

"You can't have a cremation," said Buddy, who had a little religion in him. "It isn't right."

Mickey then heard, from above, the sound of Ben's feet swinging out of bed and landing on the floor. He alone recognized that sound. He lifted his head.

"Mick," Joe said. "Have another." He poured more vodka into Mickey's glass.

"Benjie's awake," Mickey said.

The men looked thoughtfully at the ceiling.

Mickey placed his hands on the table and pushed himself up. Better get him before he comes down, he thought.

"You okay?" said Joe.

Mickey nodded. He was far from okay, of course, but he had to do what a father must. "I've got to tell him," he said. He awaited their protests ("Sit down, Mick, sleep it off, you're in no condition"), but when none came he took a breath and made his way out of the kitchen, unbearably alone, half-staggering through the rooms until he fell toward the banister, by which he pulled himself up the stairs.

He reached the top. Ben's door was closed.

Mickey stepped back and looked at his own bedroom door. It was open just a crack. He looked down: this was the very spot where Nanna's ring had dropped from his hands years before, and for a moment all the time in between—half his life—seemed to vanish, leaving him with the same feeling of tongue-tied helplessness, the same agony of indecision, of not knowing what to do next.

He pushed his door. The light in the room was strong enough for him to perceive in detail the topography of the unmade bedsheets. Those dark ridges and gullies and hills ought to be preserved, he felt, memorialized as the final sculpture left by their bodies, the last in a long history of silent collaborative efforts.

He looked over at his parents' wedding portrait. Both had died younger than Emi. He tried to remember how his father had broken the news to him about his mother, but it was a blur; he just remembered being picked up early from school, and nobody talking much. He was seventeen at the time, and not given to tears. A tough guy. Didn't let anyone near him, especially his father. Too much emotional weight there—the heave of the chest, the split fruit of his heart; nor was there any escape at the funeral: no throng to absorb one's grief, to buffer and cushion the nearness of the principal mourners. Mickey had stood next to his father at the grave, listening to the sobs, the dumb little spurts. He hated his father for that—for crying, for being able to cry.

Nor had Mickey cried at his father's funeral two years later. He had a fight scheduled the next day, and considered suppressed grief a weapon. Besides, there'd been a dozen of his father's customers in attendance, and they'd looked like orphaned children—lost, hungry, their bread taken away. How could he cry? They were supposed to be his inheritance, his new constituency: he shook their hands like a politician, leader, provider, father. But he had believed, even as he comforted them, that they would have to fend for themselves.

Alone in the bakery after the funeral, though, he had indeed cried. Cried at the sight of his father's apron folded on a shelf.

Mickey turned away from the portrait, from the bed, from the whole room. A great sense of resolve and determination swelled in his chest.

He swung around to face Ben's door.

Don't think too much, he told himself. Just sit him down and put your arm around him and hold him. Tell it softly. Let him feel your strength.

He knocked. "Benjie?"

A grunt.

"Can I come in?"

A sigh. "I suppose."

Mickey turned the knob, leaned into the door. The morning was brighter in here.

Ben, wearing only undershorts, was seated on the edge of his bed, elbows on his knees, a white bath towel over his shoulders. He smirked at Mickey's slovenly appearance—the T-shirt and trousers, the squinting, bloodshot eyes. "Must have been some party. You just get in?"

Mickey scratched his head. "I'm afraid I have some bad news, Benjie." His voice was measured, hoarse.

"You do?"

"Yes." Mickey saw terror in the kid's eyes. He wished he could spare

him, but he couldn't. "Your mother," he said. Suddenly he was aware
of the power, the grisly power of his words: they were more destruc-
tive than his fists had ever been. "Last night. Your mother—she's gone,
Benjie. She's dead."

"*What?*" Ben stood up. The towel dropped to the floor.

Mickey couldn't move. "Last night," he said, thinking that with his
words he had killed her, whereas a moment before she had still been
alive in Benjie's mind. He went on. "We were walking to the car
downtown, and two kids came up to us. Wanted to rob us, take the
car. Then something happened. They panicked, I don't know what.
One of them pulled out a gun and began firing. Your mother was hit."
The story seemed incredible to him; the power of it steeled him, he
felt like a prophet. "She died instantly," he said. "I held her. She was
peaceful. Someone called the police." He then thought he might cry—
it was like a renegade urge, the potent climax that suddenly betrays
one and shoots through one's concentration—but he managed to hold
back, waiting instead for Benjie to start, so that he himself could release and rush over and hold the kid close.

But Ben only stood there, dazed. He said, "You're telling me that
Mom was shot to death."

Mickey was stunned by the sound of that. Somehow, it wasn't ac-
curate. And yet it was the truth. "Yes," he said.

"By who?"

"They don't know yet."

"But you saw them."

"Yes, I—"

"They came up to you. What did they look like?"

"Their faces were covered, I couldn't—"

"What did they *sound* like?"

"They sounded," Mickey said, "like black boys."

"Why? What did they say?"

"Benjie." Mickey supposed the kid was just talking out of shock,
that he needed to know details the way Mickey had needed to tell
them in Flemke's office. Details covered things, softened them. Anything to cover the fact of the body. "They wore masks and sneakers,"
Mickey said. "I heard them speak. There were two of them."

"What happened? Did you try to stop them?"

Mickey opened his mouth. Somewhere in his mind, from the moment Emi was taken away in the ambulance, he knew he would have
to face that question of *why*. Why he'd done nothing, why he'd just let
it all happen—thinking that by demanding it of himself, aloud, he

would be assured—by Flemke, by the men down in the kitchen—that he was blameless, that there was nothing he could possibly have done without having made the situation worse. And blameless and faultless he'd been found. But under the scrutiny of his son (Emi's son, really, and never had he seemed more his mother's son than now), under such a cold and unforgiving glare, Mickey felt culpable, harshly implicated in the woman's death. He knew this was false, an outrageous charge; and yet he knew also that the worst was yet to come, that people—Ben included, Ben most of all—would begin to question why, why her and not him. And why indeed! Already Mickey could hear the voices, pointing out that here was a woman who had so much to offer, whose contributions would be missed, whose music had touched so many hearts; why, then, had *he* been the one to survive?

Ben stood there, as if awaiting the answer to that very question. His chest heaved. He was biting his lip.

"It all happened very fast," Mickey said. "There was no time to act."

Ben said nothing; he was building to tears. Mickey reached out his hand.

"Where is she?" Ben said.

"She's at the morgue."

"Can I see her?"

"I don't think so, Benjie." Mickey took a step forward.

"Why not?"

"Because," Mickey said. His nostrils were flared, his teeth were clenched, the whole face working to hold together. He would not tell Ben where she was shot; if asked, he would tell him the heart.

Ben nodded for a moment, took a deep breath; then he turned away, and his entire body convulsed. "Goddammit!" he said through his teeth, as if cursing himself for losing control. He hugged himself, teeth chattering. "Damn it!"

Mickey understood. God, how he understood. He swallowed hard and approached his son.

"No!" Ben said.

"Benjie."

"I want to be alone!"

Mickey stopped. He was an arm's length away.

"Leave me alone!" Ben shouted. "Go away!" He threw himself onto the bed, his face mashed against the pillow: like his mother, he couldn't bear to be seen out of sorts. "Go!" he said, his voice muffled. "I want to be *alone!*"

Though he thought he understood, Mickey was stung by the words.

It was personal, he feared. The idea was too much for him. Rejection. He backed unsteadily into the hall and found the banister with a blind hand. Grief wheezed in his lungs, and he collapsed for a moment on one of the top steps before slowly making his way down.

It's not my fault, he told himself. I didn't kill her. *They* did. In cold blood they killed her. Killed her! And for what?

He found himself in the middle of the swaying living room. The bastards! The animals! Joe was right—he'd been right all along. For nothing they'd shoot. For nothing!

Mickey raised his fists, spun, looked for a target. His vision was blurred. If only that son of a bitch were standing right here, right in front of him! He'd murder him with one blow! He'd murder ten of them, twenty! Bring'em on! Bring on every murdering little devil in the whole miserable goddamned city!

He faced the basement door—the door to Emi's studio, to her life. Her violin still down there. The music silenced forever.

It was against that silence as much as anything that Mickey let out a yell and swung with his right: the fist disappeared, the arm was swallowed up to the elbow. A clean hole. Mickey felt no pain.

"Animals!" he cried. "Animals!" He swung again with his left: another hole. The door had eyes. "I'll kill you, you bastards! I'll kill you!"

He felt himself being restrained. Joe, Buddy. They held him back. Mickey swooned at their touch; he barely struggled. There was nothing left.

"Come on," Joe said. "Come on back and sit down. That a boy."

9

It was the kind of day that takes on its own shape, that dislodges itself from the stone path of days and rises above it, like the day of a great storm, or the eve of war. There was a heady sense of lawlessness; it was a final day of sorts, a day when money didn't matter, when you could walk in the middle of the street, when shops were deserted. Ben sat on his bed. His grief (or no: his disbelief, his shock; the mere warhead of grief), which had seized him the moment he heard the news—it had been more of a reflex than something thoroughly felt, like a shriek for the pain that is anticipated at the sight of one's blood—had receded for the moment in favor of a great swell of excitement over the strange textures that were growing in and around the house: the smell of coffee, the sound of voices down in the kitchen—Joe Blank, Buddy Grossman, Morris, Shirley Finkle from next door—the urgent cry of the telephone, the reporters and camera crews milling on the sidewalk; it was the day of emergency, the day without limits. His father half-drunk, sleepless, smashing things downstairs in an extraordinary fit of rage, restrained by the other men and now calm as if shot with tranquilizers and conducting himself over the phone—to the police, to the staff at the bakery (Ben had

heard him leave a brief message with Donna, telling Nelson not to
come in to work, which made Ben jealous, he'd wanted to break the
news to Nelson in some dramatic way), to close friends of Emi who
had read the account in the morning paper—with quiet, admirable
control. There was a sense of purpose, of mission. The house had been
transformed into a kind of command post. Ben preferred to let the atmosphere flow up like smoke and reach him in his bed rather than
hurl himself into the flames by going downstairs. Despite his excitement, he felt terribly shy; he knew he'd be watched, studied. Emi's
face would assert itself in his own. He had a responsibility to that like-
ness, he felt; he must keep himself withdrawn, separate. He had gained
a mysterious fame.

He lay back on the blankets, trying to make sense of his reaction to
the news—his need to be alone, his dread of his father's touch. Mickey
had *been* there, had *seen* it; he was like a man returned from a dark
continent, a carrier of experience, of disease, leper and prophet both,
a man transformed in unknowable ways. He'd been destroyed and re-
made in an instant, a monster of assembled parts now jolted to life,
mumbling unintelligibly and holding out his arms, taking his first
dreadful, tentative steps, a creature powerful yet weak, seeking life,
the life of his son, wanting comfort, contact—it had been too much.
Ben could not bear to see his father this way, so broken; he felt even
more for him than he did for his mother, whom, after all, he could not
see, and whose absence from the world (she was to be cremated, he'd
overheard) seemed but the logical extension of those protracted absences and quarantines by which he'd come to know her best, much
as a child comes to know, even intimately, an unseen animal: the prints
in the mud, the foods which, set out, have been eaten or ignored; the
peculiar musk; the strong, exciting sense of its nearness. Such beings
were already so close to the spirit world that, should all evidence of
their life vanish, it would still be difficult to imagine them dead. And
yet he knew, too, that what had allowed him, as a child, to imagine his
mother as a kind of mythical creature, one who, confined to rooms of
ticking metronomes and bravura passages, had assumed a human form
in order to speak the frail language of violins, was the underlying certainty that she was, in fact, mortal; a certainty which, if a little disap-
pointing (it was fun to believe the impossible) had at least saved him
from being deathly afraid of her. Yet what he would give, now, to believe in her immortality!

Shot to death. There was no getting around that. Even a vampire
could be killed with a bullet. No death seemed more indisputable,

more emphatic, more final. Ben supposed it had yet to sink in, otherwise he'd be beating his chest like Mickey, screaming bloody murder. Or maybe Mickey's violence had robbed him of his own, had forced him into a more moderate role; in fact Mickey's temper had inspired calm in everyone. Still, Ben could envision himself in a courtroom, lunging at the defendant and stabbing him through the heart or neck with some crude instrument he'd smuggled past security. And though such thoughts helped soothe his unformed anger, helped massage it into something more manageable, he couldn't help but think he was lacking a normal thirst for revenge, if for no other reason than that he believed, deep down, that Emi was less to be pitied than blamed.

The idea stunned him. Like a drug, shock had drawn him into the darkness of his own mind, had sent him quaking in the face of hideous, misshapen truths. Emi had failed him since the day he was born, he realized, so much so that he could feel her death as a personal attack, the final assault on his longing for her; and when he dared to try to correct this seemingly wayward thought, he arrived at the even more disturbing conclusion that for her neglect, her selfishness, she'd gotten what she'd deserved; and that he himself, in a way unleashed by his own secret wishes, had been unspeakably avenged.

He fully expected a lightning bolt to crash through the roof and strike him between the eyes for having such thoughts, and when he found himself alive and unhurt a moment later he pledged a deep remorse. Still, he couldn't escape the feeling that there was a certain ruthless logic to her death, that the configuration of the family had been hewn to its essence: Emi reduced to hunks and crumbs of powdery rock as father and son emerged from the rubble, the dust, chiseled fine and bold as the divine figures peering from the acanthus and vines of the frieze that lined the main corridor of the Wurther. Ben recalled going there with his father on Saturdays to lunch with Emi in the courtyard during her break between classes; it was like visiting a sick person, one confined to an institution. Emi would remark on the architecture of the place, or complain about her students, the weather, her own progress, apologizing along the way for not being able to spend more time with them. Always, Ben noted, she would avoid him in subtle ways, as though to hide from him her disappointment that he was not like certain other youngsters he'd seen in the courtyard attached to their mothers' hands: a prodigy, or even gifted, or even remotely musical.

He wiped a tear from his lip. He wondered if he were making excuses, trying to avoid what he knew must be his duty as a son: to rant, to whip himself into a froth of murderous rage. What would Nelson do, he wondered, if it had happened to him? What would anyone do? Ben felt ashamed in his failure, and could only imagine that it must be cowardice. Nelson would go out and look for the culprits himself, never mind that he had no idea who they were. Ben determined to work himself into a proper frenzy. He pictured it: his parents walking, the assailants lurking, the crisscross of dark streets; and, sure enough, as the unwitting couple walked into a trap no shouts could undo, his hands began to tremble, and his heart raced as though hoping to catch up with them, stop them, turn them back from the fate that awaited them in the very next moment—

Horrified, Ben sprang up and grabbed his basketball from the floor of his closet, his thoughts hurling themselves away from the vision like a madman who has looked upon God.

The ball. Ben held it, spun it slowly in his hands, appreciating its perfect roundness, which for some reason struck him as poignant and even miraculous. He gazed into it as though it were a crystal ball in which he could see every memory: the diamond-shaped patterns of veins on her hands; the half-moon of a face as she read a book that glowed like coal under her bedroom lamp; those times when she'd hugged him and kissed him and said things that made him think, in that moment, that she really did love him and care about him, that she was sorry for not being more of a mother to him but that she knew he understood and though he might not forgive her she loved him just the same and if something happened to him she would be devastated and how could she not love him when he was her own son, but of course she loved him, and she was sorry, and she was sorry, and maybe one day things would be different and they would spend time together, maybe when he was older, yes, maybe he could come to Europe with her, or New York, and they could have dinner in a restaurant and talk and get to know one another and discover themselves in one another and celebrate their new understanding and walk down the street and laugh and be like other mothers and sons who walked down the street and laughed, or didn't laugh, but who walked together and were comfortable and natural and weren't afraid and could even be proud.

The tears fled his eyes, dripping from his chin onto the rough orange skin of the ball, where they gleamed in the morning light. He brought the ball to his chest and embraced it for a long while.

His breathing relaxed, but the rage would not let go. He'd brought it forth by effort, had given it life. It was a beating, a chant, a command to act. And he *would* act, he vowed. He would.

He put on his sweats, laced up his sneakers. He needed air. Needed to run, jump. Fly.

He went downstairs and quietly let himself out through the front door. No one saw him; even the reporters had dispersed.

He ran to the bus stop and caught the number 7. There were plenty of seats. He put the hood of his sweatshirt over his head, kept the ball locked between his knees. All the homeboys on the bus were watching him.

Ben felt toughened by his ordeal; his loss, so violent, had put him on equal footing with any of these punks. In a way, he had become one of them. They could sense it, too, he felt; they knew not to mess with him. He sniffed, twitched his shoulders. His hands were pink starfish on the ball.

Row houses, billboards, liquor stores. Bars, sub shops. Discount clothing outlets. Trash in the streets, the alleys. Brown leaves.

People got on, got off.

Ben hunched over the ball like an addict. His baby. His big round baby. No one was going to get near him. He'd already paid.

The stop to Nelson's house came up. Ben rang the bell, stepped off the bus. He stood alone on the corner, wondering why he had come down here. He felt drawn somehow, like an animal to water. The killer, he reflected, had most likely been born in this very element. Was that it? A need to zero in on something, to approach the source? To immerse himself in whatever had destroyed his mother?

He walked toward Nelson's house, the ball under his arm.

Niggas on the corner with murder in their eyes.

Don't look, he told himself. Just keep walking.

Yo—lemme see that ball. Yo!

He walked faster. His destination was in sight.

Yo, Money! Voice getting smaller. *Yo, whassup?*

Maybe Donna would be there. He hoped she was. He didn't know what they would say to each other, but he believed he could gain or discover something just by being near her. He wanted to be held.

He reached the door, knocked. Tried to look natural.

The door opened. A little girl looked up at him. Then two younger boys appeared behind her. Their eyes were wide.

"Hi," Ben said. "Is Nelson home?" He wondered if these were the kids whose drawings hung on the refrigerator.

The boys crowded near the girl. One held a doll of an avenging cartoon character, popular five years ago. The other put a thumb in his
mouth. The girl saw this and slapped his hand so that the thumb fell
out. Then she looked at Ben and said, "He's coming back." She must
have been seven or eight years old, the boys four or five. There was a
sense of even more children beyond them, deep in the house.

Ben held the basketball out to the thumb-sucker. The boy stepped
back, reinserted the thumb.

The girl rolled her eyes, stomped her foot, then grabbed the boy's
arm and dragged him forward.

Ben spun the ball on his finger. "Is Miss Donna home?" he said.

The girl shook her head.

"Where is she?"

The girl shrugged. Ben figured maybe they didn't know her as Miss
Donna.

The boys appeared hypnotized by the spinning ball.

The girl said, "He's home."

Ben turned around. Nelson was standing by the curb.

The children disappeared into the house.

Ben faced his friend. "Wanna shoot around?" he said. A crazy smile
escaped. He held out the ball.

Nelson approached him cautiously. "What you doin' here?"

Ben shrugged. "Felt like playing some ball."

Nelson looked him over. "Shouldn't you be at your house?"

Ben spun the ball on his finger.

Nelson sniffed. "How you get down?"

"Bus."

Nelson stroked his chin.

Ben bounced the ball.

Nelson looked around like he was nervous about being seen. "So
where's your father at?" he said.

"Home." The ball hit Ben's foot, bounced away from him.

Nelson picked it up.

Ben wiped his nose with his sleeve.

Nelson said, "Come on."

Ben followed him into the house.

The kids—four of them now—peered around a corner.

"Get back in the kitchen and stay there," Nelson said. "Or the big
crazy white man gonna get you."

The kids ran squealing.

Ben smiled, then bit his lip and shivered.

Nelson was still looking at where the kids had been. "I heard all about it," he said. "My mother woke my ass up and told me what happened. I was like *damn*." He shook his head. "We opened up the paper, and there it was, in print. That shit is fucked up, yo. *Fucked* up." He shook his head more rapidly; he was having trouble with this meeting. Ben felt bad for him. Nelson recovered himself and looked at Ben's chest. "Hope they find them niggas."

"They will," said Ben.

Nelson put the ball in Ben's hands. "You better get home."

Ben wanted to ask where Donna was, but for some reason he couldn't. He knew that if she were to walk through that door in the next second he would collapse into her arms.

"And better watch your back on the way to the bus," Nelson said. "Niggas'll kill you for that ball. Them shoes, too."

Ben looked out the window.

"Leave the ball," said Nelson.

"No." Ben held it tighter. He wanted kindness, a hand on his shoulder. Anything. He looked imploringly at Nelson. Couldn't somebody help him? Anyone?

"Breadcrumb." Nelson reached into his pocket. "Take this with you." He was holding the gun.

Ben's scalp tingled. There was a moment of recognition: Ben felt his mother's murder pass through him like a swallowed pill. The gun seemed to be connected to it, connected to all shootings; it was every gun ever made, yet somehow meant especially for him: his hand went out. "Thanks," he said. The gun pulsed in his grip like something too powerful for him, a girl's sex melted down and forged into a deadly chunk in his palm.

"Put that shit away," said Nelson, watching for the kids.

Without thinking, Ben dropped it into his pocket. His heart beat like a ball dribbled close to the ground. "It's—loaded?"

Nelson looked askance.

Ben scratched his head. Things were moving too fast for him. "How come you want to get rid of it?" he said. He laughed. "You shoot someone?"

"Don't even play like that, Crumb."

Ben had hardly realized what he'd said; it must have sounded like he was linking Nelson to the murder, one of those sick jokes that just comes out by surprise. But he hadn't even been thinking of Emi.

"Sorry," Ben said. He felt for the bulge in his pocket. "What I meant was—you got another one?"

"Don't worry about me. Just get your ass on home."

Ben sniffed and looked down at his feet. Then he felt Nelson's hand on the back of his neck.

"You a'ight?" Nelson said.

Ben shrugged. "I guess."

"I'll see you later then." The hand fell away. "A'ight?"

"Yeah." Ben raised his fist, tapped it against Nelson's. Yes: they were brothers. Sometimes, Ben could feel himself rising to what he imagined was Nelson's highest ideal; under Nelson's eye he could attain a kind of rare grace, a style, and so while he may have wanted to beg Nelson to let him dwell a little longer amid the shrine of photographs and splotched walls and sweet smell of dried laundry and children squealing in the sun-struck kitchen, he was bound instead to straighten his spine and walk out of there without another word, his fist half-raised, the slightest hint of street injury in his step.

"You good?" Nelson called after him.

Ben looked back. "Yeah."

Nelson raised a fist, then closed the door.

Ben stood there a moment, trying to bask in the warmth of the moment. Nelson. Could he have asked for a better friend?

He walked back to the bus stop, dribbling the ball with his right hand, almost wishing someone would get up in his face. With his left hand he reached into his pocket and probed the hole of the muzzle with a skinny finger. He was armed now, and he felt the pressure of the new obligations that being armed entailed. Was he a man or not? What excuse did he have not to avenge his mother?

His teeth chattering, he walked toward the homeboys who had called after him on the way to Nelson's. Let them just try to rob him! They were playing a dice game against a wall, laughing, but even as Ben stopped twenty feet away and dribbled the ball they refused to notice him. But why? Were their instincts really that sharp? Surely they knew he was there; and yet they ignored him. After a moment, Ben found himself wishing he could join them in their game.

He walked on, then ran when he saw the bus pulling up. There was no one but old black women aboard, and a few little kids. He was armed, and now, wouldn't it figure? there was no one around to provoke him.

He got off the bus and jogged home. Huffing down the alley, he pulled out the gun and waved it in the air. He came close to squeezing the trigger, and was pleased that he could control his fingers, that he could hold back if he wanted. The lumbrical muscles. His mother used to talk about that. The fingers.

He went around to the front and opened the door. By the sound of things back in the kitchen, no one heard him come in, or even realized that he had been gone.

Mickey tapped his fingers on the steering wheel. "Benjie?" he said. "You awake? I thought you might like to see the water."

They were driving on the eastbound span of the Bay Bridge, headed for the ocean. Emi's ashes were in a plastic container in the trunk.

The water was a dull silver with flecks of blue mixed in, the color, Mickey told himself, of Emi's eyes. Tiny whitecaps erupted and faded like stars twinkling. There were few boats out because of the cold. A speedboat rocked over the choppy water, cutting a long white slash across the Chesapeake.

"Ben?" Mickey glanced over. The kid was sound asleep. Or maybe he was faking it to avoid conversation. Either way, Mickey was grateful. In the three days since the murder (and murder it was: Mickey wasn't in the business of mincing words, of calling it, like some, the "tragedy," the "incident"), things between them had been strained; Mickey was so busy with reporters, investigators (no suspects, no solid leads, though it was, Detective Flemke told him, still "early in the game"), the crematory, with phoning his clients and vendors at the bakery that he'd barely had time to shed a goddamned tear, to say nothing of trying to comfort Ben, who had withdrawn into a puzzling adolescent silence, an impenetrable bubble from which he could see out but no one could see in. Mickey had hoped for a breakthrough today, if not in the car, then by all means at the shore, where they would walk out on the old fishing pier and scatter the ashes just as Mickey had planned, each holding part of the container and turning it over on cue.

Emi had made her wishes known years ago, and although cremation went against the traditions with which Mickey was most familiar, he'd agreed to see to it, should he survive her; they'd even shared a spooked laugh over the idea of a body reduced to ashes, though a minute later Mickey had fallen into a state of gloom, thinking about his own splendid body decaying in a box. Maybe he ought to be cremated too, he now thought, or preserved in some morbid fashion, though he had to admit that there was a certain dignity to ashes, an eloquence, a statement of modesty that seemed to honor the best in a person. Not that a burial would have been undignified. In fact, Mickey could see as how a traditional funeral may have even worked to his advantage, in that it not only might draw all sorts of interesting people from Emi's life, some with whom it'd be nice to be seen rubbing shoulders, but draw, too, a certain gentleman, one who might reveal himself in the way he stood, the way he mourned, whose demeanor at the grave (Mickey couldn't help but imagine it) might shed some light on why, near the end, the deceased (as Flemke liked to call her) had been so cold toward the man who had loved her most.

Dense metallic clouds the color of the bridge's suspension towers created a harsh, muted light; Mickey lowered the visor to keep out the glare. On the eastern horizon a white *V* passed high across the clouds. Canada geese? Yes: it must be. It was their time of year. Mickey recalled his old drives with Emi, the way he'd point things out to her. They must have made this drive a dozen times.

Mickey tried it now. "Look, Benjie," he said, pointing at the white-breasted birds. "Canada geese."

There was no reply.

Mickey bit his lip, drove on in silence. Well, he couldn't expect that the kid would be interested, and probably it was bad judgment to have tried to relive a moment that had meant so much to him even then, when Emi had gazed up at the mysterious formation and observed, with her hand on his thigh, that it was a love arrow from the north being shot across the heavens.

About thirty miles later Mickey pulled onto the gravel lot of a small general store. There was a motel across the road, then a couple of ramshackle houses, then miles of wood and field and stream.

Ben woke up. "Where are we?" he said.

"Halfway there," said Mickey. "You want anything from the store?"

"No, thanks."

"Okay then." Mickey got out of the car, heartened by this small exchange. He'd get the kid a soda anyway.

He pulled up the collar of his long coat and walked across the gravel. A bell tittered as he pushed open the shop door. The woman behind the counter looked at him; she wore a green polo shirt and a faded denim jacket. Mickey placed her at about forty, forty-five tops. It was in his nature to size people up.

"Mornin'!" said the woman. It was like a command, an attempt to startle him. She was blond, freckled, her skin and hair sea-whipped, wind-whipped. Rough lips, hands, strong white teeth. A salty, robust health whistled from her face like the menthol of a fisherman's lozenge.

"Morning," said Mickey. He looked around the place. It wasn't much. Three aisles of basic provisions. Canned soup, powdered drinks. Fishing supplies at the back.

In the far aisle, a black boy of maybe sixteen was looking up at a shelf of breakfast cereals. Mickey felt a chill. The kid looked suspicious. Mickey wondered if the woman had delivered her greeting forcefully in order to alert the boy that she was no longer alone in the store, no longer such an easy target; she seemed to sense what Mickey knew all too well: that a kid like this might be carrying in his pocket more than just a couple of nickels and a penknife. Mickey caught the woman's eye to let her know that he was aware of the problem and would stick around until the boy got the picture and beat it. The woman returned what Mickey thought was a smile of gratitude.

"Looking for anything in particular, sir?" she said, loud enough for the boy to hear.

"As a matter of fact, I am," Mickey said, matching her volume. He almost wished the boy would try something, just so he could intervene, throw a tackle maybe. He said, "I'd like a coffee and a Coke."

"What'll you take in the coffee?" said the woman, reaching for the pot. She seemed to relax some as she poured the muddy brew into a paper cup.

"A little milk, a little sugar," said Mickey. He kept his eye on her, just in case she looked up for assurance. But she didn't; no, she was good, she was just going about her business as though hoping to lure the boy into their clever little trap. Maybe she had a gun of her own behind the counter there; Mickey could picture her heaving a shotgun, taking aim like an old-time matron of a saloon. Still, Mickey liked to think his mere presence an ample deterrent; so far, the kid hadn't moved.

The woman turned her eyes in the direction of the boy. "Troy," she said. "Could you bring this gentleman a Coke?"

The boy stared at the cereal boxes a moment longer, then slipped off to the refrigerator where the sodas were kept. Mickey felt the blood rise in his cheeks.

Troy brought the cold can to the front and set it on the counter, then picked up a rag there and returned to the back.

Mickey kept his head down as he fished in his pocket for change. He supposed he ought to feel like a horse's ass, jumping to conclu-

sions and creating fantasies of derring-do. And those looks he'd exchanged with the woman—what, then, had they meant? He'd figured
everything wrong. It's your state of mind, he told himself. Still in
shock, et cetera. He gathered up his purchases and mumbled his
thanks and leaned his shoulder into the door. It didn't budge; he had
to transfer the Coke into the hand that held the coffee and pull the
door instead. Bells cackled.

Back on the road, Ben said, "What about her car?"

"What about it?" said Mickey.

"What's going to happen to it?"

Mickey sipped his coffee. He hadn't even thought of that; her car
was still parked at the crime scene, for all he knew. Or had it been
towed? He'd have to make some calls when they got home. In any
case, it was a hell of a thing to think about at a time like this. "I'll
probably sell it," he said, not only to punish the kid for having asked
such a selfish, insensitive question—obviously he was thinking of an
inheritance—but because he meant it: that car would always be tied
in his mind to what had happened, and he never wanted to see it
again.

"You okay?" Ben said.

Mickey nodded, wiped his goddamned eye. Sure, he was okay.
They'd've shot her anyhow, whether he'd told her to get out of the car
or not. Mickey dared anyone to contradict this, though of course no
one would. He alone had been there; he alone knew. Emi should never
have parked there—hell, she'd put them both in harm's way. Stupid!
And the craziest thing of all was that way down in his heart of hearts
Mickey really believed this, really believed that he wasn't responsible.
That was the horror: it was as if a lack of guilt must mean a lack of caring. But that wasn't true. He'd do anything to bring her back. Maybe,
he thought, it was the general opinion that the wrong person had died
that fueled this almost stubborn refusal to feel responsible, though of
course he had no real evidence of such a consensus. But why did he
need a *reason* to feel guiltless? Weren't the facts of the case enough?
After all, everyone he'd talked to, from Flemke to Morris to Joe to
Shirley Finkle, had *told* him it wasn't his fault, even when he'd
stopped suggesting that it was—as if they were concerned that he'd
recovered too quickly, and were insisting on his innocence as a way to
comfort themselves, convince themselves that he, Mickey, was in a
state of proper turmoil. Still, it was a strange sensation, this lack of
guilt—like probing with your tongue for a missing tooth. Always that
void, surprising and awful each time. Ah, but the hell with it! He'd

been *spared*, for God's sake. He'd have thought people might want to celebrate that; it could so easily have been worse.

"Maybe," Mickey said, "this isn't the best time to think about her car." But he understood his son. To talk about her car was to deny the gravity of things. Still, it irked him; the hint of an apparent callousness in Ben reminded him of what might be the worst in himself. He watched from the corner of his eye as Ben slumped down in his seat and looked out the window.

They drove in silence. The land was utterly flat under a sky that was taking up mellow swirls, the purple and pink of seashells. Between dried corn and soybean fields and reedy marshland lay old farmhouses, billboards hawking real estate or suntan oil, trailer parks, the odd inhabited shack, produce stands offering apples and pumpkins and Indian corn, even peaches, motels long and flat as the land itself and the occasional rambling shopping center.

Mostly, though, Mickey noticed the red leaves of the woods: sumac, dogwood, sweet gum. He thought to point them out, name them, but instead he fixed his eyes on the road until the world opened up and the smell of the sea filled the car, and the horizon ahead dropped off to nothing but white sky. Mickey breathed in. Gulls shrieked around the marshes. Then a horizontal bar of darkness rose above the distant trees: the sea, or a reflection of it. He turned down a back road. Ben, he noticed, had sat up, tense and expectant as a dog by a door. Through a narrow passage of overhanging willow trees and wild hemlock appeared a bridge that took them over an inlet and onto a narrow, sandy strip of land. There were boat slips on the inlet, a marina, a bar, a police station.

They parked in a public lot. Mickey fed the meter and retrieved the container from the trunk. "This is how she wanted it," he mumbled. The air was cold, raw, redolent of dead fish and splintered wood. The sky was white, sagging; gray substratum clouds passed one another like ghostly ships. Mickey could hear the surf, the hiss of salt bubbling on the wet sand.

They walked down the sandy path toward the ocean. A lone fisherman stood about two hundred yards down the beach, water surging up to his knees, his line taut against the current.

It was maybe sixty yards from the end of the path to the nearest tidemark. Mickey clutched the container and stepped with difficulty over the pebbly dunes that descended into a lumpy expanse of pale, tawny beach: wind-smoothed hillocks draped with long red and green ribbons of seaweed, scalloped with a million shells, bits of coral, the knocked-out teeth of the sea. Several gulls stood motionless in the sand, facing east.

Mickey spotted the old wooden pier in the gray distance. He headed toward it, conscious of his son behind him, stumbling over the sand. They arrived to find the entrance cordoned off by a rusty chain. At the end of the pier, beyond the waves, dark water licked the massive wooden legs, a white froth churning and fizzing.

Mickey touched the chain, and was almost surprised that it didn't electrocute him. He jiggled it experimentally.

"It might be dangerous," Ben said. "Maybe we shouldn't."

"It's fine," said Mickey. "This pier's been standing for years, it's not going to fall down now. The ashes have to go out to sea." He cleared his throat and added, "It's the law." He then raised the chain and ducked under it. Maybe it wasn't the best idea, and certainly he wasn't setting a great example for the kid by trespassing on condemned property, but what else could he do? He climbed the steps of the pier and advanced a few paces on its damp and rotting planks. No one could see him. He felt a thrill of lawlessness. "Come on," he called down to Ben. He turned and walked to the end of the pier, the wind swelling the back of his coat. He heard Ben's footsteps behind him.

He stopped a foot shy of the protective rail. The water was deep here, muddy. Mickey removed the container from his coat pocket. "Benjie," he called through the wind.

The kid stood there as if on a precipice. "What if this thing collapses?" he said. He was halfway out.

Mickey held up the container to remind him of the urgency of their mission. "Let's go," he said.

Ben lowered his head and started walking. Mickey held out his free hand, but quickly withdrew it for fear he might be snubbed. And who would blame the kid? A father, a husband, was supposed to protect his family; that was his job. What good was his outstretched hand if it had failed to defend his wife, failed to defend the mother of his only child? Not that he himself believed this, but he could see as how Benjie might.

"We could get arrested," Ben said, coming closer. He looked back several times as if to make sure the patrols weren't out; one hand kept playing around in his pocket. "We shouldn't be doing this," he said.

Mickey thought he understood: the kid wasn't ready. Well, neither am I, Mickey thought. Maybe, then, they ought to postpone it, wait a few more days, weeks even. No one said they had to do it right away.

And yet why shouldn't they? With burials they got the body in the ground quickly, sometimes within hours of a death. Already it had been three days. No, the time was now. It seemed that Emi couldn't really be free until they released her.

"One of us can hold this thing," Mickey said, "and the other can take off the lid. Then we can both hold it and tip it over." It was like talking clinically about a sexual act; Mickey felt ridiculous, even ashamed. Was this the best he could do for her? Shouldn't there be someone, anyone, to say a few words? He had to remind himself that she would have hated any sort of ceremony, and that this—a rotting pier, the cold, fog-ridden sea—was the simple good-bye of her dreams.

Mickey held the container over the rail. "Benjie," he said. "Take off the lid."

"Shouldn't we say something first?" Ben said.

"No," said Mickey. He felt the tears coming again. "Come on now, take the lid off." He was no longer sure of himself; he feared he might burst out crying. But he had to be strong for Ben. He couldn't fall to pieces, not now. "The lid," he said.

Ben closed his eyes tightly.

"It's okay," Mickey said. He took a step, and Ben, hearing this, feeling it, stepped back and covered his face with his hands.

"Just give me a minute," he said. He breathed in, out; the hands came down. "It's cold," he said. He sniffed. "Can we just do this? Before the pier collapses?"

"Yes," Mickey said. He held out the container and watched as Ben's hands floated to it. His fingers picked at the lid. Mickey used his other hand to help. Their skin touched: Ben's hand was warm. Mickey figured it was the hand that had been in his pocket. "Okay," said Mickey. "Pull it off!"

Ben's hands began to shake, and like an infection, the trembling spread to Mickey's hands: their fingers twitched, fumbled, and in a frozen instant they watched openmouthed as the sealed container dropped straight down into the dark, deep water.

It floated there, a tiny white object dipping and rising. Mickey stared. He couldn't speak, couldn't move.

Ben stepped back. "It wasn't my fault!" he blurted.

Mickey gasped. He leaned over the rail, searching. It was there, it was gone. He turned and rushed to the other end of the pier, a whimper of panic in his throat. He ducked the chain and stumbled back on the sand. "Emi!" he cried. He rushed the tide, his feet sinking in the wet sand. He clutched at the air. He could hear Ben calling him, alternately apologizing and denying any blame. Cold: he was now ankle-deep in the water. He shook his fists at the sea, the waves.

The container was nowhere in sight.

How could it have happened—how could he have failed her? She was trapped forever, encased; they were all trapped.

Mickey slipped and fell, then got up with surprising quickness. His coat was soaked through and his hands were raw and red, stinging like hell, the fingers dripping with wet, oily sand. He staggered back, unable to find his footing in the soft ground. Sand exploded from his wet shoes. He was overwhelmed: the ocean, the knife-colored sky, his own raging grief. There was a great power aloft in the mist. Mickey threw back his head and yelled up at it, a great bellowing syllable that encompassed all his horror.

"Dad!" Ben called. "Don't go back in!"

Mickey spat again, then turned and stumbled over the hillocks and dunes and up to the path that led back to the car, only half aware of Ben following after him at a frightened distance, the tail of a strip of seaweed in his hand like a child's blanket being dragged through the dust of a ruined landscape.

―――

"Crumb? That you?" Nelson carried the phone into the kitchen. His little cousins were playing in the living room, and he couldn't hear too well. "Where you at?"

"I don't know. Somewhere near water. A gas station. It's a long-distance call."

Nelson sensed trouble. "You a'ight?"

"Yeah. We just dumped my mother's ashes."

Nelson's heart sped up. Ben sounded lost, scared. Nelson pressed a finger to his ear to blot out the noisy shouts of the children. "So what now?"

No answer.

"Crumb."

"I think we're in Cambridge."

"Where's Bread?"

"We should drive out this way some time. You ever been fishing?"

"Where's Bread?"

"Taking a piss," Ben said. "Here he comes now. I have to go."

"Yo, Crumb."

The line went dead.

Nelson hung up. He wasn't sure what to think. Was Crumb in trouble?

No, he thought; the boy was just shaken up. Just finished scattering his mother's ashes.

Nelson shook his head in wonder. He was moved by the call, and astonished to find himself a player in what was by now a famous tragedy. He was a part of history, branded forever on the memory of the day, associated, bound, destined to survive in these unexpected ways. And yet the intimacy implied in a roadside phone call—perhaps even more than Ben's having come to him the morning after the shooting—unnerved him; he hadn't supposed they were this close, and now it occurred to him that he'd offered the gun the other day not so much out of friendship as in fear of it: it had been a way to put something between them, something blunt and cold and impersonal. But now he could see as how it may have been taken as hot, intimate. Suddenly, Nelson was unsure of his own motives. Was it because Ben's mother had been shot by a black kid, and he felt he needed to compensate the Lerners on behalf of the whole damn race? But no: that was crazy. At bottom, he supposed, he had been genuinely concerned for Ben's safety: he had seemed so unprotected.

Nelson wished he could do something more to help, to ease the Lerners' pain. He'd been following all the press about the case—in the paper, on television—and had even fantasized about apprehending the killer himself and becoming a hero and winning Bread's praise. Bread, who was probably a little ill-disposed toward blacks at the moment. Understandable, Nelson thought. Understandable.

Well, at least Mama had sent those flowers yesterday. Nelson thought a card would have sufficed—flowers would wither, die—but he was so grateful to find Mama on the better end of the transaction that he dared not argue. Still, it seemed impossible that something like this could happen to the Lerners, or that he himself should end up at such close range to their suffering. It was like he was a part of them.

A stinging came to his eyes.

He ran up to his room, angry and confused over these new emotions. He didn't want to cry.

He thought of his friends. Hawk, Rob, Chuckie Banks; they didn't know anyone like the Lerners. Nelson felt in possession of a secret treasure.

He looked at his plants, feeling more tender toward them than usual. In a way, they were his closest friends. His only friends. Well, Crumb was a friend. But he wondered about the others—Hawk, Rob, Chuckie Banks; if nothing else, he thought, they looked out for him. Bad niggas, too. All been through the system. But there was a price for their friendship. Nelson often found himself being asked to hold their shit, and Lord knew his mattress had been stuffed with every imaginable contraband. He never asked any questions, though. Didn't want them to think he was a punk.

Hawk especially. Nigga was *crazy*. But he'd given Nelson that .25 semi, the one that Crumb was now carrying, and could probably get him another one if Nelson just said the word. Nelson had accepted that gun reluctantly, considering it not so much a thank-you for past favors as prepayment for some grisly future one. Hawk had a way of casually inducing debt. A smile, a flash of gold. Nelson had never been too comfortable with the situation.

He sat next to his African violets and stroked the leaves. Maybe it was time to cut some leaves and start more plants—you could do that by placing the leaf stem in a dish of stones and water. Nelson had found that you could use the parent leaf two and three times and produce dozens of crops. Make a whole damn family. He'd given most of his plants away to relatives, for birthdays and holidays. Lately, though, he'd been considering selling them on the street somewhere, out in the suburbs. Maybe he'd take the bus to the Green Garden Nursery, check on some other plants. Amaryllis maybe. He wished he had space for a garden. A few times, driving the van, he'd stopped by Bread's house and checked out his yard. Lilies, tulips, marigold. Oriental poppy. Azalea. Fat white hydrangea.

Vegetables, too.

Nelson wondered what kind of garden he could make, if he had all that space.

Bread. The man owned property. Sometimes, Nelson wondered about the inside of the house. What was it like? He'd never seen it, of course. Never been invited.

He dipped his finger in the bowl of water that he kept on the sill. The idea was to make sure it was at room temperature before pouring it into the soil—cold water caused leaf spots, he'd found. He'd made a lot of discoveries in the past few years, all of them springing from that time when Mama was soaking potatoes, and he'd noticed that one of them, overnight, had sprouted, miraculously, a small white stubble. Water had done this. Nelson felt he had glimpsed a great secret of the universe.

He watered the plants with care. In a couple of days, he would go back to work.

It made him nervous, the idea of facing Bread, whom he feared would be changed beyond recognition. Nelson felt helpless. What if Bread turned against him? The thought terrified him. All he could do, he decided, was drive the van, make his deliveries. Do his job. No more bullshit, he told himself. He'd do his job better than he'd ever done it in his life.

10

As the investigation entered its third week, Mickey decided to shave and reopen the bakery, thinking that in doing something positive—something that didn't involve pacing the floors of his house in foul-smelling pajamas, or pausing before the colorful waterfall of clothes in Emi's closet to bathe despairingly in their fading perfume; that didn't involve burning his dinner each night so that every pot in the kitchen was now coated with a thick black skin in whose charred layers lay a record of the cook's mind adrift; that didn't involve, above all, the constant replaying of various disastrous moments of the past weeks—in doing *something*, he felt, even if that meant just pressing on and doing what he'd always done, perhaps, then, he could make the wheels of justice turn that much faster and he'd be able to begin putting this ordeal behind him.

Not that he thought an arrest would rescue him from his misery—only time might do that—but, in a way, it was the one thing to which he had to look forward, a kind of vague promise of deliverance whose daily unfulfillment had become a growing source of agitation. Lesser expectations centered around the ashes; Mickey had contacted the police down at the shore and asked them to be on the lookout for a small container of ashes washed up on the beach, intimating that he'd gone out the legally required five miles in a friend's boat. The deputy sounded less impressed than Mickey would have expected, telling him that with the way the water was turning over the past couple of weeks, such an object might turn up miles away, far out of their jurisdiction; it might even end up on the other side of the ocean. Mickey thought to drive back there and comb the beach himself, or contact the Coast Guard. It was another key to his own freedom, he thought, his own release, to retrieve that box and open it, but somehow it all seemed pointless in the end.

And so he concentrated on his work. Business was slow for the first few days, either because everyone assumed the store would be closed for a while longer, or because many customers, some of whom had known Mickey for years, were too nervous to meet him face-to-face. And who could blame them? It was odd, this relationship between merchant and customer; at times friendly and familiar, it was liable to go frightfully awkward come a real challenge, and Mickey—who down through the years had always been one to offer a word of sympathy to new widows and widowers who had finally begun to resume their routines, of which a trip to the Lerner Bakery was an integral part—did not expect the same brand of condolence in return. It wasn't so much the spectacular nature of Emi's death that tortured dialogue and turned people shyly away from one another, but rather, the roles to which they were bound. There had been, Mickey understood, a breach of contract; he was, after all, a community stalwart, and in some ways a paternal figure, inasmuch as he was a kind of provider; he wasn't supposed to be struck by tragedy, no more than by lightning. The flowers and cards that had accumulated on the dining-room table were very touching, but their bestowal seemed to earn the sender the right to avoid the bakery until the cloud of discomfort finally lifted; and while his customers, whom he could only hope hadn't, in the interim, taken their business elsewhere, showed their support in the best way they knew how, Mickey, despite himself—for he wanted their love, wanted their support—felt a burn of infamy. It was as though he had let everyone down: he saw himself as the proud athlete who, having faltered, must face the kids in the hospital, the dying children to whom he had promised the moon.

But it wasn't just the customers; it was Benjie as well. Father and son were also loath to face each other; they, too, were unsure of the rules and boundaries of the relationship; they, too, were afflicted with shame. But theirs was not the sort of godlike shame Mickey felt with

regard to his customers; this shame was a poison, a cancer, and
Mickey's understanding of it was enough to make him want to run
away forever. The two of them had been laid bare, he felt, like two
players on a stage whose painted, richly detailed backdrop has been
suddenly pulled away. Without Emi there to provide perspective,
identity, they were left with nothing but their shivering, naked selves,
so that his own lackluster person, kept half-hidden for so many years
in the shadow of his wife's career, was now left cruelly exposed.

This was Mickey's state of mind when he'd agreed to play cards
with Joe and Buddy Grossman. "It'll be like old times," Joe had told
him, forgetting, or seeming to forget, that Mickey had quit the game
in the first place precisely because it had gotten old and stale. Old
times. Hadn't it been Joe who had warned him about courting the
past, going down to Percy Street and so forth? No matter: Mickey was
too weak to fight; he'd surrender to them, he decided, sink back into
the old fraternity, back to the card games on Wednesday nights, the
table at Chen's Garden. He'd been kidding himself all along; he wasn't
any different. He was one of them. They were waiting for him, had
been waiting for years. Now he was coming home.

The men were due at eight o'clock. At seven, Mickey planted his
elbows on the bakery counter and gazed out the window. Not a customer in sight. Morris, observing that business was slow, had gone
home an hour ago, leaving Mickey alone to wait for the return of the
van. Since reopening, Mickey had yet to stick around for Nelson's arrival, preferring to close up shop an hour or two early just to dodge
any contact. It was strange: he found himself avoiding Nelson just as
he was avoiding his own son, and in contrast to his prior position he
now encouraged Ben to join Nelson in the van—"You can't sit around
the house all day," he'd told him—which enabled Ben to receive the
van keys afterward in Mickey's stead and lock them up in the register.
Thus Mickey could avoid both boys all day; and when he considered
that Ben was, as per his father's orders, reporting home promptly each
evening, he could relax in the knowledge—the hope, really—that the
boys weren't quite as thick as they'd been before the shooting.

Not that Mickey would have needed to *order* Benjie to come right
home; in a way, Emi's murder had proven Mickey's point about the
danger of certain neighborhoods, and Ben seemed to be heeding the
message. Still, Mickey felt bad about his own treatment of Nelson,
and though he refused to believe it was in any way tied to the murder, to some need to connect Nelson to the animals who had killed his
wife—a desire, really, to give the entire hoodlum element a face—he

couldn't deny a certain bitter taste in his mouth at the very sight of his delivery man, who seemed in his own way as reluctant to face his boss (could it be, again, that shyness toward the bereaved?) as his boss was to face him. Mickey reflected that the mutual aversion must have something to do with the clumsy paternal overtures he'd been making of late—the boxing hints, the attempts at locker-room banter. It was as if the charitable element of this had been somehow exposed, as if, in a well-intentioned way, he had led Nelson on, flexing his fatherly muscles, and had now abruptly withdrawn himself. Hit by tragedy, Mickey had been recalled to the basic components of his life, the near and simple things for which one becomes thankful in moments of crisis and then, a little later, examines and assesses and weighs at the expense of all else. Mickey hoped that Nelson understood, and that he could maybe view Ben as a sort of ambassador or diplomat, dispatched with goodwill from his father's high and generous office.

Mickey turned his thoughts to the evening at hand. He'd better get home, he thought, set things up. He couldn't help but feel a little giddy at the prospect of entertaining again. Chips, drinks, the smoke from Joe's cigarettes, the loud, brash talk, the jokes, the laughter; it *would* be like the old days, and was that really so bad, after all?

It took but a minute to close the store, and another ten or so to walk home. That gave him plenty of time to get washed up, clear the kitchen table and fill a few bowls with the pretzels and chips and gumdrops that he'd bought the day before.

The company arrived together: Joe, Buddy and Sam Rudin, a friendly but shady character whom Mickey had met years ago at Joe's daughter's bas mitzvah. Now, as then, he wore a gold chain around his thick, tanned neck, and the same bushy dark hairs clogged his ears and nostrils. He'd taken a two-year vacation in Pennsylvania not too long ago for loansharking, and it was generally agreed that he lent a sort of harmless flair of the underworld to any occasion. And indeed, the kitchen had been transformed by his presence: the table, arrayed with playing cards and ashtrays, had taken on an aspect of legend, like something photographed, as if the game itself were a kind of famous meal over which had been hatched some grand, notorious crime.

Straight poker was the game. Mickey dealt. It was good to hold a crisp deck of cards in his hands, and he dealt them slowly, savoring the feel of their edges, the tight pack of the cut, the snap and whisper of the two-handed shuffle and the way they glided, like a breath, when flicked across a surface. At last he had gained a measure of control; but as soon as the cards were gathered up and studied by twitchy eyes, Mickey knew that his part was over, that the evening he had merely launched would now assume its own shape and rhythm, and that the conversation—Mickey was helpless to stop it—would soon alight, like some pregnant insect, on the frail-stemmed topic of murder.

But he was wrong; there was, instead, a strenuous effort to avoid the subject, an effort facilitated by a sip of beer, a meaningless re-arrangement of cards; and it was obvious, too, that Rudin had been briefed beforehand: it seemed he was reluctant to speak at all, lest he invoke in any way the memory of the deceased. Mickey recalled a much more talkative man.

With his guests allied in a kind of cult of sensitivity, Mickey felt even more remote from them, and was plagued with new concerns that he was somehow failing them as a host. What if they were so ill at ease that they decided to leave and never come back? But no, Mickey assured himself, it must be just the opposite, for he was some-thing of a celebrity at the moment, and probably the men were feel-ing, if not a little starstruck, then certainly pleased to be in his presence. Still, it was awfully good of them to rally round him like this, considering how Mickey had more or less turned up his nose at them time and again during the long era of his marriage. He wanted to reward them for their kindness, but before he could think of a way to break the ice, to invite them into his private affairs, Joe Blank barely skimmed the topic by posing an invitation of his own.

"So," he said, eyeing Mickey over his cards, "what are you and Ben-jie doing for Thanksgiving?"

"Thanksgiving?" Mickey said. "It's Thanksgiving already?"

"This Thursday."

"Jesus." For Mickey, the holiday had sort of lost its appeal over the years; Emi was hardly ever around during the holiday season, and so the dinners became halfhearted affairs: a small young turkey to feed three or four (Morris occasionally brought some lonely acquain-tance), stuffing made from old Lerner bread, and enough Lerner fruit-cake to feed a small army. This year it would have been the same—Emi in Paris, concertizing with Shaw, then him and Benjie and Morris.

"Well, if you're not doing anything special," said Joe, "you ought to join us at my place. I got fifteen people."

"Thanks," said Mickey. It made him feel a little like a charity case, but he looked forward to being rescued from an intimate holiday din-ner with his son. He then remembered that Shirley Finkle had invited them too, last week, and that he'd accepted. Christ, he ought to start writing things down. "I'll let you know," he said.

"I just don't want you to be alone," Joe said, and Mickey took this as a soft tap on the shell.

"Yeah," Mickey said, opening up some. "Hopefully, by then, they'll have a suspect, and I'll be able to digest my food better."

Sam Rudin looked up from his cards for the first time all evening, and Buddy Grossman sipped his beer as if to appear only coolly interested, which Mickey supposed was for Rudin's benefit, a way to show Sam that he, Buddy, was a confidant for whom such information was a daily privilege.

"Well," said Mickey, warming to his audience, "so far, nothing." He presented the palms of his hands.

Joe turned to Sam Rudin. "Mickey lost his wife a few weeks ago."

"Oh?" said Rudin, eyebrows jumping. It was obvious that he'd already been informed.

"Sam's been down in Florida for the past month," Joe explained.

"This is the violinist, the shooting downtown?" Rudin said.

Joe nodded grimly.

"Sure I heard of it. Terrible." Rudin looked at Mickey. "There's nothing I can say. Terrible."

"Yes," said Mickey, unsure why the men were arranging their stories in this way. What difference did it make if Sam Rudin had been told? Everyone knew. Mickey supposed they didn't want to give the impression that they'd been talking about him.

"Don't worry," Buddy said. "They'll catch the bastard. I'd be willing to bet they catch him before the end of the year."

"It's a game of breaks," Mickey said. "We'll have to see."

"They got a description?" Rudin said.

"Not really," Joe said. "Mick was there, ya know."

"You were there?" said Rudin.

Mickey nodded.

"Imagine that," Rudin said. He shook his head slowly to his own personal wisdom of the horrid, and seemed to confer upon Mickey a special status, as though he considered his host a fellow traveler in the darker regions of experience.

"But unfortunately," said Buddy, "he couldn't get a description. The bastard was wearing a Halloween mask."

"Not that it matters," said Joe. "Who could distinguish a shvartze in the dark? It's better he had the mask—make him easier to track down."

"We'll see," Mickey said. He tried to study his hand: two sevens, queen of diamonds, two jacks.

Rudin shook his head. "Makes you wanna move to Canada. Sweden."

"Too damn cold," said Grossman.

"Things are gonna come to a head in this country," Joe said. "It can't go on like this. The whites aren't gonna take it much longer." It wasn't clear if he was including himself in this. "It's gotten to the point where every law-abiding citizen has got to be armed. You ought to consider it, Mick. Tell him, Sammy."

Rudin frowned, threw down two cards. Mickey dealt him two. Sam Rudin spoke as he picked up the cards and inserted them in his hand. "I've carried a gun for twenty-three years," he said. "And a dozen times I've had to pull it out. Never fired it, but I can tell you right now that I wouldn't be sitting here with this lousy hand losing my money to you bastards if I hadn't made that decision to arm myself. A nigger understands one thing, pardon my language. One thing. Is anyone else playing here?" Rudin's face had gone red.

Mickey got rid of his queen and picked up another seven. Full house. He hoped Rudin wasn't too sore a loser.

"The point," said Joe, "is that it doesn't matter where you go. You're not safe in your own backyard."

Mickey nodded, pleased that Joe hadn't said "I told you so" with regard to the blacks; Joe was markedly restrained, and now Mickey wondered if he hadn't brought in Sam Rudin as a kind of mouthpiece—as if Mickey might come around, might be convinced if he heard it from elsewhere. Mickey was almost amused, if not a little insulted, that Joe could ever imagine that he, Mickey, might be impressed by the likes of Sam Rudin, whom Joe obviously thought a real sharpie; but one thing seemed for sure: Joe cared; he wanted to help. And as Joe's smoke rose and collapsed, joining them all under its settling ring, Mickey felt himself letting go, sinking into the foul comfort of the love of these angry, untidy men.

"I appreciate it," he said, "but after what happened, I think the less guns in the world, the better."

"That sounds fine," said Rudin, "but it's not practical. You listen to the liberals talk about gun control, but can they guarantee our safety? Until they can, well, we've got to take it into our own hands. A man has a right to defend his life and liberty and property. When the government starts infringing on that right—which is really a basic right as set down by the founding fathers—then we're no longer living in America."

Mickey scratched his cheek. He wondered if things would be different had he been carrying a gun. Hard to say. Still, Rudin's words piqued his taste for vengeance: how nice it would be to arm himself and walk the streets and wait for some punk to give him a try.

"Ya hear that, Mick?" Joe said. "The man knows from the Constitution." He gestured at Rudin, who nodded. Joe went on: "Frankly, my friend, you've got to let go of all this feel-good crap about harmony and unity and love thy neighbor. I know that Emi—and with all due respect, Mickey, I bring up her name because this is important—but Emi would want you to have the means to defend yourself and your son and your property. Now I know I've joked with you before about her having funny ideas, and I know you're saying to yourself that she would never want you to change just because of what happened to her, but believe you me, had she lived, she'd be a different person. A more realistic person. She wouldn't want to see you have to go through anything like this again, and neither would I. Neither would any of us."

Mickey sighed. "That's fine and well," he said. "But what I don't understand is this big campaign to get me to carry a weapon."

"That's not it," said Joe. "We're talking about attitude. Forget a weapon. It's this Pollyanna attitude. You've got to take a harder look at life, Mick. See what's really there."

"You don't think I have?"

"I don't know," said Joe. "We don't really talk the way we used to. I'd like to think you have. I'd like to think you can look around and see who your friends are, and who your enemies are. Instead of driving down to Percy Street, and walking around at night in godforsaken areas. That's all. I just don't want you to get hurt."

"I don't believe I have any enemies," Mickey said.

"No?" said Joe. "The characters did this to Emi? They're not your enemies?"

"Well, sure. They're an enemy of society, I guess you might say."

"Knock it off, for Christ's sake," Joe said. "Why don't you just go ahead and say it? A goddamned shvartze took a gun and blew—"

"Hey," said Buddy. "Come on now. The man's been through enough. He ought to get away, take a trip—"

"No," said Mickey. "Joe's right. A goddamned shvartze took a gun and blew away my wife." He felt a strange rush, a euphoria; buried emotions dislodged themselves from the mud and rose to the surface, sharp and slender as pike. "Took out a gun and—" His eyes shut, his teeth clenched, his fists slammed down on the table: it was like a blurted confession. There was, inside him, a monstrous, inscrutable hate, a bile, and his need to spit it out, to rid himself of it, seemed to be taking unpredictable forms over which he had little control; he found himself at the mercy of the merest suggestions and proddings, so ready, so eager to hate; it was as if he saw a chance to wield this poisonous energy in a direction away from himself. Sure, he hated the bastard who killed Emi, but there was something else, something that had been there all along, a strain of aversion that had been excited to manic proportions. What was it? What burned inside its core? Mickey opened his eyes and slammed his fists again: ashtrays jumped, cards flinched, and the drinks he had poured—beer, diet Coke—tossed like the sea in their glasses.

"Mick."

Mickey felt Joe's hand on his back; in a moment he was calm. Sam and Buddy watched him with a mix of sympathy and concern and an odd sort of patience, like priests of some dark order observing a rite of conversion, preparing to welcome him into their fold; and Mickey, florid, exhausted in his anguish, felt himself yield to the promise of their brotherhood. He blinked his eyes like a downed fighter surfacing through the ether to find a circle of familiar, soothing, vaguely threatening faces. He felt strangely resurrected.

"Any of you gentlemen care to wager?" said Sam Rudin.

The table came alive: money was tossed carelessly into a pile. Wedding bands glinted in the light. Mickey knew he held the winning hand. He tossed in a ten-dollar bill—that was high stakes. The other men laughed at this bold move, as if finding something refreshing and humorous in it, and Mickey, knowing that the men supposed he was only bluffing badly, felt a warmth of acceptance such as he'd never known. How easy it would be, he felt, to live his life out in this way, to submit to the small, shadowed existence that had been assigned him by Nature and learn to be thankful for having glimpsed the light at all.

Buddy Grossman dropped out of the wagering, sat back with his drink. "A fella opens up a new barbershop," he said. "First customer is a priest, got the collar on, the cross. Comes time to pay, barber says, 'Father. You're a man of the cloth. You're my first customer. The haircut is free.' Priest thanks him, 'Thank you, thank you,' walks out. Next morning, the barber arrives at the shop. A beautiful bouquet of flowers by the door, with a card signed by the priest."

"I'll see your ten," said Joe, "and raise you five."

"Into the shop walks a minister. Gets a haircut. Comes time to pay, the barber says, 'Reverend. You're a good man, a man of the word. The haircut is on the house.' Minister thanks him, goes home. Next morning, the barber finds a box of candy by the door, and a card signed by the minister."

"Same for me," said Rudin. "Raise you five."

"Next customer to walk in the place is a rabbi. 'Can I get a haircut?' the rabbi says. 'Of course,' says the barber. Barber gives him a haircut. Comes time to pay, the barber says, 'Rabbi, you're a man of God, you're a good man; this haircut is free. No charge.' Rabbi thanks him, leaves. Next morning, the barber goes to open his shop, and in front of the door"—Buddy folded his hands on his rising belly—"is another rabbi."

Sam Rudin laughed, and Joe laughed too. Mickey joined them: it was like jumping into deep water, crashing into a coldness that switched almost instantly to a massaging warmth. He laughed for the first time since the murder, laughed until he coughed and had to duck down for a gulp of soda.

"Another rabbi," Buddy repeated, his belly quaking with laughter. This was one of his cleaner ones; most of Buddy's jokes were crass and tasteless and offensive, but Mickey never really made a fuss—didn't want to be a wet blanket. And when you thought about it, what was the harm? These private jokes didn't hurt anyone, not really; it wasn't like taking a gun and—

There was a sound at the back door: Mickey looked up. A slight sound, no more than a mouselike scratching under the rumble of laughter, but which registered to Mickey's senses like a crick in his neck. He knew this house, its every movement. The door opened.

It was Ben. He stood there, clearly stunned by the sight of such revelry. Mickey's first instinct was to stand up and explain everything—the cards, the laughter, the frivolous snack foods—but before he could think of a way to justify a rollicking card game spread out on the very table over which father and son had so recently eaten an almost religious meal together, glancing at each other between bites of bread and salad while Emi's violin whined below, a cantorial bleating that Mickey could almost hear this very moment, and which he now thought of as a kind of private kaddish sung to herself, as if she had knowledge of the end that awaited her—before he could even open his *mouth*, for Christ's sake, and defend his right to assemble in his own house, there emerged, slowly, from the darkness, a second figure, stepping out from behind Ben and into the white glare of the kitchen: it was Nelson, startlingly black, flagrant as a roach on a plate. He froze in the light.

The men looked up. The laughter died.

There was a frozen silence in which Mickey felt his authority—as a father, as the master of his house—crumble; the men were drawing, Mickey was sure, all sorts of conclusions, and though he couldn't say just what those conclusions were, he knew that they were somehow unfavorable and undermined his position. He then recalled admonishing Benjie several weeks ago to bring Nelson here, to the house, instead of his going "down there," where it was dangerous, but he hadn't really supposed that it would happen; and as he looked at his son, who seemed to glare back at him in defiance, he understood that the plan had been to usher Nelson upstairs—a plan that now appeared threatened by what must have seemed to the boys a veritable wall of disapproval: four middle-aged men studying them through cobwebs of smoke, their laughter gone, serious money on the table; a plan that, if it ever existed at all, was now, Mickey could see, foiled—for Benjie turned and whispered something to Nelson, who stepped back and, catching Mickey's eye, said, "Goodnight, Mr. Lerner," before disappearing behind the door.

Mickey bristled; he felt exposed, betrayed; he wanted to upend the table, turn everyone out of his house. Ben lingered in the doorway, speaking to Nelson in a coded language, then closed the door and walked past the table without so much as a nod, as if he knew he'd done something wrong, but had nonetheless scored a small triumph in having disgraced his father in front of his friends.

But why disgrace? Mickey stewed: he was aware of the men watching him; he resented their assumptions. But what did they assume?

"That was Nelson," he said, feeling a need to explain. "My driver. Must've walked Benjie home from the bakery."

"Fella that does deliveries," Joe said to Sam Rudin.

Mickey thought he detected an exchange of glances. His neck heated up. Did the men expect him to now denounce Nelson, grumble about him, threaten to see to it that he never step foot in this house again?

"You wanna finish this hand?" Buddy Grossman said.

"It's Mickey's call," said Joe. "Mick?"

Mickey was confused; he looked at his cards.

"Whore walks into a laundromat," said Buddy.

"You gonna wager?" said Sam Rudin.

Mickey quickly tossed another five into the pot.

Joe smirked. "Last of the high rollers."

Mickey raised the cards to his eyes to cover his face. Had he imagined it all—the doubts, the judgments? His anger grew; he'd been tricked, he felt, he was being tested somehow, manipulated. Buddy finished his joke, the men laughed. They seemed to have forgotten all about Nelson; it was as if they'd barely given him a thought. Yet Mickey was sure he'd been driven to this anger, driven to this new hostility that seemed to be aimed toward blacks in general and Nelson in particular. Yes: he'd been baited, lured. Hadn't he? He looked at his friends: they were absorbed in the game. Was he alone, then? Had they brought him to this place only to leave him here to find his way down? Would they rejoin him?

Mickey threw down his cards. "I'm out," he said. He tried hard to control himself, though he was shaking visibly. This confusion was maddening; he needed to be alone.

"You okay?" said Joe.

Joe's innocence was even more maddening. Mickey felt alone in his bitterness. These men were poison. Why had he even tried? What had he been thinking? They'd already pulled him halfway into the mire; he couldn't allow himself to go under completely. He had to get away. But get away from them! And yet, even as he feigned a headache and claimed that he had to talk to Ben about something or other and herded the men to the door amid confused protests ("Hey, what's the idea?") and thanked them and told them he'd talk to them later, he knew that, rather than obliterating the whole gang from his consciousness, he was doing very nearly the opposite: for with the men suddenly gone from his kitchen, having left only their crumbs and butts and haze of laughter and smoke, Mickey found himself appallingly alone, left to confront the possibility that the disease, the hatred, had not been caught, but had somehow originated inside him.

He felt a little better the next day; mornings were always better. He opened the bakery early, having left the house while Ben was still asleep. Morris arrived at ten.

Mickey spared his uncle the details of last night's aborted poker game—his outbursts, his erratic thoughts. Not that he was worried.

How could he be expected to think straight, after all he'd been through?

A man in a black hat and long black coat entered the bakery. "I'll take a loaf of pumpernickel," he said. His beard came to three points. Mickey didn't recognize him, but then it was hard sometimes to keep up with the Orthodox.

"Coming up," said Mickey. He retrieved the bread and gave it to Morris to slice. "One pumpernickel."

Morris placed the bread in the slicer, then licked a finger and swiped a plastic bag. He said:

> "I'll take a dime's worth of pumpernick
> And a nickel's worth of rye;
> A dollar's worth from the nickel pump
> So I can get to my honey pie."

He tied the bag in a knot and rang up the sale. The customer did not appear amused; he took the bread and walked out.

"They all used to laugh at that one," Morris said.

An elderly couple came in. Instead of greeting them Mickey turned his gaze to the window, through which he saw a sky mottled blue and gray. The traffic passed in both directions in volleys, salvos. Somewhere out there, Benjie was riding in the van with Nelson.

"You okay?" said Morris. Behind the thick lenses his eyes were like olives at the bottom of the glass. "You need a vacation, Mick."

"I'm fine." Mickey wasn't sure how long he'd been drifting.

The door opened. Mickey looked up. He recognized her instantly: his heart jumped. Donna. Why was she here? Had Nelson said something to her—complained that he'd been treated rudely, been turned out of Mickey's house the night before? But that was a lie! Or maybe she was here to buy bread—she didn't look angry, Mickey saw—or else express her condolences. She'd never set foot in *this* store in her life.

"Hello," she said.

"Well. Hello." Mickey felt a panic. Why couldn't she have come in while he was taking inventory, clipboard in hand, or better yet, while the place was busy, and him answering questions and directing traffic? In fact she had come at the worst possible moment: Mickey gazing out the window, Morris reading the paper, an elderly couple fondling rolls; never had the place appeared so two-bit and irrelevant.

Mickey grabbed a pencil from atop the register and put it behind his ear. Donna approached the counter. She looked lovely, the hair done up in those braids, the smooth skin, the tan cotton dress and long black coat; it was hard to connect her to her son.

"What brings you here?" Mickey said. "Oh, this is Morris, my uncle. Morris, Donna Childs. Nelson's mother."

"Good to meet you," said Morris. His eyes fixed immediately on Donna's ample bosom.

Mickey was horrified. "So," he said loudly, and clapped his hands together. This failed attempt to create a diversion was in the next moment rewarded by the cry of the phone in the back office.

"Could you get that, Morris?" Mickey said, and Morris, recalled to his usefulness—he could still answer a phone, by gad—turned and shuffled purposefully to the back, hoping, Mickey was sure, for some minor crisis of business that could be solved right then and there with the sharp, reliable tools of his experience.

"So this is it," said Donna, her eyes running along the glass counter, as if tasting every last goody in the showcase. "It's almost the same as the old bakery."

"Oh, it's a lot bigger," said Mickey. "You ought to see the back."

"I guess *I'm* just bigger," said Donna. "The other place seemed so big because I was so little." She breathed in. "Smells wonderful. *That* hasn't changed."

"You ought to smell it at night, when they're baking," said Mickey, hinting that she should judge his worth not by this empty storefront, but by the sweetness that lay in the pit of those remote hours. He spotted a tray of éclairs in the display case, and wondered if he should pull one out and give it to her. There she was, on the other side of the counter, still looking up at him with those big brown eyes; it was hard to believe she was a grown woman of forty. She'd caught up to him, it seemed. He felt twenty years younger.

"You must be wondering why I stopped by," Donna said.

"Éclairs?"

Donna laughed. "Oh, no," she said, waving her hand. "If I looked like you, maybe I'd sneak one."

"Nonsense. You look terrific."

Donna lowered her eyelids. "No, no."

"Yes," said Mickey. "You do."

"*You* look good. Let's get it straight."

"I'm dead serious," said Mickey. "You could be twenty-five."

"All right then," said Donna. She glanced upward, feigning impatience. "You just keep on talkin'. Come on."

Mickey found himself tongue-tied. What did she want him to say?
He laughed to cover his lapse. Most times he talked like this to a
woman, complimented her, she'd just blush and become tongue-tied
herself, like Shirley Finkle. Donna Childs wanted more music.

"That's all right," said Donna. "I'll let you off the hook."

Mickey knew he couldn't speak without saying too much; truth be
told, she was like a breath of life, cool as mint, a balm on his sick, burning skin. Her smile, her laugh. She didn't even know it. She was alive.

"Anyway," she said, her tone becoming businesslike. "The reason
I'm here." She reached into her bag and came up with a set of house
keys. "Nelson forgot to take these this morning. You'll see him later,
won't you? When he comes back?"

"Yes," said Mickey, wondering if Nelson had mentioned to her that
there'd hardly been any contact between them at all since the reopening. Was Donna trying to bring them together somehow?

Mickey held out his hand; their skin barely touched as the keys
landed in his palm. He closed his fingers over them, dropped them in
his pocket. Without thinking, he said, "So—you won't be home tonight, when Nelson gets in?"

"No. I have two jobs tonight. Not far from here, in fact."

"Jobs?"

"Massage. I told you."

"Right—the Japanese massage."

"I have a few private clients."

"Uh-huh." Mickey wasn't sure he wanted to hear about it.

"What do you mean, 'Uh-huh'? What are you thinking?"

"Nothing," said Mickey.

"I think somebody got the wrong idea."

"I have no ideas."

"No, no, I know what you're thinking. Something tells me I should
be offended and insulted and walk right out of here, but I won't, and
you know why? Because I've been around long enough to understand
that some people are just a little bit, let's say, narrow-minded." She'd
begun delivering this rebuke in a friendly, almost flirtatious way, and
then, as if fearing she'd surrendered too much, made sudden, crude
knives of the last two words and sank them through the butter.

Mickey didn't flinch: the confusion of emotions on her part allowed Mickey to settle into his old, steady, even-tempered self, a role
he felt came naturally to him (as opposed to the ranting madman of
the past few weeks), and which, at its highest expression, lent him

what he secretly thought of as a British manner—a reserve, a charm, a certain wit of style. "Narrow-minded?" he said. "Maybe 'uninformed' is a better term." He paused, then added boldly, "I happen to be very open-minded."

Donna seemed oblivious to his transformation into Richard Burton, though she may have felt its effect. She said, "Shiatsu has nothing to do with any kind of, you know, kinky sex, or anything like that."

"I'm sure it doesn't," said Mickey, noticing that the elderly couple was looking over their way. "Nonetheless, I'd be interested in trying it." He winked at the couple.

Donna turned dead serious. "You *should* try it," she said, alluding, Mickey was sure, to his travails, to the emotional stress that would surely ruin his health. "It's the best therapy in the world."

"Giving or receiving?"

Donna smirked like she knew he was trying to be clever, and for a moment Mickey saw the resemblance to Nelson. "If *giving* was the best therapy," she said, "I'd be paying *them!*"

Mickey laughed, but behind his back he squeezed his hands together. He'd rather give, he thought; it was no joke. His hands were strong. They wanted to work. What brilliant massages they held—and to think that Emi, rest her soul, hadn't even let him touch her toward the end!

He wanted to touch something, squeeze it, caress it, right now, wanted to grip it, bring it to life in his hands.

There then came, to his amazement, a small rustle down there in his undershorts.

"Speaking of receiving," said Donna. "Did you—get our flowers?"

"Flowers?" The conversation had shifted abruptly, and Mickey scrambled to find the suitable note, an effort complicated not only by his fear that Donna had sensed his excitement and was correcting him, but by the obvious and humiliating fact of his negligence. "Geez, we've received so many flowers and cards," he explained. "I can barely keep up with it. I apologize. There's flowers everywhere, I haven't even been able to—"

"No, no," said Donna, "I didn't mean anything like that. I just wanted to make sure you received them, that they got there." She placed her hand on her cheek, clearly mortified by this misunderstanding. "I didn't mean to sound like—"

"No," said Mickey. "It's fine. Really, I should acknowledge all this kindness. I do thank you, I really do. And Benjie thanks you as well."

Donna shook her head. "Please, don't even mention it." She seemed desperate to escape this deepening cycle of apology. "Ben," she said, grasping at the name. "How is he?"

"Oh," said Mickey, "about as good as can be expected." He scratched his head. "Of course, it's been tough. You know. A kid that age. It's tough enough already. You know—talking. Discussing your feelings, that sort of thing."

"Yes," said Donna. "I know." She sighed; they were back on safe ground. The boys. "I'm sure we could talk all day about that. Me and you, I mean." She looked away. "Yes." It seemed she might go on, confide something, but she then faded, as if her own problems must be petty by comparison, unworthy of mention. It was then that Mickey remembered—it struck him—that Donna had also lost a loved one to a gunman's bullet. Tommy Childs had been killed when Donna was just a girl.

Mickey was touched by her humility and fascinated by the idea that they were linked yet again, in this new and sensational way. He considered asking her if she'd like to meet for a coffee sometime, to talk.

Another couple came in.

"I guess I should go," said Donna, noting that the store was filling up.

"Oh, this is nothing," said Mickey. "It'll get much busier. Thanksgiving, the holidays; it's the busy time of year." Which, he reminded himself, would prevent him from taking that little trip, the getaway which everyone had been prescribing for him lately. Of course, that was always his excuse for not getting away—business. Hell, his passport was as blank as a dead man's diary: he'd never made good on any of his promises to accompany Emi on her frequent travels. "Say," he ventured. "We ought to get together sometime, have a coffee. Talk."

"I'd like that," said Donna. "When?"

Again, Mickey's tongue was caught; he'd had no timetable in mind, it was just a thought, an idea. He found himself shrugging, saying, "When's good for you?"

"Well, let's see. Thursday is Thanksgiving. How about Friday?"

"Friday."

"About seven o'clock?"

"Seven." Mickey wanted to cite a conflict. He wasn't ready for this, he felt, whatever *this* was. But the bakery closed at five on Fridays, and he wasn't good at making things up off the cuff. What else could he do? "Seven's fine," he said.

"Would you mind picking me up? Or I can meet you out here—"

"No, that's fine. I'll pick you up." A line had formed in front of the register; Mickey held up a finger to indicate he'd be there in a minute. "Friday at seven."

Donna glanced over at the customers. "Yes. Call me before—wait, scratch that. Don't call. I don't want Nelson to pick up the phone or even catch wind of this—who knows what he'll think. In fact, I'd better meet you. I can be here. Right out in front."

"What *would* he think?" said Mickey.

"Oh, you know—that we're talking about him. He doesn't like me to meddle in his life. Thinks I'm always in his business. I tell him I'm just doing my job!"

"Ah," said Mickey.

"So Friday."

"Friday it is." Mickey imagined taking her to Chen's Garden—what a scandal that would make! No, they'd have to drive to a different area altogether. He wouldn't want to be seen.

"Okay," Donna said. She touched one of her braids, smiled. "See you."

"See you," said Mickey. He watched her walk out. He was sweating, his heart was thumping. What had he done, what had he gotten himself into? But no, this was innocent, purely innocent. She wasn't interested in him—she was just friendly, that was all, she wanted to talk about Nelson. Maybe she was lonely. Maybe she would ask him, as she almost had that time in the car, to become a figure in her son's life. Ha! And even if she *was* interested, well, *he* certainly wasn't. Oh sure, she was attractive, and about as sweet as you'd like. But for crying out loud.

Still, he watched her cross the lot, wondering if she'd look back. That would be a sign, he felt. He hoped she wouldn't, and yet prayed she would. But if she did, what would it mean? And then it happened: she turned her head, and from across a distance of fifty or more yards, their eyes met. Mickey felt the long stake of doom sink through his head and burst out between his legs, nailing him fast to the floor. Donna turned away, walked briskly out of view of the window.

Mickey's palms were wet as he tended to his customers. This elation was false, it was wrong. He was on the seesaw. Up, down. He wasn't in his right mind. His wife had been killed right in front of his eyes, the love of his life, gone in an instant. He ought to be in seclusion, taking nature walks, grieving his heart out, and not feeling, as he had at various moments in the past few minutes, as though he were on the verge of something, a new beginning, that he'd somehow been lib-

erated, that Emi's death had given him—pure evil, these thoughts!—
a new lease on life.

I'm sick, he decided. Not well. He put his hand in his pocket:
Donna's keys. They were like jewels, gold. He was in possession of
something. The keys to her house. Had she really needed to come here
and give them to him? Couldn't she have left them with someone
else? But now he'd have to face Nelson—Nelson, who'd stepped foot
in his house so briefly the night before. No: he couldn't face him with
the keys. He'd be found out. Keys were intimate things, charged with
possibilities. They'd been passed. Mickey did not want to involve himself in this way, did not want to feel the gold thread of the keys connect the three of them—Donna, Nelson, himself. Did not want to
look at Nelson.

Morris returned from the back. "That was Jay Rattner on the
phone," he said triumphantly.

Mickey looked at his uncle. "What did he want?"

Morris hesitated, protective of what he must have seen as his pet
cause, then opened up, suddenly as a child, under the rare warmth of
Mickey's attention. "He said that deliveries were late yesterday, and
that when he asked Nelson what took so long—after all, he says, I got
a business to run—when he said something to Nelson, Nelson made a
comment under his breath that Jay didn't care for."

"What comment?"

"Jay didn't say," said Morris, betraying a small disappointment in his
work, as though he should have pumped Rattner for details. "But he
said that it wasn't friendly, and was muttered under the breath. It left
him with an uncomfortable feeling."

"It did, did it?"

"And so I told him if it happens again, to let me know."

Mickey sighed. "Jay Rattner's been a real pain in the ass lately," he
said. "First the rolls aren't fresh enough. Now he's getting an uncomfortable feeling."

"Maybe you should have a word with Nelson?"

"Nelson's fine," Mickey said, the defensiveness in his voice so obviously a measure of his guilt—over Nelson, yes, but also over Donna—
that he recoiled from the words as he might a punch. How could he
lay into Nelson, how could he even talk to him now that he'd practically made a *date*, for God's sake, with his mother?

Mickey put his hands on his head, closed his eyes. He was losing his
grip, he felt; he was nearing an edge, a breakdown, like the one he

would have had thirty years ago when the bakery burned, had Emi not been there to save him.

Emi. Forgive me, Emi, he called in a silent prayer. Help me.

"So that was Nelson's mother?" said Morris. "She should stop by more often."

But Mickey wasn't listening. He was on the brink of an answer. Emi. Yes: there was only one thing to do. Of course! It was wild, it was extravagant, it was downright meshuga, and yet on the other hand it made perfect sense, one might even say it was inevitable. What had merely crossed his mind once or twice before had now landed immensely like a magnificent bird. Emi—she would save him yet!

"Morris. Do me a favor and stay here until the boys come back and give these to Nelson. Tell him his mother dropped them off." Mickey handed his uncle the keys. "Can you close up yourself?"

"Where are you going?" said Morris, looking at the keys in his yellowed palm.

"I have to take care of something. Can you do what I said?"

Morris shrugged. "Do I have a choice?"

"And another thing," said Mickey. "Phone the whole staff and tell them to be here tomorrow at two. Two o'clock sharp. I want everyone here. There'll be an announcement."

He then grabbed his coat and rushed out of the store amid his uncle's questions, the great idea flaring up, iridescent and terrible, clutching him in its talons and carrying him in frantic, squawking flight toward what he hoped would be salvation.

11

It was the first time in anyone's memory that such a meeting had been called, and no one knew what to expect. Chairs and stools had been arranged in a semicircle in the bakery kitchen to seat all nine of the employees: Morris, Nelson, the six bakers and Lazarus. Ben was also present, having been told that the matter concerned him, though Mickey, who at the moment could be seen talking on the phone through the glass wall of his office, had given no details. Was the bakery being sold? Closed down?

Ben could see the fear in the immigrant faces of the bakers—all the strides they had made in this country now seemed to hinge on a single business decision. What would become of them? Their wives and children? How would they live? As they waited for Mickey to emerge from his office they fell to examining their hands, as though they were peculiar tools that they might have to turn in.

Nelson sat deep in his chair. Like the bakers, he too appeared worried, and hardly resembled the brazen outlaw who just days ago had revealed, as the van lurched past the gates of Seven Pines, a new handgun that struck Ben as so much deadlier than his own.

Ben looked around the kitchen: the huge mixers, the oven, the washbasin, the long, flour-covered worktables, the sheeter, the refrigerator and freezer, the bowls, the trays, the rollers and cutters, the bags of flour and sugar, the bottles and jugs of food coloring; every item seemed to be shining with a special urgency, like children eager to be chosen for some pageant or ball game. Ben would have thought that the employees might make a similar effort to appear indispensable.

Mickey hung up the phone and opened the office door. He appeared startled by the sight of his men all together against a backdrop of machinery, and even disturbed by their potential as a mob, but at the same time—and Ben could see this clearly—proud of the semblance of a genuine workforce at his command, and even moved to humility by his own power.

"The reason I've called you all," Mickey said, positioning himself just inside the semicircle, "is that there's going to be some changes around here for the next couple of weeks." He looked at the bakers to see that they understood, unaware that their English had improved vastly over the past few years, and the bakers, who could not be sure that they were being looked at for that reason, steeled themselves for the worst. "I'll be going away on Wednesday for about two weeks," Mickey announced. "And while I'm gone, the bakery will be managed and run by Benjamin."

Ben's mouth fell open. Had he heard right?

Mickey looked at Ben and winked, hinting at an old father-and-son prankishness in affairs.

Ben dared to glance at Nelson, who was now looking back at him with the sidewise smile that seemed to convey the same odd mix of superiority and wounded pride that he showed whenever Ben burned him with a jump shot. But there was something else there too: a sly, conspiratorial nod at the prospect for anarchy. Ben shied from the smile as Mickey, hands behind his back, proclaimed that he expected everyone to treat Ben with the same respect that one would give any employer.

The bakers did not seem to know whether to feel relieved or insulted by the new arrangement. They all turned to Ben as though in an effort to see him in a new light: he'd always been this young kid hanging around, a snotty kid sometimes, the boss's son, a natural target of jokes in foreign tongues, of dark, sadistic, scar-faced smiles; and now it was him to whom they'd have to answer. Ben looked back at them, hoping to earn their respect in a solemn nod; these were essentially docile men, but something in his own lack of confidence brought out a glint in their eyes that seemed mutinous and even deadly.

Lazarus, meanwhile, remained impassive; though he was a paid employee like anyone else, his unique position set him apart from the laborers, and he enjoyed a mysterious independence from authority. The decision would not affect him either way; Ben knew that his mind, as usual, was lost between the pages of some thick black holy book, and that he was no more likely to resign in opposition than play peacemaker should there be a kind of labor uprising in Mickey's absence.

Morris, no doubt relieved that the burden of responsibility had not fallen, as perhaps it should have, on him, raised his hand halfway in the air. "If you don't mind my asking," he said, "where in the hell are you going?"

"Away," Mickey said. "By myself. I haven't had a break from this place since I can remember."

"But to pick up and leave on such short notice?" said Morris, gripping the armrests of his chair.

"I'll be back."

Morris didn't seem to hear. "You're picking up and leaving on Thanksgiving?" He looked around to see if anyone shared in his dismay. "Can you imagine?" he said, his eyes blinking behind his glasses. "Thanksgiving."

The bakers, who had always observed the American feast day with a strict, studious enthusiasm, now regarded Mickey with suspicion. What sort of American was he?

"You'll get along fine," said Mickey. "It's not like we've ever really celebrated Thanksgiving." This drew further looks from the bakers, but Mickey was unfazed. "Well," he said, eager to wrap things up, "any questions?"

There were none. The silence lingered, and Ben regretted that Mickey's plan, of which Ben himself was the chief beneficiary, had gone over so poorly. Then Lazarus raised an imaginary glass and, in the halting oratory with which he still occasionally blessed wedded couples and thirteen-year-old boys, nodded to Mickey and said, "May you relax, enjoy and have a wonderful time."

"Thank you," said Mickey. "Meeting adjourned. Benjamin, I'd like to see you in my office."

Ben noticed that he was Benjamin now, and despite himself he felt the weight of those syllables like medals of recognition on his breast. He knew the workers were already plotting against him; already—he could feel it—their indignation was giving way to the suppressed excitement of students who have been presented with a shaky substitute teacher. He would be tested, abused. Or would he? For if he were really in charge, he would have the power to alter their lives. Yes: it would be easy, so easy. But the sudden authority at his disposal—it felt like a smooth lead pipe in his hands—had filled him with a kind of mercy; it was *too* easy to destroy them, and as he stood up and proceeded to his father's office, the eyes of the room upon him, he felt in his shoes the grim dignity, the good fight, of a despised and embattled leader.

Mickey's office was a mess. The desk, which Ben had never really considered before, was covered with papers, and still more documents—bills, consignment sheets, valuable receipts—were pinned under the telephone.

Mickey came in and closed the door. "Don't mind the crew," he said as his workers filed lethargically past the office window and out through the front of the bakery. "They're all good fellas." He smiled; Ben might have been a total stranger applying for a job. "Please," said Mickey. "Have a seat."

Ben sat in the chair facing the desk, the chair normally reserved for those whose sluggish job performance required a little pep talk from the boss. Many had ended up in that chair over the years, and Ben could actually feel, through the seat of his pants, the heat of all the anxiety that had been left there.

"I didn't mean to catch you off guard," said Mickey, sitting casually on the edge of the desk, crushing papers. "In fact, I made the decision at the last second. I had planned to announce that we'd be closing up while I was gone. Then it hit me when I was standing there in front of everyone: why not let Benjie run the show?" He smiled, and Ben had a feeling he was lying, that he had made the decision much earlier.

Ben scratched his head. "Where are you going?"

"I'll get to that in a minute," said Mickey. "First things first." He stood up, swung around to his chair and lowered himself slowly into it. Each movement, it seemed, was calculated for emotional effect. "Are you feeling up to the task?" he said, clasping his hands behind his head. There were great amoeba-shaped stains of perspiration under his arms.

"What's the task?" said Ben, eyeing the sea of papers.

"Well," Mickey said, "I'm not going to lie and tell you it's the easiest job in the world. Your old man didn't get these gray hairs for nothing."

Mickey had never referred to himself as "your old man" before. Ben didn't like it. "I don't want gray hair," he said.

Mickey laughed. Ben was surprised: Mickey usually didn't respond well to wisecracks. He seemed nervous.

"I don't think you'll have to worry about gray hairs," said Mickey, pulling himself up to the desk. He planted his elbows on some complicated forms that Ben imagined would soon be pursuing him in dreams. "Maybe you'll get a little indigestion," Mickey conceded, "but that's all. You shouldn't have to worry too much with the suppliers, but if you feel we're running low on anything—I'm talking flour, yeast, eggs, sugar, margarine—here's a list of numbers."

He went on to explain the whole works, from the inventory chart to the list of hotels, country clubs, nursing homes and restaurants to which Nelson made deliveries. "Keep track of workers' hours here," he said, magically pulling up the correct sheet of paper. "Wholesale accounts get billed," he said, now waving a thick pad with numbers all over it. Ben kept nodding, responding to his father's bizarre new faith in his ability, thinking it was maybe some kind of extravagant apology for all that had been wrong between them over the years and especially in recent weeks, a reflection of Mickey's desire to patch things up, lest he be left all alone come the day when Ben would no longer be dependent upon him. Or maybe he was trying to deepen the dependence—or at least prompt enduring filial ties—by drawing Ben further into the business, condemning him to the bakery, as it were.

Mickey said, "I'll leave you with your pay in advance so you can buy groceries, and also the van keys and my car keys."

Ben was stunned. The car? Mickey had passed into an exquisitely reckless state, and Ben knew he must not draw attention to it with displays of excitement. Let him think he's being completely reasonable, Ben told himself, and more gifts may follow. "Well," said Ben, feigning uncertainty, "I mean, okay."

Mickey turned cautious. "It's not always a picnic," he said.

"I know," said Ben. Then a sobering thought. "What about when you come back?" he said. "What happens then?"

Mickey smiled, and there was a twinkle in his eye which seemed to indicate that if things went well while he was away, Ben would retain his position, and father and son would rule the empire together. But then the twinkle faded, and Ben was struck with the thought—as perhaps Morris had been struck—that Mickey had no intention of returning.

"Where are you going?" Ben said. There was the slightest quavering in his voice.

Mickey looked down at the papers on his desk, began moving them around. "Paris," he said. A pencil rolled off his desk. "Figured I'd put your mother's plane ticket to use."

"Paris?"

"Then I figured I'd stay on for a week or two," Mickey said, "maybe give us both some time to clear our minds." He chuckled. "Maybe we need to get away from each other for a while." He chuckled more emphatically to make light of that.

But Ben knew he meant it. And though he himself felt the same way, the words cut him.

Mickey looked up. "What do you think? Good idea?"

Ben shrugged. "I guess." He didn't feel so well all of a sudden.

Mickey turned back to his papers. "Good." He squinted at a pink sheet. "I'd better get over to Overland Farms and straighten out this bill." Overland Farms supplied the eggs.

Ben swallowed hard, determined to talk business in an even tone. "Why not just call them?"

Mickey folded the pink sheet, tucked it in his shirt pocket. "When you're talking money"—he looked Ben not quite in the eye, but a little above it—"you want to be face-to-face. I've learned that the hard way." He paused to let a history of sour business deals conducted over the phone settle cloudlike over the desk. "The telephone isn't a substitute for a handshake. Sometimes you've got to sit down with people and look them straight in the eye. You have to be direct. Firm. Understand?"

Ben nodded.

"Good," said Mickey. "And one other thing. Keep your eye out for characters. A suspicious-looking fella comes in the place, and you get a bad feeling, don't hesitate to trip the alarm under the register. You know what to look out for."

The next few days were spent going over the finer points of running the bakery. Father and son spent more time together over this period than they had in what seemed like years. The talk, however, was confined strictly to bakery matters, and all the unsaid things gathered darkly around the edges of their words. Ben wanted desperately to reach out to his father, assure him that he wouldn't regret his decision, thank him and reward him in advance with some small demonstration of competence, but as the man didn't seem overly concerned (Ben supposed he'd made an impression after all, on the days he'd filled in for Mickey behind the counter), as he betrayed no real reservations about handing over the reins ("If I can do it, you can," he'd said), Ben was left with a nagging frustration, the only cure for which was to convince himself that Mickey harbored secret doubts, and that he, Ben, must not so much reward the man as prove him wrong. For some reason he could not accept that his father believed in him.

At points during Mickey's sermons, be it on the maintenance of machinery or the particulars of the company bank account, Ben fell into a kind of trance of admiration for his father, thrilled to discover at every turn some new complexity of his character, his knowledge; he had, Ben witnessed, created a system—imperfect and antiquated, perhaps, but an elaborate universe nonetheless, and there wasn't one piece of equipment or one slip of paper that didn't bear his stamp. The tentacles of this business reached further than Ben had ever imagined, from the granaries of the Midwest to the cane fields of the Caribbean; there was even a bottle of vanilla extract whose beans had come all the way from Madagascar. The whole world, it seemed, was contained in this inconspicuous bakery, and Mickey Lerner was its master. And yet all the stuff of this universe—the machinery, the ingredients, the utensils and inventory and supplies—seemed to create a barrier between them, seemed to encircle Mickey in a protective aura of accomplishment through which something as simple as the reaching out of one's hand seemed next to impossible.

Ben was grateful, then, when Mickey asked him for a lift to the airport. Emi had always hired a car; airports were emotional places. Ben tried to imagine the scene at the gate. Would Mickey open his arms? Would his eyes moisten, turn to glass? Ben yearned for an embrace, but as the moment grew closer he began to fill with dread; a display of emotion, he felt, might weaken him in his father's eyes, might make him seem something less than the tough cookie on whom Mickey was counting. But more than that: an embrace at the airport would be almost premature, as if to seal their contract in advance of the trial period (and that's what this tenure was, Ben thought—a test) would be to sanction the very worst.

On Wednesday morning they drove to the airport. Ben had spent all of Tuesday at the bakery under Mickey's eye, and things had gone smoothly.

The beltway was jammed, but once the traffic picked up Ben still drove slowly. Mickey, slumped in the passenger seat, looked awful; he hadn't slept the night before, and Ben could only wonder if he was having second thoughts. Though maybe he was just worried about the flight (he'd never been on a plane for more than an hour or two), and the prospect of making his way, alone, in a foreign country. He didn't know anyone in France.

By the time they arrived at the airport, Mickey's eyes were closed.

"Where do I go?" said Ben, looking around in confusion at all the terminals. "Dad?"

Mickey's eyes popped open, and he gathered himself up in his seat. "United to New York," he said. "There it is."

"I see it," said Ben, thinking that he should offer to carry Mickey's suitcase, which Mickey had spent a long time packing the night before. The sight of the seldom-used suitcase provoked a strange sadness. What dreams had inspired that long-ago purchase? Even filled, the suitcase was a joyless object; the idea of a man reducing himself to what could fit inside, and then struggling with the weight of it, was as sad as it was trampishly comic. Ben tried hard not to feel sorry for his father, who had seemed so strong and invincible while lecturing in the bakery. "Where should I park?" he said.

"That's okay," said Mickey. "Just let me off in front."

Ben felt something inside him buckle. "Don't you want me to—to go in with you?"

"This'll do," said Mickey. He seemed anxious to get away. He unfastened his safety belt and unlocked his door. "I'll call you tomorrow."

It was all happening too fast; Ben wanted to clasp him, hold him back.

Mickey pulled up the collar of his overcoat and opened his door. In a moment he was outside the car, peering in. "Could you pop the trunk for me?"

Ben pulled a lever. The hatch clicked. He wondered if he should get out and help. He hesitated, then opened his door. When he stepped into the cold air the trunk slammed shut. Mickey stood there, ashen, holding his suitcase. Ben took a step as if to walk around to the back of the car, wanting to at least part on a handshake, but Mickey held up his hand, a gesture that said "halt" as much as it said "farewell." Ben bit his lip. Slowly he raised his own hand. Mickey nodded, then turned and walked to the terminal. Ben stood and watched as Mickey inclined his shoulder toward the weight of the things he'd chosen to take with him.

12

Hawk passed the bottle—a malt beverage called Powerhouse that Nelson pretended to enjoy. And really it wasn't so bad, in fact it got better the more you drank. Nelson tilted his head and guzzled.

"Yo, Little Man," Hawk said, laughing. The nickname was a comment not on Nelson's size (though he *was* the smallest of all of them), but rather, Nelson assumed, his perceived lack of experience. "I *never* seen you drink like that."

Chuckie Banks gave Nelson a hard look in the rearview. Sharp chin, Chinese eyes. Toothpick twitching.

Hawk clapped his hands in delight.

Rob said, "What that nigga doin'?" He was in the passenger seat, too fat to turn his head all the way around.

Nelson winced; drink dribbled down his chin. Hawk laughed, Chuckie Banks did not. Nelson wiped his face, passed the bottle up front to Rob.

Chuckie said, "Don't be spillin' that shit on my leather interior."

Hawk laughed, adjusted his dark knit cap. "Nigga," he said, "this ain't even your own car."

They were driving west through a corridor of boarded-up storefronts, disabled cars and hollow-looking row houses, heading toward a world that Nelson knew so much better than the others. The bakery lay a few miles ahead; so did Crumb's place. Further out, Seven Pines.

"Yo, Chuck," said Rob. "Where you steal it from?"

"Just enjoy the ride, Buddha Man," said Chuckie Banks. He declined the bottle.

"Nex' time," said Rob, "make sure the radio work." He pushed dead buttons. "Damn."

Nelson could never be sure when they were joking. Had the car really been stolen? But if it hadn't, why would they pretend otherwise? To impress him? Tease him? The difference meant everything, Nelson thought. Chuckie and Rob weren't entirely known to him. Fortunately, they both seemed subordinate to Hawk, whom Nelson had known since they were little kids. Kevin Hawkins, the craziest kid on the block. For some strange reason—and Nelson had never rushed to question it—Hawk had remained a fiercely loyal friend, and Nelson sometimes felt he commanded a small moralizing influence over him. All of which argued—he hoped—for a certain immunity from violence at the hands of Rob and Chuckie Banks.

Hawk reached for the bottle. He closed his eyes and brought the small round mouth to his lips. Nelson watched him, and was struck by a vision of deep religious suffering, as of a solemn libation, ambrosial and deadening. There were fires, Nelson saw, fires that the alcohol would either quench or fuel.

Hawk lowered the bottle. "We need some grub, y'all."

Rob turned his head. "Yo, Little Man. Can you get any more of them pastries?"

Nelson felt a chill. "Not tonight," he said, cursing himself. Damn! He should've known better than to have ever pilfered sweets from the bakery and given them to Rob.

Chuckie said, "What pastries?"

Rob said, "Nigga drive a truck, deliverin' *baked* goods." He said it almost proudly, intimating connections to inner retail circles. "Work for this white man, deliverin' product all over the metropolitan area." He turned his head a little more. "Ain't that right?"

"Yeah." Nelson hoped they didn't think he was all high and mighty, all big on himself because he had a job. In truth, he had mixed feelings over the recent developments—Bread leaving, Crumb assuming power; he wondered what would happen.

Even Mama had thought it a crazy thing. "Mickey Lerner went *where?*" she'd said, and then got into a strange mood—lost her appetite and everything. "For two weeks?" she'd said. She seemed angry, confused, as if she couldn't believe it either—the idea of Crumb in charge!

"Yo," said Chuckie, glaring at Nelson in the rearview. "Can you hook me up with a job?"

"Me too," said Rob. "Can you hook us up, Little Man?"

"Naw," said Nelson. "Ain't no openings."

"Not yet," said Chuckie.

Rob laughed.

Nelson sank further into his seat. Shit. These punks didn't know what he had in his pocket—a .22 he'd bought off Phil Withers, this fifty-year-old crackhead from down the street who'd come up to him near the bus stop peddling a whole box of cologne and some new shoelaces and hinting that since he was sick with the virus he was putting a lesser emphasis these days on self-defense and was willing to sell off his gun to buy a few more day's worth of "medicine" from the dealers down on Fulbright Avenue. "Now I know you'll play me straight," he'd said, "you a good man, your mama a good woman, I wouldn't make this offer to none of these murderin' fools 'round here. Can't even hold people up no more," he'd added as the furtive trans-action was made right there on the corner, Nelson having just gotten paid. "Too slow." It did cross Nelson's mind that he could, in fact, take the gun and run off, but he didn't want to have to watch his back every time he stepped out of the house. Withers could be lying in wait with a blood-tinged needle, and in any case Phil Withers's judgment of him (crackhead or no, the man had been around fifty years, he knew something about people) was flattering in its way and made Nelson want to reward him for his faith. But when it came time to hand over the money Withers's yellowed eyes went soft with a dazed, queasy lust, and as he clasped the paper, his lower lip moistened with a de-sirous white foam that frightened Nelson and sent him backing off without a word, turning and running two long blocks to his house, where, breathless, he found that the gun contained four bullets.

Even Hawk didn't know about the gun, and now Nelson consid-ered what it would be like to take both Chuckie and Rob from be-hind, right now, execution style.

"Fuck the pastry," said Chuckie. "Wish we had some weed."

"Yo," said Hawk, turning to Nelson. "You got any more of that weed I gave you?"

Nelson had to think for a moment. Hawk was always giving him weed, some of which he smoked but most of which he got rid of for fear it would damage him genetically; he'd read an article about that in *Time*. The seeds, however, he saved. "Naw," he said, rubbing his chin. "Smoked it all."

"All of it?" said Hawk. He made a face. "Didn't even save none for your boy?"

"Sorry," said Nelson, frightened. Hawk was drunk.

Rob said, "Hawk, man, you gonna stand for that?"

"Why you didn't save none?" said Hawk.

"I forgot," said Nelson.

"Yo," said Chuckie Banks. "Don't get no blood on my upholstery."

Rob shook his head. "Nigga play *me* like that? Shit."

Nelson's throat dried up.

Hawk laughed. "Little Man so drunk, he don't know *what* he sayin'. Ain't that right, Little Man?"

Nelson remained silent. He understood that Hawk was rescuing him.

Rob said, "When Little Man get home his mother gonna sniff his breath and whup his ass. Ain't she a Jehova's Witness?"

"What?" said Hawk.

"You said she a Jehova somethin'—mistress, mattress—"

"Naw, man," said Hawk, "I said she a Japanese mass*euse*. Why you gotta act so stupid?"

"Little Man's mother Japanese?" said Rob.

Nelson giggled.

"She can cure people's disease with her fingertips," Hawk announced, glancing at Nelson for verification. "It's all about pressure points."

"Yo yo Little Man," Rob said. "I got a disease on my dick. Can your moms touch it and make it better?"

Nelson stopped giggling.

"Yo," said Hawk.

"She do the Japanese thing, I'm the Buddha," Rob said matter-of-factly. "Whassup? Huh, Little Man?"

"Yo, nigga," said Hawk. "I'll put a slug right in your fat mother-fuckin' head."

"Not on my leather," said Chuckie.

"Think I'm lyin'?" said Hawk. He pressed his finger into the back of Rob's head. "Do you?"

Rob sniffed like a hurt child. "Shit, Hawk. My mother go to church. Prayin' for me. You know wha'm sayin'?" He turned his head as far as he could. "Yo, Nelson. Respect." He offered a giant hand. Nelson took it.

They were on the edge of town. Crumb's house wasn't far. Nelson, still trembling from a confrontation in which he had failed, as usual, to stand up for himself, said, "Make a left at the next red light." He noticed the bottle in his own hand.

Rob lit a cigarette.

"Where we goin'?" said Chuckie.

"I know this white boy," Nelson said. "Might have some weed."

There was a silence, in which Nelson sensed the impact of his words: none of these punks knew any white boys. For the moment, Nelson was head scout on the frontier.

"Where the fuck we at?" said Rob, confused by the darkened houses, the trees.

Nelson felt his heart beating deep in his coat. "Make a right at the stop sign," he said. "Then a left."

Hawk said, "I never smoked no white-boy weed. Shit prob'ly got *strych*nine on it."

"Yeah," said Rob. "White boys be smokin' any damn thing. Jus' bring us back some Twinkies, Slim."

Nelson's remark about the weed was, of course, a lie, but it was the only way to get Chuckie to take him over there. Dropping by Crumb's was essential, he'd decided, a way to impress the guys with his worldliness and at the same time gain respite from their violence. And Crumb: he'd have something to think about, finding Nelson at his doorstep with some serious homeboys waiting in a car. Now that Crumb was his temporary boss—an incredible and even humiliating development—Nelson felt driven to such a display, thinking too that a little intimidation might go a long way in the event of a dispute in the workplace.

Hawk said, "Yo—can we come in too? I never seen no white people house."

Chuckie glanced in the rearview. Rob shifted his weight.

"Naw," said Nelson, sensing a conspiracy growing around him. In a way, he felt as protective of the Lerner house as he did of his own. He appealed to Hawk. "Y'all got to hang back." He said this in a hushed tone, jerking his head to indicate the hoodlums in the front seat, hoping to flatter Hawk's sense of leadership. "Be better if I go in alone."

"Why?" said Hawk, not getting it. "They prejudice?"

Nelson cursed under his breath.

"Who prejudice?" said Rob.

"Nobody," said Nelson. "Yo, stop here."

Hawk said, "Little Man says he got to go in alone." It was a command.

"Shit," said Rob, but he didn't go any further.

Chuckie Banks eyed Nelson in the rearview. "Make it fast, then, Truck-Drivin' Man."

Nelson dared, in his drunkenness, and with his sense of Hawk in his corner, to challenge Chuckie's gaze. "A'ight then, Chuck," he said, watching in fascination as Chuckie finally blinked and looked away. His scalp tingled with a fantastic terror.

He got out of the car and walked up the small hill to the steps leading to Ben's front door, looking back a few times to make sure no one made a move.

Steam rose up from the canned chicken soup that Ben had overcooked on the stove top. For the first time in his life he was left completely alone, and the sensation of freedom was so great that he was exhausted by it, unable to think of anything extraordinary to do beyond blasting the gas jets in a rage of solitude. He couldn't even think of a place to go to in the car; under any other circumstances he might have picked up Nelson and just driven around, gotten some beer and looked for girls, but now that he was technically Nelson's boss, he wasn't too sure if that would be proper.

He could hear the hum of the refrigerator, the swish of distant traffic, the creaking of the house's bones.

He looked at the clock. Mickey would be somewhere over the Atlantic by now. What if the plane were to go down? They hadn't even shaken hands. Ben felt he ought to have learned something from Emi's death. He'd never told his mother he loved her, and though it hadn't seemed to matter when she was alive—she was always in motion, too fleet for such clinging words—the unsaid things weighed heavily upon him. He'd always thought that familial love was something understood, and that to express it in words was as silly as praying aloud, as though you wouldn't be heard otherwise. Now he wished he had said something specific to both parents, or that they had said something to him.

He took his dishes to the sink and let them crash. Tomorrow, Thanksgiving, would be his first real day on the job. Tonight, the bakers would be hard at work on all the pies and cakes that had been ordered, and customers would have until four o'clock tomorrow afternoon to pick them up or purchase other last-minute items. Ben

decided against dropping by the bakery in the wee hours to throw his
weight around, though certainly it was his prerogative. He'd take the
"hands-off" approach for now.

He went up to his room. He was tired, and a little anxious about
tomorrow. He'd brought home some papers to review for the purpose
of familiarizing himself with the ledgers, thinking he could enter the
information onto his computer and maybe play around with the numbers, improve on them.

He sat on his bed and was about to kick off his shoes when he heard
a noise coming from downstairs. He stood up and listened. What was
it? He grabbed the gun from under his pillow. It was after eleven.
Then he heard it again: a distinct rapping on the front door: three military knocks. Was it the police? He looked at the gun, confused. Was
it Shirley Finkle?

Ben placed the gun in his pocket and went downstairs to the door.
He looked through the peephole. It was Nelson.

Ben hesitated in his surprise, then opened the door before he was
sure he wanted to.

"Breadcrumb," said Nelson. He was wearing a dark hooded sweatshirt and an oversized black ski jacket; his face was mostly obscured.

"Hey," Ben said. "How'd you get here?" He then noticed a car idling
in the middle of the street.

"Got my boys with me," said Nelson. "Whatchoo doin'?"

Ben shrugged. "Just getting ready for bed." He thought he smelled
liquor. "Got to get up early and open the bakery." There were at least
two people in the car, he saw. The orange tip of a cigarette bounced in
the dark.

"Can I come in?" said Nelson. His eyes appeared bloodshot and
jaundiced in the porch light. "Never *did* see the inside of your house."
He turned and made a signal to the car.

Ben stood aside as Nelson entered.

"We was just drivin' around," Nelson said. He stopped and looked
at the furniture, the walls, hands deep in his coat pockets.

Ben closed the door, locked it.

"Your own castle," said Nelson.

"For a little while anyway."

Nelson nodded at what he saw. "You the king now," he said. It
sounded somewhere between accusation and suggestive reminder.
"You got the power."

Ben's palms were moist. "It's only temporary," he said. "Things'll be pretty much the same." He meant it as reassurance, that there'd be no radical changes, but Nelson seemed to take it as notice that there'd be no benefits.

"Don't tell me you gettin' all serious now," he said.

"Hell no," Ben said, and laughed. But he wasn't sure what Nelson expected. Deliveries still had to be made, after all.

"Maybe you can give me a raise."

Ben laughed, hoping it was a joke, or to turn it into one if it wasn't. "I'm not *that* powerful," he said. His shoulders twitched. "Want something to eat?"

"Got any pastry food?"

"Naw," said Ben. "Want some soup?"

Nelson shook his head. He stepped back and looked thoughtfully at the wooden balusters of the staircase, which seemed to lead to golden places in his imagination. But the house could not be said to be opulent, even by Nelson's standards: what might pass for pricey antiques were simply old pieces left by Mickey's parents, their value accidental.

Ben glanced at the window, fearing that Nelson's friends might come to the door.

Nelson turned to him, his eyes now drawn to the bulge in Ben's pocket. Ben covered it with his hand.

Nelson laughed; his eyes became purple-rimmed slits.

Ben tried to laugh with him.

"Armed and dangerous," said Nelson.

Ben blushed. "People don't usually knock on my door at eleven at night," he said. "Better safe than sorry."

"Hey," said Nelson, shrugging immensely, arms out at his sides. "That's what I'm sayin'. "

Ben wondered if Nelson was carrying his.

Nelson dropped his arms and turned, surveying the room more aggressively: the antique lamps, the glass swan and bronze mortar and pestle on the coffee table, the antique barometer on the wall above the television and the series of Japanese watercolors (a robed woman on a bridge, mountains and sea behind her) that Emi had brought back one year, her only contribution to the room. Nelson stalked, ogled, tasted with his eyes, his nose, his tiny ears.

"What's in there?" he demanded, nodding toward the basement door, which was boarded up with plywood where Mickey had punched it in.

"It's my mother's practice studio."

Nelson rubbed his chin. The reference to the dead seemed to subdue him, and Ben saw an opportunity to draw out his sympathy.

"Want to see it?" Ben said. He went to the door and turned the knob. He hadn't seen the studio since Emi's death, but he'd have to pass through it sooner or later because the laundry room was down there, and now he wondered if he wanted Nelson to come with him because he was afraid to go down alone.

He opened the door slowly. He could see that Nelson was hesitant, which piqued his own courage. He motioned with his head and went down; in a moment he heard Nelson's steps behind him.

When his mother was alive, Ben would not have dared enter the space like this—there had been rules. Emi saw her practice sessions as metamorphic events, matters of extreme privacy. She wanted to create the impression of spontaneous perfection; the hours and hours of practice were a matter almost of shame, and she wished to close everyone and everything off from them.

"This is it," Ben said, arriving at the bottom of the stairs. The room was even more spare than he remembered it: a music stand (it still held the score on which she'd been working), a chair, a bookcase filled with compact discs and manuscripts and music books, and, in a corner, a small desk. The violin, which would have netted twice what Mickey had gotten for her car, had been put away for safekeeping in some locker at the bank. But basically the room looked untouched; there was a morbid sense of preservation in all of it, as of ghoulish expectations that she might return.

Nelson entered the space as though it were sacred ground, and Ben could see, in the glaze of Nelson's eyes, a few dim flickers of compassion. Ben was encouraged by this, but there was still the faint stench of alcohol and the car waiting outside and the unworldly quality of Nelson's presence.

"It's like a tomb," Nelson said. He looked at the score on the music stand but did not touch it. "When the Egyptians made mummies," he said, "they put a person's favorite things in the tomb. They believed the things would go with the person to the next world."

Ben thought of the violin, trapped in a locker.

"I know about Egypt," said Nelson. Under his vast hood he seemed like an oracle. "They put bread in the tombs of the pharaohs."

Ben wondered what he'd take with him to the next world, if he could.

"Bread shaped to look like animals," Nelson said. "Even pyramids. Egyptians *invented* bread."

"I'd take my ball," Ben said.

Nelson rubbed his chin.

"Maybe," Ben said, "you can play your old games. Maybe if you're good in this world, you get a second chance. But if you're bad"—he thought of the last game of his career, that disaster versus Columbus—"if you're bad, you have to relive your mistakes every second."

"Maybe," said Nelson, "I'll get to play all the games I had to miss." He looked at Emi's chair.

"What do you mean?"

Nelson sniffed. "I told you. The scouts was watchin' me. High school." He sniffed again.

"Then you got hurt."

"Yeah." He looked Ben in the eye. "I got hurt."

Ben felt a tingle of fear. They'd been through this before, Nelson elusive and mysterious, but now he seemed ready to tell, and Ben prepared himself for the biggest lie yet; he firmed his jaw so as not to betray his doubt, knowing that this was a direct challenge, an arrow aimed at the very heart of their friendship. A test. "What happened?" he said.

Nelson's mouth twisted into a half-smile, the toughness of which was slackened by the wet, drunken fatness of the lower lip. He then reached down near his belt, and Ben's heart jumped, but Nelson only pulled up his sweatshirt over his skin, revealing, to Ben's astonishment, a long, sickle-shaped scar that arched from his popcorn-shaped navel to his pectoral. No wonder he never took his shirt off on the courts, Ben thought. The scar tissue was a few shades lighter than his skin, a mix of rose and purple and the milky translucence of ice; it was raised weltlike, a giant earthworm, swollen, indelible.

"What happened?" Ben said.

"I got cut," said Nelson, running a finger along the ridge, a note of elation in his voice, as if he knew he'd been doubted all along, and that every claim he'd ever made would now have to be reexamined in a new light. "I was walkin' home from a game, no shirt on, lookin' like I'm motherfuckin' homeless and shit, and these three Walbrook niggas come up and ask me for money. Like I got it. Tall nigga pulls this blade." He shook his head. "Next thing I know, he swings that shit up. Slashed me like a tire, yo."

Ben stared.

"Lost half my blood," Nelson said. "Had to sleep on my back for a year. Couldn't play ball, nothin'."

"Damn," said Ben. He couldn't stop staring.

"My mother said God and the angels gave me this mark so they could find me better. When the bandages came off she cried, and when she stopped crying she said, 'Now you got proud flesh.' "

"What's that?"

"It's the skin around a cut—flesh that swells up. That's why it's called proud."

Ben nodded. He wanted to touch it, but Nelson dropped his sweatshirt.

A car horn sounded.

"That's for me," said Nelson. He seemed strangely vulnerable now. "Got to go."

Ben led the way upstairs. When he reached the top step he was startled by another horn blast. Nelson was still on the staircase, pulling himself up slowly.

Ben went to the front door and opened it, but did not look out at the car. Nelson was coming toward him, hands in his pockets, craning his neck for one last look at the room.

Ben gazed at the floor as Nelson walked by. A dangerous heat passed between them, or so it seemed; Ben felt relief when Nelson was beyond him. He looked at Nelson's back. "I guess I'll see you tomorrow morning," he said.

Nelson stepped outside. "A'ight then, Breadcrumb." He turned, and the porch light barely illuminated his shrouded face. "Or should I call you Bread now?" The half-smile.

Ben placed his hand on the inside doorknob and looked at a spot just above Nelson's eyes. He smiled. "Whatever you prefer," he said, in a voice touched with the kindness and distance of an employer. He did not recognize it as his own.

13

The darkness was vast; all was sky and ocean, two great depths
flooding a night that stretched halfway across the world. The lights
in the cabin were soft, like honey aglow, insisting on sleep, but Mickey—blanket on his knees, vodka tonic in hand—remained awake, one
of a small number of passengers keeping a kind of priestly watch, as
though the safe arrival of the flight depended expressly upon their
vigilance. He yawned, sipped his drink. If he fell asleep he might have
a nightmare, might shout out and disturb a peace that had taken on
an almost religious cast: babies asleep in their mothers' arms, couples
head to shoulder, elegant old people sleeping in perfect silence; a con-
gregation of pilgrims, of children of the heavens. Not that he wouldn't
be tended to, of course, comforted, should he suddenly lose his grip;
ever since the swell of the engines had sent the plane speeding down
the runway (Mickey gripping the armrests, eyeing the long, flimsy-
looking wings), from which it lost contact and climbed slowly—
slowly—into a cold, clear night, leaning now, so that the bowl of the
world tipped to the side, spilling out a treasure of tiny pulsating lights
that flickered like candles for the dead before the plane straightened
out and climbed even higher, now pushing toward the sea, away from

land, from light—ever since he'd been *seated*, really, buckled in for take-off, Mickey had been under the care of a nice-looking stewardess, a girl young enough to be his daughter, who seemed to have recognized in him a certain helplessness the moment he appeared in the aisle: the lone traveler, stunned eyes blinking in the cold light as people with heavy bags cleared their throats pointedly before shouting for him to move it.

He set his drink down on the tray. The calm with which he did this concealed a great distress, and Mickey reflected that even the stewardess had little idea as to the true dimensions of his predicament. He himself could hardly grasp it. He felt terrible over what he'd done to Donna Childs—he hadn't even paid her the courtesy of a phone call—and could only hope that the pain he must have caused both of them might satisfy what Mickey was sure must be the demands of his wife, who would not, he was certain, have been pleased with the way things had seemed—*seemed*—to be shaping up between himself and Donna. But this journey would erase all doubt. He was heading to the city of Emi's birth, her youth, the one place in the world where he felt he could mourn her without distraction, with a purity of spirit. The source of her.

But the questions lingered. Handing the bakery over to Ben, for instance—what had it meant? It was a reckless decision at best, and now he could only wonder if he'd done it with the intent of ruining himself, so that he might start completely anew. The idea terrified him. He did not know whether his actions were aimed toward destruction or salvation; the two ends seemed hopelessly interchangeable.

Like a soldier heading into an unwinnable war, Mickey felt he had committed himself to disaster. He had no plan, no concrete goal; he was, he feared, adrift, making excuses, improvising, and insofar as he could not, at this moment, give any better account of himself than that he was half-smashed in an airplane, he was tempted to consider the possibility—it made him laugh, it was so farfetched—that he was going to Paris to end his life. But in a moment the laughter subsided, and his entire body trembled.

He lifted his near-empty glass and held it steady to prove to himself that he was in control. The items in his suitcase, the money in his pocket; why would he bring these things, he wanted to know, if his aim was to die? He'd even brought Flemke's office number, so that he could keep pace with the investigation. Still, he couldn't help but feel at least a little attracted to the idea that he might have motives hidden even to himself. In transatlantic flight he was possibly no longer the man he knew; he could be anybody. For what seemed the first time in his life, he felt like a man of substance. If Emi's death had lent him a brief fame and burnished his features with the harsh wisdom of a veteran, it was yet another distinction granted by *her*; this, however, was a chance to fashion his own singularity. In imagining, even in jest, that he was going to kill himself, he had attained a kind of presence, and it was from the mysterious depths of this new bearing that he raised his hand and hailed his stewardess for another drink.

But this effect wouldn't last; how could it, if the suicide were only a fancy? But it was more than that, he told himself. It was an idea, even a proposal. *Suicide.* It was a word that cut to the heart of things, a word to be whispered. Mickey could grapple easily with such terms now. Death was something he'd held in his hands. Was it really so fantastic, then, this notion of suicide? Was it really so remote? His life had become little more than a series of unbearable tortures; and what was he, what did he have to offer, to give, that it was necessary for him to go on? Why live with all this turmoil? Maybe, he thought, his death would even liberate Benjie somehow, relieve the kid of the constant sight of so ordinary a figure, the model of his flesh, murderer of his potential, reminder of his limitations. Oh, maybe that was being too hard, but the fact remained that if he were to flirt with such serious stuff as suicide, he'd better damn well make an airtight case for it. He was no martyr, no, but he did believe in sacrifice, and there was nothing he wanted to do from here on out that wouldn't lead to some good. He'd done enough harm, he felt. And so he imagined it: attending Shaw's concert, then going back to his hotel room and quietly ending it all with the sleeping pills that Dr. Abel had given him (for the bad nights, Abel had said) and which he had yet to take, wary as he was of the effects. He was no pill-taker, never had been; didn't even take aspirin. Yet he had brought the pills. Why? What had he been thinking? Mickey honestly couldn't say; his best guess was that he had packed for any and all eventualities.

He closed his eyes, wanting to sleep without dreams, to sleep the sleep of the dead. Again he wondered: courage or cowardice? Dissipation—now *that* was cowardly; he could let himself go in a heartbeat, he felt—drink and eat to excess, kill himself slowly; that would be easy. But to actually take one's life in a single moment: that could only be an act of courage; for what was there to stop him, if not fear? As he examined this question, he closed his eyes and slipped almost immediately from consciousness, then slipped again, further, and was already snoring lightly by the time the stewardess arrived with his drink.

Hours later, he was awakened by what felt like a sharp turbulence; he opened his eyes, and was shocked to find that the plane was absolutely still.

He looked out the window: they were over land. England, he heard someone say. For a moment Mickey forgot all else. *England*. Below, a great blanket of clouds lay in the predawn darkness: England was completely blotted out by what looked, from above, like the rocky surface of an ice planet—clouds shaped like plowed snow, rippled, curdled, a sea of swans piled frozen, lumps, feathers, the whitest unmoving smoke. Mickey thought of the villagers on the ground, who would never know this beauty, who would look up and see only a vault of gray.

Europe. I made it, Mickey thought. I did it! He suppressed a giggle, surprised at this burst of excitement and realizing at once that it was unbecoming in a man his age. There were children on this flight who'd probably made the trip a dozen times, and so any delight he may have secretly enjoyed over this feat of travel ought to be snuffed out by the years it had taken him to get there: his pleasure could only remind him of so much pleasure deferred. He was like a man awakened after a long sleep to a new life, only to realize he had precious little time left to enjoy it. The chatter of passengers taunted him; they had places to go, lives to live. Yet in a certain way, Mickey saw himself as their superior, a man beyond life. It gave him a peculiar thrill to imagine that he had come here to commit suicide, though in his heart he knew it was little more than a joke, a crazy idea fueled by too many drinks; truth be told, he didn't have the guts.

Soon the plane was dipping into the clouds, and when land came within sight—strange white houses with red rooftops, gray rain-soaked fields—Mickey knew that he had arrived in a place of dire consequence.

The old, familiar excitement returned. It was the same excitement he'd felt when, standing by the basement door, listening to Emi play, he would place his hand on the knob, poised to intrude. This sensation was personal, his own; it had nothing to do with the more universal thrill of arrival. For an entirely different reason, he once again felt distinct from the crowd. Who else on board stood to discover so much in Paris? Whose story could compare to his?

He gripped the back of the seat in front of him as the wheels touched the ground.

There was applause. It was morning. Mickey looked around for his stewardess, to thank her, say good-bye, but she was nowhere to be seen, and as he filed out of the plane with everyone else, he could feel, like a heavy hand on his shoulder, the return of his anonymity.

The airport was much bigger than he'd expected. Words on signs were different—Mickey understood nothing. Announcements in French issued from the loudspeakers. People spoke to one another with no regard for his understanding.

The strange language added to his sense of torture, of persecution; it was like an attack on his sanity. He was alone, completely alone, glimpsing the life that he'd always feared was in store for him: the solitary man, old and confused, the world around him menacing, inscrutable, leaving him further and further behind.

He followed the other passengers through a series of document checks (security was tight on account of some recent problems with Arabs, you couldn't spit without hitting a cop or a soldier) and then to the baggage area, where he waited and waited in a dwindling crowd, fearing his bag would never emerge from the tunnel, so that when it finally did he felt a shock of recognition, and reached out for it as though it were a person.

He went to a window marked CHANGE and handed over three hundred dollars in traveler's checks. He'd brought a few thousands' worth, and carried three credit cards. The transaction went smoothly. Mickey took a small pleasure in each successive triumph over the language barrier, embracing the challenges like an athlete and finding that all the worries he'd rehearsed so intently on the plane had fled to the edges of his thoughts, leaving nothing but the moment at hand. The idea of taking his own life now seemed especially preposterous, and he was embarrassed for having toyed with it. He was now convinced beyond a doubt that there was something here for him to discover, something about his wife; indeed, it was as though she were leading him through all of this, and as he entered a waiting taxi (which seemed planted there by the curb, waiting in the rain just for him) he pulled from his wallet a scrap of paper, kept in the envelope with the plane ticket, on which Emi had written the name and address of a Paris hotel, along with the address of the place where she and David Shaw were to perform. Mickey handed it over to the driver, who glanced at it and nodded.

"L'Hôtel Dakar?" he said.

"Yes," said Mickey. *"Oui. Merci."* If he'd ever wondered what sort of place Emi chose to stay in when she was abroad, now he would know. He hoped it wasn't too pricey.

He gazed out at the scenery along the rain-slicked highway: gray loomings of modern office buildings, high-rise hotels of black glass, housing developments that looked as though they were thrown up in a hasty response to a refugee problem; hardly the hills and forests and rolling manors and country houses that Mickey had always imagined surrounded the great city in lush, green, ever-widening concentric circles. As things on the outskirts of town grew bleaker and denser with drab apartment buildings, Mickey began to worry. Was this Paris?

The taxi entered the city like a rodent. Mickey had never seen such filthy streets. And the people! Nothing but blacks and other dark-skinned types. Arabs? Turks? Soon the driver slowed and pointed to a white building on a corner. Attached to it was a lit sign with the words HÔTEL DAKAR burning red through the drizzle.

The place looked like a dump. And the area! Blacks everywhere (blacks, here in *Paris*!), half of them dressed in brightly colored African robes, absurdly out of place among the white buildings, the flashing lights, the cars whizzing along rain-glazed boulevards. The sidewalks, meanwhile, had been taken over by foreign street vendors, who were busy arranging their tattered, orphaned wares (clothes, shoes, books, dishes, tools, batteries, you name it) upon thick blankets, and the trash cans—sealed, Mickey figured, to prevent terrorist bomb attacks (Arabs—what else?)—overflowed with the garbage placed atop them by careless passersby. Mickey turned his gaze to the elevated tracks splitting the dirty street in an infernal eruption of steel, thinking how easy it would be to forget he was in one of the great capitals of western civilization.

He paid the cabbie and got out, unsure what to think about Emi's choice of lodgings.

Or maybe this wasn't her hotel at all, but someone else's; someone she had meant to call on, meet. And what about Shaw, he wondered; where was David Shaw staying? Certainly not *here*. Shaw traveled in style.

Mickey pushed open the door and entered what he supposed had to be called the lobby. There was a wooden desk, two chairs, a small wooden table and a pay telephone.

"Bonjour," said the man behind the desk. His skin was as black as Mickey had ever seen on a man; his European sweater and jacket

seemed wrong on him, a corruption of his nature. *"Puis-je vous aidez?"*
"No French," said Mickey. "English."

The man smiled, showing an octave of white teeth. "You are American?"

"Yes I am," said Mickey, striking a patriotic note. Emi had often said that foreigners, all foreigners, despised Americans, and that Americans consistently shamed themselves abroad. He'd always taken it personally. "How much for a room?"

The man seemed to respect Mickey's no-nonsense approach, and the figure he quoted was satisfactory. It took Mickey some time to figure out the money, and he could feel the man's patience bearing down on him as the coins and bills jingled and crinkled in his clumsy white hands. He placed the francs on the desk, along with his passport.

"Thank you very much," said the man, placing a key beside the money. The exchange seemed to have put a distance between them. When the man looked up and smiled, there was something false in it. "Please sign," he said, producing a pad and pen. Mickey took the pen, hesitated; the handing over of the key had thrown him off, had reminded him for some reason of Donna. It was an unexpected and unwelcome thought—he was here to concentrate on Emi, after all—but the guilt over his treatment of Donna, coupled with his desire to make amends, exceeded for the moment all other feelings, producing in him an odd resentment of his wife: he found himself *wanting* to find fault with her, that he might ease the burden on his conscience with regard to Donna Childs—Donna, who was alive, and who was perhaps feeling, even at this very moment, the sting of his disappearance.

Mickey signed the register with a steady hand. The man looked at the passport and said, "Thank you, Monsieur Lerner, and have a pleasant visit."

Mickey blushed at the sound of his name, and felt a pang of humility at the man's obvious command of English. "Thank you," he said. If Emi had come here before, he thought, this man would surely recognize her. Mickey pulled out a photograph of his wife from his wallet—an old photo, true, but then she hadn't changed all *that* much, and how many white women came into this place anyway—and offered it to the man, watching him carefully. "Do you recognize this woman?" he said.

The man studied the photograph, then looked at Mickey. "Are you the police?" he said.

"No," said Mickey, in such a way that he might be the police indeed. "Has she been here before, that you know of?"

"I think," said the man, "that she has been here, but I cannot be positive. What is her name?"

"Emilie Lutter," said Mickey. He spelled it.

"I can look in my records," said the man. "But with all respect, why do you ask?"

"I'm her husband," said Mickey.

"Yes," said the man, and nodded gravely.

Mickey was dumbstruck; he hadn't meant to convey any such meaning, but the man had understood him instantly, and though this understanding seemed to point to exactly what Mickey had thought he needed in order to justify his feelings toward Donna—that Emi had, indeed, been unfaithful—the imminence of so enormous a confirmation sent him reeling, which told him that he hadn't really believed it after all, and was thus wholly unprepared to take it on, like a fighter going into the ring stone-cold.

"I will check for you," said the man, who seemed pleased to find himself the pivot of an international intrigue, though Mickey could see, beyond this new sense of duty, a kind of glimmer of superiority, even of contempt for his new guest, and not simply because he would, if his findings turned up the worst, be more or less an accomplice to Emi's disloyalty—it was *his* hotel, after all—but because, as a man, as a competitive animal, he would naturally find something distasteful about monsieur, that he could not keep his woman in line, that he'd journeyed thousands of miles for the sake of her and all but admitted to his own male inadequacy.

"Thank you," Mickey said, his voice straining against his anger. Room key in his fist, he climbed the winding, uneven staircase, feeling certain that he was being mocked.

On the third-floor landing he observed a dark-skinned man enter a room ahead of an older white woman dressed in a long coat with what looked to be a black teddy underneath. Mickey could hardly believe it. This place was worse than he'd thought. Prostitutes! Pimps! Mickey knew that his wife had had something of a fascination with the underclass, but to stay here in this hotel, this flophouse, well, that was taking things a mite too far. Certainly it was too seedy a place in which to conduct a love affair, though Mickey could see as how some people might derive a certain thrill from it. But he could not in a million years imagine Donna Childs conducting an illicit affair here or anywhere else; she was a woman of strong moral fiber, Mickey felt. He really ought to call her and apologize, explain, but he didn't want to compound his offense by lying to her, which is what he would end up doing, what he would *have* to do, seeing as how he had no clear idea why he'd stood her up, fled, save maybe that he felt he was in some danger from her, and how could he possibly tell her that?

Mickey entered his room, which was not much bigger than a boxing ring. Bed, night table, dresser, toilet, shower. On the wall above the bed hung a framed aerial photograph of an outdoor arena filled with tens of thousands of people dressed in white. Tall light towers illumined the scene, their bulbs so bright under the dusky sky that even in a photograph they hurt the eyes. It was entitled *Mecca*. Mickey found that he could not look at the picture without feeling an almost dizzying sense of dislocation.

He lay on the bed. How could Emi stand it? How could she stand to travel so far from home, to be so deeply alone in foreign rooms? For there were times, he knew, when she'd gone to obscure cities, places where she knew no one, where she'd had to spend days at a time surrounded by the unfamiliar. Had she felt as he felt now—like a child lost, a child forgotten? For he was far, far from home, far from his store, his house, his family and friends, his garden and room and car and autumn birds, far from everything he had ever known, and there was no one, no one at all, to comfort him.

He could hear sounds coming from the next room; thumps and grunts, one and then the other. Occasionally there was a female whimper.

These seemed to Mickey the loneliest sounds he had ever heard.

He brought his knees to his chest. What did they know, what did *anyone* know about making love? He alone knew what it was to love a woman, and all attempts by men in bedrooms and hotel rooms could only fall short of the standard he'd set in those early years with Emi. He saw her now, youthful and girlish in just a T-shirt that came to midthigh, her hair wet from her bath and smelling of cherries as she combed it in the bedroom mirror. How graceful she was when she didn't know he was watching her! The small eager breasts, the white, hairless legs; how he liked to walk up behind her and lift the shirt and peek at the small, goose-pimply buttocks, press his groin against them as she tilted back her head and opened a mouth full of imperfect European teeth. And who better than he knew how to grip her by the shoulders and gently drive her to the bed, in such a way as to make her feel, each time, that her innocence was being taken? Whose prick? Whose tongue? Yes, he knew what it took to please her, to keep her coming home, and when she bounced so slick and warm astride him and ground her bone into his and cried out into his mouth as his fingers pressed each knob of her spine right down to the dangerous dark button of her backside, his mastery was clear to him—for who else could make her see such colors, who better than he could play this wild clarinet?

But when they eventually fell asleep, her hand resting jealously between his legs as though protecting a rare monopoly, he could sometimes wonder, and more than wonder—just as he did at receptions or parties, when, in conversations, he'd stand silently by her side, feeling for the life of him like some strapping buck whom she'd purchased at an auction for one obvious purpose, while the other guests regarded him from over the rims of their wineglasses and deigned to take him seriously—if she loved him not with her heart, as he had suspected during their times in the garden, or driving to Pennsylvania on a Sunday in autumn to pick apples, but with that small, urgent cunt, which, even if it failed to develop other, more exotic cravings (though such a failure seemed almost impossible), would then at least, in time, relent; and what good would he be to her then?

Strange: he had not, in those days, ever supposed it might be *he* who'd become restless and get wandering eyes. But it was only recently, when she became so distant, that he had started to think— *really* think (of course he'd always had casual thoughts)—about other women. Yes: she'd driven him to it; and as he listened to the sickening creak of bedsprings through the wall, he dared to seek comfort in the idea of Donna Childs, thinking too that in having very nearly elicited from the man downstairs testimony of Emi's infidelity (he'd all but laughed in my face, Mickey thought) he had earned, God help him, the right to indulge this tender, awkward preference. For Donna *existed*; she lived and breathed. And what greater recommendation was there? That she was attractive and warm and intelligent and had a wonderful laugh, well, this was secondary, it was icing on the cake; nor did it hurt, in terms of her appeal, that she was swathed in the forbidden—so much so, in fact, that Mickey was all but resigned to the knowledge that he might only ever be with her in this sad little way: alone in a darkened room, the blankets pulled over his head.

But as he tried to summon her to his imagination, the sounds from the next room grew louder: thumps, grunts, gasps for air, noises that sounded less like a session of love in a cheap hotel room in Paris than an exchange of blows in a West Baltimore gym. It was as if Tommy

Childs himself were in training on the other side of that wall, sparring, preparing for a rematch, rising from the dead to defend the honor of his daughter; and as Mickey placed his hands over his ears, the noise grew louder still, beating him further against his pillow, pummeling him at last into the depths of memory.

14

Lou Glazer was all over him the minute he walked in the door. "Where the hell've you been?" Glazer demanded, in that high, loud, deaf man's voice, which, along with his lazy right eye and the thick tufts of hair that stuck up like wings at the back of his white trainer's shirt, had probably given him plenty of reason to become a fighter—as if having grown up among cutthroat Greeks and Poles and Italians in East Baltimore weren't reason enough. He followed Mickey to the locker room, which smelled strongly of crotches, buttocks, armpits, feet, powders, hair oil. Two young, thin Negroes whom Mickey didn't know were getting dressed there.

"Hey, smart guy," Glazer pursued. "You got your first fight tomorrow. Or did you forget?"

"I didn't forget," Mickey said, turning the combination lock. His hand was shaking, in grief and in anger: he'd just finished bawling his eyes out at the bakery, and that hadn't been in his fight plan.

"Two days you've been gone."

"My father died." The locker popped open.

"Your father died." Glazer nodded, folded his arms, rocked on his toes. He'd heard it all before. "So," he said. "How many times did you fuck her? Huh, Lerner? How many times?"

Mickey was embarrassed by this sort of talk, but he liked what it assumed about his experience, liked that the Negroes might think him a studhorse. He said, "He had a heart attack."

Glazer clucked his tongue.

The Negroes snickered.

Mickey turned his body away from Glazer to change into his leather protector and trunks. "Check the obituaries if you don't believe me," he said.

Glazer wasn't buying. "Think I wasn't eighteen once?" he said.

Mickey looked at his trainer: skinny legs, bulky middle, that clean white tunic; no, he could never have been eighteen. He looked like the eternal Italian barber.

"Call my house you don't believe me," Mickey said. "There's a whole crowd there. My uncle and some neighbors and some people my father knew. I told them I had to go to the store for some aspirin. They think I'm at the store. The funeral was this morning." There must have been something in his voice, because Glazer shifted his weight.

"Well then," Glazer said. "If that's the case, maybe you shouldn't be here." He clasped his hands together. "I mean that really is a terrible thing." His voice could not find the right note for sympathy; like his eye, it seemed to have been knocked out of alignment from too many punches. He said, "You want to cancel?"

Mickey shrugged.

"What?" said Glazer.

"No."

Glazer nodded grimly, then took from his pocket a pair of used, smelly wraps, which caused Mickey to turn and hold out his hands. Getting wrapped always reminded him of that day, several years before, when Noah Brown, the bakery's kosher supervisor, had beckoned him to the back of the store while the elder Lerner was busy with a customer. Noah pulled from a silken bag a small black box that was connected to a long leather thong, and Mickey, feeling small in the face of such a mysterious and presumably powerful object, allowed Noah to place the box on his arm. He repeated, at Noah's whispered command, some foreign syllables that rumbled the back of the throat, then watched again as the old man wrapped the thong around his forearm and middle finger and uttered another blessing.

It happened but once, and was never mentioned again: it may have been an obscene act. But whenever Glazer wrapped his hands, Mickey became aware of a similar sanctity, a secrecy, as of some ancient ritual; and Glazer was always solemn, winding the bandages round and round with great care.

"Okay," Glazer said. "Lerner?"

Mickey had been drifting; he hadn't wanted the wrapping to end, and now Glazer was holding his finished hands, waiting for Mickey to pull them away. When Mickey didn't, Glazer dropped them.

Mickey stared at the hands. They were now calibrated weapons, weighted, packed. He said, "You gonna at least tell me who I'm fighting?"

Glazer looked askance. "Kid named Thomas Childs. I told you, don't worry about it. Just do what I tell you, you'll be okay." Then he was gone, quick as a fly: he raged into the gym and went after a wheezing, bloated Clayton Grimes, who was sluggishly shadowboxing in the mirror, appearing somewhat less fierce than he did in the promotion posters that covered the peeling gray walls of Glazer's office.

In the main area there hung four big bags, which, amid so many carnal smells, resembled things hanging in a slaughterhouse; on one of them a light-heavy named Warren Hurt was taking out serious frustrations, grunting, occasionally butting the bag with his head or shoulders as it swung back toward him. Like most of the fighters here, Hurt was essentially a violent man, in whom the gym prompted a grudging discipline; so that by the time he returned to the street he was, far from tranquilized or ennobled, often ready to kill somebody.

By the time Mickey finished his calisthenics, the speed bag was free. He walked past the ring, which was elevated three feet off the ground: the two kids inside it, headgear falling over their eyes, danced endlessly. Along the perimeter of the space, fighters skipped rope and shadowboxed. They all knew who Mickey was—he was conspicuous enough—but no one went out of his way to talk to him. Mickey took it in stride. He knew they saw him as Glazer's favorite boy (which was dead wrong: Glazer favored no one, loved no one), and if this cost him their friendship, it also spared him their wrath: it was the colored kids who got whipped with towels and shoved into the lockers.

He stood before the red pear, tapped it, roused it, then stroked it until it blibbered and blurred. He could forget himself, could surrender completely to his own crafted rhythms. He watched his fists, slow and pendular in a shiver of red.

After this, he headed for the giant salamis. These were for power.

Mickey sent his bag swaying lazily, the chain squeaking from where it was attached to the ceiling. He wasn't a grunter; he swallowed his grunts, not wanting to draw any attention to himself, but also out of a kind of sexual shyness. His gray T-shirt grew dark with sweat as he directed his punches with increased purpose. At points he feared he might begin to cry if he stopped punching. His father had loved salami. He used to eat it sliced thick, with mustard and olives on rye toast.

He shadowboxed and skipped rope. Normally he felt his body trimming and tightening into perfection as the rope whipped over his head, but as he faced the mirror and observed himself, all the uncertainty in his life—the bakery, the house, the prospect of living alone—came straight at his chin, blows that were so quickly absorbed into his concerns about tomorrow's fight that he felt he could not go on training unless he knew more about his opponent. But for some reason Glazer wasn't telling. Mickey didn't think Glazer would pit him against a top-notcher, an ace, not in his first fight anyway. But was Glazer that careful? Who was Thomas Childs? Despite himself, Mickey felt the first small stirrings of fear; his feet stuttered, and the rope snared his ankle.

It was time to spar. Glazer whistled for Hurt, who, though not a middleweight, had been one not long ago; he was only three pounds heavier than Mickey, but found himself on the other side of the class cusp. He was gaining weight now, wanting to move up to cruiserweight; at six feet two, he had room for more pounds. He was twenty-three years old and his face was already flat as a photograph.

Glazer gripped Mickey's jaw and fed him a mouthpiece, then strapped him into his headgear. Again, Mickey thrilled at Glazer's firm touch. He ground his teeth on the mouthpiece, enjoying the weight it gave to his skull. He saw his hands eaten up by two red gloves. Glazer secured these, then took a dollop of Vaseline on his finger and drew a cross on Mickey's face: a stripe down the nose and across the brow.

On the other side, Glazer's assistant, old Abe Lackman, outfitted Hurt. Mickey scraped his shoes in the rosin box and stepped nimbly into the ring. He met his opponent in the center and touched his gloves.

The other fighters stopped their workouts to watch. They all knew that Mickey was fighting tomorrow (Hurt was fighting too, as was a kid named Leonard Roach), and Mickey sensed a kind of familial pride in the way they gathered around the ring. To please them he danced a little with Hurt, but that wasn't his style; he was a flat-footed puncher, not so much a bull as a rock: patient, willing to wait for an opening, a mistake. He kept his fists high, his head down. He knew that Hurt—stronger, more experienced—was under orders to take it easy. Mickey planted his feet and initiated with a lead, then let Hurt toughen him up with body blows. There was pain, the gasp of lost wind, the need, at first, to vomit, but once beyond a certain threshold the blows became like cramps that come only with laughter: no pain in between, just a giddy bracing for it. More impressive than Hurt's punches was Mickey's ability to absorb them. Having lulled Hurt into that game, Mickey suddenly went after him, jabbing, feinting. Now he moved his man back, landing harder stuff, and as Hurt went into his shell Mickey pounded the arms, wanting to pry them open to get to the meat. Glazer was yelling something at him, and in the very instant he turned to look at Glazer he saw a flash of shattered light and found himself on his back, his chin tingling, his skull bruised where it had slammed on the canvas.

A towel full of fumes was passed under his nose by crooked-nosed Lackman, and Mickey could hear Glazer yelling at Hurt. Mickey knocked the towel away and stood up too fast. Wobbling, he saw that the onlookers had been roused: they shook their heads, smiled, slapped each other's backs, mimicked Hurt's delivery. Mickey winced at Glazer's fingers on his lips, then coughed up the mouthpiece as though he had swallowed it. The headgear came off to a blast of air and noise. Glazer told him he'd had enough. "Save it for tomorrow," he said.

The next day, Mickey escaped the house again on another flimsy pretext. He had a feeling Morris was on to him—Morris had remarked offhand the night before about the puffiness around Mickey's eyes, and later had caught him shadowboxing in his room—but still Mickey lied. He felt guilty as hell, boxing all through the mourning period, but what was he supposed to do? Glazer had gone through a lot of trouble to nail down this fight, and Mickey had trained his heart out.

He drove down to the gym, where Glazer was waiting with Hurt and Roach and Abe Lackman. They all got into Glazer's car, the three fighters in the backseat, Mickey in the middle.

As Glazer and Lackman talked up front, Hurt and Roach chatted across Mickey's knees about neighborhood things. Then the conversation got around to the fights, and Hurt poked Mickey in the chest. "You're money in the bank," he said. He was a few years older, and Mickey respected his wisdom, though he was afraid of him personally. "They gonna put you against bums, make you look good for the white people. Turn you pro fast as they can."

Roach, his knees scissoring, listened studiously.

"You'll never have to be any good to make money," Hurt said. "Just good enough to be a good white bum. They always room for a good white bum."

Roach nodded.

Mickey tried to ignore it. He said, "You know anything about Thomas Childs?"

"That your man?"

"Yeah."

"Prob'ly a bum."

"Yeah?"

"Or maybe not." And at this Hurt closed his eyes and stretched extravagantly.

None of the fighters had ever been to Dundalk before. It was working-class to the bone: tidy row houses, corner bars, Old Glory hanging from front porches. Hurt began fidgeting a little; Roach stroked his chin.

They pulled up to the hall, one of those Legion halls that are often rented out for weddings or fund-raising events. The proceeds from this exhibition, the fighters had been told, were to go to a local hospital—the proceeds, that is, which remained after the promoter and the managers took their cuts.

The place was already half-filled with thick-necked men, their bellies burning with beer and Polish sausage, with the sparks and fire of the workplace. In a dark corner of the arena, Mickey noticed, there sat a small group of Negroes.

The mood in the dressing room was funereal. Hurt and Roach were subdued, almost prayerful, hardly their usual belligerent selves. Mickey changed into his pine-green trunks and took a brief rubdown from Glazer, who told him to relax, to just fight his fight—as if he *had* a fight, as if he'd fought a dozen times. Mickey just nodded.

"Jabs," Glazer said absently, slapping Mickey's shoulder blades. "Don't chase him."

"Okay." Suddenly Mickey was on his feet, with Glazer helping him into a long, threadbare purple robe. He shuffled, threw a few punches at the air, touched his toes, bent his knees. Glazer reached behind him to put the hood over his head.

Mickey heard his name being announced, but the fella got it wrong—he said Leary instead of Lerner. Mickey looked at Glazer to see if he noticed this. Glazer smiled slyly. "It's got a better sound to it," he said. "Better for business." He turned his head at the sound of scat-

tered boos and catcalls, and his fleshy, battered face grew dark. "It's
time," he said. Mickey threw a sloppy combination at the air, then followed Glazer through a doorway and down an aisle toward the ring,
where, under the lights, a referee and a ring announcer stood looking
at him, and where Thomas Childs, rangy, unknown, his face hidden in
the hood of a glowing white robe, was being aided through the ropes
by his colored handlers.

Glazer removed Mickey's robe, then inserted his mouthpiece and
greased his face while Lackman arranged the water bottle and towels
and bucket by the stool. Mickey touched his head—no protective gear
there. A face wide open. He looked around: there must have been
over a hundred and fifty people on hand, most of them white. They
eyed Mickey with a mix of curiosity, pride and blunt expectation.
Mickey looked down at his shoes.

Glazer pawed his head and said into his ear, "I know you've had a
tough couple of days, kid. Now go and take it out on the shvartze."

"Leary!" called the referee, a fat, middle-aged man in a striped shirt.
With a push from Glazer, Mickey trotted to the center of the ring to
meet Childs, who was still huddled with his seconds. In a way, Mickey
was glad to be Leary; it took the edge off his guilt, helped him separate himself from his actions.

Childs was skinny, sleek; he had a part in the middle of his hair and
a pubescent mustache. But his arms were long, and when he shook off
his robe his muscles rippled. His face was unreadable. He stared at
Mickey and flashed his mouthpiece. Mickey felt a chill down his back.
When Childs met him up close, Mickey saw dull, shifting eyes and a
perfect nose, preserved either by lack of experience or a refusal to be
hit.

The referee went over some rules, wished the fighters well and ordered them to touch gloves. Childs tapped Mickey's glove without
looking at him and went back to his corner to wait for the bell.

The lights that had been rigged above them were hot, bright; as
much as anything else they gave the fight the semblance of an event.
Glazer was barking instructions and rubbing Mickey's neck when the
bell rang. Childs charged to the center before Mickey left Glazer's fingertips. The crowd responded favorably to Mickey's slow advance.

Childs kept his hands low, jiggling them at his sides. Mickey forgot
about everything else; the past and the future fell away from him. He
was left with only his body.

He stepped in and jabbed. Childs snapped his head back, avoiding
the punch, then countered with two lightning jabs, both of which

Mickey barely picked off with his mitts. His own quickness surprised him. That, and the lack of power in the punches. Childs uppercut, missing completely, then crossed to the face. Mickey felt his nose go numb; the sensation forced tears. An uppercut landed under his heart. Mickey covered up, felt a small storm on his arms and at the top of his head. If Childs was scoring, Mickey felt a moral advantage in having had his nose struck first. The crowd, however, was less encouraged: they booed loudly, a thunder to accompany Childs's rain, and through it all Mickey could hear Glazer screaming at him to get out of there.

Mickey pushed Childs off, and brushed his own nose with his glove to make sure it was still attached. He got in close, jabbed and feinted in the textbook fashion. Both corners were yelling for their guys to mix it up; both sensed a vulnerability in the opponent. Mickey jabbed, then hooked with his left, catching the chin. His right followed to the nose. Bull's-eye. Childs sailed back into the ropes. The chest was open, and Mickey charged in, nailing the solar plexus and the heart. Some in the crowd had risen. Childs gasped, leaned into the ropes. Mickey roundhoused to the head; sweat jumped from Childs's scalp like bugs. The ref was on top of them. Fans stood and pumped their fists. Childs's face looked dented. "Finish him off!" Glazer yelled. Childs's trainer was hollering for jabs. Mickey went down low to work the body. Glazer screamed for him to pound the head. Childs hit Mickey's ear like a baby banging a drum. "The head!" Glazer screamed. The crowd picked up on that. Mickey straightened and nailed the sinuses. Childs clung to Mickey. Mickey dug again into the gut. The ref separated them and said something to Childs. Childs nodded that he was okay, but his legs were rubber. The ref stepped back. Mickey went to the body, and Childs sagged into the ropes again, covered up, waited. Mickey did not pursue. Childs staggered forward and embraced him, punching weakly at his kidneys. Mickey slow-danced with him, draping his arms over Childs's shoulders. He breathed and closed his eyes to the shouts. The ref separated them. Mickey assumed a stance à la Benny Leonard, waiting for Childs to come to him. Childs shuffled and bobbed, but did not come. The bell rang.

Mickey returned to his corner. Glazer wiped his face with a towel as Lackman aimed the water bottle erratically, squirting everything but Mickey's mouth. Mickey knocked it away. Glazer was livid: "Why did you let up? Huh? You were one punch away!"

"He didn't go down."

"You didn't go in for the kill!"

"I can take him," Mickey said, panting.

"Then take him," said Glazer.

Mickey came out more aggressively this time, to the renewed delight of the crowd. The first round had just been a tease, they seemed
to think; its promise would now be fulfilled. Mickey scraped the canvas with his shoes, rolled his neck, flashed his mouthpiece.

Childs looked refreshed, even confident; his corner had recon-
structed him. Maybe this wasn't a bum after all; maybe the first round
was just so much subterfuge. Mickey tried some exploratory jabs, like
poking at something that might or might not be alive. Again he sensed
Childs's lack of power. Then he was struck on the chin; he staggered,
and in the corner of his eye saw the small group of Negroes lean forward in their seats. Childs came again to the body. Mickey tried to
clinch, but Childs backed up. Mickey followed him. He charged into
Childs's right hand, but kept coming, and they mixed it up, trading to
the body before their skulls collided in a *klonk* that sent them both
reeling. Mickey recovered and fired, smashing the nose, and followed
that with a hook. Again, Childs was on the ropes: his eyes and his nostrils were slits. Mickey noticed blood on the canvas. He looked at
Childs. It was hard to tell from where he was bleeding, he was so dark
and sweaty. Mickey pawed at him harmlessly, thinking he might be in
real trouble. What had he done to him? Again came the cries to put
him away. The ref got closer. Sweat poured into Mickey's eye. Pausing
to wipe at it, he was struck on the throat. Mickey caught his breath
and fell into Childs so that he could wipe the eye. His glove came
away bloody. The eye blurred up. He tasted blood on his lips. It was
his own.

He would never fully remember what happened next; all he knew
was that he had thrown himself at Childs, wanting the skull, the soft
food beyond it. He was blind, swinging his fists as though trying to
break through a darkness to light, coming closer to something, a brink,
a moment of shattering release in which he would howl like some
wild, soaked animal, his torso wet and shiny as a carnival in the rain.
His face and chest were spattered, his trunks streaked with blood;
Childs was a bronze font, a twisted, drooling sculpture, sprinkling the
ring with an unholy water that drove Mickey's thirst to madness.
Mickey punched and punched, continually finding the snapping head,
urged on less by the crowd than by his own burning need for relief. To
kill! He yelled and pursued his target, connecting again and again until
at last it fell away from him as the body crumpled into the ropes. He
gave chase, but was pulled away. Childs fell forward and lay in a heap.

The ref waved his hands. A doctor climbed through the ropes, his box shining under the lights. The crowd was on its feet, cheering, jubilant, fists pumping, a hungry tribe drunk on enemy blood. It took Mickey a moment to understand what had happened.

Glazer was beside him. He grabbed the bloody, gloved hand, raised it. The crowd roared.

Childs was motionless. The doctor called for a stretcher.

Mickey's heart pounded. A damp towel was pushed over his face: everything went dark. Abe Lackman's gravel voice broke over the shouts of the crowd: "A tiger! We got a tiger!"

The mouthpiece was pulled from him, and all at once Mickey felt naked.

He broke away to get a look at Childs, who was surrounded by doctors, seconds, family members. The eyes were still closed. A woman held his hand. His mother? She was weeping, praying.

Mickey stared. His mouth tasted of metal. What had he done? God, what had he done? His hands were numb inside the gloves.

Thrown debris piled up in Childs's abandoned corner. Mickey wanted to reach down to Childs, touch him, bring him back. The woman holding the downed fighter's limp hand looked up at Mickey with a tear-streaked face. "You killed him," she cried. "You killed my baby!"

Mickey couldn't speak. The woman turned back to the boy on the canvas, begging him to come to—"Please, Tommy, don't leave your Mama"—as the doctor aimed light into the peeled-open eyes, one and then the other, looking for a response.

No, he wasn't dead, he couldn't be dead. The doctor was calm, methodical. He'd seen this all before. Hadn't he?

Mickey told himself that he wasn't solely to blame for this: the crowd had willed it, yes, and the ref had held back. It was a conspiracy. Why hadn't the fight been stopped sooner? Why hadn't Childs's people jumped into the ring? Mickey felt the tears stinging at his eyes. What would it mean, what would it make him, if Thomas Childs were to die?

Mickey gritted his teeth; he feared he might break down. He himself had no one—no mother, no father. He wanted to reach out to the woman, to Childs, to everyone, throw himself at their mercy, but was stopped by the pat of a hand on his behind. "Let's go, kid," came a voice. It was Glazer. "He'll be fine. Come on now. Gotta get you cleaned up."

Childs was still unconscious, as far as Mickey could see.

"Mick!"

Mickey jumped at Glazer's command and followed him out of the ring and up the aisle, fixing his eyes on a spot at the back of Glazer's head, thinking insanely that if he looked back at the ring, Thomas Childs would surely die.

Around the edges he saw the proud, beaming faces of the patrons, some of whom called out his name.

He woke up in the dark, in a strange bed in a strange room. He knew where he was. He checked his watch, which—he now remembered—he'd set ahead for Paris time. It was a little after five in the morning: he'd slept for more than fifteen hours.

He turned on the bedside lamp, the taste of the memory still on his tongue. Poor Tommy: never the same. It had been Tommy's last fight, just as it was Mickey's last, though Mickey felt that he himself, unlike Tommy, hadn't quit the game so much as fled it. Its demands were more than he could abide; he'd been a decent athlete, true, but never what he'd call a competitor; he'd thirsted not for victory or blood, he'd decided, but for contact, for the equitable exchange, the physical conversation; and yet he had nearly killed a man. This was a promising sign in Lou Glazer's opinion, but Mickey had had enough. Something awful had been unleashed. He'd *felt* it, felt the killing frenzy of the crowd invade him, possess him, urging him on as though he were their son, one of their own, and God knew he had craved that, yes, he was aware of them, every single one of them, a whole proud and rabid family of men promising him their sweaty, brutal love.

Later, as Glazer rubbed his back, praising his savagery, he'd been terrified (Childs had been taken to the hospital, that was all anyone knew), believing he'd tapped into something ungodly within himself, and that the only way to repent for his actions was to suppress the thing that seemed so central to what he was.

He never fought again.

Still, the memories haunted him. Two days after the fight he hopped into his father's Pontiac (his car now) and drove down to West Saratoga Street, to Tommy's peeling row house, armed with some Marvel comic books and a bag of lollipops (sucking candy, easy on the jaw), the two things that he himself would most liked to have received, had *he* been recovering in bed. At the door he was greeted by Tommy's mother (she'd been curt on the phone, he'd thought, but now she seemed glad to see him), who led him to a back bedroom where Tommy, his face so swollen that Mickey hardly recognized him, lay shirtless in a bed, thumbing through the pages of a high school yearbook.

"Tommy," said his mother. "Somebody's here to see you." She smiled at Mickey, then turned and was gone.

Tommy didn't look up. "My mother told me you were coming," he said. "Ain't like I'm dyin' or nothin'."

"That's good," said Mickey. These were the very first words between them, but it seemed to Mickey that they'd known each other for years.

"What are you doin' here then?"

Mickey shrugged. "Happened to be in the neighborhood." It was meant as a joke.

"Heard your father died."

"Yeah." Mickey had mentioned this on the phone to Tommy's mother, hoping it would soften her heart. Evidently it had.

"That's rough," said Tommy. He turned a page.

"Well," said Mickey. "Just dropped by to see how you were."

Tommy raised the book a little, as if to obscure his beaten face. He said, "If you'd've lost that fight? Your people would've come after both of us. We'd be two dead motherfuckers, strung up side by side."

"They weren't my people," Mickey said.

Tommy didn't seem to hear him. "That's why I let you beat me," he said. "I was more afraid of that crowd than I was of losing. Figured I could save both of us, you know?" He lowered the book and looked at Mickey for the first time, the puffed eyes gleaming with challenge. "Decided to go down," he said. "Sacrifice."

Mickey waited for a sign, an indication that Tommy was only kidding, but none came, and Mickey was forced to confront the grisly spectacle of a pride so ravaged that it had, even more than the punches, turned the beaten fighter into a kind of awful giant insect, a brown, slit-eyed creature flat on its back, gone hideous with self-loathing and having no other recourse than to look daringly into the eyes of its enemy and with sheer roach defiance utter the most outrageous lies imaginable.

Mickey was horrified: he'd never seen a shame laid so bare, a humiliation so artlessly concealed; his instinct was to go along with it, aid Tommy in his bitter quest to be believed, and could only hope that his own reaction to this incredible news—that Tommy had thrown the fight to avert a riot—was somewhat less transparent than the news it-self. "Yeah," Mickey said. "But next time you want to throw a fight, don't make it so obvious."

The comment floated there like a still balloon, and any irony it may have contained—and it was hard for Mickey to restrain himself com-pletely from irony, he had his pride too—inflated it all the more, so that Tommy, lying punch-drunk in a camphorous vapor of balms and liniments, would yet be able to detect it; and when Mickey remained silent, as if allowing his meaning to sink in (though in fact he was speechless out of fear, of a lack of knowing what to say)—as Mickey stood there at the foot of the bed, clutching the comics, the candy, he sensed that his pride had indeed reached Tommy, reached him like a blow, absorbed with what Mickey supposed must be terrific pain, a pain made all the more apparent in its being expressed not, as he might have expected, in a violent outburst, but, to Mickey's mind, something far more appalling: a smile, or rather an attempt at a smile, at once confessional and smug, innocent and sly; it told far too much, and Mickey could not face it: eyes lowered, he laid his gifts at the foot of the bed and mumbled a farewell. Tommy said nothing.

A similar feeling came over Mickey now: a need for air, a need to escape this drab little room. He rolled out of the bed, determined to stay in motion until Shaw's noon concert. Moving, he would not be caught by memories, though even as he showered and dressed he could not help recall the few occasions, over the next couple of years, in which he'd met up with Tommy Childs socially. He'd called him at Christmas, and though they'd met a few times for burgers at a colored joint not far from Tommy's block called Papa Bell's, it became clear to Mickey that they were too different to ever become close. Tommy now had a baby girl, was married, and in any case the fight had ruined any chance for a real friendship, seeing as how Tommy couldn't let it alone, harping on it and embellishing until he'd arrived at the belief that he'd actually been ahead on points when the bout was stopped. It was then—and later Mickey would reflect how he'd seen it coming all along—that Tommy challenged him to a "friendly" fight (though it didn't sound very friendly) right there on the parking lot in back of Papa Bell's, in the presence of several young Negroes who gathered round the two with scavenger interest, hands deep in the pockets of their winter coats. As Tommy squared off, Mickey stepped back and waved his hand, a gesture which, Mickey knew, appeared to their audience—much to Tommy's satisfaction—as a cowardly backing down; and though Mickey was in a sense happy to provide Tommy with this false redemption, he felt badly misused, so that when the Negroes had dispersed, lobbing laughter and taunts, Mickey knew that he and Tommy had come to the end of things. Tommy had tried to smooth it over—he sensed Mickey's anger—but it was too late; the tension was too much to bear, it had become dangerous, and Mickey never called Tommy Childs again. The following Christmas, though, he did send a card, and a few days later got a call from Tommy's mother, who told him that Tommy's wife had left him and that Tommy had "gotten into some trouble" and was now living with his aunt and uncle in Durham, North Carolina. Mickey felt bad for her, poor woman, and resented Tommy for breaking his mother's heart. And then there was Tommy's ex-wife, a pretty, full-figured girl whom Mickey'd met once, briefly, and who later began shopping at the bakery. She'd probably never have recognized him had he not introduced himself as an old friend of Tommy's ("He's probably mentioned me before, Mickey Lerner, we fought once, a few years back"), and if she was a little cool toward him—understandable, Mickey thought, given what he'd done to Tommy—he at least had an admirer in her little daughter, to whom he'd often give a free éclair and a playful, fatherly tickle under the chin.

Through the window, Mickey saw that the rain had stopped. He put on his coat, grabbed his wallet and street map and went down the steps to the lobby, where the same man who had checked him in was back on duty, seated at his desk. He looked at Mickey with some interest.

"Good morning, my friend," he said. "Ça va? Did you have a good night?"

There was something knowing in the man's voice that gave Mickey pause. "Yes," he said. "Slept like a rock." He wondered if he looked shady, leaving at such a furtive hour, but judging from what he'd seen of this establishment, his own movements must be fairly unremarkable. Yet still the man watched him.

"I have your answer," said the man.

Mickey wasn't sure what he meant. "My answer?"

"Yes—what you asked me. About your wife."

"Yes," Mickey said, snapping to attention. He bristled at his lapse—to think that the question had been less than foremost in his mind!—and feared that the man, in recognizing Mickey's preoccupation with

other things, would feel vaguely let down, even embarrassed for having made an effort to research the matter, and would now punish him
by divulging the worst.

What if Emi's name were there, Mickey wondered, the signature
right alongside that of a lover—what would he do? He wanted to stop
the man, give himself time to prepare, but he couldn't speak, and was
even more alarmed by the way the slight smile on the man's shining
face seemed to reflect something of terror in his own.

"Emilie Lutter," said the man. The smile disappeared. "I looked for
this name in my books. And I must tell you that it appears in my
records not at all."

"You mean she was never here?"

The man shook his head.

Mickey nodded. *"Merci."* His relief faded into an odd disappointment: if Emi were innocent, what did that make *him*?

He walked out into the street, agonizing over what seemed to be
his growing disloyalty to his wife. He'd come here to mourn the
woman—so he'd told himself on the plane—and only after his
thoughts had strayed toward Donna, where they were smartingly re-
pelled by memories of Tommy, did they crawl, slither back to her. He
stood on the corner, battling his confusion. It really was a hell of a
thing, to wish that your dead wife had had an affair just so that you
could be free to pursue your own desires. A hell of a goddamned
thing.

The thought frightened him into walking, moving. Move, you don't
get hit, he told himself. Keep moving.

He pulled out his map and tried to read it as he passed under street
lamps. Shaw's concert was at a cathedral on the other side of town.
Mickey found the spot where he presently stood and traced a route
with his finger. It was a long trek. He walked on, amazed that he had
the streets of Paris to himself.

He passed two or three streets when he was hit by a smell: fresh
bread, so strong that he could almost feel on the back of his neck the
wavy breath of ovens. As he walked on—as the buildings became
older, more elegant, more of what he had imagined the city would
be—the smell grew in its intensity; the entire city was undergoing a
secret mutation, giving off its scent like a bush at a crisis in its life
cycle. Everywhere he looked he saw the source: bakeries and pastry
shops, one after the next, street by street. Mickey stopped by the window of a *pâtisserie* and peered in at the glass cases, but it was too dark
to make out what was inside.

Around him, the city was coming to life; the traffic picked up on the boulevard (the headlights of the cars the color of egg custard), and people—white people, French people—appeared on sidewalks with dogs or shop keys. Darkness was fading, now a deep blue that was indistinguishable from nightfall. Before him, the *pâtisserie* lights went on, and he saw, through the window, a display of pastries—rows of them in crinkly boats of paper—that triggered in him an alarm which sounded from the depths of his professional pride. This was pastry as Michelangelo must have dreamed it. When the woman inside unlocked the door, Mickey rushed in. His eyes and nostrils widened. Strawberries, chocolate, peaches, almond cream; jewels of blueberries, cherries. And then: lemon meringue, vanilla, hazelnut, mocha. The golden butter of apples, of milk.

Mickey looked up at the woman behind the counter. She was big and broad-shouldered, with a wide, masculine face and large, fleshy hands. Her vast bosom, piled high under a sexless white smock, resembled in shape the round loaves of bread that lined a wooden shelf behind her. She looked down at Mickey and, with a smile that may only have been a grimace of impatience, said, *"Monsieur?"*

Mickey straightened up and scratched his head. "I only speak English," he said.

The woman nodded. "Yes," she said. "What can I help for you today?"

Her accent, her way of speaking, stirred memories of Emi's accent, when she'd first come into the bakery. The improvement in her English during the first year of their marriage had been, for Mickey, a measure of the life she led away from the house; she'd come home from trips with new words and phrases, revealed to him in conversation like new bedroom tricks that she had learned from someone else; it got so that he could no longer locate his own influence in her speech.

"Monsieur."

"Yes," said Mickey. He pointed to a plain, chocolate-covered éclair, curious to know how it stacked up against his own éclairs, which enjoyed a reputation back home. *"S'il vous plaît,"* he added. He placed some coins on the counter; the woman took what she needed and handed Mickey an éclair wrapped in wax paper. Slowly he pulled it apart: the pastry was thick, not too soft, and the inside was a smooth, cold, creamy yellow, a color painful to the teeth. Mickey's heart sank. *This* was an éclair. Too often the shells of Lerner éclairs would harden, and the custard inside would lie shyly in the hollow, a dried, quivering curd, instead of melding with the dough, stretching gooily with

the pull of it. Words failed him: his tongue was stunned, just as his ears
had been stunned so many years ago, when he first heard the sound of
Emi's violin.

Other customers arrived, and Mickey stood back and observed the
commerce. There was no friendly conversation flying across the
counter; just an exchange of greetings and the transaction itself. Food
was serious business, Mickey saw. It was respected. People waited in
line. The woman behind the counter was crucial to the way of life
here, and with her polite efficiency—the weighing, the wrapping, the
making of change—she seemed to control the tempo of the entire
city.

Mickey wondered if he ought to approach her and introduce himself as an overseas colleague. Though wouldn't that be disingenuous
somehow? For he couldn't deny it: he'd never felt any real passion for
his bakery; and as a baker he'd never had any sense of his place in the
world. And now that he saw that there might be something more to
what he had been doing all along, that he may have figured in a spiritual way in the life of his community, somewhat as Emi had in hers,
he found that it was too late: the past refused to light up and become
something different than it was. There was no reviving it.

The woman behind the counter, by contrast, appeared to be ani-
mated by an unwavering knowledge of her purpose. Mickey yearned
for that understanding. For Emi, there had never been any question.
Her purpose was clear. Mickey knew it was too late for him to become
something else. He had to make sense of what he already was. But he
felt ashamed in the face of the woman; he felt small, even fraudulent.
Sure, he did a decent business. Sure, the bakery had been recognized,
cited. But what about him? What was he?

He walked out of the place, chewing sorrowfully on the last bite of
éclair. Everywhere, now, he saw *boulangeries*, all of them open for
business. They were not set at the back of a parking lot, like his own;
they were an aggressive presence on the street, an essential part of
things. They were life.

He walked faster, impatient for the start of Shaw's concert. Maybe
the music would calm him, ease his troubled mind. He had to go back
to his boxing days, to those workouts at Glazer's Gym, to recall a time
when he'd been able to create his *own* peace.

15

David Shaw's fingers pressed into the lungs of the piano as though intent on reviving it from a drowning, and the cathedral flooded with the sound of Schumann. Mickey stared up at the stained glass and frescoes and ghastly iconography. He was seated at the back, having arrived a few minutes late, but he supposed he would have chosen a seat at the back anyway. Far from calming him, the music and the awesome architecture of the cathedral made him feel even smaller. He turned his gaze to the massive crucifix that dominated the backdrop for Shaw's piano: a slumped, bloodied Christ. It was an ironic venue for a concert in Emi's honor, but of course Emi herself had performed in many cathedrals. Mickey had attended a recital of hers at the Cathedral of St. John the Divine in New York some years ago—his first time in a church—and had found that the acoustics and imagery had given rise, within the music, to voices.

And it was the New York concerts he remembered best. Most poignantly he remembered a concert she had played a few years back at Avery Fisher Hall as part of the fall concert series, and how he had driven up on a last-minute whim (she had no idea he'd be there) and been lucky enough to find a man in the lobby who was selling a single ticket to a concert that had, to Mickey's mild surprise, been sold out well in advance. Even more lucky, he'd brought his opera glasses (a birthday gift from Emi some years before), which, because Emi had always arranged for him a seat close up, he'd never really used, but which now came in handy, as he'd ended up sitting, for fifteen bucks, in the very back row of the highest balcony.

Through the glasses, he was able to experience his wife in a new and unusual way. It seemed he had captured her, isolated her in this secret circle, in this tunnel of perverse and artificial nearness at the end of which she became a documented subject, a target. There was something inescapably exciting and predatory about seeing her this way: he felt he were seeing her for the first time, a woman with whom one becomes instantly obsessed. There she was, coming onto the stage amid applause like spilled diamonds, clad in a long black gown, hair braided at the sides and pulled back and tied invisibly together behind her, lips uncharacteristically painted and surrendering a small smile as she acknowledged the nods of the principals and the first violinist and shook hands with the conductor. It was a violin concerto—Beethoven, if Mickey remembered correctly. Emi had the full power of an orchestra behind her, but the world for Mickey had been reduced to a single face—a face that was innocent of his presence, but which had made itself beautiful nonetheless: it was the face he never saw while she was gone, the face of other cities, other rooms. In observing her in this detached yet intimate way, he imagined that afterwards he, a stranger, would pursue her past the fountain outside, call her name, and that she would turn, and that in the instant before recognition, when either of them could be anyone, he would discover in her eyes some essential, elusive quality, the individual herself, unguarded, stunned for a flicker of a moment into her youth, into the girl she once was, before she knew him, before she was known, some aspect of her that he feared was gone from his sight forever.

But this dream, and all the romantic exaggerations it encompassed, was wrecked as soon as he lowered the glasses at the conclusion of the first movement, for it was then that he saw the larger picture: the modern and even ugly concert hall (Emi had called it that herself) and the agitated look of the performers, many of whom seemed trapped in their metal chairs, resigned meekly to their instruments, appearing uninspired and about as anxious to get it all over with as a good deal of the mostly white-haired, palsied audience, season-ticket holders who, as Emi had observed more than once, showed up out of a bland sense of obligation to high culture and made so much noise between movements that it was a wonder the conductor didn't turn around and give them a lecture. But it wasn't until the end of the concert, when Emi and the others took their bows and walked off the stage as the audience clapped for a curtain call, that Mickey saw, to his disgust and embarrassment, a shocking number of people heading for the doors. Yes, here, in New York, he saw them streaming into the aisles, their backs turned as Emi and the conductor acknowledged with truly heroic civility the desperate applause of the hearty, grateful few; Mickey thought immediately of the people who left in the eighth inning of a ball game, or at the two-minute warning—ingrates, frauds!—but this was far worse, for there was no traffic to beat here, no packed parking lots; nothing but a group of performers standing, as Emi stood, to receive their due after pouring out their goddamned hearts. This inexplicable behavior seemed to epitomize what Emi meant when she uttered the word "Americans." Mickey felt bad for her; she had played magnificently and deserved better. But more than that: he felt he had glimpsed something from which he ought to have been shielded; he wanted to believe in the great halls, the high pageantry, the opulence and grandiosity that he'd always associated with her music; and as the stage cleared and the hall all but emptied, he told himself that this was a fluke, that her music was as alive and vital as it had ever been, that it still mattered, and that elsewhere—in Europe, in Asia—the ideal survived, flourished, and that someday soon she would once again be ankle-deep in roses.

He had remained seated, staring down at the empty chairs, the program notes scattered in the aisles. He decided against surprising Emi; he'd rather grab a quick bite alone and then hightail it out of there. It wasn't so much that he would not want her to know that he'd witnessed what was, from a certain standpoint, a disaster, as it was his need to deny that the concert had ever occurred in the first place. A tear burned in the corner of his eye, but why or for whom he could not be certain; all he knew was that in that very moment, seated alone in the empty concert hall, the ushers making their way through the rows, retrieving programs, he had never loved his wife so much.

And now here he was, in Paris, attending a concert in which she was supposed to perform, but which now (as he read in the program notes, which were written in French and English) had been altered drastically. *Today's recital is lovingly dedicated to the memory of Emilie Lutter.* Mickey wanted to be moved by the gesture, but the reduction of Emi's memory to a line of small print on a cheap piece of paper depressed him. And yet wasn't it a damn sight more than he himself had managed to offer?

Watching Shaw, Mickey recalled the memory lapses that Emi had spoken about that day in the garden. What if Shaw were to suddenly black out? Mickey looked around. All these unsuspecting people! He felt in possession of an explosive secret, like knowing about the presence of a bomb. Shaw's hands: how much longer could they go on? Mickey felt the mounting of an unbearable tension, and just when he thought he might have to get up and run breathless from the cathedral, the music stopped, and applause rained down.

Mickey laughed inwardly: of course Shaw would be perfect. Why wouldn't he be? He was a master.

Shaw, expressionless, wiped his brow with a handkerchief. Mickey sized up the crowd. A hundred and fifty people, give or take; the same number of people that had seen him put away Tommy Childs. Ah, but this was a polite group. Would they turn on Shaw if he were to fail? Would they pelt him with coins? Scream bloody murder?

Mickey felt a passing barbarian pride in the arena mobs he had known.

The audience quieted down and waited for Shaw as Shaw had waited for them. In a moment, the sound of Ravel flew up like a pigeon to the light.

Shaw.

Mickey grew restless. If Shaw deserved applause, didn't he? Hadn't he done anything in his life, didn't he deserve to be honored, even just once? What about how hard he'd worked all these years? And hadn't that work enabled Emi, back when they were starting out, to pursue her career?

He agonized in his anonymity, and felt more restricted than usual by the protocol of concertgoing—the silence, the waiting, the rules of applause. He watched the great Shaw, resplendent in the light, under the dying Christ, enraptured in his music, a god.

Mickey longed to be adored.

Shaw was triumphant, and, after walking off, returned glistening and glowing to shouts and persistent applause. *Clap-clap-clap-clap.* Mickey joined in because it was awkward not to. There was a vague flavor of rally. The faces in the stained glass were looking down with disapproval, Mickey thought.

Shaw played another piece, then stood and bowed deeply, wiped his brow and walked off. Mickey waited to see what would happen.

The audience finished clapping and stood, gathering their coats. Mickey stood, but did not go out. How could he not say hello to David Shaw? But he felt a kind of slow dread of such a meeting; few had known Emi better than Shaw. If anyone had the answers, it was David Shaw. He was the person in whom Emi would confide.

After a moment, Mickey was the only audience member remaining.

Shaw appeared, alone, still wearing his tuxedo under a black overcoat. Despite himself, Mickey's spirits rose; there was the old tingle in his bones, the faint twitter in the heart.

"Mr. Lerner!" Shaw said.

"Mr. Shaw," said Mickey. It was their standard greeting; in response to some undefined tension in the relationship they had never arrived at a first-name basis, adopting instead the mock formal.

Shaw approached jauntily with an outstretched hand, his face still radiant and hinting of stage makeup. As usual, he seemed to be bathed in a different quality of light. Mickey smiled, his only regret being that there was no one around to see them together.

"What a surprise!" said Shaw, and Mickey could see that he was full of that erratic energy that had worried Emi toward the end. "Are you here alone?"

"Yes," Mickey said.

Shaw frowned. "It was a very modest and humble tribute," he said. "But heartfelt, I can assure you."

"I enjoyed it very much," said Mickey. "And thank you for the flowers. They were beautiful. I haven't had a chance to thank everyone for their kindness."

"Please, don't mention it. But tell me—have they found anyone yet? Any leads in the case?"

"Not yet," said Mickey. He'd call Flemke tomorrow, he decided.

"And where are you staying?"

Mickey scratched his head. "Oh, just at a hotel." He stopped short of a description. "And you?"

"I'm staying with a friend in the Marais. Rue St.-Paul?"

"Ah," said Mickey, embarrassed by Shaw's presumption of his knowledge of the city. Shaw could be oblivious that way.

"Emi used to stay at the most dreadful hotels. She refused to spend a lot of money on a room."

Mickey laughed knowingly. "I can imagine."

"Shall we have a coffee?"

Mickey was surprised by the offer, but tried not to show it. "Sure," he said, mystified and even a little disappointed that Shaw seemed to have no other plans. They walked out of the cathedral and into gray daylight.

In the square in front of the cathedral Shaw was gawked at by several people who had attended the concert. Mickey corrected his posture and sucked his features into a tense portrait of literacy as he and Shaw descended the steps and made their way toward the river.

"And your son?" Shaw said, as they crossed a bridge. "He didn't come with you?"

"No."

"Where is he?"

"Home."

"And how old is he now?"

"Eighteen."

"Eighteen," said Shaw. He fell silent, as if in observance of the journey into manhood that Emi would never see. Shaw, Mickey surmised, knew very little about Ben; Emi would not have told him much. Mickey saw opportunities for harmless invention.

"He's thinking about colleges," Mickey said. The river rushed brown beneath them. "Just taking some time off at the moment."

"Oh?" said Shaw.

Mickey thought he heard surprise; perhaps Emi *had* revealed things. But what had she said? Mickey lowered himself into his coat and hoped Shaw would drop the subject. Shaw did. He went on about the weather, as if Benjie's name had never come up. Mickey felt vaguely persecuted.

As they arrived at a second bridge, Mickey spotted, in the distance, as he had on the way, the Eiffel Tower, and then, much closer, Nôtre Dame, which he recognized from the picture on the cover of his French phrase book. Ancient and weathered, the cathedral stood immense on its isle like some grand, decaying beast. People milled around it with cameras, and innumerable birds were perched on the heads of the sculpted figures in its walls; and when Mickey saw, at the back of the structure, the skeletal effect of the flying buttresses, the image of a dinosaurian carcass was complete.

Mickey looked around. The cathedrals, the bridges, the domes and spires looming in the fog—all seemed trapped within some insidious encroachment, a disease on the outer rim of things; Mickey perceived a ring of fire slowly eating its way to the center. He remembered the Hôtel Dakar: his suitcase, his clothes: had he locked his door? Yes—he never forgot to lock up.

He was relieved when they had crossed the river and entered into a labyrinth of narrow streets. The shuttered windows with pots of marigold and geranium, the endless storefronts bright with food and clothing and art, the people in their suit jackets and smart hats and blue jeans and scarves and dresses, walking with a sense of purpose and destination; for a moment Mickey could believe that this was the truer existence, and that things like poverty and suffering were but a kind of itchy static, a crackle of bad reception creeping into the song of life.

They wandered into a mostly residential area: streets lined with crooked, sagging dwellings, the narrow sidewalks untouched by tourists. Shaw was commenting on how much safer it was to walk Parisian streets than those back home; but he expected that here, too, things would sink into an American state of violence. Mickey listened, nodding, but his attention was then arrested by the sight of a *boulangerie* across the street that looked as though it had been there for centuries. The building was in disrepair; paint had peeled off the shutters of the windows above. The shop itself appeared to be closed, though breads could be seen in the windows. It was places like this that gave bakeries a bad name, Mickey thought. Old and decrepit. Still, he was curious, and suggested to Shaw that they have a look, thinking too that the sight of such a quaint and harmless shop—so clearly inferior to the Lerner Bakery, which Shaw had visited on several occasions over the years—might raise him somehow in Shaw's esteem.

Standing before the window, Mickey made blinders with his hands and peered in. Nothing but bread in the dimness, the brown crusts split and gridded, dusted with flour or pocked with olives, nuts, flakes of oats. Each loaf appeared so dense and heavy that any elderly person might have a problem getting one home.

Mickey approached the door.

"It's closed," said Shaw.

But the knob turned in Mickey's hand. The door gave, and Mickey stepped inside. Shaw came in behind him.

The bakery was fragrant with bread, and filled with an unusual warmth; not an electrical warmth, but the primitive warmth of fire. Mickey felt drawn to it.

Shaw said, "Perhaps we shouldn't be in here."

"Hello?" Mickey called into the darkness. There was no answer.

"Maybe they stepped out for a minute," said Shaw. He looked around. "I wouldn't leave bread like this unattended. It's absolutely gorgeous. Expensive too," he added, pointing to a chalkboard with the prices written out. "Can you imagine leaving your shop unattended back home?"

"I don't have bread like this," Mickey said. There was a hint of anger in his voice. What was so gorgeous? These were big, ugly, wheel-shaped loaves, none of which looked as though it could have proceeded from a modern electric oven such as his own; they seemed begotten rather than made, sprung from the elements, each bearing, on its bottom, the imprint of a hearthstone. Mickey recalled his father placing bricks on the rack of the old gas oven at the house, and how the letters on the bricks showed up on the crust of his home-baked breads. The bread was supposed to bake better that way, but as a child Mickey hadn't been able to taste the difference, and even now he'd sooner put his money on the state-of-the-art ovens, which were calibrated to bake bread just right. He'd thought his father an old fool, with his bricks in the oven and his suspicion of bleached flours and fast-rising yeast.

Shaw was looking at a shelf of round breads that were scored with the severe, slanted lines of tribal masks. He turned and said, "Maybe something's wrong."

Mickey knew what he meant: an empty register, a body in the back.

A noise came from the doorway behind the counter. Mickey felt Shaw's hand on his elbow. Footsteps sounded on a staircase, coming closer. Then a figure appeared in the doorway. Mickey could feel Shaw's heart jump at what looked to be a ghost, a dead man—but Mickey knew in an instant that the striking pallor of the man's face and hands was flour.

"*Oui?*" said the man. He came closer, and Mickey saw a man about his own age, broad-backed, slightly hunched, with wide, blinking eyes. His hands and arms were white to the elbows with flour, and faint yellowish stains stretched across his white apron.

"*Bonjour,*" said Mickey.

"You speak English?" said the man.

Shaw stepped forward and began speaking rapidly in French; the man looked at Mickey with growing interest.

"You are a baker?" the man said to Mickey. "In America?"

Mickey blushed. Shaw smiled encouragingly at him, as if to coax him toward a dialogue; he seemed proud of the atmosphere he had created, and Mickey felt a kind of athletic pressure to perform. Shaw was ready to be amused, entertained; but there was also an impresario's pride in his eyes, and it was to this that Mickey responded. "Well, not a baker exactly," he said. "I own a bakery." Never had he put it that way; he'd always said "run a bakery." But the word "own" had chosen itself, filling the air with biblical reverberations, the music of shekels and asses and slaves.

"You own a bakery," said the man, "but you do not bake the bread?"

Mickey shrugged. "I have bakers."

"So you are not a baker."

"No," said Mickey. He laughed, but when Shaw didn't join in he became alarmed. Was Shaw siding with the baker? Surely a man like David Shaw would see nothing admirable in a man covered in flour. "I'm a businessman," Mickey said, more for Shaw's benefit. Hell, he had deals all over the city. A dozen clients. This fella here, this baker, was a toiler. It didn't take a genius to see the difference.

"This is a strange idea," said the man. He stepped up to the wooden counter and planted his elbows. "A bakery owner who does not bake."

"I don't think it's very strange at all," said Mickey. "As a matter of fact, I'd say it was pretty normal."

"I do not mean to insult you," said the baker. He came out from behind the counter and met Mickey face-to-face. "My name is Dulac," he said. He held out his hand.

Mickey had no choice but to reciprocate. "Mickey Lerner." Dulac's hand was smooth with flour and pleasingly warm. Shaw had faded back a few steps, a spectator.

"I hope, Monsieur Lerner," said Dulac, "that you do not feel, how shall I say, too important for baking?"

"Too busy, is more like it."

"Busy, busy. Everyone is busy. But are you too busy to realize that civilization was built upon man's need for bread? The cultivation of wheat—this began everything. And when the Romans perfected the rotary mill? Well. This was one of the greatest and most important advancements in engineering and technology that the world has ever known."

"Well," said Mickey. He glanced at his watch.

Dulac picked up a loaf of sourdough. "This"—he moved the loaf up and down to express its substance—"is the stuff of revolutions. Revolutions! For when there's not enough of it—ah, but I do not have to tell you! History itself is here. The course of human events!" He looked Mickey in the eye. "Here," he said, coaxing with his head. "Take it. Hold it."

Mickey received the loaf. Christ, it must have weighed as much as a newborn. Shaw appeared beside him. Mickey passed the bread. Shaw held it stiffly for a moment, then handed it to Dulac, who seemed convinced—Mickey could see it in his eyes—that the passing around of his bread had linked the three of them in an almost religious way.

"You will not," said Dulac, "find a better bread in Paris."

"Why no long loaves?" Mickey said. "Baguettes?"

"The baguette," said Dulac. "Everyone is concerned with the baguette. What is this? A stick! Something slim and fashionable. It is not even French—it is Austrian. A recent import." He shook the sourdough loaf. "But this—this is authentic French bread. The bread my grandfather ate!"

Dulac's passion had gained a slight lunatic edge that Mickey feared might undermine them both.

"For me," said Dulac, "there is more to bread than mix and bake, mix and bake. I must know everything about my bread. I visit the fields. I want to know the machinery—the tractor, the mill. All of this is important. And the water: what is the source? It must be pure water from the spring. Bread is something that is alive; we must take great care with it. I cannot support anyone who calls himself a baker and is not concerned with every detail that goes into his craft."

"I guess my philosophy is different," Mickey said. He felt it beneath his dignity to explain himself, but with Shaw nearby he couldn't resist tooting his own horn a little. "I feed people," he said. "Hundreds a day. My bread is shipped all over the place, from nursing homes to country clubs to office cafeterias to religious institutions. I feed the rich and the poor, the young and the old. To be frank, my customers could care less about the process. Half of them couldn't chew a crust like this, and the other half couldn't afford it even if they wanted to. And as for myself, I don't have time to visit fields. Look, I appreciate what you're trying to do here, don't get me wrong. It's very nice. It's just a matter of choice. You feed the few, I feed the many." Mickey laughed to take the edge off his words; he knew he had scored a triumph. "It's funny," he said. "I used to do some baking myself, years ago, the way my father used to. I think I nearly went crazy, sitting there waiting for the dough to rise." He laughed again. "Just wasn't my speed."

Dulac nodded; he seemed defeated. Mickey felt bad for him and his quaint little shop. The Lerner Bakery, meanwhile, bordered on an industrial works; it was unfair to make comparisons.

"I will show you something," said Dulac. "Something very special." He went behind the counter, disappeared, then came up with an old stone bowl, holding it with both hands cupped around the bottom. "In this bowl," he said, "is a sourdough culture that dates from the reign of Napolean."

Mickey's nose twitched.

"My great-great-grandfather used this bowl," said Dulac. "All of my sourdough bread starts here." He offered the bowl. It was stained brown, and Mickey could smell the pungent yeast that survived there.

"Yes," said Mickey, suddenly remembering. "My father once told me something about starters. You take a piece of dough from your batch, let it ferment, and use it to rise tomorrow's dough. And so on and so on. He said that breads were like families that way—tomorrow's loaf is the child of today's. You could have endless generations of bread by always saving a piece of dough and using it next time. I haven't thought about that in years, but I remember being very taken by the idea. That bread could give life to bread." As he spoke, he became aware of Shaw listening to him. He went on. "My wife was a musician. A violinist. Legacy is an important thing in music. My wife could trace her lineage of teachers back to Vienna, to Mozart's time. It's interesting to think of bread that way. In terms of pedigree."

"Yes," said David Shaw.

Dulac put away the bowl and took up the sourdough loaf. He tore it in half with his big baker's hands. Crumbs flew like sparks. "Taste," he said. He pulled off a piece from one of the halves and handed it to Mickey. Mickey tore that in half and handed a piece to Shaw.

Mickey put the bread in his mouth and chewed. It took him a moment to capture the taste—he hadn't eaten a piece of bread in God knew how long—and though he didn't want to believe it could be true, that there could be such a range in quality of something composed of flour and water and yeast, he had to admit that he'd never tasted a bread quite like it: a tangy, sour, fruity flavor that seemed to prove Dulac's point about cheap flours, fast-rising yeast and water from the city pipes. There *was* a difference; it was there, you could taste it. Mickey knew his own breads probably wouldn't stack up in a taste test of gourmets, but then, hell, he'd never claimed to have entered any Grand Prix of bread-making. And the truth of the matter was, most people he knew wouldn't even know what to *do* with a hearth-baked wheel of sourdough: the damn stuff didn't even come sliced.

"Delicious," Shaw said.

Dulac puffed out his chest. "I baked it myself." He passed out more bread. "Though perhaps that is obvious. As you can see, I am the only one here. My baker left to open his own place. I wish him well. But for the moment I am without help."

"Can't say I know the feeling," Mickey said. He sympathized with Dulac's plight, but couldn't resist another jab. "I have a full staff. Six bakers and a delivery man. And also a man who stays all night with the bakers to supervise the—" He stopped; Lazarus was too complicated to explain. "Anyway, my son is taking care of things while I'm away."

"A family business," Dulac said. "This is very special. You have a son, you should teach him how to make real bread, true bread."

Mickey tried to laugh this off; he was embarrassed by Dulac's fervor.

"I do not have to tell you," said Dulac, "that traditional baking is in danger. The corporations are destroying us." His eyes gained a wild, messianic light, and Mickey realized that this man was vying for his soul. "I have seen what passes for bread in your country," he said. "I have seen what mothers feed their young. Understand, Monsieur Lerner, that you have the opportunity, the power, to improve the spirit of your people. Of *all* people." His eyes then flashed, alert to something. He sniffed the air. "My bread!" And without another word he turned and rushed to the back and disappeared.

Shaw gazed thoughtfully at the old stone bowl. "And all this time," he said, "I thought the baguette was French."

Mickey said nothing. He couldn't figure if he'd gotten the better of Dulac in their discussion or not; he wanted another shot at the man, a chance to further his point.

"Shall we go and have our coffee?" said Shaw. "Our tea?"

Mickey said, "I'd hate to leave this place unattended."

"I wouldn't worry," said Shaw. "He'll probably be up in a minute." He seemed eager to get out of there.

"A tea?" Mickey said.

"Yes," said Shaw. "Or a whiskey, if you'd prefer."

"Well," said Mickey. He felt hesitant about leaving.

"Because," said David Shaw, a nervousness entering his voice, "I would like to speak with you about something."

Mickey looked at the pianist. "What is it?"

Shaw shivered momentarily in his coat, then raised his chin. His eyes were moist with meaning. "It's about your wife," he said.

16

At the well-lit bus stop there stood the usual crowd of white-uniformed ladies who worked at the nearby nursing home, and rather than spit on the ground and curse under his breath as they took their damn time getting up the steps of the bus, Nelson stood by and made a courtly gesture with his hand, as though admitting all of womankind into the plush interior of his own winged chariot. Smiling, he thrust his other hand in his trousers pocket, jingling the change in a jaunty way before pulling out a few good hard coins and, upon boarding, dropping them briskly into the slot with the confidence of a man who can smell dinner on the table. It was a pleasure to pay for his ride, a pleasure to feel the driver's curious gaze pass over the gold buttons of his suit jacket, and a pleasure especially to walk tall and proud down the aisle amid looks and glances ("Is that the same young man who usually gets on here?") and take his seat among the weary laborers and idlers and thieves whose grimy clothes and haggard faces threw his own suit and smile into such startling relief that he became aware of a palpable light radiating from his breast.

He'd just completed his first full day behind the counter—a promotion, was how he'd explained it to Mama—and things couldn't

have gone better. The ring of the register, the communion with customers, the exchange of money for goods; moving product, it was
called. Commerce. Nelson found he had a knack for it: he could move
product. It damn sure beat fighting traffic in the van, and he could
only hope that Crumb wouldn't get bored too quickly with making
deliveries.

Crumb. No sooner had he returned from his route and sought assurance that things were going well in the bakery than he shut himself up in his father's office, where he could plot in private more ways
to change things, more ways to exercise his new power. He was wild-
eyed, inspired. What would it be next? There was a sense of reckless-
ness, of revolution. Nelson wasn't sure what to make of it; all he knew
was that when he asked his new superior if he'd like to go out for a
drink after work—Nelson having developed, with his increase of position, certain fuzzy ideas about lounges and beers and unwinding
with colleagues—Crumb put him off in a polite, impersonal way, saying how he was "too busy."

Nelson decided not to take it too personally; eventually, he figured,
Crumb would get off his pedestal. In the meantime, Nelson was determined to go about his job as best he could, and hope that Hawk
and company would sort of fade out of the picture. He sure didn't
need any trouble coming round his door, now that he had himself a
position.

He hadn't spoken with Hawk in several days, not since the night
they'd driven out to Crumb's; he recalled how, after he'd returned to
the car without weed or money or food, Rob and Chuckie (and Hawk
too, though less ominously) had wanted to go inside. It had taken
everything to dissuade them; he'd ended by promising to take them
back there some time in the future, though of course he never would.
In Nelson's opinion, these boys were ready to do something crazy, really crazy; you could smell it on them. It was time to get out of Dodge.

And yet he knew, as the bus approached his stop, that he would
come home to Mama's hard face, telling him—and all it would take
was a look—that Hawk had called, had stopped by. Mama could be
harsh in her judgments—she'd never liked Hawk, even when he was
a little kid—and Nelson almost looked forward to defending his old
friend, if only to ease the guilt he felt over avoiding him.

The bus pulled up to the curb. Nelson exited into the chilly night,
feeling vaguely depressed. No matter how well things went at work,
he realized, he would still be delivered, afterwards, to this dreary
place: the elevated tracks, the garbage-strewn alleys, the leaning util-

ity poles and their dipping wires, the vacant lots spangled with glass; the daily sluggish push of humanity, thousands of weary souls heaving themselves blind onto buses; the crush of discount shoppers on the avenue (EVERYTHING 99¢, the windows proclaimed), the little children swarming on sidewalks as young mothers, their chests dusted with talcum powder, shouted after them, grabbing their hands and dragging them through the doors of the beauty salons which spewed invisible clouds of tonics and treatments and dyes that burned into Nelson's lungs; the sirens, the shouts; the occasional crackle of gunfire.

Meanwhile the customers at the bakery flashed jewelry, thick rolls of cash. Nelson liked to imagine that one of the older, wealthier women would take a special interest in him and remember him in her will. Not that he was counting on such a miracle, but it was fun to think about, and in any case—if today were any indication—he was certainly capable of making his own way in the world (nine bucks in tips he'd made: that was an extra fifty a week), and if things continued to go well, and he saved his money, he might soon find himself ready to get his own place, get a car. Make his own life.

He zipped up his coat to cover his suit jacket. No sense advertising his turn of fortune.

He reached his street and turned the corner. It was strangely quiet, and darker than usual: a street lamp was out. Approaching the house, he was startled by the toot of a car horn, but kept walking as though he thought it was some dealer trying to call him over. Then he heard the voice: "Little Man!"

Nelson stopped: he was caught. He muttered a curse. Did he ever really think he'd be able to rid himself of Hawk?

Slowly, Nelson turned.

Hawk was in the passenger seat, his face barely lit by the tip of a cigarette. Slumped at the wheel was Chuckie Banks.

Nelson walked over. He was scared, but didn't dare show it; Hawk was prone to suggestion, and Nelson knew that if he acted casual, Hawk's pride would force him to behave likewise: he would not want to seem too reliant on Nelson in front of Chuckie Banks.

"What up?" said Hawk. He rolled the window all the way down.

"A'ight," said Nelson. He met Hawk's outstretched hand. The grip was insistent, advisory; Hawk's fingers locked with Nelson's and fell away silkily.

Hawk said, "Where you been? Didn't your mother tell you I been callin'?" There was the slightest hint of urgency in the voice, a nuance meant especially for Nelson, waged just beyond Chuckie's hearing;

Nelson heard it as a desperate plea, as of some terrible need to be saved.

"I been busy," Nelson said. "Workin'. Christmas comin' up, so, you know. Overtime."

"You need some money?" said Hawk.

"Naw," said Nelson.

"Naw," said Chuckie Banks. "He a *work*in' man. Whassup, Money?"

Nelson didn't dare meet Chuckie's eyes.

"You wanna make a few bills?" said Hawk.

"I'm a'ight," said Nelson, trying to guess at the scheme. Drugs? A holdup? Whatever it was, Hawk wanted him in, as if his stabilizing presence would somehow prevent things from going too far. Nelson felt a disappointment over Hawk's calculations, less for Hawk's willingness to bring him into harm's way (he could almost be flattered by that) as for the idea that Hawk had ended up at the criminal mercy of Chuckie Banks.

Hawk said, "What you doin' in them kicks?"

Nelson looked down regretfully at his new dress shoes. "Workin'," he said.

"Yo, Chuck. Check this nigga's footwear."

Chuckie's sharp face emerged from shadow like a blade. "Thought you drove a truck," he said.

Hawk reached for Nelson's coat zipper and yanked it down. The suit jacket lay revealed like a final skin.

"Damn," said Hawk. "My boy all pretty and shit."

Nelson gave a laugh, but he was burning with shame. He closed the coat, struggled with the zipper.

"Thought you drove a truck," Chuckie said.

"I do," said Nelson. But already he could see the guys trailing him to work, and then, later in the day, coming in all loud and crazy, scattering elderly customers.

He said, "My boss put in a dress code."

Hawk sniffed. "Is that cologne you wearin'?"

"Naw," said Nelson. But the smell was all around them.

Hawk sniffed harder, cringed. "Damn," he said.

Chuckie laughed: he and Hawk slapped hands, and Nelson could see, in the ceremony of their handshake—a prison handshake, rich with the inflections of secret brotherhoods—evidence of a fast and furious bond.

Nelson shivered. All at once he longed to be a part of them.

Chuckie said, "Yo." He started the engine. "I told you, he a mama's boy. Nigga prob'ly turn us in."

Hawk ignored this, looked up at Nelson. "You in or what?"

"What's the plan?" Nelson said.

"Yo, I can't be tellin' you 'less you in."

"Come on, Hawk. You know me better than that."

Hawk shook his head slowly. "I don't know sometimes, bro."

Nelson sensed he was being punished for something, but what? It was true that he and Hawk weren't as close as they used to be, that things had changed since high school. But whose fault was that?

"Maybe we different people," said Hawk. "You doin' what you gotta do. Makin' chump change. A'ight then. That's you. I stick with my boys, but that's me, you know wha'm sayin'? That's me. That's *my* code."

Chuckie pumped the gas. Fumes spilled up from the tailpipe.

Nelson coughed.

Hawk turned to Chuckie. "Yo, let's go over that girl Denise house. They a party tonight."

"Denise?" said Chuckie.

"Yeah. She the one got pregnant by that nigga name Shawn, live on Turner Avenue."

"Oh yeah. Den*ise*."

Nelson felt himself fading away in the ensuing fog of exhaust. Hawk and Chuckie were laughing now, their bond growing stronger by the second.

Hawk looked up. "A'ight then, Style. Better get inside. I think somebody waitin' for you." He nodded toward the house.

Nelson turned. He saw the curtains close in the front window. Had Mama been watching?

Chuckie laughed. "A'ight then, Workin' Man." The car went backwards, stopped, then surged ahead with a screech, and all Nelson saw as it passed was a blur of Hawk's face in the passenger's seat, eyes tightly closed, head thrown back in an agony of laughter.

Nelson stood there numb in the cold and dark, trying to grasp what had just happened. He held his stomach. The breath had been knocked out of him.

He ought to feel relieved to be rid of them, he told himself. Wasn't this exactly what he had hoped for? And hadn't it come much easier than he'd imagined?

He walked to the front door of his house, weak-kneed, fumbling despairingly with his key. His eyes stung; his vision was split, slanted. Inside, Mama stood waiting for him in her blue nightgown, arms tensely folded. She'd been in a foul mood all week.

"Was that Kevin Hawkins I saw you talking to?" she said.

"What if it was?"

Mama's nostrils widened. "I told you, I don't want you hanging around that boy. You hear me?"

Nelson looked down at his shoes.

"I said, You hear me?"

"Ain't you gonna ask me how was my day at work?"

"It doesn't matter how your day was, not if you're going to come home and mess with that Kevin Hawkins. Now give me those clothes so I can wash them in time for tomorrow."

Nelson felt his fists tightening. He could hear Hawk laughing at him. Hawk and Rob and Chuckie Banks.

"Nelson?"

"Stay out my business!" he shouted. Enraged, he rushed past his mother and ran up to his room, where he slammed the door and stood trembling under the bare lightbulb.

The room enclosed him. He stared at the map on the wall, and saw a picture of his own mind: a once-solid mass having come apart, chunks uncoupling and floating slowly out to sea.

"Nelson?"

Mama was at the bottom of the stairs.

"Leave me alone!" Nelson called.

He removed his jacket, his shirt, let them fall to the floor. Then he pulled off his T-shirt and, once again, looked down and faced the horrible fact of his scar. He still wasn't used to it. He traced the line with his finger, like playing a sad, slow melody.

Why? Why him? What had he ever done?

Denise: the name flew at him, but he would never know its heat, this affliction had killed his spirit, had filled his ears with imagined shrieks and gasps, with whispers and laughter and mean sentiments of pity. A small scar, that would have been okay, might've even had some sex appeal. But this was a monstrosity. What girl would ever want him, his body split like that; and what girl, for that matter, wouldn't roll her eyes at the small honest change in his pocket—chump change, Hawk called it—or at Mama spying on him through the curtain?

He recalled with longing all the good times with Crumb—the games of hoop, the long, breezy rides in the van in the hot summer;

Crumb had been the closest thing he'd had to a true friend, he real-ized, and it shamed him to think that he could be so lonely for him now. Still, he hoped that the situation would improve, that they could go back to the way they were just a week before—Crumb respecting him, looking up to him, seeking his company, his words, his strength.

Benjamin Lerner sat back in his father's chair and put his feet up on the desk. All the papers that had been piled there were now neatly arranged in vertical files, and a record of the week's transactions shone impressively on the screen of his computer. He'd entered the data of the past year's receipts and statements, and now at the click of a but-ton he could project profits, track inflation, budget, strategize, envi-sion. In three short weeks he had implemented a host of changes that he felt would make things run more efficiently; sure, he'd hit a few snags here and there, but not a day went by when he didn't come up with some new idea, be it rearranging the items on the shelves for a more attractive presentation, or keeping his gun hidden in the desk drawer, where it would always be on hand at the end of the day, when he was alone in the back counting money.

He eliminated certain unpopular products, raised and lowered prices of others. He suspended all transactions with grocery stores— selling on consignment wasn't very profitable to begin with, and when you added all the driving back and forth, the time, the gas, the hassle, well, he couldn't imagine what Mickey had been thinking. Without the deliveries to stores, volume decreased, and so when two of the bakers began making noises about going to work for a new catering outfit, Ben forced the issue by cutting back their hours. As soon as they quit, Ben installed Lazarus as a baker at a little better than a baker's wage. This saved even more money—Lazarus was now, in ef-fect, doing two jobs at once, baking and supervising preparations. It was a wonder that Mickey hadn't thought of doing this years ago.

And then there was Nelson. Ben had been certain that Nelson would resist the idea of surrendering the van keys and working the counter, but he was wrong: Nelson took it as a promotion. He began to dress differently—white oxford shirts, dress shoes, a blue suit jacket the shade of billiard chalk—and developed in just a few days an air of high professionalism, mixed with a small dose of street hustle, the fast-talking come-on that was like a language all its own. The result of

all this was that many customers, whether charmed or faintly intimidated or just out of plain racial guilt, were making larger-than-normal
purchases, and Ben saw no reason to tamper with Nelson's enterpris-
ing approach. The best thing about it, of course, was that he wasn't
paying Nelson a penny more; the extra money now came from tips,
and of all the ideas that Ben had hatched, it was the tip jar which he
considered to be his masterstroke. Customers thought nothing of
dropping in a few coins, and Nelson always rewarded them with a
smile and a thank-you, which filled a good number of them—Ben
could see it in their eyes—with that warm humanitarian feeling people get when they have a pleasant exchange with a black person. By
the end of the week, Nelson had pulled in an extra forty, fifty bucks.

Deliveries, however, were not nearly as fun as he'd imagined, back
when he used to tag along with Nelson. It was pretty boring, really,
driving around all day, and demoralizing to arrive at country clubs and
nursing homes (using the service entrances, he could avoid the sight
of the filthy rich or the forsaken old) and approach the tie-wearing
banquet managers and white-linened kitchen help, who, as though
sensing his arrival, were invariably assembled in a fierce tableau of
labor and industry, looking for all the world like a lean enemy army
that might someday conquer his own.

No longer did he dream of speeding down the highway with the
radio on full blast, or crossing state lines in a blur of rattling metal; the
van was not a toy, but a vital piece of equipment, to be maintained and
handled like everything else that had come under his control.

His only real regret was over the tensions that had entered into his
relationship with Nelson. Or was this mostly in his imagination? Sure,
things had changed between them—Ben, by his own admission, had
set a different tone, or rather, had been the first to respond to the demands of the situation—but he certainly harbored no ill feelings, and
could even believe, during moments of bustle behind the counter,
amid shouted orders and brisk teamwork, that their friendship had
simply been raised to a professional level. And hadn't he done everything he could to downplay his power? Hadn't he coated his com-
mands with humor and gratitude? With joking, self-effacing remarks?
Hadn't he gone out of his way?

It was one o'clock—time for somebody to get lunch. Ben got up
from the desk and walked around to the front, where Nelson was
waiting on a customer, wearing a big, wide, toothy smile that had been
growing over the past couple of weeks, and which had now reached

such grotesque and mocking proportions that Ben feared the customers might take offense. But they noticed nothing; in fact it put
many of them at ease.

"What'll it be today, sir?" Nelson said to Irv Gould, an old crank of
about seventy with bushy red eyebrows. "Rye bread lookin' good—I
recommend gettin' two, 'cause you're liable to eat one on the way
home."

"The seeds get stuck in my teeth," said Gould. He was one of the
few customers who wasn't impressed with Nelson's style. "And I like
to keep both hands on the wheel when I drive."

"That's fine too," said Nelson. "Can't blame you."

"I'll take a plain wheat bread," said Gould.

"Sliced?" said Morris.

Gould waved his hand in the affirmative. Morris set the loaf on the
slicer and turned the switch. The store rattled with the noise.

Gould took his bread and left without leaving a tip. Nelson made
an effort to appear oblivious; quickly he pulled out a rag from under
the counter and began wiping the countertop.

"I'll go and get lunch," said Morris, glancing at Nelson.

"That's okay," said Ben. "I can get it."

Nelson shook out the rag and folded it with care.

"You've been getting it for the past week," said Morris.

Ben felt Nelson's eyes on him. "Okay," he said, trying to make it
seem natural. "Okay. You can go. I'll have a chicken sandwich, potato
salad and a Coke."

Morris wrote this down on a pad. "What about you, Nelson?" he
said.

Nelson placed the folded rag in his pocket. "Chicken sandwich," he
said, his voice low, hooded.

"What was that?" said Morris.

"Chicken sandwich."

Morris scribbled frantically.

Ben took out a bill from his wallet. "It's on me today," he announced. As Morris walked past him he handed over the money.
"Don't take all day," he whispered hotly.

In a moment Ben found himself alone with Nelson. There were no
customers.

Ben sighed. "Slow day, huh?" he said.

"It's a'ight."

"Probably pick up later."

"Yeah." Nelson rubbed his chin. "Probably."

Ben noticed that Nelson never looked at him anymore when he spoke (he can't face me, Ben thought; can't stand the idea that I'm his boss!), never responded with more than a few words. Ben felt he ought to be shown more respect, but then too he believed that he had certain responsibilities to his staff, such as being a good communicator, the kind of boss with whom you could have a cup of coffee in the office and chat about a ball game. In this capacity he was obviously falling short.

He said, "You watch any games last night?"

"Naw."

It was frustrating: he wanted to talk to Nelson the way they used to talk, but feared that the mere sound of that language, like the snap of a hypnotist's fingers, might transport them to former roles. Ducking that risk, he had now become what Nelson had long suspected was his truer, hidden self—the snake-oil salesman who could stand tall in Donna's kitchen and portray himself as the soul of rectitude. He knew that Nelson despised his new persona—despised *him*—and his only response was to avoid his old friend as much as possible.

Things had gotten so quiet, so tense with distrust, that when Ben saw the squinting figure of Shirley Finkle making her way through the cold to the bakery door—normally a dreaded sight—it was like an answer to a prayer. Nelson's mood seemed to lighten too: Shirley Finkle meant an easy sell and a dollar in the tip jar.

"Well, good afternoon," she said, her head bobbing as she looked around at the paper snowflakes hanging from the ceiling by a special transparent string that Ben had purchased at a party store. The flakes were still flinching from the draft that Shirley had let in. "When your father comes home, he'll never recognize this place," she said, and Ben had a feeling she was referring more to Nelson's presence behind the counter than anything else. "Have you heard from him?"

"Yes," said Ben. "He left a message last week."

"Saying what?"

"Not much, really. Just that he'll be back soon, and to call him at his number if there's an emergency."

"What in the world is he doing over there?"

Ben shrugged. Mickey hadn't said, and Ben didn't particularly care; he could only hope that his father's return might be delayed, and that, in the time that remained, he himself could gain some kind of unofficial but compelling custody over the bakery, like that of a squatter, or a devoted stepparent.

"How do you like that," said Shirley, shaking her head. "And he expects you to keep running this place all by yourself?"

"It's not by myself," Ben said. He gave a jerk of the head to indicate Nelson. "I've had some help." He looked at Nelson to flash him a smile, but Nelson was looking into the tip jar, counting the coins with his eyes.

Shirley continued shaking her head, and Ben wondered if she was hurt that Mickey hadn't contacted her, or sent a postcard.

"Anyway, it's fine," said Ben. "He trusts me."

Shirley sighed, looked around some more.

Ben wasn't sure what to make of his next-door neighbor. She'd wanted so badly to be a heroic presence in the wake of Emi's death, but it just hadn't worked out; only once since Thanksgiving had she invited Ben over to dinner, and that had been a minor disaster: everything about the evening, from the lemony scent of cleansers to the big smile frozen on Shirley's face, had suggested nervous preparations and efforts to make him feel at home, and it soon became eerily obvious that the Finkles were imagining that Ben was a sort of grown orphan whom they had adopted. Their childlessness cried out from between the layers of Shirley's wet, sliding lasagna, shrieked up from the gloss of the kitchen floor, quivered within the silences that descended on the table like an overly attentive waiter. The Finkles watched with wonder as he used his silverware, and seemed to be on tenterhooks as he chewed. When he remarked how good the food was, they looked at each other as though their doubts as to whether he had ever enjoyed a home-cooked meal had been confirmed. It was only when he announced that he couldn't stay for dessert because he had to go to the bakery to do some paperwork that he knew their fantasy had been spoiled: he wasn't so needy and helpless after all, and as he walked out the door trailing thank-yous, he sensed that there had been something improper about the whole event, like a date between friends or co-workers that would always be remembered as a bad idea.

Fortunately, Shirley seemed to have erased the evening from her mind. She examined a tray of pastries, still shaking her head over the idea of Mickey gallivanting in Paris, or maybe she was noticing that the prices had gone up a quarter.

Nelson looked up from the tip jar as if he had just noticed the new customer. "Hey, Miss Shirley, how you doin' today. Got your eye on that raisin bun?" He pulled out a sheet of wax paper from the dispenser, ready to make the move.

Shirley giggled. "Not me," she said. "I'm starting next year's diet a little early."

"You got to indulge sometimes," Nelson said. "Life is way too short."

Ben could see Shirley relenting under the pressure; she'd rather buy some buns and throw them out at home than turn down Nelson. "Well," she said, "now that you put it that way!" A tremendous and startling smile broke out on her face, causing her eyes to close.

"How many?" said Nelson. "How about half a dozen." He began to bag them, one after the other. "I'm sure your husband'll be glad to come home to somethin' good and nice."

"What, I'm not good and nice?" said Shirley, watching as Nelson loaded the bag. "I'm not nice to come home to?"

"Now I didn't say *that*," said Nelson, and he and Shirley shared a bouncy, shaky laugh, under cover of which Shirley deposited a dollar in the tip jar.

"You boys be good," she said, setting out the exact change, and then she turned and hurried out the door.

"Nice lady," said Nelson, looking down at the tray, at the six shiny spots where the buns had stood.

Ben kept himself from saying something like "good job"; he just stood by and let Nelson feel he was being noticed.

Another customer entered: beard, black hat, black coat. Ben had seen this man a few times over the years, but he didn't know his name.

Nelson, full of momentum, was ready to win him over. "How you doin' today?" he said.

"Good," said the man, without inflection. He was big, thick, his heft and bulk full of appetite, voracious for books, texts, parchment, for fleshy excesses of the marriage bed, the crushing surge of fatherhood. His beard came to three points; red lips twitched in a nest of hair.

Ben went over to the register to free up Nelson, who followed the man to the other end of the counter.

"May I help you with anything?" Nelson said.

"Yes," said the man. "A loaf of rye bread."

"One loaf of rye," said Nelson. It seemed he might push for more, but he held back; the Gould rejection would not be far from his mind. "Want it sliced?" he said.

"Please," said the man.

Nelson put the bread through the slicer, then peeled off a plastic bag and licked his finger to open it. As he slid the sliced bread into the bag, the man cleared his throat.

"You really shouldn't put your hand in your mouth and then touch the bread," the man said. "It's unsanitary."

Nelson looked up at him. "I didn't touch the bread," he said politely. "I just touched the bag."

"Yes, but you first picked up the bread with your fingers. If you've been licking your fingers and picking up bread all day, I would argue that that is an unsanitary practice."

"No need to argue," said Nelson. He tried a laugh, but Ben could see he was trapped. Ben felt trapped himself, caught between loyalty to his employee and service to his customer.

"I'd like a different loaf," said the man.

Nelson held himself together. "Okay," he said. "No problem." He reached for another loaf.

"I'd prefer if you washed your hands first," said the man.

"Wash my hands?" said Nelson. He chuckled, shook his head.

The man's face gained some color. "I'm sorry, is that too much to ask?"

"I didn't hear you askin'," said Nelson. He remained gracious, instructive, but his blackness alone seemed to tinge all of that with menace. "You want to ask me, there's a way to ask."

The man said, "I'd like to speak to the manager. I'd like to speak to Mr. Lerner."

Ben interceded, fingering the knot on his tie. "I'm the manager," he said. "Benjamin Lerner."

"You're the manager?" said the man. "And you allow your employees to handle bread in such a way?"

Ben hardly knew what to say, and could only hope that Nelson would keep his head. "I'm sorry," he said. "It won't happen again."

The man narrowed his eyes. "Perhaps the Health Department would be interested to learn of your unusual practices."

"We apologize," said Ben, his knees shaking at the very idea of the Health Department. They'd closed down a big area bakery a few years back, citing roaches, mice. Rumor had it that it was a political move; someone had wanted the place to go down. The big winner, of course, had been Lerner's. Now Ben could see his own business facing ruin. He said, "I can guarantee we'll clear up the problem. In the meantime—" He pulled out a piece of wax paper and with it placed two loaves of rye into a bag. Nelson stood there watching. His hands were in his pockets.

"No, thank you," said the man as Ben placed the bag on the counter.

"This is not how I prefer to conduct business." He shot Nelson a look, then turned and walked out of the bakery.

Nelson stared after him through the window.

Ben decided to act like nothing serious had happened, though he knew he'd have to take some sort of action. It was incidents like this that snowballed and came back to roll over you.

"Tellin' me to wash my hands," said Nelson. "That nigga got to be out his mind."

"Shrug it off," said Ben, almost grateful that he'd been afforded this opportunity to rally behind Nelson. "The guy was an asshole. Don't worry about it."

Nelson shook his head; Ben could see he was getting himself worked up.

"I'll get some plastic gloves," Ben said, "those disposable ones. Personally, I don't care, but, I mean, we sure don't need any hassles from the Health Department." He sighed. "Look, it's no big deal. It's not like we need his business." This statement was a direct contradiction to remarks Ben had made during a staff meeting the day before, when he said that there was no such thing as an unimportant customer.

Morris came back with the food and sat in his folding chair by the bread slicer. When Ben told him what happened, Morris looked surprised.

"I've been licking my fingers for fifty years," he said. "Never had a complaint."

"There you go," said Nelson, as if this proved his point. He grabbed his chicken sandwich and went to the far end of the counter.

Ben canceled afternoon deliveries so that he could be around just in case the man returned. He told Morris and Nelson that he had a lot of paperwork to do, but he knew Nelson didn't believe him. The day passed without further incident, but Nelson, his spirits dampened, had ceased to be upbeat with customers.

When after three days Nelson still hadn't rebounded, Ben knew he had to do something. He called Nelson into the office just before closing and told him in as friendly a tone as he could to have a seat. Then he sat at his desk and clasped his hands behind his head. "Something tells me," he said, "that you're still pretty upset over what happened the other day."

Nelson fidgeted in the chair and looked around.

"I've been thinking about it," Ben went on, "and if it's okay with you, I'd like to put you back on deliveries."

Nelson glanced up at the ceiling.

"Of course, it's entirely up to you," Ben said. "I just want you to be as comfortable as possible. I mean, in the van, at least you won't have to deal with as many assholes."

Nelson stroked his chin. "If you want me to drive," he said, "I'll drive."

Ben considered that his talk two weeks before about teamwork and being a team player had maybe rubbed off some. "Great," he said. "I never really got the hang of driving that thing anyway." He reached into his pocket and pulled out the van keys. Nelson became alert at the sound. Ben gave the keys a little friendly jiggle in his palm. "Like old times," he said. "Think you remember how to drive it?"

"Yeah," said Nelson.

Ben placed the keys on the desk: it was like a dare for Nelson to grab them. When Nelson didn't make a move, Ben took the keys, got up, and offered them. Nelson held out his hand, and when the keys had been passed, Ben felt instantly that he had made a terrible mistake.

17

Mickey stared at the fire. It had been three weeks since he'd learned the truth about his wife, but even now, watching the hypnotic dance of the flames (it is alive, this fire, Mickey thought, it is more alive than me, and yet I have created it), the words of David Shaw came back to him, and despite the tremendous heat—a heat like he'd never known—a chill passed over his skin.

"It's about your wife," Shaw had said as they walked out of Dulac's bakery under a bone-colored sky. Shaw then informed him that he knew of a place not too far away where they could talk, as he cryptically put it, alone, and Mickey, as he followed Shaw's brisk steps, could not bring himself to utter a single word of inquiry. And didn't he already know? It seemed almost cruel that Shaw should now tell him of Emi's deeds (he suddenly recalled a remark of Shaw's at the Halloween party: "We must talk some day," he'd said), and Mickey wondered if the pianist, who would have witnessed her liaisons firsthand while traveling with her, needed simply to unburden his conscience.

They entered a dark, mint-scented room of red rugs and pillows—the best tearoom in Paris, Shaw said, and Shaw would know—and were led to a corner table, where Mickey lowered himself with a small protest from his joints on the low, cushioned wicker seat. The usual reds of November—leaves, apples, Indian corn, the remnant clouds of sunsets smeared red-orange across a turquoise rim of sky—were displaced by red visions of wine and desert sands: a moody, sensual setting, deepened by the heavy red draperies that hung unmoving over the windows, pressing the darkness in toward some central erotic idea. As Shaw ordered two teas from an Arab waiter—Shaw's bomb was imminent now—Mickey thought to preempt him by claiming a knowledge of Emi's secret life, in hopes of saving both of them from the pathetic charade of disclosure.

He heard himself say, "I know what you want to tell me," and wished immediately that he'd held off, waited for the tea at least, so that he could have something to hold, to duck down into. His hands squirmed on his lap.

"You do?" said Shaw. He seemed surprised, even disappointed. "About Emi?"

"Yes," he said, a little ironic wink in his voice, "I couldn't help but notice how she was acting toward the end."

He sat back and waited, confident not only that he'd struck the perfect note—a man of appetites reclining in his knowledge—but that the bomb of adultery (here it comes, he thought) would release him from the role of celibate widower in mourning and permit him to look up and admire the tall redhead in the black skirt who was being seated on the other side of the room.

Shaw touched his ear, that faultless musician's ear, and inclined it a little toward his companion, as if he hadn't heard right. "You mean you knew?" he said. "About—her condition?"

Mickey kept his jaw firm, but a certain suspense in his eyes unmasked the would-be playboy. Condition? He knew she'd been under stress, a little frustrated—but a *condition*? "What do you mean?" he said, forcing a smile so as not to seem too surprised or concerned.

Shaw pulled a cigarette from his shirt pocket and lit a match: a flame snapped into existence—like something born in hell, Mickey would later think—then quickly reduced, and with it the room, the city, the entire world seemed to concentrate itself into what was now a tense moment of ignition, a moment on which so much suddenly seemed to depend. Mickey watched the blue light swim toward Shaw's fingertips as he held the tiny droplet of fire to the end of the cigarette, until at the last possible moment the tip burst into a brightness that intensified like a frightening idea. The match, black and twisted but still showing a glimmer of blue, fell straight down into a clear glass ashtray, where it broke in half, sending up a single strand of smoke, a musical note heard only by the dead.

Shaw exhaled slowly. "I think you ought to know," he said, "if you don't already." He paused, as if to decide the best way to tell it, and then, with the suddenness of one ripping a bandage from a wound, said, "Cancer," then exhaled and tapped his cigarette insistently until a finger of ash dropped off into his open palm. "Breast cancer," he said, now pulling on the cigarette as though it contained his next words. The bald bronze head smoked, it seemed, from everywhere, even the eyes. "She was very sick. Very sick." He nodded, his eyes fixed on the ashtray. "Yes, in fact I believe she was terminal." He paused again, then brought the cigarette to his lips and inhaled slowly.

Mickey felt a voice gurgle and die in his chest. There was no possible response to this. If he had questions, they were buried under the weight of his disbelief. Follow Shaw, he thought; keep your eye on him. Shaw looked up, and so did Mickey: the waiter had arrived with the tea. Steam rolled dizzily from the glasses, which were set down before them. Shaw stirred his tea with a spoon.

"I take it," said Shaw, "that you didn't know." He glanced at Mickey.

"Keep talking," Mickey said.

"Yes. Well, I know this must come as a tremendous shock." Shaw sipped his tea, the cigarette unraveling wildly between his fingers. "But please, let me explain. She confided in me—you cannot imagine how it felt, knowing what she was doing to herself, and my having taken a vow of confidence. But I can now see that there was nothing to be done. She was convinced that her way was the best."

"What way?" said Mickey, trying to contain himself. "What are you talking about?"

"Please," said Shaw. "I know you're confused, I know you're shocked, upset, I understand, but please, let me explain. You will see that she did have her reasons. I debated over and over whether or not to say anything, but I realized that I would go straight out of my mind unless I talked with you."

Mickey's mind raced. Was Shaw trying to tell him that Emi would have died anyway, that the shooting had simply hastened the inevitable, had in fact saved her from a long and painful end? Or did he simply want to rid himself of an awful secret, pawn it off on its rightful owner, so that he, Shaw, could be free?

"I urged her to tell you," said Shaw. " 'Tell your family,' I said. I urged, I pleaded—"

"Yes," said Mickey. Shaw's nervousness brought out in him an eerie sobriety. "You urged her. Now tell me what happened."

"I'm trying," said Shaw. "It is very—difficult."

"Go on."

Shaw closed his eyes for a moment, opened them. He was verging on tears—he blinked rapidly, went for his cigarette—but Mickey felt no pity, only a detached fascination with the man's humanity, which had always been kept from him, hidden behind the reputation, the loftiness of the name. "Please," Shaw said, and Mickey felt a sudden shock of intimacy: he was joined in suffering with the great David Shaw: all at once his soul cleaved to the man's voice, so that when Shaw spoke, Mickey could feel the vibrations in his own lungs.

"She found a lump in each breast. We were in Chicago. This was in May. She saw a doctor there. He did a biopsy."

"Cancer," said Mickey. To utter those syllables was to gain entry into another world. Mickey felt cut off from everything he'd ever known. He was in the region of disease, of darkness. He could not get past the word: *cancer.* He thought of a crab, a scavenging creature skittering sidewise through her blood. From there, he had to move backwards, from the texture of the word to the lumps themselves (a lump: why hadn't he noticed it?), two deathly curds floating in those small round globes, tethered by sprouting capillaries, nourished by blood.

"It was cancer," said Shaw. "In both breasts."

Mickey shook his head. It all made sense now, and yet he understood nothing. Why hadn't she told him? He felt himself sinking into new depths of despair; he might fade from the world, crumble like ashes and blow away.

"I don't believe it," he said.

"I'm sorry," said Shaw.

Mickey's hands turned to fists on the tabletop.

"Please," said Shaw. "Please don't hate me for this."

Hate? Mickey was confused; he stared at Shaw, whose face seemed darker than before, as though ripening with a full knowledge of the word.

"It wasn't me," said Shaw.

Mickey felt a chill. Had he missed something? What was that look in Shaw's eyes? "What do you mean?" said Mickey.

Shaw drew a long breath. "She was determined," he said, in a tone of grim confession, "to beat the disease. But she did have one important option." He fingered the cigarette, as if debating whether or not to pick it up. "At least, *I* saw it as an option." He ground the burning tip into the eye of the ashtray. He said: "A double mastectomy."

There was a silence in which Mickey mumbled the horrible words. If he understood correctly, Emi was faced with the sort of radical surgery—and Mickey knew of a few of his customers who'd been through it—that would rip the muscle from her chest and shoulders ("It could take quite a while," the doctor would tell her, "before you'll regain your strength, and even then you may never have quite the endurance you had before") and render her unable, for a time at least (and a day would seem a year to her), to play her violin. Mickey could see it: Emi running to a dozen quacks and crackpots and God knew what sort of acupuncturists in her will to avoid the knife.

Damn her! How could she be so stubborn? How?

"But of course," said Shaw, "to her mind, surgery was out of the question—it would mean the end of her career."

Mickey's fists shook under the table. It was suicide!

"She had a lumpectomy in Chicago, then immediately sought alternative treatments. The doctor warned her that it was likely they hadn't gotten it all, that it could spread, that they needed to remove the breasts, get it all before it was too late. But she didn't want to hear of it. She took vitamins, shark cartilage, herbs, tonics. She meditated."

"Suicide."

"That's why she wouldn't tell you," said Shaw. "She knew you would have that reaction—she knew you would try everything in your power to see to it that she underwent surgery."

Mickey was speechless. It was true: it would have been a battle royal.

"She was concerned for you," said Shaw. "She didn't want you to worry, to agonize; she believed she would live—she was determined to live. Even as she was dying she believed she could spare you the knowledge of her suffering. She hated herself for being diseased. She was ashamed. It disgusted her. She didn't want to be pitied, God, above all she didn't want that. Please don't hold anything against her. I'd rather you blame me. She's been through enough—"

"No," said Mickey. "I should have known. I should have known!"

"No—"

"She was my wife!"

"I—"

"I should have noticed something, should have picked up on the signs—and there were signs, plenty of signs. I had to be blind!"

"No," said Shaw. "Don't blame yourself. I should have told you, I should have said something!"

"I didn't read the signs, I didn't even save her that night on the street. I failed twice. Twice! Twice her life slipped from me. I didn't want her dead!"

"No."

Mickey felt Shaw's hand on his arm: he saw nothing, he was sailing headlong through a fog. "And to think"—he let out a mad, miserable laugh—"to think that I thought she was avoiding me because she was seeing another man!" He smacked himself in the head with the heels of his palms and fell away from the table and to his feet.

"Please don't go," said Shaw. "I can tell you that there was no one else—no one!"

Oh, but if only there had been, Mickey thought, if only she hadn't been all alone in her illness—if only there had been someone to save her! "I failed her!" Mickey said. He turned, staggered, groped for the door, the red room spinning, Shaw's voice fading, and was struck by the cold of the afternoon, the dull white light. He saw a wide, empty path of sidewalk and chased it.

The storefronts blew past him like a silver train: windows: whole birds draped on ice, wings and eyes still wild with flight: pigs rotating slowly over fire: pink pianos of meat hanging heavy from hooks. Every human face seemed infinitely strange, every glance an attempt on his life. He was nothing, he was nowhere. People held baguettes on their shoulders like rifles and seemed to be marching. Mickey flung himself against them: they parted for him, they barely knew he existed. Where is she, he cried to himself; where is my wife? He came to a corner, turned blindly into another street. Cars sped past, blurs of color. The city was unforgiving in its design, streets radiating in all directions from mad, whirling circles of traffic into which he saw himself charging and being swept under, rolled lifeless into the gutter. *Emi!* How could she be so gone from this place, so utterly gone? She'd left nothing. Nothing! There was nothing of her: she was nowhere. Mickey stopped, wheeled. *Bear with me,* she had pleaded. How she had tried to make him understand! And God, how she'd taken his arm on that walk from Shaw's—and how he'd felt her behind him when she was ordered out of the car, not seen her but felt her, the last he knew of her in this life, a heat behind him, the brush perhaps of her hand on his back.

He was ready; he could do it. He was at the very edge of his life, a life that, aware it was threatened, surged forth: his entire body seemed to rise. His senses were heightened to a painful degree; he heard every footfall, the grind of every car, saw every red petal of the endless potted plants on windowsills and latticed iron balconies. It was too much, too much! He must act: then it would all be over, the universe in some minute way would be corrected, restored to a certain balance. He looked around. He had nothing at his disposal: not even a penknife to cut his wrists. And the pills—the pills were back at the hotel. Damn it all! He must do something—but what? Run out into the street? A bus approached: Mickey stepped off the curb, poised himself for a sudden bolt into its path. The bus came nearer, nearer. Mickey took a breath—it was upon him, one more second, go!—and then a huge rumble of steel, the wind of it knocking him back a step. His fear thrilled him—he'd come that close! He felt like a child at the beach, daring the crashing waves, standing before them as one might stand before the very face of eternity.

As he walked on, his terror deepened his resolve. Perhaps he could go down into the metro, leap onto the tracks. It was strange: the impulse was within him now, he couldn't shake it. He was like the nonbeliever who arrives at God through the mere repetition of a prayer. He'd flirted with it, and now it was real.

But what awaited him? If there was some sort of hereafter, how would he be received? Would Emi be there? Would they meet? Would their souls collide, brush each other in a moment of recognition that was beyond the senses? Would she forgive him?

He found himself on a familiar street; he'd come this way with Shaw. Dulac's bakery should be just down the road—and yes, there it was. It was hard to believe that only an hour before he was inside that crumbling old place, lecturing on his business with such confidence, such relish, such desire to ground Dulac, with his sad stone bowl and odes to round peasant loaves, into dust. Poor Dulac, he thought, alone in his humble little bakery, crushed by the American. Mickey's heart went out to him. The arrogance! Could he ever stop causing people pain?

He must apologize to the man, he felt; make that one final gesture. If he could undo one bad thing, he thought, if he could set one thing right.

He opened the door of the bakery. Again, there was no one there. Mickey looked at the round breads, the faces of which seemed to be watching him. The work that Dulac must have put into a single miserable loaf—poor man!

"Dulac?" Mickey called. There was no answer.

Mickey ducked under the counter. There were no more barriers in this world, he was beyond them, there remained only one, the membrane that separated him from death. He went through a doorway into a dark corridor, off of which he discovered an ancient stone staircase.

"Hello?"

Again there was no response.

The steps wound down into blackness. Might Dulac be down there? Mickey perceived that warmth again, as of fire; and as he descended, round and round, the heat grew, and he could smell burning wood and the earthy mud of yeast and grain. He touched the massive stones of the walls. They were cool despite the heat. Mickey reached the bottom—it was still too dark to make anything out—and turned a corner to find what seemed to him the source, somehow, of all awful things: a large brick oven that seemed to be built into the stone wall, a roiling furnace around the edges of whose closed door burned a steady orange glow.

"Hello?" he called again, though it was clear there was no one about. "Monsieur Dulac?"

The room, he now noticed, was very hot. There was a single worktable covered in flour; it held a half-filled glass of water and the old stone bowl and had a look of grave permanence, as of the workstation of some solitary prisoner. Cloth-lined wicker baskets were stacked here and there on the dusty stone floor; dozens of jugs of water lined two walls. A lightbulb directly overhead, from which a long string hung down motionless in the heat, marked, along with the large mixer, the only nod to modernity: its meager light dropped Mickey's shadow like a ball before his feet. There were no windows, no sense of the world above. Mickey could not imagine a more wretched place, a place that could better reflect what he felt.

"Yes?" came a voice.

Mickey looked up: there, standing near the bottom of the stairs, half in shadow, was Dulac.

"You have come to speak with me?" said Dulac. "To continue our talk?"

Mickey wasn't sure if it was an invitation. "I can leave," he said. "You're probably busy."

"Ah yes, busy, busy." Dulac walked around to the oven. "So you have seen my—how do you say it?—my pride and joy. Yes?" He opened the chamber door: Mickey's eyes widened at the sight of fire and bricks.

He could smell the fire, could hear its gallop. Dulac shut the door.

Mickey felt the sweat break out all over his skin; and as Dulac held forth on the benefits of fire (the heat did not seem to affect him), Mickey removed his coat and slung it over his shoulder, his mind reaching toward a vision fed not only by the flames of the oven and the passion of Dulac's homily ("All of life springs from fire: we are but the dust of exploded stars: only where there is heat can there be life"), but the force of his desire to mortify himself to the core of his being, that he might finally be good enough for death. Yes: a sentence of fire and darkness and isolation, of hard labor as an inmate right here in Dulac's cellar. He wanted to sweat, to suffer, to deny himself all pleasure until the pain was so great that even a death by burning would seem a godsend. *This* was what he deserved.

When Dulac paused for a breath, Mickey came out with it. "If you need a baker," he said, "I think I can help you."

"Help me?" said Dulac.

"Help you bake."

"Ah, but Monsieur Lerner, we have had this discussion. You are not really a baker."

Mickey understood the game: Dulac required total submission. Mickey saw it as part of his own martyrdom. "Yes," he said, "but I'm willing to train." He thought of Glazer in his white smock, wearing him down with orders, working him to the point of collapse. He'd been at Glazer's mercy. Why not Dulac's?

"So," said Dulac, still guarded. "My words today convinced you?"

"Yes," said Mickey. He felt the lie pass into Dulac's belly.

Dulac, lips puckered, looked Mickey over as he might a piece of machinery, nodding as if to the whispered judgments of bakers past. "I suppose," he said, "that we can make a try."

Mickey wanted to laugh—as if Dulac were doing *him* the favor! "Thank you," he said, wincing inwardly. Already he could taste the further humiliations in store for him: the fanatical Dulac haunting him, intruding on his solitude, peering over his shoulder, testing water temperatures, poking at the dough, becoming violent when something wasn't perfect.

"*Bon,*" said Dulac. "How much time will you have?"

"I don't know," said Mickey. "I'll have to see—"

"Do you have a place to stay?"

"I—"

"You may stay here," said Dulac. "In the back." He pointed to a passageway opposite the staircase. "I have a room there, it is empty now.

It is small, but it contains everything you will need. A bed, a bath. Everything."

Mickey shuddered at Dulac's efficiency, his resolve; he was like a little scheming demon, a fisher of bad men. He had it all worked out so prettily: it was as if he'd planned for Mickey's arrival years ago and had been waiting in the dark ever since.

"It's good?" said Dulac.

"Yes," said Mickey. "It's good." This was it, he thought, the final act. He would give himself to Dulac, would surrender the small remainder of his life to this infernal place.

Already he looked forward to his death.

18

Ben stood behind the counter next to Morris. He'd barely slept the night before, worrying about his decision to hand Nelson the keys to the van, but now he could relax a little: it was three in the afternoon, and the phone had yet to ring. Ben had instructed his contacts to call him if there were any problems with deliveries, any problems at all, wanting to send a message to everyone that here was a hands-on manager who was on top of things, doing his job.

Customers came and went; there was little pizzazz or excitement to things, and Ben gained a new appreciation for the work that Nelson had done. He could see how sales might slip, but on the other hand, the atmosphere was much more relaxed; without Nelson behind the counter, customers were able to assert their old, fussy, demanding personas, were more likely to confuse themselves into purchasing more than they intended. Six of one, a half dozen of the other, Ben thought.

When things slowed down around lunchtime, Ben told Morris he was going out for an hour or so. It was a mild, sunny day; a caravan of white clouds was stalled in a blue sky. Ben walked home coatless through the broad alleys, which seemed dirtier than he remembered.

Neighbors of different colors, some of whom he'd never seen before, reached up to the long banners of drying laundry that divided their yards in two. Aside from the usual Orthodox, there were now Indians, Koreans, Hispanics, blacks. FOR SALE signs had been popping up like dandelions. People were dying, moving away, even the Finkles next door were talking about moving to Florida. Ben wondered if Mickey would want to move some day.

He opened the gate and entered the backyard, indulging a small fantasy of ownership. He stepped onto the yellowish lawn, paced it slowly, enjoying the feel of property beneath his feet. The bird feeders were empty—Ben made a mental note to fill them with crusts of bread. And the garden—maybe he ought to do a little digging on Saturday, turn the soil over.

He went inside and fixed himself a tuna sandwich from one of the cans that Mickey had left for him. Then he went upstairs and jerked himself off into a wad of toilet paper, doing it real fast and without fantasizing, as though it were any other hurried bathroom act. Who had time to make a big production out of it? He had a business to run.

Girls would come in time, he told himself. He looked forward to the day when all the college grads would come home to find the Lerner Bakery expanded into a booming corporation. Let them have their business schools, Ben thought, let them have their ivory towers; he lived and worked in the real world. The bakery was his university. When those kids came home with their useless degrees, they'd be coming to *him* for a job.

He washed his hands and paused in front of the door to his parents' room, which he'd kept shut since Mickey's departure. At first he'd shut it because he didn't want to be reminded of his mother—it was bad enough having to go through her studio to get to the laundry room— but now, with Mickey gone for nearly a month, it was fun (well, maybe not fun, exactly, but interesting, amusing) to pretend that they were both dead, pretend that everything—the house, the bakery—was now his and his alone. Keeping the door closed facilitated the illusion, which was not to say that he couldn't open it if he wanted, since he was pretty much over Emi's death, though it was also true—no sense denying it—that he'd been too busy with the bakery to give her much thought, which after all was maybe the whole idea to begin with.

But whatever reason he had for throwing himself so feverishly into his work, be it to please his father or forget his mother, or both, the fact remained that the work was *his*, and when he left the house and strode proudly back to the bakery in his shirt and tie, he felt as grown up as he'd ever felt in his life, a young man of responsibility and accomplishment and vision, showing just the right trace of concern at the corners of his mouth to suggest a weighty matter of business lying unresolved on his office desk.

The store was empty save for Morris, who looked unusually small and frail behind the counter. Ben shuddered at the thought of having left him there alone.

"Everything okay?" said Ben, as the door closed behind him. "Go ahead and take a break."

"Benjie," Morris said. "Looks like we got a small problem."

Ben froze. "What is it?"

"Jay Rattner called."

Ben touched his tie.

Morris took off his glasses. "He said that Nelson was a little late with his delivery, and when he said something to Nelson about the lateness, Nelson used abusive language." He put his glasses back on. "Jay said he's going to take his business elsewhere if the situation doesn't improve."

"What does he mean, *improve?*"

"He doesn't want Nelson coming into his place anymore," said Morris.

"Shit," Ben muttered. He looked at his great-uncle. "So what are we supposed to do?"

Morris took his glasses off again, rubbed the lenses with a paper napkin, and, in a voice whose grave matter-of-factness was mysteriously tied in with the wisdom of his years, said, "It'll be your decision, Benjie, your father left you in charge—but all things considered, I think you ought to let him go."

The words were barely out of Morris's mouth when Ben spotted the van entering the lot.

Ben cursed, but he knew Morris was right. Nelson was a goddamned time bomb.

Morris faded toward the far end of the counter as Nelson entered the bakery carrying a stack of empty boxes.

Ben's throat went dry. To think that all the work he'd done had come down to this, that all the good things had mixed and stewed and somehow spawned this one horrible event. And for what? It wasn't *his* bakery—not really. Why had he made the effort? Why should he be put in this position? It would be easy—even satisfying, in a way—to let Nelson ride roughshod over clients and customers while Mickey frolicked in Europe; easy to blame Mickey for this whole state of af fairs. But there was too much at stake: if the bakery suffered, it would impact on everyone. He thought of the bakers, and the old customers whose habits had hardened; where would they be without Lerner's? And then there was his own reputation to consider. He'd won a lot of praise lately, and had taken all the credit. What would people think if he were to piss it all to hell? His leadership had never really been tested until now, and he remembered something his father had once said—how he never considered the bakery his own until the fire, until he'd had to save its life.

Nelson dropped the boxes on the floor and rubbed his hands together, the clipboard clamped under his arms. He acted as he always did, as though nothing unusual had happened during his route, and this darkened with possibility all the other times he'd behaved so nonchalantly. Ben considered that he really had no choice in the matter.

"Hey, Nelson," Ben said. "I'll take the clipboard. And the keys." Nelson handed them over without a word—this was routine. He was still wearing his conscientious blue jacket and pressed oxford shirt. It would be harder to fire him in those clothes, Ben thought.

Morris took up a broom.

"Nelson?" Ben said. "I'd like to have a chat with you in my office." The uttering of this phrase to a rogue employee had been foremost in his administrative fantasies, right up there with thwarting an armed-robbery attempt. Funny how little he relished it now. "Just for a minute," he said, and ran his eyes quickly over Nelson's person, checking for any bulges. There were none.

Nelson glanced at Morris, who was sweeping the floor with inordinate gusto.

Ben was aware of risks in performing the deed in a small, enclosed, out-of-view office, but he felt strongly that this was the only way to conduct affairs: man-to-man, in private.

Nelson followed him through the office door. Ben decided not to close it.

"Please, have a seat," Ben said. He sat behind his desk and gripped the armrests of the chair. For some reason he thought he should offer something—a drink, a cigarette—but all he had at his disposal was a bag of chocolate candies in the shape of coins, wrapped in gold foil. A holiday gift from Shirley Finkle. He opened the desk drawer, where he had stashed the candy, and was startled by the sight of the gun. He grabbed the mesh bag and closed the drawer.

"Chocolates?" he said, holding up the bag. To his surprise, Nelson reached out and took it.

"Thanks," Nelson mumbled, staring at the gold as though it might be real loot. Ben felt that his game had been thrown off; Nelson was supposed to refuse politely, an indication that he knew what was coming and was prepared. Ben now realized that Nelson was expecting not his walking papers, but an apology for the way he'd been treated lately—or worse, a bonus, or even a raise. It was, after all, the week before Christmas; everywhere in the business world employees were being invited behind closed doors to receive white envelopes. Ben watched with dread as Nelson unwrapped a chocolate.

Then an idea came to him. He saw a way out.

"You know, I've been thinking," he said. "All this stuff about putting you back on deliveries. You already know deliveries. And you know the counter. That's half the business. What I was thinking was, why not learn the other half?"

Nelson looked up with interest.

Ben smiled and motioned with his eyes at the glass window, behind which the oven and mixers and tables were framed in a way that suggested exciting opportunities. "Right over there," he said, and pointed toward the kitchen as though it were the promised land.

Nelson looked there too.

"You learn that end of things," Ben said, "and you'll be the one person here who knows the whole works. The one person who could maybe start up his own business someday."

Nelson turned to him. "How much money would I get?"

"Well, I'd assume you'd make what the other bakers make."

"How much is that?"

Ben laughed automatically. "Money can be discussed," he said.

"I'm here."

Ben scratched his head. "I'm not really prepared to talk money at this exact moment," he said. He could smell his own sour armpits. "I mean, I'll have to think about it. But what I'm saying is, I think maybe we can come up with something fair."

Nelson bit into his chocolate coin and chewed with infinite patience, now a man of closed-door negotiations, of proffered candies and bargaining tables, of agreements hammered out. He said, "I don't know about them nighttime hours."

Ben sighed; obviously Nelson wasn't getting the picture. Time to be a little more direct.

"Look," he said, rubbing his temple to suggest hard battles fought on Nelson's behalf. "I'm trying to do you a favor."

Nelson stopped chewing. He sensed a change.

Out with it, Ben thought. Just pretend you're in his corner and you'll be okay. "What I mean is, I got a couple of phone calls today." He looked at Nelson to see if his meaning registered, but the face was a blank. "From Jay Rattner," he said.

Nelson glanced upward.

"You want to tell me what happened?" said Ben.

Nelson shrugged. "I don't know what you talkin' about." His voice was higher than normal. He smacked an invisible insect on his head and looked angrily at his hand.

"I'll tell you then," said Ben. "I got a message saying that you were maybe a little rude to him when you made your delivery today."

Nelson's jaw dropped. "He called you up and said that? Accused *me*?" His face twisted into a scowl of righteous indignation. "Said *I* was rude? And you gonna believe *him*? Take his word over mine?"

Ben sighed: the force of Nelson's argument was too much for him. He knew that Nelson must have said something to Rattner, and in a way he couldn't blame him. Ben had dealt with Rattner firsthand; he'd seen him in his tie and white shirt, pacing the slick floor, berating the cooks and dishwashers, his nerves pressed to the surface of his skin by all the complaints he received from the members. He'd even seen Rattner scold Chef Willie in front of Willie's sweaty, grease-splattered men, their paper hats all slightly askew on their flashing heads. Rattner was a son of a bitch.

Ben said, "Okay. Just tell me what happened."

"What?"

"Just tell me what happened. What was said."

Nelson's mouth gained that sly smile, and when he shook his head it was almost pity. "Don't matter what I say, 'cause I *know* whose side you on."

"I'm on your side," Ben said, and some real passion came out in his voice, causing Nelson to squirm. "I want to keep you here, but I've got to do business at the same time. Don't you see the position this puts me in?" It was the worst thing he could have done—appeal to Nelson for sympathy. Had he been firm and forthright, he'd at least have gained some respect. Nelson was now looking at him with sheer contempt. "Can't you see?" Ben said. He was pleading now, but he couldn't help it. "I've got people threatening to stop doing business with me. I've got people talking about the Health Department, and who the hell knows what else. What am I supposed to do?"

Nelson said nothing.

Ben's undershirt was soaked. He struggled to keep his voice even. "Will you accept the position I've offered you?"

Nelson said nothing.

Ben tried again. "Will you?"

Nelson sniffed. "S'pose I say no?" he said. "Then what?"

"Then," Ben said, and he felt the words rise in his throat like a meal he could no longer keep down, "I think . . ." His throat seemed to close up. "I think I'll have to"—He pulled words from the air—"make a decision." Fearing the sound of that, he added, "But this is stupid. I told you, I want to keep you. It's just that—" He felt all his resolve drain out of him, felt the almost pleasurable gush of failure. "Look," he said. "How about we forget this whole conversation. I'll talk to Rattner. Maybe the three of us can sit down and talk it over."

"Keep me?" Nelson muttered. He was looking at his hands. "What you mean, *keep* me."

Ben had a flash vision of Mickey relaxing in a hotel room. Strolling a park.

His hands turned to fists under the desk. "Then it's your choice," he said.

Nelson laughed, shook his head.

Ben's neck felt hot, tight. He thought he might choke.

Nelson dropped the laugh. "I want to talk with your father," he said. He nodded at the phone. "That's what I want."

It would have been easy, at that moment, to lay all of it at Mickey's doorstep, but Nelson's appeal struck a nerve. "My father has nothing to do with this," Ben said, and some of Nelson's righteousness found its way into his own voice. "Okay? I'm in charge here. This is *my* business." No, he couldn't call Mickey: something larger was at stake. "I'm running things here," he said. He felt as though he had just committed Mickey to an overseas death. "This is my show. Understand? Mine. So if you want to stick around, you'll do things my way. I don't give a shit about what's fair. Nothing's fair. You can do what you want." He was shaking. "Do we understand each other?"

Incredibly, Nelson seemed unnerved by Ben's passion. In a voice laden with defeat he said, "So you tellin' me I'm fired."

The word was too awful, too charged with consequences: Ben refused to recognize it. "You bake, you stay," he said, determined to leave it in Nelson's hands. "You don't, you walk." He shrugged to express the absurd but undeniable fact of his own power.

"So," Nelson said. "You givin' me the option to quit."

"Or to stay. However you want."

"Why don't you just say it?"

"I've said what I had to say."

"Go ahead, Crumb."

Ben hooked a finger around the handle of the desk drawer. He said, "Do you stay or not?"

As Nelson raised his hands, Ben's finger tightened on the handle. Nelson appeared as he had on that night of the eggs, hands above his head as he stepped out of the van: hands renouncing everything, hands clean of sin. "You the boss," he said.

Ben ground his teeth, and in a sudden burst of anger in which he saw his parents' faces rise up from the depths and distances in which they'd placed themselves, he blurted it out: "You're fired. Okay? You're goddamned fired!"

There was a silence. Ben's finger was white and bloodless on the drawer handle.

Nelson grinned, shook his head. "Breadcrumb." He tossed the bag of chocolates onto the desk and stood up.

Ben couldn't speak.

Nelson went to the door, and as he placed his hand on the knob he turned. "Watch your back, Little Man," he said, and then he was gone.

Ben was numb. What had happened? What had he done?

Hands fumbling, he opened the bottom drawer and retrieved the strongbox, which held over three hundred dollars in cash. He took all of it and went to the front, where, through the window, he could see Nelson walking across the lot in a slow, proud, wounded way, almost limping.

"What happened?" said Morris. He was at the far end of the counter, gripping the broom handle as though it were the one sturdy thing in the world.

Ben ignored him. He stood there and pictured himself running after Nelson and handing him the money, insisting he take all of it. But somehow he knew, standing there, watching Nelson, that maybe it wasn't the best idea.

19

The chill passed with the recollection of how he had gotten there (had it really been three weeks?), and Mickey, his eyes burning from the brightness of the fire, grabbed the long wooden peel, shoveled in another naked ball of dough and closed the chamber door. Three weeks, he knew, because he'd been paid three times, despite his insistence that he didn't need the money (*"Merci,"* he'd said, "but really, it isn't necessary"), which Dulac seemed to take as the patronizing refusal of a wealthy industrialist who perhaps pitied him his little shop, insisting for his own part that it was a point of honor to pay a man a wage for services rendered, even if that man were the billionaire sheik of Araby. So Mickey took the money—it was so extravagantly useless in his hands, this silken stuff, the bills like the leaves of some mighty fallen argument for living—and kept it, for lack of any other ideas, under his mattress upstairs. If nothing else, it was a way to keep track of the days, which ought by now to be lurching toward Christmas, though Mickey could not say for sure how many, no more than he could describe the sights and sounds out in the streets, whose shop windows must now be decked with garlands, pinecones, red and gold tinsel, the occasional string of lights. It was a dark, solitary existence indeed, a daily communion with fire and water, with grain, a life of monastic ritual whose laws of habit, of repetition, had given him a strange unthinking satisfaction. All thoughts, all passion, had been forwarded to his hands, so that, watching them work, he felt relieved of emotion, the hands now the carriers of his burden, the twin writhing animals of his soul. In the pure act of doing, of making, he had entered a state from which he had no desire to emerge.

Only once did he break the spell, having gone out to buy some food—apples, olives, dates, a big bag of nuts—that he kept in his sparsely furnished room ("The room is good?" Dulac had said, turning on the light, and yes, it was good), though mostly he subsisted on bread and water. After marketing, he stopped in a tobacco shop and purchased a phone card, then went to a phone booth and called the answering machine at the bakery, on which he left a number where he could be reached (in his room there was a telephone that tended to explode at ungodly hours, Dulac bright and alert on the other line, making sure Mickey was up and ready to go to work), adding that overseas calls were expensive and not to call him there unless it was an absolute emergency. In making contact, he had put at stake his very solitude, the splendid anonymity for which he'd traded his life. To be without name or country, to exist solely through his work; this was a fragile mode, one that, now threatened by a call from home, seemed even more precious, and that he sought to further imperil (it seemed necessary, somehow, to hold a knife to the throat of that which he valued most—a way of earning it, he felt); and so he searched his wallet for Detective Flemke's number and called him too, leaving a message similar to the one he'd left Ben, telling Flemke to call him only in the event of an extraordinary development.

So far, though, he had not heard from either party; the threat to his seclusion seemed to have passed.

He scooped out another blob of dough from the mixer and slapped it on the table. In the silence he could hear the faint snap of the fire.

Outside, the night sky was beginning to change. Mickey thought of it as a kind of reverse ripening, the dark fading to light; or better, a heavenly fermentation, a rising of the celestial batter. Whenever he saw the first hint of light at the bottom of the stone stairs—it was like a human presence—he stopped what he was doing and rushed up them so that he could watch this hopeful sight from the bakery window: the arrival of another day, the gradual emergence of color, the soft conversion of things that made him feel, if but for a moment, the imperceptible rotation of the planet. Often he studied his reflection in the window: his bare chest and belly dusted with flour and spores of yeast and riveted with sweat, forming vertical stripes that reminded him of a prisoner's linen.

He would skip today's sunrise, however; there was too much work to be done. He wiped the sweat off his chin and looked at the tall pyramid—taller than himself—of cloth-lined wicker baskets by the wall farthest from the oven, where the air was a few critical degrees cooler, allowing the dough inside the baskets to ferment more slowly. Still, the room was hot as blazes, and Mickey, as he often did, stripped down to his boxers and sprinkled himself with water.

Dulac trusted him outright; he'd been impressed by how quickly Mickey learned the basics, and was obviously comfortable enough with the situation to leave Mickey alone, and though he never really commended Mickey on a job well done, he had yet to complain either, which for Dulac was the same as the highest praise. It barely occurred to Mickey that the breads he baked were being purchased, eaten, carried home through Paris streets; he had very little contact with the goings-on upstairs, and when he did think of his bread being wrapped up by Dulac and carried off in the arms of strangers, his heart filled with a strange joy that he quickly, guiltily suppressed. This was meant, he cautioned himself, to be a life of sacrifice. He did not want any distractions.

He listened to the fire. Next to the oven lay a pile of timber—hickory, cherry, apple, a mélange of delicious fresh-cut hardwood that Dulac imported weekly, wood whose sinewy meat Dulac felt imbued the fire with the perfect character, just as the wooden staves of a cask will bend the note of a wine. Each morning Mickey loaded the wood into the oven and fired it as Dulac had taught him, with a little kindling and a single match, and each time he felt himself verging on an awful vision, as of some historical nightmare—a madman raging in a charnel house of war, heaving the bones of the slaughtered into the furnace.

Sometimes he would keep the chamber door open and gaze in at the terrible force he had unleashed. It seemed odd, even heretical, that fire could be tamed, that it could be used for the good; he'd only ever known the destructiveness of it.

20

Watch your back, Little Man. Ben couldn't get the words out of his head. Oh, Nelson was out there; of that he was sure. He knew, could feel it. Nelson in the backyard, waiting. Or else out in the front, crouched in the azaleas. Ben pulled the blankets over his head. It was two in the morning. Should he call the cops? Explain what had happened?

The mere suggestion of police involvement seemed to push his fears to the brink of realization; he dared not pick up the phone.

He placed his hand under the pillow and gripped the gun, which he'd have to take with him everywhere now. Watch your back meant watch your back. He wasn't about to take any chances.

He was trapped. How could he go outside? How could he go to the bakery? What was to stop Nelson from showing up here, there or anywhere?

And yet underneath his terror Ben could feel a relief, could already see the benefits from a business standpoint. Nelson—no sense denying it—had become a liability. Things would run much more smoothly without him. Ben comforted himself with the thought that Nelson had *wanted* to be fired. Didn't it make sense? He'd never really been happy at Lerner's. Maybe, now, he was even grateful. Wasn't it just possible?

Ben decided to walk to the bakery around four or five o'clock (the coast would be clear by then, he thought), and load the van with whatever he needed for the day's deliveries, using some of yesterday's bread if enough fresh stuff had yet to be baked. Then he would drive to a secret, far-off spot where Nelson would never go, maybe sleep in the van for a couple of hours before calling Shirley Finkle to ask her if she would give Morris a hand behind the counter (on several occasions she'd offered to help out, and though he'd refused her each time, Ben knew she'd be thrilled to finally get the nod). Then he'd make his deliveries; and by afternoon, with any luck, he'd have thought of something else, a further strategy to elude Nelson.

The initial plan went off smoothly. He arrived at the bakery at five and gave each of his men a warm pat on the back, hoping vaguely to elicit their loyalties in the event of a showdown on the bakery floor, though he didn't really expect that Nelson would be rash enough to try anything there, not with so many potential witnesses around. Still, it made him feel better to imagine that the bakers were behind him. He collected what he needed for deliveries and drove out twenty or more miles, out into the county's vanishing farmland.

He parked on the side of a back road and watched the sun rise through bare black trees. The air outside was sharp and cold and full of earth, the sky soft with the first lavender light. On the other side of the road he could make out a long, white wooden fence, a hill of pasture, a farmhouse, a barn. Something in this landscape filled him with longing. He knew that the eggs and grains that were delivered to the bakery came from factory farms that in no way resembled this one, but for some reason he felt a need to make the connection; it was the same feeling he'd had at the shore, when they'd gone to scatter Emi's ashes—that desire to immerse himself in the eternal: the sea, the sky: a yearning to be both fathered and mothered, protected, to be held close to a beating heart.

He shut his eyes, and as the morning grew and the grass and fence posts gained a roseate light, Ben felt himself become enclosed, if only for a moment, in the immense pink paws of the world. When he opened his eyes he saw that the light had spread bluish white, like the milk of the cows that were now standing motionless in the pasture. He wished he wasn't alone. He wished his father would come back.

He drove toward town and stopped at a phone booth. Shirley Finkle, as he expected, was ready for action, claiming she knew the bakery like the back of her hand, that she could work the counter with her eyes closed.

At around noon he headed over to Seven Pines, wondering, not too seriously, if Nelson were somewhere on the grounds, waiting in ambush.

He parked the van by the service entrance, suddenly nervous about speaking to Jay Rattner, who, as Ben entered, could be seen raging through a fog of steam and smoke, men in white paper hats chopping and dicing twice as quickly in his wake. Rattner: alive and well and unaffected; business as usual.

Rattner: twenty-six, gourd-nosed, balding in mysterious patterns, his big keg-wrestling body gone soft and pear-shaped in the confines of what Ben imagined to be a lonely apartment decorated with mementos of fraternity pranks and famous beer blowouts. There would be posters, framed beach photos (Rattner tanned, fit, tennis-handsome, but with the first beery signs gathering ominously at his drawstrings), rented video tapes on the coffee table, maybe an aquarium. A hairy bathroom smelling of a strong, male-animal piss, a shipwreck of dishes in the kitchen sink.

Rattner, Ben knew, began working at Seven Pines as a busboy ten years ago. He stayed on as a waiter all through college, where he studied something like hotel management; a prodigy of sorts, he was offered the lucrative position of banquet manager upon graduating. Money, power, responsibility, prestige. That was Seven Pines. But now he looked miserable, beleaguered, a petty administrator in a rumpled shirt and tie, a colonial magistrate among savages. The kitchen staff, if they weren't humorless, would be capable of enjoying him, especially upon those rare occasions when he tried to prove himself a man of the people, loosening his tie to talk sports and women with the fellas, peppering his speech with street terms that came off like bad dance moves. No: Rattner would be loved by no one, not by the hundreds of club members who paid him to make their affairs and luncheons flawless, nor by the men who toiled in the steam and slosh of the kitchen and bore the brunt of his frustration.

From across the kitchen Rattner spotted Ben and headed toward him, a look of anxiety and anger in his close-set eyes.

"Did you get my message yesterday?" he said.

"Yes," said Ben. "What happened?"

"What happened?" Rattner laughed like a child imitating a machine gun. "Your delivery man told me he was going to blow my fucking brains out, that's what happened."

Ben shivered under his coat. Had Nelson really gone that far? Ben steeled himself: Let it be Rattner, he thought. Rattner instead of me. He said, "What did you do to tick him off?"

"Ha!" Rattner seemed outraged by the question. He grabbed the pen and clipboard from Ben's hand and signed his name violently on the delivery memo. "What did I do to tick him off? He's a fucking psychopath! He threatened my life, for Christ's sake. I'd call the police if I thought it would do any good." He shoved the clipboard and pen into Ben's chest. "Are you defending him or what?"

Ben looked down at the signature. The paper was ripped.

"Huh, Lerner? Because I don't need this bullshit. Okay? This has been going on for months. Months! I told your father about it, but I guess he didn't think it was that important. And now you. Like father, like son. It's no wonder he left you in charge. The man obviously doesn't care about his business. It's all a fucking joke!"

Ben took a breath; in the wind of Rattner's bluster he felt a sudden homicidal bond with Nelson, a bond intensified by the regrettable fact of their breach. He squared his shoulders and said, with a faint note of accusation, "Nelson doesn't work for me anymore." Just hearing the words brought the emotions to his throat.

Rattner blinked. "You mean—you fired him?"

"Yes," said Ben. He had to struggle to say nothing else.

Rattner stood there for a moment, then hit himself in the forehead. "Great. That's just fucking great!" He looked up at the ceiling, laughed, then, taking tiny steps, made a little circle, repeatedly striking his head.

Ben watched him, fascinated by his terror. It hadn't occurred to him that by firing Nelson he would bring others into his own sphere of danger. He had expected Rattner to cheer. He said, "I thought you'd be happy."

"Happy?" said Rattner. "Happy? Now he'll *really* want to get me!"

"Don't worry," said Ben, more to himself. For a moment he considered what it would mean to enter into some sort of alliance with Rattner. He tried to think of a way to open that discussion, knowing Rattner might already be suspicious of him. Carefully he said, "I don't think Nelson's very happy with me either," but it came out sounding too much like an appeal, and he quickly placed his hands behind his back, as if to withdraw the offer before it could be rejected. Then, as he watched Rattner process his words, he feared just the opposite response—feared a quaking Rattner latching onto him, bumbling, panicking, then betraying him at a critical moment.

A crooked smile formed on Rattner's lips. "He's not happy with you either?" he said, lifting the box of bread. *"Good."*

Fear shot up Ben's spine. Rattner was now backing away.

"Maybe," Rattner called, "he'll get you instead."

Ben completed the rest of his deliveries in a daze. As he drove back to the bakery, he kept seeing black male figures that may or may not have been Nelson—at bus stops, walking across parking lots, in the backseats of cars. The closer he got to the bakery the more the van seemed to stand out, so that by the time he reached the lot he felt as though he were inside a parade float. He had to remind himself that it was broad daylight, that there were people around. He walked slowly from the van to the bakery doors, hand on the gun in his pocket. Danger seemed to demand slowness: he may have been walking past a phalanx of growling dogs. Upon reaching the door he resisted the temptation to rush in; instead, he paused, his back to the lot. He counted silently to ten, rushing the last few numbers. Then he opened the door.

Shirley and Morris looked up at him. There was one customer at the counter, a black woman in a purple dress and a camel-colored coat. She turned to him.

Ben's hand froze in his pocket. It was Donna Childs.

Dulac had informed him that it was the day before Christmas, but this meant little to Mickey, other than that the shop would be closed tomorrow. For now, he was eager to get on with the business of baking his last batch before the holiday. Most of baking, he'd learned, was in the waiting, but as a baker (and he supposed now he *was* a baker, God knew he'd baked enough bread for an army in the past few weeks), the broad intervals of time no longer taunted and tortured him, as they had years ago, when he'd tried to bake at the house. Waiting was now part of what he did. The sculptor, Mickey considered, did not sit in anguish while his clay baked in the oven; he dreamed about his next piece. Mickey found himself thinking of ways to improve his next batch, small experiments he might perform with time and temperature and measurements. Sometimes he would take up the razor blade and create new patterns with which to score the bread by tracing them in the air: cat's whiskers, stars, diamonds, suns.

Baking had taught him another thing: how to give up control. He thought of this each time he surrendered a raw lump of dough to the hearth: the bread belonged to the fire now. Only a small percentage of bread-making occurred in the oven, he reminded himself, and so it seemed to him that he was in fact more a maker than a baker, though of course Dulac would argue that he was now many things: botanist, chemist, philosopher, artist.

Mickey fired the oven and stripped down to his undershorts. The flour-dusted stones were cool under his bare feet. He wrestled a gobbet of dough to the table and began massaging it, using Dulac's technique. The first few times he'd done this he'd thought of Glazer's training table, the working of muscles, but lately he was getting other ideas. This could be woman. Thighs, buttocks. Deep, soulful flesh. He pressed and kneaded, using his hips. The hour was buried in darkness. He rolled the flesh, parted it, folded it over, pressed it into itself. It tensed, relaxed, grew fragrant with its pleasure. It stretched, gaining glutinous, sinewy muscle, then contracted into a shuddering, swollen mound.

When he cut the dough into pieces and gave it over to the fire, it was very nearly a human sacrifice.

Slowly, the room filled with the smell of baked bread.

Mickey licked splotches of flour from his arms. He paced the floor, his skin getting warm. He sucked in his stomach, rolled his shoulders, held his fists to his temples and threw some soft jabs at a phantom opponent. He could taste yeast in his gums.

The hour subsided: darkness wearied under the weight of a new light. Mickey could feel it.

He slid in the peel, removed the brown loaves from the oven and deposited them on the rack to cool. Heat bathed him, but he felt a sudden, bracing bodily chill; looking down, he saw that his prick had escaped from the vent of his shorts and was now swaying to and fro, like some instrument for measuring spiritual presence.

Mickey was shocked: he'd forgotten how big the thing could get. He couldn't remember the last time it had been so hard. It looked electric. His gripped it in his hand to keep it from moving. His palm was warm.

Without thinking he grabbed one of the loaves and tore off a small chunk. Steam rambled out. He placed his hands around the hips of the bread and held it in front of him. His legs trembled.

He entered slowly. The heat inside made him shiver. Walls of wheat collapsed, ripped. Guiding the brown hips, he eased further in, until he could feel the hard crust against his belly.

He closed his eyes and threw back his head. He thrust and squeezed, causing scales of crust to flake off and fall to the stones.

Donna, he thought. He could see her.

His fingers had dug through the cracked skin. His arms bulged. Pungent yeasty smells rose up and spread throughout the room.

He backed his lover against the wall and pummeled. Crumbs spilled. He arched his back, and with a silent gasp felt himself dissolve.

Why was she here? What did she want? Ben hadn't seen her since before his mother's death, and if he had ever longed for her during those rough few days afterwards, he felt himself shrink back at the sight of her now, though in fact he was moving forward, smiling. "Miss Donna," he said in a voice to match the smile, and his hand shot out in front of him in a burlesque of corporate surprise: she may have been a client.

Her gloved hand communicated nothing. Ben kept up his smile, hoping it would sway her agenda, which he did not suppose friendly. "May I talk to you?" she said.

Ben swallowed: it was as if a high school principal had showed up in his home. Morris and Shirley looked on with glum expressions.

"Sure," said Ben. "Come with me." He led her to the back, aware that Morris and Shirley were following him with their eyes. There was no doubt who was in charge here. Ben cursed both his uncle and his neighbor, and grasped at the thought that in Donna's presence no real harm could come to him.

Once in the office, Donna pulled off her black gloves by the fingers. "He doesn't know I'm here," she said. She wore red nail polish and matching lipstick. She said, "I came by myself." Her rose-scented perfume was heavy with suggestions of rendezvous. Ben felt a lover's dread: what if Nelson came in? He looked at Donna—the perfume, the glossy lipstick, the removal of her gloves—and threw his trust into her experience. He asked her to have a seat, then shuddered as she delicately lowered herself into the same chair from which Nelson had taken his dismissal. She held her handbag on her lap.

Ben sat behind his desk, hoping to regain something of the authority that her scent seemed intent on denying him. "Well," he said, fingering a pen. He tapped it on the desktop. "What can I do for you?"

Donna sighed. "I know you must be busy," she said, "and I don't want to take too much of your time."

"Not at all," said Ben. Her reverence gratified him, eased him into a sense of paternal command: the desk now seemed a broad extension of his own belly, a war chest filled with benevolent holiday promise. He rested his hands on the surface of it.

Donna looked down at her handbag. "Nelson told me a month ago that your father went away on a trip," she said, "and that the very next day you gave him a promotion."

Promotion. Ben was moved by this reminder of Nelson's gratitude. "Yes," he said.

Donna continued as though reciting a prepared speech. "I know that he's been very excited about it. But yesterday he came home early. I knew he was upset. I asked him what happened, but he wouldn't say a word—just changed his clothes and went out the door. He didn't come home last night, and I haven't seen him today."

Ben nodded, suppressing the mean little hope that Nelson had run away, or else—terrible!—that something bad had happened to him. But Donna didn't seem *that* concerned; Ben got the idea that maybe this wasn't the first time Nelson had pulled this sort of thing, and that Donna, worried as she might be, was making a supreme effort to hold herself together.

"I was hoping," said Donna, "that you could tell me what happened."

Ben cleared his throat. What could he possibly say? How could he tell her that he fired her son? "I think," he said, "that he just decided it was time to move on." And wasn't this true, in a way? Hadn't he given Nelson a choice?

"Move on?" said Donna.

"Do something else, I guess," Ben said, displaying his palms to illustrate the limits of his office, thinking too that if the conversation ever got back to Nelson, it would appear that Ben was acting on his behalf. "It was his decision." But the moment he said this, he realized it might look as though he were protecting *himself*, lying to Donna to save himself from charges of unfairness. There could be, in Nelson's eyes, no worse offense.

"Are you sure he didn't do something?" said Donna. "Get himself into trouble?"

Ben hesitated: was she offering him a way out, he wondered; was she prepared to disbelieve Nelson and side with *him*? Ben cautioned himself to be careful; maybe Donna knew more than she was letting on.

"Now I know you two are friends," Donna said, "but I want you to tell me honest. He got himself fired, didn't he."

Ben scratched his head, feigning dilemma.

"Tell me what he did," said Donna.

Ben knew he would have to come clean—Donna was watching him closely—but he refused to concede any wrongdoing. "Nelson didn't see eye to eye with some people," he said, fighting to keep an even voice, "and when I offered him a different position where he wouldn't have to come into contact with them, he decided he'd rather not work here."

Donna nodded. "I think I see now."

Ben looked down at the desktop. What did she think she saw?

"Let me ask you one thing," said Donna. "Does your father know about this?"

"Yes," Ben said, without hesitation, wanting her to think that the decision was sanctioned from above while still retaining for himself some semblance of rule. "We discussed it."

"He must have done something awful bad," said Donna. "Nelson, I mean."

Ben glanced up at her: she was looking at him with pleading eyes. Yes, Ben thought: she is my ally. He felt he could tell her everything—about the tension between him and Nelson that was like a heat in the room, about Nelson's resentment of his power and his own efforts at diplomacy; the business with the Orthodox customer, the threat against Rattner; everything. But he wouldn't; he wouldn't have to. He could tell it all simply by downplaying the situation, by appearing to protect Nelson. "No," he said. "It wasn't Nelson's fault." He shook his head, sighed. "It was a combination of things."

"That's okay," said Donna. "I don't mean to put you in this position. I know you're his friend."

"I wanted him to stay, I really did—"

"I know you don't want to talk bad about my child," said Donna. "I just wanted to make sure I was right."

"But he really didn't do anything bad."

"Please," said Donna. "Don't think I don't know my own boy. I

know he can get an attitude about things. Sometimes he just doesn't
know how to act. Even when he was little, he gave me fits. He was always thinking people were against him. Teachers, classmates. Thought
I was against him." It seemed to Ben that Donna was pleading with
him as though he were her equal, someone she could confide in, trust.
"It's those troublemakers he hangs around with, the ones from high
school. That's the problem. Bad influences. They make him think he
has to act a certain way."

Ben nodded in understanding.

"That's why I was so happy when he started bringing you around."
She dug into her handbag. "I'm sorry if he's caused any trouble." She
came up with a small package wrapped in red paper.

Ben's throat went dry.

Donna fondled the package. "I know it can't have been much of a
Christmas this year," she said, her rueful tone encompassing the hard-
ships of both families, "but we all have to be strong. I know you will."
She placed the package on the desk and looked down at it.

Ben took the gift in his hands. "You didn't have to do this," he said.
He could feel her watching him as he opened the paper with tender,
almost sepulchral care, and his heart heaved as he pulled from the nest
of paper a pair of blue nylon gloves. "Thanks," he said. "I really needed
these."

Donna looked worried. "You're sure they're okay?"

"They're perfect," said Ben. "I lost my other pair just last week."
That was true. "Thanks." He set the gloves down on his desk, and was
startled at the sight of them: they were like two hands. Looking up, he
saw that Donna still wore a faint expression of uncertainty.

Ben then realized what this was all about: she was waiting for him
to offer to take Nelson back. She'd humbled herself, apologized, accepted the blame on Nelson's behalf. She'd given a gift.

Ben wanted to be angry—this was bribery, after all—but he felt too
sorry for her. She'd put herself on the line, and deserved at least some
kind of hope, even false hope. Ben dared to give it to her. "You know,"
he began, and something in his tone caused her to clasp her hands
tightly over her bag, "maybe when my father comes back we can all
work something out. I mean, if Nelson would be interested." It was a
risky proposition: he was buying time, buying off Nelson's vengeance,
but only for a while. He could never bring himself to submit the matter to Mickey, who'd trusted him to do a good job and not to mishan-
dle things.

Donna seemed to be considering the offer with caution; Ben supposed that she didn't want to appear too eager. Then she shook her head and said "No."

Ben looked at her. Did she mean it? Or did she expect him to insist?

"What's done is done," she said. "Maybe it's better if we all try to put this behind us."

Ben was astonished: it seemed that Donna was genuinely determined to block access to Nelson. Was it pride? Ben's heart sank. How could he ever appease Nelson without Donna's help? What could he do to sway her?

He opened the desk drawer and pulled out Nelson's last paycheck, which he'd kept for fear that mailing it might seem too coldly bureaucratic, a final insult. But more than that: it was the last card in his hand, the last shred of anything that could give him a sense of being in control. That Nelson had yet to come in to pick it up was a doomful sign to be sure, but to surrender it to the vast uncertain universe of the mails seemed infinitely worse.

"Here," Ben said, placing the envelope on the desk. "Before I forget. Nelson's pay."

Donna stared at the envelope.

"I was going to mail it today," Ben said, "along with his Christmas bonus, but since you're here . . ." He dug into the strongbox and pulled out a roll of twenty-dollar bills. This was rainy day money, on hand for emergencies or impulses. Counting it on some evenings, he'd had visions: a new sign for the front window, or a surveillance system from which he could monitor the goings-on in the front while he tapped at his computer. Now, like one calmly administering a painful injection in one's own arm, he counted out two hundred dollars, placed the money in another envelope and set it next to the paycheck. "I know it's not very much," he said, his Adam's apple rising. "But I hope it'll come in handy."

Donna pursed her lips. She held back emotion like a sneeze, letting it detonate silently inside her. Her gloved hand went out and collected the envelopes, but she could not round out the smoothness of the act; the moment was too charged with her need, and in a flash she stuffed the money into her bag, the hand now fumbling spasmodically among tissues and cosmetics. "Thank you very much," she said. "Thank you very, very much."

Ben said, "You'll make sure he gets it?"

"Yes," she said. She was all nervous movement now. She checked her watch, closed her bag. "Thank you very much."

Ben felt a sudden agitation, an emptiness. Something had fallen away from him.

Donna stood up. Ben stood too, but his tongue wouldn't work; all his words seemed woven in the money that Donna had taken.

"Please," he managed to say. "Make sure he gets it."

"Okay," said Donna, heading for the door as though her very next breath depended on it. "You have a Merry Christmas and a Happy New Year." She then stopped, and without looking at him, said, "And tell your father I said—hello."

"I will," said Ben. He came out from behind the desk, hoping to gain some kind of assurance—an embrace, a squeeze of the hand, something to tell him that everything would be okay, that the threat of Nelson would fade—but before he could reach for her she was out the door and gone.

Mickey was sweeping the floor when Dulac lumbered down the steps carrying two boxes of unsold bread.

"It is typical on Christmas," he said. He dropped the boxes and kicked them so that they slid one after the other into the wall. "I don't like to waste, but it is better to bake too much than not enough." He wore dark pants, a light-blue shirt and a sleeveless navy pullover. "Ça va?" His face was pink from a fresh menthol shave; he was clean, barbered, robustly three dimensional against a flat gray backdrop of stone.

"Ça va," said Mickey. "Almost finished." He held the broom in one hand and began sorting utensils on the worktable.

Dulac brushed some dust and crumbs from his pullover, in such a way that made Mickey aware of his own nakedness. "Do you have any plans?" said Dulac. "For Christmas?"

"Not in particular," said Mickey. He wondered if he might be invited to join Dulac on a train to Lyons, where the baker had an ex-wife and two grown children whom he visited on holidays.

"You mean," said Dulac, "that you will stay alone?"

Mickey shrugged. "I don't mind." He smiled.

"And what about your family?"

"They'll be fine," Mickey said. He began sweeping again.

Dulac nodded, but he looked uneasy. "And how much longer do you plan to stay?"

Mickey felt a sting of rejection. Was Dulac asking him to go? But why? Was his work not good enough? "I haven't really planned on anything," Mickey said.

"No?" said Dulac. There was frightful moral purpose in his whisker-less cheeks. He squinted. "No plans to return home?"

Mickey understood. Dulac must be wondering about his home life, his family back in the States; the son who was running the business. But what right did *he* have to judge? Wasn't he, Dulac, separated from his children too? Hadn't he left them to pursue his art?

As a man who demanded to know everything about what went into his bread, it made perfect sense that his bloodhound nose would now turn its attention on the man who was baking that bread. Dulac be-lieved that meanings traveled through the craftsman's hands, that a bread contained the soul of the baker. And what sort of soul, he seemed to be asking, was this?

Mickey looked down at the small hill of flour at his own feet. "I'll go," he said, "when you decide it's time for me to go." He took a breath and awaited the worst.

"Très bon!"

Mickey looked up. Dulac was coming toward him, smiling. He slapped Mickey's bare back and coughed in the ensuing cloud of flour. "Ah, very good!" he said. "Then you will stay. I was afraid you would leave for the holidays and never return."

Mickey's head spun in his effort to adjust to his swiftly changing fortunes. So Dulac wanted to keep him after all!

"I must go," said Dulac. "I will be gone for three days. You will watch over the shop?"

"Yes," said Mickey.

"You will be okay?"

"Yes."

"Bon. There is not much you must do. Just make sure the door is locked. We will open in three days. Yes?"

"Yes," said Mickey. *"Bon voyage."*

"Merci, et Joyeux Noël." Dulac bowed.

Mickey bowed awkwardly. "Same to you."

"Au revoir." Dulac turned and went back upstairs. Mickey was warmed by the man's good wishes, and even more by his trust. Dulac had faith in him.

Mickey cleaned the bakery meticulously, so that not a single crumb remained. By the time he was finished it was nightfall; already Dulac would be with his children, sitting down to a rich, gamy dinner.

Mickey felt the hint of an encroaching loneliness. There was no baking to be done, not for days. What else was there for him to do? How could he remain in the ecstatic rhythm of making, of giving? He felt like a man who has trained and trained for an event, and was now ready—but for what? He looked over at the boxes of bread. Strange: back home he'd think nothing of throwing out a couple of boxes, he did it all the time. But these loaves were living things. Earth the father, fire the mother; he'd arranged the marriage with his hands and then midwifed the babes through long, flaming births. Their heaven resided in the human body: humanity was their kindred element, the idea toward which all dust aspired. Mickey could not abide the thought of his bread disintegrating in a garbage heap, never to realize its high purpose. Maybe it was crazy, but he loved these loaves, and felt responsible for their fate.

He knew just what he must do.

He went to his room and put on his coat, then returned and grabbed the boxes and carried them round and round up the old stone steps and out the bakery door into the cold, moonless night.

The streets were empty, silent: the city could have been occupied again, under curfew, or else abandoned, the enemy nearing the gates. But it was only Christmas.

He walked to the boulevard, eager to find someone, anyone, to whom he could offer one of these fresh but aging loaves. Emi had once referred to France as the country that murdered God—a reference to its anticlerical revolutions, Mickey had gathered—but on this night it seemed wholly consecrated, everyone shut in with their loved ones. Mickey felt useless, very nearly absurd. His hands ached. The bread was suffering in the cold.

Mickey then got an idea. He set the boxes down and held up his hand, hoping to spot a taxi in the approaching stream of yellow lights, or that a taxi would spot him; and in the next moment, sure enough, a small gray taxicab veered from the flow of traffic and bore down on him, stopping with a screech at the curb. Mickey opened the door and shoved in the boxes, then got in himself. He pulled from his wallet the wrinkled piece of paper on which was written the address of the Hôtel Dakar and handed it to the driver, a bearded African in a tweed jacket. "S'il vous plaît," Mickey said.

It was a long drive through the city; at one point Mickey could have sworn they'd doubled back, that the driver, aware that his passenger was a foreigner, an American, was trying to cheat him, though it was possible too that the driver hadn't much more idea of where he was going than did Mickey, seeing as how the roads seemed to have been laid out by a hundred independent planners, each with their own vendetta against sense. Wide, tree-lined avenues and boulevards radiated like spokes in all directions from various central points marked by monuments and statues, the spokes connected by impossible networks of winding, narrow streets, like so many cobwebs on a wheel. Still, Mickey could not be sure of the driver's intentions (the fare was running up nicely, he noticed), and so, by way of advising the driver that he was aware, thank you very much (I might be American, he meant to say, but I'm no sucker), of a certain odd circuitousness to their route, remarked that it must be awfully confusing to drive a taxi in Paris; to which the driver replied in hobbling English that in fact these roads represented a great achievement of order: it was, he communicated (Mickey strained to follow him), the work of one man, a supreme architect of the nineteenth century whose job it was to transform a rapidly growing city plagued with inadequate roads, a crumbling sewage system and dilapidated neighborhoods into a clean and coherent place in which to live and conduct business. "He take place of poor people and destroy, make better place," the driver said. "People very rich want something nice, they don't want so much factory and things not so nice. Paris was become city of two millions, very big. There is how you call, *Révolution industrielle*. More and more peoples. This man make a project very great. He work for the rich one, but the poor one is benefit too. Everybody has better city."

Mickey was awed by the story of this architect—to think, that a single man could be responsible for so enormous, so monstrous a design!—but then his thoughts turned almost immediately to the men who actually did the work, who'd toiled and sweated and died, like the builders of St. Petersburg, swallowed by swamp. Emi had told him the story, she had been there, it was, she'd said, the most beautiful city in the world. But what of *them*, Mickey wondered; what of the makers, the builders? They were forgotten. Mickey closed his eyes for a moment, as if to communicate his blessings to all the unsung workers of the world, blessings made all the more poignant by the dawning notion that, in his own small way, he, Mickey Lerner, was architect *and* builder, a master, really, of his own destiny. He looked out the window and watched an entire history, of which he knew nothing, pass before his eyes—cathedrals, palaces, libraries, museums, all housing such historical riches, such momentous bric-à-brac, that a lesser baker might have been overwhelmed, suddenly doubtful of his vocation, the tools and ingredients of whose art were so simple and basic compared to the manifold hammers and saws and wrenches, the hewn stone and tempered steel and wood of the carpenter and the mason. He watched the light of great buildings shimmy on the river like the hips of some old and gifted whore, and recalled his impression of Nôtre Dame, which he now spotted in the distance, a golden, glowing rock: yes: the decaying beast beset by birds and tourists: a carcass. No sooner did this image come back to him than the quiet grandeur through which they were driving subsided and a kind of low and hungry swarming began: hookers, blinking lights, dark, scar-faced men standing in groups on the sidewalk, the smoke of burning lamb filling the air with the perfume of another land, another time. Now Mickey recognized the place: the elevated rails, the tattered blankets of street vendors, the steep, narrow lanes and fish-scented markets of the Africans: the Hôtel Dakar came into sight.

"Stop," Mickey said. "I'll get out here." He thanked the driver, paid him, then stacked the boxes on his lap and made his way slowly out of the cab. He kicked the door shut and stepped onto the sidewalk, where he placed the boxes side by side, less certain of his plan than he'd been just a minute before. Should he shout like a street vendor? Wait quietly for passersby? He wondered if he might be out of his mind, standing on the street in the cold, but the purity of his impulse assured him that he was right on target. All at once he felt a great surge of love: he wanted nothing more than to give of himself: that was all.

A group of blacks was approaching from up the hill. Mickey grabbed two loaves from one of the boxes and held them over his head. *"Le pain,"* he said. The voice was small, tentative; he took a breath and tried again: *"Le pain!"* The blacks—two men, a woman, a child—were upon him; he thrust out the loaves. *"Le pain!"* The blacks looked at him, looked at the bread, walked on. Mickey felt a pang of despair. The bread was dying in his reddened hands.

Two men passed across the street. *"Le pain!"* Mickey cried out at them. "Free! *Bonjour!*" He waved the loaves. The men glanced at him, walked more briskly.

An hour went by, and Mickey had yet to give away a single crust of bread. His fingers, his feet, his ears and nose; all was numbness and cramps and stinging. He stacked the boxes to keep the bottom one warm, then took off his coat and placed it over the top box. He rubbed his hands, blew into them. How could it be? How could he be left with all this bread? Did the people not trust him? Was bread foreign to their culture? Mickey could remember the days of credit-book customers, of giving away far less worthy bread than this. He sat down on the cold pavement and clasped his hands around his knees. There must be someone out here who would take the bread, he thought, someone who was hungry, who had mouths to feed at home. Mickey was embarrassed to think of the image he'd had of himself, distributing loaves to a grateful mob, and wondered if there hadn't been a self-serving motive after all, a desire to be appreciated, loved, recognized, revered as a hero of sustenance. He hoped it wasn't true—he didn't *think* it was true—but his being left ignored on the sidewalk like this seemed to argue that he was being punished for some covert sin of pride.

He felt himself falling toward a dark, numbing core; his eyes were frozen shut, or so it seemed; he could not open them, didn't want to open them. His thoughts lifted, faded away, save for one frost-covered idea: that this is what it must be like to be dead.

Some new and dangerous form of sleep had captured him; Mickey felt nothing. The boxes towered above his hunched, shivering frame, a leaning temple at whose foot he appeared to be praying.

21

"**Y**o Little Man," said Hawk, eyeing Nelson in the rearview, "what takin' this white boy so long? You said he gonna come out by ten o'clock."

"He'll be here," said Nelson, staring at the deep creases on the back of the head of Chuckie Banks, whose steadfast silence—to say nothing of the liquor they'd drunk, or the cold Christmas air seeping through the windows of Chuckie's car—gave Nelson the shakes, and made him wonder, for what seemed like the hundredth time that night, just what, exactly, he'd gotten himself into.

From the moment he pulled open the door of the Lerner Bakery and went limping blind and dazed across the lot to the bus stop (*fired*: it seemed to him the lowest, cruelest, most grievous word in the language), breathless, gasping, his heart beating with such alarming rapidity that he thought he might, as a crowning humiliation, collapse and die right there on the asphalt in full view of the bakery windows—from the moment, really, when it became apparent that Ben Lerner meant to squeeze him out, get rid of him, he knew—yes, even then—that he would have to act; and as he climbed onto the bus and let himself drop like a stack of newspapers into the first available seat and drew his coat around him to hide the grotesque spectacle of his blue jacket and shiny black shoes, there arose one idea that might save him from buckling under this new world of disgrace and impotence and want, a world he would now have to bear, in anger, on his shoulders. One idea: revenge.

In his bewilderment, though, he'd gotten the days mixed up. He'd counted on Mama being at work, but when he walked into the house she was right there, dusting the photographs in the living room. She looked up at him with surprise, and must have seen his own stunned expression, hard as he tried to conceal it.

"What are you doing home?" she said.

"Got off early," Nelson said, his voice too rushed, too high. He tried to correct it. "Things got slow. What about you?" He assumed a casual, conversational pose in the doorway. "Shouldn't you be at work?"

"I'm off today," Mama said. Her eyes narrowed. "I'd've thought this was the busiest time of the year at the bakery. Holiday time."

Nelson was angered that she didn't seem to believe him, that she should suspect him so readily—angered, really, that she was, as usual, right. But he knew if he got defensive it would only look worse. "Things just got slow," he said, and, unable to meet her penetrating gaze, walked past her (not too quickly), trudged up the stairs as though it were any workday but bracing himself with each step for the eruption of Mama's voice below, demanding from him the "truth" (a voice that never came, which was more ominous still), went to the bathroom and took a long mournful piss during which he studied his face in the mirror and saw what Mama must have seen: a defeated, frightened young man, wounded, lost, prepared to risk everything for the recovery of his pride.

He turned away from the mirror. How could he face Mama without telling her the truth? What if she confronted him? What should he say? For that matter, what *was* the truth? Nelson felt a great pressure inside his skull. He gripped his head in his hands. *Fired.* And yet he could no sooner denounce Ben Lerner for *his* actions, for bowing to outside pressure, or even, one might conclude, for his own latent racism, than take the blame himself; Mama's fondness for Ben was, Nelson felt, still his own proudest achievement, so much so that he even considered, for a moment, going back to the bakery and apologizing and, if need be, begging Ben to rehire him (if he could only speak to Bread, he thought; Bread would understand), but the very thought of it—and he could see it clearly, could see himself groveling there in the office, Crumb frowning behind the desk—made him wince with disgust and burn even hotter for retribution. If Ben hadn't put him back on deliveries in the wake of that incident with the Jewish man, if Ben hadn't bowed to pressure, then that run-in with Jay Rattner ("You know how to tell time, Nelson? Three o'clock means three o'clock. Not three-ten or three-fifteen. Three o'clock: big hand on the twelve, little hand on the three. Got it?")—that fateful exchange on the back lot at Seven Pines, Nelson ten stupid minutes late with the rolls—never would have happened. He couldn't believe that Rattner had snitched on him to Ben, though admittedly he himself had possibly gone overboard in threatening to shoot Rattner, not that Rattner didn't deserve it, he did, damn right he did, especially now.

Nelson went to his room and changed into jeans and a sweatshirt and sneakers that were beginning to fall apart. He could forget about buying a new pair; could forget about buying a lot of things. He'd already spent fifty bucks on Christmas gifts for Mama and his aunt and his little cousins—the boxes were right there in his closet: silk scarves for the ladies, dolls and comic books for the kids—and then there was the hundred he'd given Phil Withers a few weeks ago for the gun. Financially he was way in the hole. So what now? Without money he was nowhere. It was as if his entire life had been taken from him.

Somebody was going to pay, he told himself as he kicked his discarded clothes into a heap by his door.

He reached under his mattress and pulled out the revolver. He'd bought it strictly for protection, but now he could feel in its solid weight other possibilities. He spun the pregnant cylinder. Could it be that another life was calling him? The gun felt *right* in his hand; like holding a ball, he was somehow connected to his potential. He wondered if Crumb ever had the same feeling, holding *his* gun. No wonder Crumb had the nerve to fire me, Nelson thought. The irony wasn't lost on him, that he'd given Ben that gun, had provided him that security.

"Nelson!" came Mama's voice.

Nelson muttered a curse.

"Nelson!"

"What!" Nelson shouted. He gripped the gun.

"I want to talk to you!"

Nelson said nothing.

"You get down here right now. Do you hear me? Nelson?"

Nelson closed his eyes, placed the gun to his head. He was perspiring, his stomach burned. If all else failed, he thought, there was always this.

"Nelson!"

He lowered the gun, then took sudden aim at the full length mirror on the back of his door. For the first time—and he'd struck such poses before in mirrors—the effect was convincing.

"Nelson!"

The phone rang: Nelson froze. What if it was Crumb? But there was nothing he could do: Mama had already picked up.

Nelson opened his door, tried to listen. This was it, he thought. Crumb calling to explain himself, complain, appeal to Mama's sympathy. Or maybe—*maybe*—he was calling to apologize, to make Nelson an offer.

"Hello?" Mama said. "Hello? Who is this? Hello?"

Nelson listened as Mama hung up the phone in anger. "That's the third time in a week!" she said, so that Nelson could hear. "Now who'd be calling here and hanging up like that!"

Nelson felt a tingling in his spine: Mama's tone implied that it must be Hawk, and Nelson filled with hope. A day before he would have dreaded such a call, but now it was like a godsend: Hawk was anxiously reaching out to him through the weeks of their separation, trying one last time to make contact, to recover what had been lost. Nelson felt terrible for having put Hawk off—and who else but Hawk to give him another chance, to instruct him in the meaning of loyalty!

A new world opened up in Nelson's furious mind: money, opportunity. Yes: Hawk would give him a chance. Hawk would forgive him.

Nelson put on his coat, stuffed the gun in his pocket. He had to get to Hawk. His one friend in the world.

He rushed out of his room and down the steps. Mama was waiting for him at the bottom.

"Where are you going?" she said.

"To get some food," said Nelson. He squeezed past her and reached the door.

"Nelson!"

"I'll be back," he said. He leaped off the stoop into the cold and fading afternoon, and ran toward Hawk's place down the street.

Hawk's smart-mouthed sister Stephanie answered the door. As usual, she rolled her eyes at the sight of Nelson. "Kevin!" she hollered behind her. She was fifteen, dark-skinned, still a little chunky with baby fat but, in Nelson's opinion, good to go, though of course he himself would never try anything, which was maybe why, he thought, she treated him so bad. "Kevin! Little Man at the door!" She slipped Nelson a coy smile. "So why they call you 'Little?' Is it 'cause you ain't got nothin'?"

Nelson smiled bashfully. "They just jealous," he said. "But that's between you and me."

Stephanie's eyes lit up. "Oooh!" she said, regarding Nelson as though he weren't quite real. There was cruel laughter in her eyes. "Ke-vin!" she called. "Nelson said you jealous!"

Hawk appeared in the doorway. "What up?" he said, as if they'd just seen each other yesterday.

"You been callin' my house?" said Nelson.

"Naw," said Hawk.

Nelson didn't believe him. "You got a minute?" he said.

"Nelson said you jealous, Kevin."

"No I—"

"Said his thing bigger than y'all's."

"Shut the fuck up," Hawk told his sister. "Go back to your stinky-ass room."

"This is my house too," said Stephanie. "I can stay here long as I want." She folded her arms in defiance.

Hawk tried to smack her head in a half-playful way, but she deflected it.

"You hit me," she said, "and I'll call my father."

Hawk laughed. "Your father wouldn't care if ten niggas fucked you in your fat stinky butt," he said as he stepped outside. "Why you think he never calls you?"

Stephanie looked mortified. Nelson knew that it was his own presence which had stirred Hawk's wrath toward his sister—Hawk was still hurting, he sensed—and that he himself had no other choice than to watch Stephanie suffer because of him. He wished there were something he could say in her defense, but found himself laughing uneasily with Hawk when she bit her lip and ran off to cry.

"So," said Hawk. The laughter was gone. "Figured you must've hit the big time."

"Naw," said Nelson.

"How come you ain't at work?"

Nelson shrugged. He couldn't look at Hawk's face. Hawk will enjoy this, he thought. But he had to come out with it. "They fired me, yo."

"Fired you?" Hawk seemed truly shocked. "What the fuck for?"

Nelson realized that Hawk might in fact be disappointed in him.

"They set me up," he said, with some urgency. "It was a race thing." He spat. "Racial discrimination." And wasn't it true?

"Yo," said Hawk, shaking his head. "That is *fucked* up."

Nelson was encouraged. "So, you know," he said, "if you still got somethin' goin' on, you know, some kind of money thing, I'm just puttin' the word out that I'd be interested, seein' as how I ain't got no kind of, you know, income and whatnot." He was looking straight down at his shoes. "You were right. I chose the wrong side."

"Naw," said Hawk. "You was just being true to your nature, that's all."

Nelson looked up.

"Everybody different," Hawk said. He shrugged. "You you, I'm me. Human nature."

Nelson smiled, shook his head to suggest a wise knowledge to the contrary. "People change," he said. "Sometimes, all it take is one incident." He knew Hawk was skeptical, that he believed, even needed to believe, that Nelson had too much sense to get himself mixed up. But Nelson felt he could no longer afford to live up to those expectations. "Yo: I need some real money," he said, "I got to get the fuck out my house. My mother drivin' me *crazy*." He wanted to flatter Hawk, win him over. "See, you had it all figured to begin with. I put myself in other people hands. Now I'm just—cut off." And then it hit him yet again: he'd been fired. It was sinking in slowly, in awful increments, like a stake being driven in deeper and deeper.

"Yo," said Hawk, and Nelson had a feeling, from the hint of sympathy in Hawk's voice, that he was in for a letdown. "If it was up to me, I'd let you run with us, but Chuckie want to put his homeboys in."

"In what? What is it?"

"Can't say."

Nelson waved his hands to express his infinite understanding. "That's cool," he said. "A'ight."

Hawk sighed. "A'ight, I'll tell you, but you can't say shit to *nobody*."

Nelson shrugged.

Hawk shoved his hands in his jeans pockets and bounced on his toes, fighting the cold. "Chuck know some niggas who gonna hook us up, you know, in the trade. So now we got to get a team together. Street level and upper, you know, management. But like Chuckie say, we can't be bringin' in nobody who can't be trusted."

Meaning, Nelson figured, someone who wasn't alert and savvy and honest and loyal. But Nelson desperately saw himself as all these things, thinking too that his experience behind the counter at the bakery made him especially valuable from a business standpoint. *Businessman*. Was it his imagination, or was Hawk already eyeing him as a potential manager, someone to keep the books, handle the money? Is that why Hawk had been calling him?

Nelson said, "Well. I *am* looking for a job."

"I don't know, bro. This is serious business."

Nelson looked away. On the corner, some young kids were hanging out: bulky coats, wool caps: a radio throbbed on the ground by their feet. "If you and Chuck partners," he said, "maybe you gonna need somebody neutral to cut the money, pay the bills. Keep things on the level." He paused to let the logic of his words awaken any doubts Hawk may have harbored about Chuckie Banks. "Wouldn't cost you too much, either."

Hawk laughed, shook his head. "I don't know. Chuckie think you soft, yo."

"Why—'cause I never been locked up?"

"It ain't just that. You never showed him nothin'. Chuckie always be watchin' niggas. He say you never stand up for your *own* self—that time when Rob was fuckin' with you in the car? How somebody supposed to expect you gonna stand up for *them*?"

Nelson was stunned: this verdict was too much to bear. He thought to protest, to claim that the reason he hadn't stood up to Rob was because Hawk had insisted on doing the talking for him (which was exactly what had happened), but Hawk would only turn that around somehow, make him look even worse, and in any case Nelson wasn't sure that he himself would have acted differently had Hawk *not* intervened. But why? What was it about him that made him retreat inwardly, even while armed, at the first sign of a threat? How could such a person survive? Or was that in fact the key to survival? But if word got around that you were soft, how many nights could you expect to walk home alone untouched? He thought back to the knife attack that he'd barely survived—his mistake, true, he'd walked through the wrong neighborhood, he should've known better—and how Hawk, visiting him in the hospital, had sworn revenge, and had later tried so hard to get him to go back to that area, to the very spot on the street where the knife had split him open and sent the blood streaming all over his skin: Let's go, Hawk had said, just the two of us, wait a whole damn week if we have to until one of them niggas walks by: Hawk had wanted to do the shooting himself. And wasn't it always like that? Wasn't Hawk always rushing to defend him? Always there to steal from him the chance for glory? For the first time, Nelson saw the cunning of it: Hawk could look bold and tough without having to do a damn thing, because he knew—damn right he knew, it went all the way back to when they were kids—knew, just as sure as he knew the time of day, that Nelson, fearful of the consequences—"sensible"—would refuse to go along, would talk him out of whatever violence he was bent on, which allowed him, afterwards, when he'd cooled off, to proclaim to himself, if not to the world, that he'd have done it if not for Nelson.

"I ain't soft," Nelson mumbled. His new understanding of Hawk seemed to kindle in him the very courage in which Hawk and Chuckie found him lacking. "A'ight?"

Hawk shrugged. "Sorry, Little Man," he said. He glanced back at the door. "Wish I could help you."

"I ain't soft, Hawk."

"Prob'ly didn't even say nothin' to them people who fired you."

Nelson's voice was small. "You wrong," he said.

"If that's me? I'd be takin' niggas *out*."

Nelson glared at his friend. "I bet you never took nobody out in your life," he said. His scalp tingled.

"Nigga, you crazy."

"Who, then?"

"Nigga, you don't even know me."

"I know you as good as anyone." Nelson, his blood racing, looked Hawk square in the eye, daring him to deny it, daring him, no, forcing him, to read the deeper meaning of his words, which was that Nelson knew his soul, yes, knew that he, too, was a punk, a mama's boy, and that his reputation was built on nothing but bluster and lies. "I *know* you," Nelson said, fearful that he might not bring it off, wondering if it was too late to swerve, to turn it into a joke, but no, it *was* too late, he'd committed himself, he had to go through with it, he was, he knew, lost, he had only his voice, his words, they were taking him to the heart of things, he would follow them, he would die with them. He said, "I know what you about."

Hawk looked back at him, as if searching his eyes for a sign that would tell him how to respond, then threw back his head and clapped his hands together and threw out what struck Nelson as a laugh born of terror. "Little Man," he said, but the laughter took over, cascading over his cold and shivering body like a liquid armor. Nelson was fascinated: it was as though he had thrown a stone into darkness and broke a window that he hadn't been too sure was there. Hawk's laughter—

loud and insistent enough to cause the kids on the corner to turn and
look over at them (a tacit threat, Nelson supposed: Hawk knew those
kids, they might be at his disposal)—Hawk's laughter shattered his
own myth. Nelson saw a chance to gain the upper hand.

"You wanna see somebody take somebody out?"

Hawk kept laughing. "You *know* me," he said. "What the fuck that
supposed to mean? You a faggy or what? How you wanna know me,
yo?" He clapped his hands. "Talkin' 'bout 'I *know* you' 'n' shit. I always
knew you was a faggy. Who the last girl you was with?"

Nelson ignored this. "The white boy who got me fired," he said. "Jay
Rattner. I'm gonna shoot the motherfucker." Just uttering the words
seemed to push him to the brink of the act; he pulled the gun an inch
from his pocket, gave Hawk a glimpse of the butt. "Know what I'm
sayin'?"

Hawk stopped laughing. "Boy, you crazy."

"Come with me then," said Nelson. "We'll see whassup. See who's
soft."

"Yo. You ain't got to prove yourself to me."

"It ain't about you," said Nelson. "I'm doin' it for my own situation,
a'ight? I just thought maybe you'd want to come along."

"I don't know, yo. I can't be riskin' no trouble right about now."

"It's on me," said Nelson. "You ain't in no risk."

"I don't know," said Hawk. He seemed to be thinking.

"Then you'll see," said Nelson. "Then maybe you can get me some
work."

"A'ight then," said Hawk. "Maybe I'll go with you. Maybe I'll bring
Chuck along too." He rubbed his chin. "You gonna need a car, right?"

"Don't matter," said Nelson, trying not to betray his excitement
over having gotten what amounted to an audition for Chuckie's crew.
Just like that, he had set an enormous thing in motion; he could not
entirely believe in it.

"When?" said Hawk.

"I'll call you in an hour," Nelson said. He turned his head, spat a
white pill of saliva on the pavement, shoved his hands in his pockets
and walked away, not sure whether he was more haunted or relieved
by the specter of his "good sense" hovering just over his shoulder. He
walked faster to see if he could outpace it.

"Is that him?" said Hawk.

A lone figure was striding up the gravel hill toward the employee
parking lot of Seven Pines. The lot commanded a vista of the entire

club—the rambling, hilly golf course, the dining hall, the pool, the tennis courts—and Nelson had seen the same figure emerge from the dining hall. He knew at once that it was Rattner, but something had kept him from pointing this out to Hawk and Chuckie. Now it was too late: having already identified to them Rattner's BMW (Rattner had his own marked space on the lot), it would be impossible to deny that the man about to step into that car was someone other than his quarry.

"Yeah," said Nelson, his throat dry. "That's him." They were parked several spaces away from Rattner's car, one of the few that remained on the lot, which was maybe a hundred yards from the dining hall. Nelson almost hoped that Rattner would become suspicious at the sight of Chuckie's car and retreat down the hill before Nelson could get out and accost him.

Where was his nerve? As recently as an hour ago he had been ready, urged into the rhythm of things by the music blasting out of Chuckie's new car stereo as the bottle was passed along like an idol, weaving, Nelson perceived, an invisible thread through all of them, drawing them closer to the bloody moment at hand; it was like an initiation, an echo of the fraternal ceremonies that Nelson had learned of at college: the blindfolded floggings, the ritual mutilation. But all through it, Chuckie Banks had remained silent, and Nelson began to fear that it might be some kind of setup, that Chuckie was thinking about Rattner's wallet and car, that new BMW there, yes, Nelson could see it, Hawk was in on it too, they'd let him smoke Rattner and then smoke *him* and run off with the spoils—but no, that was crazy, they wouldn't hurt him, they didn't even know how to get out of here, they'd need him, he was just trying to think up excuses for getting out of it, he was afraid, God he was afraid, he knew the spotlight was on, knew Hawk was counting on him ("You can do it," Hawk had said to him, winking), that Hawk, ever loyal, had persuaded Chuckie to come, had probably had to convince, no, *promise* him that Nelson would distinguish himself, that he would prove himself worthy of a position, that he could be trusted in matters of honor. And so Hawk, too, had a stake in this, Nelson realized; had a promoter's stake in Nelson's success. It was too awful a burden.

Christmas night, he'd told Hawk two days ago; Christmas night was the night. He knew that Rattner would be working late on Christmas, as he did on other holidays, and that he'd be coming, as he was now, up the hill, alone and defenseless in the dark. Nelson was glad for one thing, that he'd at least done his duty as a son and nephew and cousin this morning under the Christmas tree. He'd gotten a nice cotton shirt from Mama (he could barely face her: he knew the shirt was supposed to be for work) and a duffel bag from Aunt Tina, though Mama did seem strangely preoccupied, and Nelson couldn't help but wonder if she hadn't phoned Crumb over at the bakery and gotten *his* side of the story. Was she waiting for him to come out with it, then? Giving him a chance? Nelson had decided to stay quiet.

Rattner pulled out his car keys, jingled them in his hand. He didn't seem to notice Chuckie's car.

"A'ight then, Little Man," Hawk said.

Nelson swallowed hard against the sickness. Why was Chuckie so quiet? But there was no time to think: Rattner was ten yards from his car.

"Go!" said Hawk, and at the sound of his voice Nelson opened the door and watched his feet swing out and land soundlessly on the ground. The moment had seized him; there was no way out.

"Yo," Nelson said. He pulled out the gun and walked toward Rattner, who wore a long dark coat over a white shirt and black pants.

"What in the hell?" Rattner said. He stopped and raised his hands.

"Just shut the fuck up," Nelson said. He had to act fast; someone could come out of the dining hall at any moment. "Get down on the ground."

Rattner fell to his knees. "Oh God," he said.

Nelson glanced back at Chuckie's car: four eyes watched him.

"Take my wallet," Rattner said. "Take my car. I swear I won't tell anybody. Please—"

"I said, be quiet!" Nelson tried to summon his hatred for Rattner, but such thoughts were blocked both by panic and the wild hope that Hawk would rescue him—that, true to form, Hawk would intervene and do the job *for* him, prove *himself* to Chuckie. Wasn't it possible? Shouldn't he hesitate a moment longer, give Hawk the chance to leap from the car and push him aside?

"Little Man!" came a voice from the car. Chuckie's? Nelson heard the engine start: they were ready to go. All he had to do was pull the trigger and run to the car: they'd be gone in a heartbeat.

Rattner's wallet lay by his side. Nelson knelt down and with his free hand took out the cash to make it look like a straight robbery.

"Yo!" came the voice.

"Please," Rattner said, his cheek pressed against the ground. "Please don't."

Nelson placed the muzzle of the gun next to Rattner's eye. "You shouldn't have done it," he said. "Shouldn't have fucked with me. You fucked me up, Rattner. You hear me? You fucked me up!" Yes, he thought: you fucked me up: my life is nothing: I have no choice. "Fuck you, motherfucker!"

"I'm sorry," Rattner cried. "I'm sorry. I'll give you anything!"

"Little Man!"

"Fuck you!" said Nelson, his finger poised on the trigger. He averted his head and closed his eyes and squeezed.

The gun went off, and no sooner did Nelson feel the jolt go through his hand and up his arm than he heard a screech of tires. He opened his eyes: Chuckie's car was flying off the lot and down the driveway.

Nelson looked down: Rattner was motionless. The gun was still pointed in the direction it had fired: an inch above Rattner's head. The bullet had traveled into the darkness of the golf course, had burrowed somewhere in the frozen hills.

Chuckie's car was gone.

"Shit!" Nelson said. He tried to understand. For some reason he'd raised the gun an inch before firing, but Chuckie and Hawk could not have known that; they could only have assumed that Rattner had been hit—and so why did they flee? Had they seen someone coming? Nelson looked around: there was no one.

Rattner was still playing dead.

"Yo," said Nelson. "Get up."

Rattner didn't move.

"Yo. You ain't dead. Get up."

Rattner opened his eyes. "Please don't kill me," he said.

"I need a ride," Nelson told him. "Let's go to your car."

"You can take the car."

"I don't want your car. I just want a ride."

"You're going to make me drive you somewhere and shoot me."

"Yo, it's too cold out here to argue. I ain't gonna shoot you if you do what I say."

Rattner got up slowly, brushed off his clothes.

Nelson hardly knew this dangerous gangster who was walking Rattner to his car; he felt as though he were a figment of Rattner's imagination, a grisly manifestation of Rattner's opinion of him.

They got into the car, which was so loaded with state-of-the-art features that for a moment Nelson did consider, not too seriously, dumping Rattner on the side of the road and taking the thing for a spin. "How much this cost?" said Nelson, flinching as the automatic locks fired shut.

"A lot," said Rattner.

"How much?"

Rattner's Adam's apple rose, fell. "If anything happens to me," he said, "you *will* get caught. I've already told several people that you threatened me. Word travels. Some of the top judges and lawyers in the state belong to this club." He started the engine, whose low growl seemed to confirm his extravagant claims. Headlights speared the darkness. "Millionaires. They'd put so much money on your head you'd have half the city on your trail. Or maybe your buddies would turn you in. Weren't you just with some buddies? Wasn't there a car?"

"You seein' things, Rattner."

"I thought I—"

"Yo, just drop me down by Northern Parkway, and stop askin' me questions. And don't try anything—just keep your hands on the wheel. I got you covered. You hear me?"

Rattner's boldness withered; he swallowed, nodded.

"And turn up the heat in this motherfucker." Nelson slumped down in his seat. So that was it, he thought: it had been a setup after all. Hawk and Chuckie would wait for the reward to be posted for information leading to the conviction of the killer, then go to the police and say how he, Nelson, had bragged to them of the murder. That there had been no killing and would therefore be no money was of little consolation to Nelson; his best friend had sold him out.

He clutched his gut. He must be the sorriest, most pitiful human being on the face of the earth, with the possible exception of Rattner, who was now chauffeuring his would-be assassin down to Northern Parkway. But even this did not cheer Nelson; had he in fact shot Rattner and been caught and locked up, he'd be, he thought, no worse off than he was now; for what did he have? He had nothing. And Rattner—the man who started it all in the first place, the man who'd gotten him fired—would wake up tomorrow morning and get in his expensive car and go to work and at the end of the week bring home a nice fat paycheck.

Nor did he expect that Rattner's soul would be improved by this ordeal, or that he himself would be repaid for the mercy he'd shown Rattner.

He said, "If I was you, I'd start paying attention to how I treat people. Specially the brothers in the kitchen. I know you got pressures, but yo, these are human beings. Just 'cause they black don't mean they your slaves and shit."

Rattner didn't respond.

Nelson fidgeted in his seat. "See, you quiet 'cause you know I'm right." He was becoming irked at himself as well as Rattner. How could he take this self-righteous stance, when he'd just tortured the man, fired a bullet right past his head? If only he could be himself, he thought. He needed some time alone.

Not another word was spoken until they arrived at Nelson's stop. Rattner pulled over to the side of the road and closed his eyes, either awaiting a bullet or else thanking God that the episode really was coming to an end. "Thank you," he said, "for not hurting me."

Nelson detected some sarcasm there, but he knew Rattner was, at bottom, grateful. He opened the door.

"You're welcome," he said. "Now just make sure you don't go to the police. I got friends too." He stared hard at Rattner, who was gazing straight ahead. "We're even now. A'ight?"

"Yes," said Rattner.

"A'ight then." Nelson then remembered something: he reached in his pocket and pulled out the bills he'd taken from Rattner's wallet. "This belongs to you." He dropped the money on the seat between them, then got out and threw the door. He watched as Rattner made a U-turn and sped off.

What next? He was still a mile from home, and now it troubled him to think that he'd told Rattner to let him off here so that Rattner wouldn't see where he lived. As if Rattner couldn't have guessed! And what was Jay Rattner to him anyway?

He began running down Park Heights Avenue. No one was around. The sky was clear, chinked with stars. The night would only get colder.

As he got closer to his street, Nelson wondered what would happen. For sooner or later he would have to run into Hawk.

22

Mickey screamed, opened his eyes. Where was he? Was this real? Night; a street. How long had he been there? Was he really awake? He looked at his numb, bluish hands: they were still attached: they had not, he was relieved to find, been torn off him like heels of bread and—eaten? Strange dreams! He looked around: there was no one. He seemed to recall people—Africans, the people he'd seen on the street—gnawing at his body and digging, with children and dogs, through the boxes, which he saw were still there, just as he'd left them, one atop the other. Mickey cringed, gathered his strength, and with a great effort raised himself to his feet. The bread was nearly frozen. Ruined. It was not even fit for dogs.

He thought to take the boxes back to Dulac's, revive the bread somehow, but of course that was impossible. He decided to let the boxes stand there, a ragged monument to himself. Maybe the birds would come for it, the dirty-breasted pigeons that, on his first day here, had, on some inaudible cue, exploded from the many-figured gallery of a cathedral he'd passed on foot, a plague of beating gray that cast a stormy, fast-moving shadow over the cobblestones.

He walked down to the boulevard to hail a cab back to Dulac's. The need to give of himself had reduced to a dull pang in his loins; the rest of his body ached with emptiness.

It was a long ride. Light, shadow, darkness, light; the city rushed by in flickers, it beat its wings; its changes passed over his face like a story.

All he had wanted was to give, and now he felt as though he'd killed something, that in abandoning his precious bread to the cold he had violated the cardinal law of fatherhood. They were his creations, individuals of a sort, unique beings for whom he was unconditionally responsible. He had meant well, God knew he'd meant well. He wished there was something he could do, something to quench this hunger not only to give—and more than give: to make, nurture, provide—but to salvage what he'd ruined, to embrace what he had forsaken, to redeem himself and be, finally, good: if only, he thought, he could be good.

It was almost midnight when he arrived at the bakery. As soon as he walked in he noticed, on the highest shelf, a single loaf of bread that Dulac had either forgotten to toss into the boxes or else had left there on purpose for him to find and eat; in any case it struck Mickey as a miracle, a second life, and he reached out for that loaf just as he'd clutched at his suitcase that first day in Paris, when it had finally appeared on the baggage carousel, a lost part of himself returning to him, making him whole.

He took down the loaf and held it close. A strange impulse invaded him, dire and primitive, derived, it seemed, from the substance of the bread itself; it entered through his fingertips and flushed throughout his blood. Without thinking he went back outside with the loaf in his arms, and damn all the cabs and street maps that might point him out the way. He would follow his nose, yes, like an animal he would sniff and wander, and though he was lost on a darkened avenue of swirling trash and leaves, of glass-enclosed phone booths and empty shop windows, he knew, not only from the breeze but from the way the street seemed to be aiming itself, and him, toward a huge wall of blackness, that he was headed, inexorably, for water; and sure enough, he came out of the avenue as though it were a dense wood (and in fact there was a stand of trees to his left, a park of some sort, a *jardin*) and found himself looking upon a vast black clearing, through whose heart ran the great river: it was at his feet, encountering him. He looked around to get his bearings: the gold rock of Nôtre Dame was at a frightful distance—he was far behind it, on the edge of things, a speck on the rear margin of the city.

He walked out onto the nearby bridge and looked over the railing.

The chill water rushed incessantly under innumerable bridges toward
the floodlit opulence of the quai des Tuileries, whose lights it would
carry and deposit along the great stone embankments that guarded its
icy flow, before finally shaking the city off its glinting reptilian back
and winding in the shape of an improbable intestine to the Channel,
the sea.

Mickey felt the cold air blow crystals into his lungs, and watched
with a great unnameable piety as his fingers tore off a small piece from
the loaf and let it drop over the rail: it fluttered down, where the idea
of its flight was stolen by the black, glassy water: it went sailing now
in a kind of horizontal flight, aloft on the current. Mickey's chest
heaved with feeling. What was it about this act that compelled him to
repeat it? What buried knowledge or memory? What essence, what
truth?

It was as though he were heeding some ancient tribal call to the
water, some timeless urge of the species to cast off one's sins. His
hands labored, sending a riot of feathers into the night, fluffs of yellow that took to the water like ducklings. He was rending himself, bit
by bit, until he found himself rising up in a high ecstasy of contri-
tion—for what, he couldn't say—up like ashes to the speckled vault
of night.

He descended to his room, too weary and cold to undress, too exhil-
arated to sleep. He wanted to talk, to touch, wanted to test himself,
experiment with his new purity. Wasn't there someone out there with
whom he could seek some kind, any kind, of communion? Anyone?
Was he really this isolated, this estranged from the world? He sat on
the edge of the bed and stared at the telephone. Should he pick it up,
he wondered, put another call through to Donna Childs? Maybe he
would have the nerve, this time, to speak to her, though the mere
sound of her voice—"Hello?" she'd said: "Hello?"—had, when he'd
dared to push those buttons a few days ago, been comforting enough,
connecting him, if only briefly, to a hazy, dreamlike region of happiness that was itself like a distant land. Besides, he'd had nothing to say;
he barely knew the woman, truth be told, and now, as he lay back on
the bed, he regretted having made contact at all—not because it violated the terms of what was supposed to have been his penal servitude
(somehow it had ceased to be that), but because it spoiled the sanctity of what, for him, had become an almost holy seclusion, numinous,
divine. But even this existence seemed to have run its course: out on
the bridge he had come, he knew, to an end.

The fires had gone out on the hearth; the bricks were cold, the oven was at rest.

Mickey lay back on the whorl of sheets and blankets that after a month smelled deeply of his own smoky musk. The moment he closed his eyes the phone rang. Mickey bolted upright. Past experience told him it must be Dulac, calling to check on things; but as he reached for the receiver and lifted it and pressed it to an ear that still flamed crimson with cold, he was seized with a panic of unpreparedness, a blurry fear of consequences which he hadn't the time to—

"Hello?" he said.

"Is this Mr. Lerner?" An American voice.

"Yes it is."

"Sorry to disturb you, Mr. Lerner, I know it's late there. This is Pete Flemke."

"Yes," said Mickey. In an instant, the wall between his separate lives had been shattered: he gripped the receiver. "Detective."

"Yes sir. I'm calling to let you know that there's been a couple of arrests in the case."

At first, Mickey wasn't sure what Flemke meant. And then it hit him: "You mean—you caught them?" He wasn't sure how he was supposed to sound; he hardly even knew what he felt. "Who are they?"

"I'm not at liberty to disclose that right now, sir," said Flemke, sounding more coldly formal than Mickey remembered. "It's procedure, unfortunately. Anyhow, the arraignment is at eleven o'clock tomorrow, downtown. I don't expect you'll be able to make it, but if you want some quick answers, you'll find them there."

Mickey placed his hand on his forehead. The world had swept in, had flooded his room. Waves of memory came crashing down on him, receding now, pulling at his ankles, his knees. He felt himself floating among wreckage, the shards and splinters of his former life.

"Do you have any questions, sir?"

Questions? "No," said Mickey. He was dazed, adrift on the bed, clinging to the receiver, to the voice within it. "Thank you." There was silence on the line. Mickey watched as his hand returned the receiver to its cradle: it was like a quiet act of violence. No: he would not allow himself to be *drawn* back home; he would return on his own terms. And hadn't he been prepared to do just that, before Flemke's call? Hadn't he been filling with a certain anticipation, a sense of imminence? Mickey felt vaguely cheated of his initiative. He did not want to return for the sake of what was.

And yet the call had set him in motion: he swung himself to his feet and began packing his suitcase with an excitement that betrayed a suppressed desire; he was ashamed of the fervor with which he gathered his things; it seemed to argue an almost childlike relief at the prospect of return, undermining the integrity of what he'd believed, not a day before, to be his essential, his truthful existence: the solitary man, toiling with dust and fire and water. It was as though he'd been unleashed, delivered from a spell, a trance; but even as he scribbled a note for Dulac on the pad on the nightstand expressing his thanks and his regrets for having taken sudden leave, he felt the tremors of the first jittery alarms sounding in his conscience. Like one who has overslept, he froze for a moment upon the realization: he had missed something: something had suffered from his neglect.

A fresh panic overtook him. What awaited him at home? Would everything be the same? He reminded himself that no news was good news, that Benjie would have called had there been trouble. Weren't those the instructions? And wouldn't he have taken the first flight home, had Benjie needed him?

Mickey stopped: he thought he smelled smoke: but no: it was only the faint burnt trace of ashes, of scorched brick. The smell was in his nostrils, buried in his skin; he would carry it with him always.

He placed the last items in the suitcase. He would go to the airport, exchange his ticket for the next flight home and pay the difference in cash. There was no time for long good-byes, and in any case he found he was eager to remove himself from his experience precisely so that he could recollect it; already he looked forward to the savor of these memories.

The suitcase bulged with smoky woolen rags, his sweaters and shirts, the raiment of this short, strange life. It took strength to walk away from something you loved, and as one who knew what it was to have the world torn asunder in an instant, he was pleased to be able to declare this break himself, feeling, as he buttoned his coat, a sense of urgency, as if he were responding instinctively to a far-off call, marshaling himself for some great patriotic sacrifice, some grim adventure of return. His old life had reclaimed him: soon he would be swept into the hubbub of airports and clerks and rocky flight, of crying children and unwieldy bags; already he could feel in his bowels the drop in altitude, the immense waiting of the ground, the wheels touching, the wing flaps opening tense as an animal's fear. Suitcase in hand (it seemed lighter, the bag: his arms had gained muscle from so many hours of kneading), he turned off the light in the room and went to the foot of the stairs, where he looked, for the last time, at the workspace in which he had discovered consolation. It was pitch-dark, but he thought he could make out the forms of the table and, behind that, the oven, which, even at rest, had about it the faintest glow, a breathy, billowy memory of its own light.

Mickey extended his arm in the darkness, wanting to touch the vestigial glow within, the heat that he had created and suffered. His hand trembled slightly as he held it out; his fingertips disappeared into the vast black sea of shapes and came back, five pale pearls of light, the tang of yeast still fast under the nails.

23

Mickey had been to the courthouse only once, to get married; and it was on account of Emi that he came there again.

His transit had been so relentless that he'd barely had the chance to fathom not only the unsettling shift of place (it didn't seem right, somehow, that one's feet could land on both continents in the space of a day: was the world really as small as that?), but a sense which had struck him the moment he stepped off the plane in New York; a sense of a kind of national violence: the air itself was different, charged. He had arrived in a big, electric, unruly place, the pitch and pace of which tormented him with visions of chaos.

He was stopped by an armed guard at the courthouse doors. With his rumpled clothes, frosty beard and overstuffed luggage, he looked like an aging street revolutionary come to settle a score with the government. But when he identified himself as the husband of Emilie Lutter, whose case was supposed to be heard today (he dropped Flemke's name), and explained that he'd just arrived from overseas, he was respectfully admitted through the metal detector, suitcase and all. It seemed strange to him that he should be allowed to proceed, that the guard was directing him to the appropriate courtroom;

strange to be trusted not to open the bag and pull out a blunt object (a shoe?) and lunge at the suspects. Did he not look the part of the vengeful husband?

No one seemed to notice him as he approached the door. He loitered for a moment, trying to listen to the chatter of the reporters as they spoke in low tones into tape recorders and microphones. He heard the name of his wife (as ever, she had become the property of others, a name for the papers), but could make out little else; he strained to listen, amazed by his own calm, yet fearful that it might not hold, that the very sight of the suspects would send him leaping headlong with outstretched, murderous hands. But in the next moment there came a commotion: the group made a stampede toward the door, causing Mickey to back out of the way. What was happening? The door opened, and Mickey, fighting for position, could see, through the small crush of reporters and flashing cameras, a short procession of court officers, followed by a young, haughty-looking black boy—he couldn't have been more than fifteen—dressed in an orange jailhouse jumpsuit, hands bound in steel in front of him. Behind him, another black boy appeared, also in a jumpsuit, his head down, followed by what must have been his court-appointed lawyer, a young bespectacled white man with a sandy mustache, whose dark, inexpensive suit reflected the dim drudgery of a career on the brink of uncertain change. That explained why Flemke had been mum, Mickey thought; the suspects were under age and therefore protected by idiotic laws. He followed the surging crowd, trying to get a look at the culprits, to catch the eye of one or the other (the gunman must be the first one, Mickey thought; the second, more subdued, probably had a plea bargain in the works), though certainly there would be time for that, plenty of time for penetrating looks and sizings up, there was a whole trial ahead, assuming these boys had pleaded innocent.

As the crowd moved toward the elevators, Mickey had an urge to identify himself to the reporters, draw their attention, then punish them by refusing comment. *He* had more of a right to those boys than did any newsman, he felt; but he kept his distance. The absurd youthfulness of the suspects seemed to mock his anger, shame it. What could he do? What could he say? He was then struck by a sudden image of them as bastard angels sent to perform an act of mercy on a dying woman—an image he quickly dismissed, though he was still gripped with a need to touch them, to lay his hands on them, not so much to beat their hard young faces to a pulp as to fix them in his sight, to hold them and demand from them with his eyes an explanation, demand their very souls, urge the very life-light of them to the surface for a single devout reckoning.

Yet somehow this desire went beyond vengeance, went beyond even the boys themselves; but before Mickey could make a further inquiry (for there *was* something, he felt; something he must get at), the elevator car opened and the two suspects were swallowed, along with the attorney and two officers, by the closing doors. The reporters gathered in front of the neighboring elevator, into which they threw themselves the instant the doors opened up, and Mickey, responding to their excitement, had no sooner thrust his arm out to repel the closing doors and join them in their pursuit than he heard his name being called behind him. He turned to see Flemke—a big Saint Bernard of a man with sagging, fleshy jowls and enormous hands—detach himself from a group of tough-looking red-nosed men and stride hugely toward him.

"Looks like you're a minute late," Flemke said, seeming to note, in his detective's manner, Mickey's suitcase, his growth of beard. Mickey felt he was being examined, but for what? He shook Flemke's hand firmly. "You just get off the plane?" Flemke said.

"My feet've barely touched the ground," said Mickey.

Flemke laughed with what Mickey thought was a kind of local reverence for a cosmopolite; a laugh—nervous, polite, a little too hearty—that Mickey recognized as his own: it was the same laugh he'd used so often in the company of Emi's set. Mickey hung his head as Flemke briefed him: the suspects, both fifteen years old and charged as adults with murder in the first degree, had pleaded not guilty; the trial date had yet to be set; the district attorney would be in touch with him soon regarding his possibly testifying. Flemke then added confidentially that the case was a strong one, what with the recovery of the weapon and the taped confessions. "Of course," Flemke said, "with the jury system these days, you never know."

Mickey nodded, sighed. He wasn't too crazy about the idea of taking the stand—he'd been through enough reenactments in his mind, he didn't need to be led through one in real life—but he'd do whatever he was asked. He looked up at Flemke to communicate this reluctant willingness, but his eye was drawn beyond the detective to the doors of the courtroom, from which emerged what appeared to be the grandmother of one of the suspects, a hefty middle-aged woman in a green dress, an old blue pelerine and a black pillbox hat that made Mickey think of the words "Sunday best," sobbing into a crumpled tissue, her elbow held by an elderly, slightly stooped black man in a dark blue suit—either her father or pastor, Mickey supposed—who took slow shuffling steps (she was supporting *him*, Mickey now realized) and then stopped and turned his head to the doors, through which now issued—Mickey's heart rippled with bitter compassion at the sight—a young woman in her early thirties, wrapped in a gray trench coat that seemed to betray the very poverty it was meant to conceal. Not a material poverty, necessarily; rather, an inner poverty, a lack of that intangible, undefinable something that allows one to function in the world, to be at home in it. The broad corridors, the high-sounding inscriptions on the walls quoting various Europeans, the oil portraits of the titans of American justice, the rooms designed and furnished to the specifications of a single great idea—these things had nothing to do with her, she looked lost amid them, dislocated, cut off from some simpler past. As a mother—and she must be the mother of one of the suspects, Mickey thought—she had failed; and Mickey could read the shame in her dazed face as the well-tailored white man by her side whispered patiently in her ear.

And where, Mickey wondered mordantly, where, pray tell, was the father?

"The next right," Mickey told the cabbie. "You can let me out on that parking lot."

There it was: the bakery. He felt he was looking at it for the first time, or rather, that he was *seeing* it for the first time, seeing it as a symbol of himself, the way one might glance at a pair of one's favorite shoes on the floor and feel a jolt of identification.

Through the windows he could see Morris alone behind the counter.

He paid the driver and dragged his suitcase from the seat with the grunt of a man for whom airports and courthouses and the heft of luggage may well have been routine. "Thanks," he said, and slammed the door. The report sounded across the lot.

Mickey approached the bakery slowly. He'd never known this feeling in his life, this strange triumph of return. For the first time, he would be able to measure himself in terms of the impact of his absence. He was aware of his volume, his weight, his relationship to air, to gravity. What should he expect? What if nothing had changed—if his being away hadn't mattered in the least? What if he hadn't been missed at all?

But when he entered the bakery—when Morris looked up at him and had to take off his glasses—Mickey's heart leaped to his throat, so moved was he by the sight of family, of one of his own. Some people, he knew, went away for years before they saw their kin again, but Mickey wasn't ashamed to feel a little choked up after being away for a single month. A month could be precious, God knew; there were only so many left in a life.

"I'll be damned," said Morris.

Maybe it wasn't a mob scene and cheers and "For He's a Jolly Good Fellow," but the look on Morris's face was worth all of that. For the first time that Mickey could remember, the old man's face lit up: the child in him rose to the surface just briefly, and in that flicker of boyish light Mickey felt a strange longing, as of a desire to make good on promises, to live up to a heroism that seemed to have been heaped upon him the moment he walked through the door.

Mickey set down his suitcase and looked around. Everything appeared just as he'd left it, save for maybe the snowflake decorations. The breads and cookies and cakes were all set out in the usual way. Yet Mickey was aware of indiscernible changes, like how you can walk into your room and know instantly that someone has been there.

"Where's Benjie?" he said.

"In the back."

"Is everything okay?"

Morris put on his glasses, and his face grew ashen with what Mickey realized was anger. "We've managed," he said.

Mickey was chilled by his uncle's manner; just a moment before he had seemed so pleased. It was as if, at his age, he hadn't the time to stick with any one emotion for too long: he was at the end, and there was so much to feel, so much he had never allowed himself to feel until now. Mickey longed to reach out to him, but Morris took up the broom as if in defense of that, then turned his back and began sweeping the floor with slow, calculated strokes.

Mickey scratched his nose. "They caught the kids that killed Emi," he said.

Morris stopped sweeping, but kept his back turned. "Is that right?"

"Got both of them. Yesterday. Two kids."

"I'll be damned," said Morris. He turned around to face his nephew. "So is that why you're back, Mickey?" It was like an accusation.

Mickey nodded. "Yes," he said. "Partly."

"We thought maybe you were gone for good."

"Well, I'm here." Mickey knew that his uncle had a million questions ("Where were you? What have you been doing?"), and that something in his own bearing—the suggestion of an obscure fame—must have caused the old man some pause.

"Shvartzes?" said Morris.

"What?"

"The killers."

"Two kids," said Mickey. "They're caught."

"Good," said Morris. "You can run, but you can't hide."

"I'll go see Benjie," Mickey said. He walked to the back.

"They ought to take and execute the bastards," Morris said. "The old-fashioned way, a bullet right through the heart. They ought to—" He had fallen out of earshot.

Mickey looked around: the kitchen area appeared clean, orderly. The office door was closed. Mickey reached for the knob, then, on second thought, raised his fist to knock. He stood there for a moment, unsure of himself—he hadn't even thought of what to say, how to act—and then watched helplessly as his hand rose up and rapped with confidence upon the wood.

"Who is it?" came a cautious voice.

Mickey hesitated. What did his hand know that he didn't? "It's your father," he said. His voice, strong and clear, surprised him.

There was a click, and the door opened slowly. Ben appeared in the crack, looking much older than he had in November. He wore a white shirt and a tie that Mickey recognized as one of his own, and in the eyes lay a faintly harried, hunted look, such as Mickey had worn during *his* early days at the bakery, down on North Avenue, when customers would corner him with demands and complaints, and papers would pile up on the desk.

"Dad," said Ben. There was, Mickey thought, a note of awe in his voice.

"Son." Mickey felt like he'd been waiting all his life for this simple exchange of monosyllables. He thought to open his arms in an embrace, but was distracted by the sight, glimpsed over Ben's shoulder, of a stunning tidiness that was almost harsh on the eyes. "What in the world happened in here?" A computer—Ben's computer—sat flush on a miraculously paperless desk. "What the hell did you do?"

"Just organized things," said Ben. He seemed eager to ask questions, but retreated instead into what seemed to Mickey a kind of shy respect, not unlike that with which he had greeted his mother when she'd return home after a similar length of time. He went to the desk and turned a switch on the computer. "Look," he said.

Mickey felt a sting of anger, though maybe it was hurt pride as much as anything—the idea that his mess had been cleaned up by someone else. He positioned himself behind the desk chair and looked over Ben's shoulder at the list of options on the screen. How in the hell was he supposed to make sense of all this *narrishkeit*, as his father would say, all this hocus-pocus?

"Everything's here," Ben said.

Mickey sighed. What would Dulac say about computers?

Ben moved a plastic gizmo on a pad, maneuvering it in a series of intelligent clicks, bringing up all sorts of charts and figures. As he explained what it all meant, and how he'd done this, that and the other thing to cut waste and save money, Mickey's head began to swim. The colorful graphics gave Ben's arguments indisputable weight, and Mickey found himself trusting the kid's decisions based on the mere fact of technology. The glow of the screen became a hearth, around which they had both gathered for warmth; Mickey tried to listen as Ben described, with eloquent logic, how each change led to profit, but under the screen's glow Mickey fell instead to admiring his son's profile ("He looks just like you!" Shirley Finkle had often told him) and the sound of his voice, in which Mickey could hear his own tone and inflections, his own youthful pluck in the face of adversity.

Mickey wondered how to spring the news of the arrests. Gravely? Joyfully? It wasn't exactly what he'd call "good" news, and yet somehow it was. He said, plainly, "You know, Benjie, the police caught those two kids," wondering if it had already broken in the papers.

Ben said nothing, and Mickey knew he was thinking the same thing that Morris had thought: that this was the reason he'd come back; that otherwise he may never have returned. But of course it wasn't true; he'd missed his son, had been desperate to come home to him.

"What have you been doing all this time?" Ben said.

"Did you hear what I said? They caught the killers."

"I heard you."

Mickey felt the kid was on to him somehow, and didn't want to give the impression that he was avoiding the subject. Though why should he feel defensive? He'd gone away for the good of all of them. Couldn't Ben see that? Mickey felt a chill. This wouldn't be easy, he thought. And yet it moved him that Ben seemed to have felt so deeply the blow of his absence.

"I met a very interesting man in Paris," Mickey said, and the next thing he knew, he was preaching like Dulac himself, singing the praises of wood-fired ovens and organically grown wheat, thinking that as much as these new ideas might upset Ben's ledgers, they were in any case vital seeds that would eventually take hold in his imagination and lead him, one way or another, to the serenity that Mickey had found while baking overseas. "We can do better here," he said. "We can turn out a better product. I want to try and communicate something, try to—" He stopped; he couldn't explain it like Dulac. And there was so much he wanted to express! "A single loaf," he said, pulling at the air with his hands, grasping for the words, the inspiration that would enable him to convey the meaning of a single speck of grain—"is a living thing."

Ben kept his eyes on the screen. "What are you talking about?" he said.

Mickey sighed. "I'm saying we need to maybe change the way we make things."

Ben turned his head and looked up at him. "Change? What do you mean?"

"I just told you. The very philosophy behind—"

"But what about all I've—everything is—how can you want to change it? I've—"

"Benjie."

"You always said that the idea is to produce the highest volume in the shortest amount of time for the cheapest cost. I've done that."

Mickey was taken aback. The kid was vehement, on a mission of his own.

"This is a business," Ben said. There was a severity in his tone which seemed to carry this verdict beyond the bakery and into the realm of the personal. "That's all you ever meant it to be, a business. You can't change it now."

"Why not listen to what I'm saying," said Mickey, "instead of flying off the handle?"

"I've done too much," said Ben. "You can't just barge in here and take over."

"Barge in?" said Mickey. He laughed. "This happens to be my bakery."

"If it's so important to you, then why did you go away for so long?"

"That doesn't mean it isn't mine."

"It means," said Ben, "that you don't really care about it."

Mickey was staggered. "Of course I care about it," he said, his voice straining to impart deeper meanings. "Why do you think I want to improve it?"

Ben looked crestfallen—he was speechless, his mouth agape—and

Mickey immediately saw his own error. To suggest improvements was to degrade all that the kid had done.

"Listen." Mickey walked around to the front of the desk and sat down in the chair. Funny: before he'd left, it was Benjie in that chair and him behind the desk. "Don't get me wrong," he said. "You've done a lot. I don't mean to turn everything upside down."

Ben gazed at the monitor.

"So what about everything else?" said Mickey, his voice bright with the insistence that all was well between them. "Any problems? The staff? Everyone okay?"

Ben was motionless for a moment, then sighed and typed something on the keyboard, the way an athlete might walk off pain. "Three people are gone," he said, still typing.

"What?"

Ben sighed, read over what he'd typed, then went on to explain that two of the bakers—the Chinamen—had left for greener pastures, and that Lazarus—old, owl-eyed Lazarus of the night—had been installed in their place.

"Lazarus?" Mickey said. "Baking?"

"And supervising," Ben said. "Kind of kills two birds with one stone. Three birds, really, since there's one less baker now."

"And he doesn't mind?"

Ben shrugged. "He likes it."

"Well," said Mickey. It was, when you looked at it, a pretty smart move—it saved money and made for a leaner, more efficient staff—but Mickey was concerned that maybe the kid had been too ambitious, that this little shake-up was only the tip of the iceberg. He braced himself for more. "Anything else?" he said.

"No," said Ben. "I mean, I canceled the store consignments, which weren't the least bit profitable—that's how I could afford to lose a baker, cutting the volume like that—but of course you could start them back up if you wanted, which I wouldn't advise you to, since it's not worth it, which I can prove to you on the computer, if you want. And Nelson quit. Here, look, I'll show you the consignment figures. Say we make seventy-five percent off each item—"

"Just a second," said Mickey. It was crazy, but the news of Ben's brazen business decisions (which in any case were probably sound; Mickey had to admit that the kid was on the ball) did not stun him half as much as the item about Nelson that he'd tried to slip in there unnoticed. "You said Nelson quit?"

"It was his decision," said Ben, with an odd emphasis. "Anyway, I covered the deliveries."

More money saved, Mickey thought. "He get a better offer?"

"I didn't ask," said Ben. "Maybe he just wanted to do something else. Maybe he was tired of deliveries."

Mickey scratched his head. He seemed to recall hoping, in the back of his mind, that Ben's new position might, among other things, hasten the collapse of that ill-boding friendship, but now all he could feel—it hit him all at once—was an immediate threat to his contact with Donna Childs. He knew this was a selfish thought—Ben had probably taken Nelson's departure hard, God knew it wasn't easy to be both a boss and a friend, not every boss could be loved, or even liked, hell, your better ones were probably even hated.

"Well," Mickey said, more for Ben's sake, "I'm sorry he had to go."

The phone rang. Ben picked it up.

"Lerner Bakery," he said.

Mickey watched his son with a growing pride. The computer, the desk, the professional, confident manner on the phone—

"Uh-huh," Ben said. He turned his head slightly. "Uh-huh. Right. No." There was a long pause. "Uh-huh. Yes. Okay." His hand dropped: the receiver slammed down.

"Careful with the phone," Mickey said. "Who was it?"

"Nobody," said Ben. "Just some customer asking stupid questions." He rubbed his head.

Mickey laughed—he knew the feeling. "You okay?" he said. The kid looked a little pale.

"I'm just tired," Ben said.

"You've been working hard, huh?"

"Yeah."

Mickey nodded. "How about we close up early and go home. Have an early dinner."

Ben looked at him. "Close up early?"

"We can do that, you know," Mickey said.

After having seen what had been done at the bakery, it came as little surprise to Mickey that the house should be in tip-top condition. Plants watered, floors clean, kitchen sink empty of dishes. Ben had even made two neat stacks of mail on the table by the phone: a small stack for Emi (junk mail, mostly) and a big stack of bills for him. Mickey examined Emi's stack—don't get rid of your mother's mail,

he'd said, there might be something important—and found himself
unable to throw any of it out. It was strange: before he'd left, he'd had
no trouble tossing out her mail; now, perhaps because the flow would
be slowing, each piece had the weight of a rare collectible.

In the kitchen he put a pot of water on to boil. There were a couple of boxes of pasta in the cupboard, and also some olive oil, a jar of
capers and a container of sun-dried tomatoes. In the refrigerator he
found some old garlic and a jar of black olives. Tomorrow, maybe, he'd
go food shopping.

"Dad?"

Mickey turned. Ben was standing in the doorway, wearing only a
pair of undershorts. Mickey's first impulse was to turn away in modesty, but he then realized that Ben's appearance was perfectly normal.
He looked at his son, trying hard not to betray his sudden discomfort
with the raw body, the plain physical fact of his own child. Nipples
like twin birthmarks, hair shooting up like flames on the bony chest,
a light fuzz creeping below the coin slot of a navel; Mickey hadn't
seen the kid's bare hide since the day after Emi's death, when he went
into his room to break the news, but even then he hadn't noticed the
hair, the marks of an approaching manhood that now seemed to pit
them against each other.

"Did you like it?" Ben said. "France?"

"Sure," said Mickey. He smiled. "But I'm glad to be home."

Ben scratched at the hairs below his navel. "I think we should move
there," he said.

"You want to move there, huh?"

"Or somewhere." A thumb found the elastic band of his shorts. "I
bet we could move to another state or even another country and start
up a business."

Mickey laughed. "We'll think about it," he said. He might have been
fielding a small child's request for a horse.

"I'm serious, Dad."

It was the "Dad" that grabbed him. Mickey took a harder look at
this young man, this lean bundle of ideas. What was inside him? Why
this urge to move, to get away?

Mickey saw the danger—saw the kid spreading his wings and flying
the coop. He was eighteen, almost nineteen. An adult. Mickey stiff-
ened: would he lose Benjie too?

"Take a couple of weeks off," said Mickey. "You've worked hard, and
you've done a real bang-up job."

The water had come to a boil. Mickey opened a box of spaghetti and emptied a loose bundle of stiff golden spindles into his hand. He said, "I just want you to know that I'm very proud of you, son." He turned, and was startled to find that Ben wasn't there.

After a moment he heard the footfalls on the stairs, and the slam of a bedroom door.

Mickey ate alone: Ben had shut himself up in his room, saying he wasn't hungry, that he had a headache. Mickey figured he was angry at him for something, or maybe he was just uncomfortable with the situation; they hadn't had a meal together in a long time, after all, and neither of them, Mickey supposed, would really know what to do or say.

After dinner, Mickey sorted through his mail. Bills, bills and more bills, a few late cards of condolence from customers, a dozen mail-order catalogs and sweepstakes offers, a dozen more bank and stock statements. The waste of paper that went on in his name impressed him greatly. And Emi—she was obviously still alive to her creditors. Mickey searched her pile, thinking he might alight on something personal—a letter, a postcard, something to revive her name in a small explosion of controversy, that he might recall her, just for a moment, with the immediacy and intensity which only jealousy can fuel—but there was nothing. Mildly disappointed, he went up to bed.

Ben's light was out. Mickey stared at the phone, tempted to pick it up and call Donna, but in a failure of nerve told himself that it would be better to try her during the day, at work, where at least Nelson wouldn't be a factor.

He fell asleep, then woke up at dawn: for a moment he thought he was in Paris, that it was time to get up and kindle the hearth. He felt a small regret when he realized he was home.

Restless, he shaved and dressed and walked over to the bakery to see what was what. The bakers, including a whistling Lazarus, who wore a white apron over his black suit, were hard at work, mixing and cutting and shaping. Mickey stood unnoticed by the office door, watching; as ever, he was amazed at the industry that went on in his name, even when he wasn't there.

"Good morning, gentlemen," he said.

The bakers looked up, and like a string of firecrackers their faces lit one after the next with recognition. They stopped what they were doing and came toward him, some of them still holding their cutters. Mickey stepped back, and was then surprised—though why should he

have been surprised?—when the men surrounded him with big peasant smiles and slapped his shoulders.

"I want to hear all about it," said Shirley Finkle as Mickey moved some
trays around in the display case. It was a few minutes before opening,
and Shirley, who had been knocking at the glass—who had damn near
fainted like a starstruck bobby-soxer at the sight of Mickey coming
out of his office to the front—had just now informed him that, as
she'd been lending a hand behind the counter ("I tell ya, I've been in
here so many times I could have done it with my eyes closed!") and
checking in on Ben daily ("He knew better than to stay out all hours,
not with eagle-eye Shirley right next door!")—that, seeing as how
things would have been so topsy-turvy without her, she, more than
anyone else, deserved the first full account of his adventures.

"Very nice trip," said Mickey. "Very interesting." He wondered if the
DA would phone today. Hadn't Flemke said he would?

"Nice? Interesting?" said Shirley. "You can do better than that. Let's
have some details!"

"Details," said Mickey.

"Did you parley-voo Fran-say? Did you climb up the Eiffel Tower?"

"Not this time," said Mickey. "I'm afraid I wasn't much of a tourist."
He was aware of the effects that his new worldliness was having on his
neighbor, and tried hard to appear like the simple man who had spent
forty years behind the counter. "How's Gilbert?" he said.

Shirley didn't seem to hear him. "Didn't you take any pictures?"

"Pictures?" said Mickey.

Shirley shook her head in wonder, as though forgoing picture-
taking was a foolish, bullheaded and devastatingly masculine act. "You
are something else, Mickey Lerner. Some-thing *else.*"

Mickey rubbed his nose. "Next time," he said, "I'll take a camera."

"The hell with the camera," Shirley cried. "Take me!" And she began
to laugh in that giddy, whiskey-sour way of hers.

Mickey laughed with her.

"So," she said, "What's going to happen with Benjie, now that you're
back?"

"Benjie?"

"Is he staying here to work?"

Mickey shrugged. "Whatever he wants."

"He's not going back to making deliveries, is he?"

"No," said Mickey, reminding himself that he now had to hire a delivery man. "He'd be helping me run the show, just like he's been doing."

Shirley shook her head. "The way he handled himself, I tell ya, I was amazed. Little Benjie Lerner."

"Yup." Mickey watched through the window as a bus pulled up at the stop.

"Is he coming in today?" said Shirley.

Mickey looked at her. "No. I figured I'd give him a break, some time off to rest." Mickey had no sooner completed the sentence and begun to wonder again what he'd do about deliveries when he saw through the window a figure stepping off the bus whom he thought might be Nelson: a young black man in a hooded coat, the kind Nelson often wore.

Was Nelson dropping by to visit, to chat about his new job? Ask for his old job back?

Mickey almost hoped it was the latter, but when the man failed to enter the bakery, Mickey figured that it wasn't Nelson after all.

24

As he approached the bakery, Nelson was shocked to see, standing behind the counter, not the lanky figure of Ben Lerner, but rather—he could hardly believe his eyes—that of Mickey Lerner, Bread, in the flesh, *there*, as though he'd never even been gone. Nelson quickly moved out of sight of the window; he had planned to ask Crumb to do him a big favor, but the sight of the elder Lerner, home safe and sound from distant lands, filled him with unexpected emotions.

He went inside the adjacent drugstore and walked the aisles, trying to think. Did Bread know about the firing? What had he been told? What did he believe? He picked up a candy bar, unwrapped it, took a nervous bite. He knew he was being watched by the cashiers. He grabbed a pack of Wrigley's and walked on.

It had been a crazy twenty-four hours. By the time he'd gotten home from Seven Pines (he'd ended up wishing Rattner had driven him all the way to his house, it was a longer walk than he'd imagined, and colder than he'd thought), he was ready to go straight to bed, but when he turned the corner at Washburn and Percy, he saw, under the street lamp, a group of young teenagers, two or three of whom were astride bicycles, their attention focused on a bouncing, hooded figure in the middle whose words seemed to hold them spellbound.

Nelson knew, even before he saw or heard him, that the speaker was Hawk. Was he talking about what had happened? But that would kill the theory that he was waiting to go to the police, to finger Nelson and collect some money; he'd be quiet then. Drawing closer, Nelson wondered if Hawk was not only discussing the evening's events, but taking credit for the shooting. And wouldn't that just be like Hawk? But that still didn't answer the question of why he and Chuckie had fled in the car, and Nelson, noting Hawk's rapt, loyal audience, wasn't sure if this was the best time to confront him.

"Yo—there he is," came a voice from the group, and Nelson froze in his tracks as five or six faces—Hawk's included—turned to him, their eyes all aglow like some ominous constellation.

As if summoned, Nelson advanced, hands deep in his pockets. *He* held the cards, he felt; if Hawk had told lies and built himself up as a brazen killer, he would know better than to antagonize Nelson, who, angry and deranged (so Hawk must have seen him, given what had happened at Seven Pines), might dare to contradict him. But as he got closer, Nelson saw in the faces not hostility, or scorn, or amusement, but rather—and he'd seen the look before, in Crumb's eyes—a kind of awe, a fear, a reverence; glances were exchanged, there were whispers; and Nelson knew, as the group parted eagerly to let him through to the center, that Hawk, standing there like a minor god, his angels scattered, had told his, Nelson's, story, told it with relish, perhaps even pride, had, perhaps to ease his guilt over having abandoned him, remained, in this peculiar way, loyal; had given credit to Nelson.

"Yo," said Hawk. "Nelson. Yo, man. You a'ight?"

"What happened, Hawk?" Nelson said icily.

Hawk glanced around at the kids, who were gathering again, an audience now to this meeting of neighborhood giants.

"Yo, man," said Hawk, shaking his head. "Chuckie just took off. The boy panicked. The second that gun went off, he just put on the gas."

"Yo, Nelson," said one of the kids. "You really shoot a white man?"

"Naw," said Nelson.

The kids looked at one another knowingly, as if this denial was the ultimate confirmation of Hawk's story.

Hawk took Nelson aside. "Don't worry," he said. "These niggas ain't gonna say nothin'."

Nelson laughed to himself. Had there really *been* a murder, it would have been Hawk after all who'd have done him in. In bragging of Nelson's exploits, Hawk's loyalty had taken its final idiotic turn: the whole neighborhood had been informed. And yet Hawk seemed to think nothing of it—he probably even supposed he was, in spreading the word, *helping* Nelson, building a wall, a fortress, protecting him somehow from the law.

"Yo," said Hawk, turning to the kids. "Y'all need to go now. Me and Nelson havin' a private conversation."

The kids didn't move; they were, Nelson saw, staring at *him*, as though awaiting from him some sign that would tell them how to proceed with their lives.

"Y'all better go," Nelson said, and watched with disbelief as the kids, without so much as a grumble of protest, backed off, turned and dispersed, running, riding, occasionally looking back.

"So what happened?" said Hawk. "How'd you get here?"

Nelson spat on the ground. "Took the white boy's car," he said. "Left his ass there on the lot. Took the car down to that chop shop over near Rogers Avenue. Lucky for me, somebody was there to take it off my hands."

"Damn," said Hawk. He shook his head. "I can't believe it."

"What did you expect?" said Nelson.

"Not this," said Hawk. "I didn't think you'd do it, yo." There was a fear in his voice. "I didn't think you'd do it."

"Then why," said Nelson, "did you bring Chuckie?"

Hawk took a step back. He looked away from Nelson as he spoke. "I didn't think you'd do it. I thought it would just be, you know, something to do. For entertainment. Thought you'd go soft at the last minute, embarrass yourself in front of Chuck. That way you wouldn't be askin' me anymore to run with us. See, I couldn't be tellin' you no without givin' you a chance. I thought for sure you'd ruin your own chances, get me off the hook. I told Chuck, I said, 'Yo. This nigga ain't gonna shoot nobody. Shit just gonna be for laughs, you know?' Now Chuckie think you a crazy nigga. Made me promise I can't have nothin' to do with you if me and him gonna work together."

Nelson listened to this, nodded. "And what did you tell him?"

"Yo. I got to look out for my own self too. You mixed up in some serious bullshit. I mean, it ain't nothin' personal. But yo. I'm tryin' to get my life together."

Nelson nodded some more. So that was it: he'd scared everyone off. He wanted to laugh, to shout: totally isolated now, he had only himself: it was like a second chance. Having come within an inch, literally, of murder, he now found himself rid of all the vile influences that had led him to that point in the first place. It was crazy, but he felt he'd been given a gift.

When he awoke the following morning he felt like a new person. He knew Mama would get on him again about his not going to work at the bakery, but he was determined to beat her to the punch by finding another job. And would it really be so hard, so impossible to find work? Hadn't he done it once before?

He took the bus way out Falls Road to the Green Garden Nursery and asked the white lady in charge if she was hiring. He knew she recognized him as a customer—he'd bought his African violets there, and had inquired once about some narcissus bulbs, which he'd once read could grow in a bowl of pebbles and water—and knew, too, that on several occasions she'd watched him study the plants with the special intensity of one who sees beyond the spectacle of blossom, sees straight down the pistil and into the secret ovary. The air smelled of pine, of wood chips, of the basil, sage, rosemary and sweet bay that grew in tiny white pots, of roses and hibiscus, of red and yellow marigolds. It was December, but everything was growing here; the whole nursery was crawling and creeping with life. Yes: this was where he belonged. He would learn the names of all these growing things, these strong-smelling flowers and shrubs, would learn how to care for each and every one of them. Who could deny his will, his enthusiasm? Still, he had expected rejection—there was, he knew, this kernel of anxiety that rattled loudly through his body whenever he tried to appear composed and professional—and was therefore stunned when the lady told him that she was looking for someone to perform general duties—potting, watering, pruning—and handed him an application and told him to come back as soon as possible.

He'd filled out the application on the bus, dreaming of a future of flowers, vegetables, bushes, trees, of dirt under his nails, of the rainbow mist of sprinklers. Who knew where it might lead? Who knew what he would learn?

And he would learn. He'd listen and watch and ask questions and learn everything he could. But when he came to the part on the application requesting a recommendation from a former employer, he stopped: all his hopes collapsed in a heap of regret and bitterness. How could he ask for a good reference, after all that had happened?

Well, he'd thought after a moment: Crumb owes me. And wasn't it

true? Didn't Crumb owe him at least that much? Finally he convinced himself that Crumb—if not by coercion, then out of his own
guilt over the firing—would almost certainly provide him with a
glowing, perhaps even breathtaking reference.

But now, creeping through the aisles of the drugstore, he felt a deep
dread. Crumb was not there, and Mickey Lerner, who was, might, for
all he knew, turn on him (for Ben would have told him stories, if Jay
Rattner hadn't already), order him from his store with a stern, rigid
finger.

Nelson grew defensive over this imagined treatment. What about
his side of things? The way he'd been treated? And what right did
Bread have to judge him, when he hadn't even been there, when he
didn't even know the facts?

Nelson paid for the candy bar and gum and walked out of the store,
his blood running hot with the righteous indignation of the falsely accused. He had nothing to fear from Bread. He'd enter the bakery a
proud man and demand justice, make Bread understand that it was in
his interest to write a good recommendation, lest the weight of
protest come crashing down upon his store in some fiery, time-
honored form.

Nelson took a breath, raised his chin and advanced to the bakery
door. Bread was alone, he saw. That was bad; with people around he
might be more agreeable, more cooperative. Nelson considered coming back when things were busier, but he needed to get back to the
nursery as soon as possible.

Bread would have to be dealt with.

"Well, look who it is!" the voice called out as Nelson opened the
door. A hand shot out over the counter.

Nelson was confused. "Hi, Mr. Lerner," he said. He shook the man's
hand, and was thrilled by the strength of the grip. Somehow he wasn't
quite Bread anymore; he was someone else. Something bigger. "How
you doin'?"

"Doing well, knock wood." Mr. Lerner rapped the glass countertop
with his knuckles, drawing brief attention to the bright buns and pastries underneath. "How about yourself?"

"I'm good," said Nelson, fingering the folded application in his
pocket. What did Mr. Lerner know? What had he been told?

"Benjie tells me you left us."

Nelson stroked his chin, looked askance. "Yeah. Morris okay?"

"He's fine. You get a new job?"

Nelson shrugged. "You know," he said. "I got an opportunity." A heat broke out on his back.

"Is that right?"

Nelson pulled out the application, unfolded it. "Yeah," he said. He couldn't meet the man's eyes. "I got this application. They want me to get a reference. You know. Something nice." He was aware of a slight anger in his tone. He laid the paper on the counter between them: it looked shabby with its creases.

Mr. Lerner picked it up, looked at it. "The Green Garden Nursery," he said, raising an eyebrow. "You're interested in gardening, are you?"

Nelson stroked his chin. Did Mr. Lerner know that he'd made special trips in the van, just to admire his garden?

"So they want a few words of praise, do they?"

Mr. Lerner took a pen from his pocket and bore down on the paper, and Nelson felt his entire future squirm under the point. Should he stop him, ask him what he intended to write?

But he knew it was too late. The man was writing slowly, intently; his concentration demanded silence.

Nelson swallowed. Should he say something anyway? Ask about his trip?

"Here you go." Mr. Lerner slid the paper across the counter.

Nelson quickly folded it. He'd read it outside.

"You know, Nelson, if things don't work out over there at the nursery, and I'm still looking for a delivery man, maybe we can work something out."

"Thanks," Nelson said. But he knew—just as Mr. Lerner must have known—that he would never return. He wondered if he'd ever see the man again.

"By the way," said Mr. Lerner. "If you're not busy tomorrow, why not stop by my house? I'll be baking some bread and puttering around in the garden, weather permitting. If you want to taste some real good bread—"

"Maybe I'll do that," said Nelson. He doubted he would, though; it would be awkward, with Crumb around, and besides, it was Saturday, which meant ball games on television. Still, it might be nice, especially if Mr. Lerner was going to be working in his yard. He said, "I better get going." He met the man's eyes and gave a shy smile, then quickly looked away. This was just how they'd met, back when Nelson was hired: Mr. Lerner handing him an application over the counter. Now they'd come full circle.

Nelson took one last look at the bakery—the baskets of bread, the glass cases, the counter, the corny snowflake decorations; already it was a place deep in his memory, viewed from a distance, a pinpoint of light at the end of a wistful backward vision.

His reverie was broken by a voice: "So long." Mickey Lerner raised his hand like a man taking an oath.

Nelson mirrored that. Then he turned and walked out.

It now seemed odd to him that no one had mentioned Ben. Had Mr. Lerner avoided it on purpose? Had they both avoided it? Again he wondered what the man knew.

At the bus stop he unfolded the application. He closed his eyes, opened them, and read.

Nelson is hard-working, honest and dependable. He is responsible and a pleasure to work with. He was a valuable addition to my staff. I can recommend him without hesitation.

Nelson read the paragraph several times, occasionally glancing back at the bakery. No one had ever said these things about him. He wasn't sure what to feel or think. Did Mr. Lerner really mean it? He wanted to shout with joy, but something stopped him. The words, the praise. Suddenly he wasn't sure if he deserved it.

He'd done a lot of things. Time and again he'd gone off his route to play ball or just to drive around; he'd invented traffic stories to explain lateness, burned unnecessary gas. There'd been abuses, lies. If anything, he deserved to be punished. Taken to task. It was crazy, but he wished Mr. Lerner had hauled off on him. He wanted to be taken aside, dealt with, forgiven. It sickened him to think that he'd gotten over on his former boss.

In his great confusion of feeling he vowed to do everything he could to live up to the man's opinion of him. He did not want to make Mickey Lerner a fool.

On the bus heading to the nursery, he read the incredible words again and again.

The moment Nelson walked out of the bakery, Mickey began to second-guess himself. Should he have made the invitation for tomorrow more definite? Nelson, as he well knew, was his only link to Donna, and though he had planned, just as soon as he got up his nerve, on calling Donna at work (some kind of massage place downtown: he'd look it up), it made him sick to think that he'd just seen his former employee for the last time, that he'd blown the chance to build a bridge to a woman whose beauty had come back to him at the first sight of her son (he saw it now, the resemblance: the eyes, the nose), and whose ready laughter—he remembered it well—still rang in his ears like the bells of the bakery door on a quiet day: the sound of hope, of the entrance of possibilities.

Though maybe, he told himself, maybe such a casual invitation warranted—why not?—a follow-up phone call; sure: he could call Donna on the pretext of reminding Nelson about Saturday, and, if she sounded the least bit receptive to him, suggest that she might like to come along too. Or maybe he ought to propose something else, a more intimate get-together, offer it as a sort of apology for his having stood her up in November—yes, he ought to at least call and apologize, tell her how he'd been so terribly confused, and that he wouldn't mind, if it was okay with her, talking about it, which was, of course, true, he would like to talk, he couldn't remember the last time he'd sat down with someone and talked.

No sense sitting around; it was put up or shut up. Still, it bothered him that he could be yearning for Donna when he'd yet to sit down and talk with his son—Benjie being home alone, up in his room, withdrawn as if in protest of his father's return, which comprised a threat to the new life he'd carved out for himself at the bakery—but he assured himself that the kid would reject him anyhow, that he needed a few days, maybe even more, to get used to the idea of relinquishing his power, no, sharing it, sharing his power with the man who had granted it, the man who had hastily outfitted him and then left him alone in the jungle wilds of business. And yet Mickey'd have thought the kid would have shown at least *some* gratitude, having been given such a rare opportunity.

He called Morris at home and asked him—told him, really—to come in, that he had to make some deliveries and would be gone for a couple of hours.

Cathedral Street, Mickey thought, his hands tight on the steering wheel of the van. He remembered the place exactly. And hadn't Donna herself suggested that he drop by sometime, for a massage? Not that she had really meant it—there was such a thing, after all, as just being polite—but it did provide him with a humorous opening line ("You told me I ought to drop by sometime"), which was better than nothing, and though he'd never been a great one for quips and cranks, he could see as how a man of his hard experience ought to at least have the nerve to give it a try, to charge headlong into battle with both fists swinging. And while it did seem incredible to him, what with all he'd been through, that he should be intimidated by the prospect of meeting Donna Childs, it was this selfsame nervousness that assured him his feelings were genuine, and that Donna, the very thought of whom could put a foolish, self-conscious grin on his face, was the one person in the world for whom he'd put off a talk with his son.

When he arrived downtown, it occurred to him that he would have to pass within blocks of the spot where Emi was killed. As he drove nearer, he felt a physical revulsion, and though in the weeks following the murder he would not have been able to bring himself to come here, he did have a rich and even proud history of returning to a scene: after his bakery had burned, he used to visit the site regularly, as if on the chance that the building had risen from the ashes the night before. It was always strange to see that empty space—and strange, too, to be faced, each time, with that sudden snatch of alleyway and the backs of the row houses beyond it, whose windows were now painfully exposed.

Now he had an even grimmer scene to visit. He turned onto the street where the shooting had taken place, then parked the van just yards from the spot and got out.

Two months had passed, which was not enough for him to be able to say that it felt like any less. Two months was still yesterday. And as he stepped onto the cracked, disjointed pavement, he could recall, like a macabre rhyme learned in childhood, every last detail, from the sound of their own footsteps to the car keys being passed to him as they walked more hurriedly ("I'm not wearing the right shoes"—her gallows humor was never riper) to the moment of the confrontation itself, right here, yes, by this slab of curb. Mickey swallowed hard and lowered his eyes to the ground.

A chill of expectation shot through him. But he was met instead with an utterly blank tablet of concrete; and as he walked along with tiny steps, searching the ground like a cartoon detective (all he needed was a magnifying glass), his heart dropped with the realization that it was gone, the blood was gone, washed away by weather or the hard bristles of a scrub brush.

Mickey stood there dumbfounded. The absence of blood was haunting, even worse than had he seen it in great splotches; it seemed to reflect something of his own guilty wish to be done with her. He tried to tell himself it was a vanishing act on her part. And besides, hadn't he made it his business to stop by here? Albeit on the way to see another woman. But hadn't he come with the solemn heart of a pilgrim?

Mickey returned to the van and drove on to Donna's, but the visit had put a damper on his ambition. As he parked, he found himself in the grip of the same morbid desperation with which he had searched in vain for blood. He wanted to find in Donna a trace of something that might crush him—no, not crush him: deliver him: a word, a sign. How he dreaded the thought of finding nothing!

His heart pounded as he approached the building, a converted row house that—Mickey read the names by the buzzers—was home to a nutritionist, a yoga instructor, and, on the third floor, the Qi Healing Center. Mickey buzzed the third floor.

He was admitted without question; it was as if someone were expecting him. He walked up the long flights of steps and rang the doorbell. The door opened, and a young, pale girl with hair like rope and a ring in her nostril stood looking at him with surprise.

"Oh, I thought—may I help you?" she said.

"Yes," said Mickey.

"Do you have an appointment?"

"No. I was just here to see Donna Childs."

"Would you like to make an appointment with her?"

"An appointment?" Mickey said.

"Your name?"

Mickey hesitated. It had been a long time since he'd uttered his name; but when he announced himself he felt, just as he had felt when entering the bakery yesterday, a jolt of expectation, as of some awareness in others of his small renown.

"I'll get her," said the girl. "Come in."

Mickey entered the office. It wasn't much: your basic reception area, behind which hung a simple white curtain with a slit down the middle, through which the girl disappeared. The walls of the office were bare, save for a sign with prices written out. Forty bucks an hour they wanted. Mickey placed his hands behind his back and puckered his lips in search of some absent tune.

The curtain parted again, and there she stood: it was like a vision. She wore a white robe tied at the waist, like one of those martial arts outfits Mickey remembered from the kung-fu programs he used to watch, years ago, on the old television from Diamond Electric that Jack Diamond had sold him at a fantastic discount—

He stopped himself, hurled himself into the cruel, unforgiving moment of encounter. She was looking at him blankly: he tried to smile.

The white fabric (her slippers, too, were white) seemed to shimmer against the darkness of her face, her hands, seemed to cool something fierce about her. Mickey could not speak.

"Hello," Donna said uncertainly. They were maybe ten feet apart. "Are you here to make an appointment?"

"Well," said Mickey. "You said to drop by anytime." He smiled, trying to recall for her their last conversation, their tender moment in the bakery. "So—do you have any time?"

Donna remained aloof. "I usually don't take walk-ins," she said. "Most people call in advance."

Mickey laughed automatically. "Just thought I'd take my chances."

"What are you wearing?"

"What?"

"Underneath your coat. Because you need to be wearing comfortable clothes."

"Oh, these are comfortable," said Mickey. He was wearing his usual work clothes. A shirt and trousers. What could be more comfortable than that?

"Usually I ask that people wear loose-fitting clothes."

"Well," Mickey said. "I think I lost a couple of pounds getting up all these steps."

Donna touched one of her braids—it was the next best thing to a smile—then quickly withdrew her hand. "I have another client coming in twenty minutes," she said. "So we can do a short session now, or you can schedule something longer for later."

"Short is fine," said Mickey.

"This way," Donna said. She turned and disappeared behind the curtain. Mickey followed her into a short corridor with doors on either side. Donna opened the door on the right.

"Nice place you have here," said Mickey.

It was an empty room, save for a couple of rubber mats on the floor, a stack of bath towels and a portable stereo on a small table. There were no chairs.

"So," said Mickey. "How've you been?"

"Good," said Donna, closing the door. "I'll need you to remove your coat, and also your shoes."

"My shoes? You sure?" Mickey was thankful he'd put on clean socks this morning. Sometimes he didn't.

"And lie down on the mat. On your front. And empty your pockets."

Obviously, Mickey thought, she was perturbed with him, and this more than anything else—the small room, the likelihood of an intimate physical exchange—seemed to connect them, give them a thin cushion of history against which Mickey could relax. And yet the threat was implicit: he may well have lost his chance with her.

As Donna took his coat and hung it on a hook on the door, Mickey removed his shoes and placed his keys and wallet next to the mat. He felt like a damned fool, crawling around on his hands and knees with his tuchis high in the air.

Donna set out a towel on the mat, then lowered herself to her knees.

"I do appreciate you taking me," said Mickey. "On such short notice."

"When did you come back?" Donna said. She jumped up and went to the stereo.

"Yesterday," said Mickey. He awaited more.

Instead, there came a soft, meditative chanting of voices from the stereo.

"Head down, hands at your sides," said Donna. "Palms facing the ceiling."

Mickey obeyed.

"Close your eyes." Donna walked over, knelt beside him. "And breathe deep." Her voice hovered near. "Inhale."

Mickey surrendered himself to Donna's expertise, to the chanting voices. He breathed in, and felt her hands warming the muscles of his back.

"Exhale."

Mickey exhaled.

"Inhale. We're going to release your *qi*," Donna said. "The vital life force. Exhale. *Qi* makes up the universe in the five elements:

"Wood. Inhale.

"Fire. Exhale.

"Earth. Inhale.

"Metal. Exhale.

"Water. That's right, breathe on your own. Your entire body is relaxing now. Good. The *qi* flows throughout your body through what we call the meridians. Sometimes it gets blocked. So we go to points along the meridians and apply pressure to release it."

Mickey felt her fingers dig deep into a space beneath his shoulder blades, pressing, pressing. She was on her knees, leaning over him,

using her weight, distributing it. Mickey grimaced when there was
pain, but didn't dare yell out; there seemed to be an understanding
between them, a trust. Mickey knew he was expected to cooperate,
knew instinctively that he must breathe into the pain. His body had,
it seemed, become *theirs;* she commanded as great a knowledge and
mastery and tenderness over it as he would want to command himself, and though he had his doubts about this business with what she
called the "vital life force"—blood it wasn't, but rather, something invisible, an energy, it flowed, it got stuck, it went this way and that, up
and down the meridians, a bunch of hocus-pocus, Mickey thought,
with the meridians and the flowing and God knew what else—though
he was, and always had been, a believer in doctors and blood tests and
X rays and the whole nine yards, he had to admit that he felt a definite release of something, he wasn't sure what, a tension maybe, but
more than that, a pain, as of some hostile emotion that was eating
away inside him, and he remembered her saying something about disease, yes, that time in his car, down on Percy Street, her saying how
one could prevent disease, and it occurred to him that he had yet to
tell Ben about Emi's cancer, for that matter he had yet to tell Ben a lot
of things.

"Relax," Donna said. "Breathe." Her voice was so near that Mickey
could feel the lightness of her breath, and it was this strange conflict
of sensations—the thought of Emi, of Ben, on the one hand (but why
tell him about the cancer—what would be the point?), and then, on
the other, the exquisite comfort of Donna's gentle voice, of her firm,
knowing touch—which produced in Mickey a kind of panic, a fear
that something might happen, that they were getting too close, that,
just as they had lapsed into this hypnotic dance of breathing and
touch, of the intuitive interplay between giver and receiver, so they
were headed, now, for absolute danger: his breath quickened: her
hands covered his scalp, his ears: he feared he might, right now, at her,
their, compulsion, turn and grab her and smash his full rough lips
against hers; and so it was out of a sort of mortal desperation that he
invoked the one name that could possibly veer them off course.

"Did I mention," he said, "that I saw Nelson this morning?"

"Nelson?" Donna's hands stopped working.

"He stopped by the bakery," Mickey said. "Had a job application for
a nursery, wanted me to write a few words of recommendation. I
didn't know he was interested in plants."

"What?" said Donna. She removed her hands from his body; the
spell had been shattered. "A job application?"

Already Mickey regretted what he'd said; already he longed for what he'd just destroyed. "Yes," he said. "For a nursery."

Donna sighed. "I had a feeling that's what this was all about."

"What do you mean?"

"Nelson," she said. "You came to explain to me why he was let go. You could have just said so."

"I'm afraid you've lost me," said Mickey. He rolled over, away from her, and pulled himself up into a sitting position. Donna was on her knees, watching him closely.

"I thought," said Donna, "that you were here to explain why Nelson was fired."

"Fired? Nelson? I was told he quit."

"Told?"

"Last night, when I came in, Benjie told me Nelson had decided to leave."

Donna tilted her head. "So you mean to say that you knew nothing about this?"

"Not a thing," said Mickey. He was shocked. "I've—been away." A prickling heat spread out on his back. "You're sure about this? Fired?"

"It happened a few days ago. Ben told me—" She stopped.

"What?" said Mickey. "What happened? What were you told?"

"Nelson wasn't about to tell me anything," said Donna, "so I went to talk to Ben. Of course he was careful about what he said. But I got the feeling that there was some kind of incident. Kind of thing where Nelson did something he shouldn't. I couldn't get any straight answers. I didn't expect to. But I thought for sure that you knew. I didn't think any of this could have happened without your consent."

Mickey tried to recall if Nelson had behaved in an unusual way this morning, if there had been any signs that he himself should have noticed, but he was so overcome with anger and confusion and embarrassment that he could hardly remember his own name.

"Now what was this about a job application?" said Donna.

Mickey shook his head. "I'll get to the bottom of this," he said, and as he got hold of himself enough to tell her what little he knew about Nelson's bid for a job at the Green Garden Nursery—and he could see, even as Donna listened to him, that he had been discredited in her eyes—as he tried his best to ease her doubts over whatever had happened to Nelson at the bakery ("I'm sure he'll get the job," he said, "I gave him a good recommendation"), indeed, ease his own misgivings about it, his anger ran hotter than ever. Ben had misled him, lied, allowing him to make a goddamned fool of himself to Donna. What sort of father, Donna must be thinking, would allow his teenage son to run amok like that, firing people indiscriminately? What sort of father, what sort of employer, person, man?

Mickey rose slowly and unsteadily to his feet. Whatever Donna had accomplished with her massage had now been ruined: his nerves were shot. Where a moment before he had been prone on a mat with Donna's hands in his hair, he was now standing tense as a soldier, facing that woman through the bitter knowledge that her son—her only child, for whom she worried and fretted and prayed—had been dismissed from *his* place of business without his even knowing it. Oh sure, the situation could be rectified, that would be easy enough, but Mickey felt as though he'd been caught out in some terrific lie. As an employer he'd been less than faithful: he ought to have been in touch.

"I'm sorry about this," he said, patting down his hair.

"Maybe," said Donna, "it's for the best."

Mickey wasn't sure he understood. Did she mean to say that she preferred there be no such connection between the families, no conflicts of interest that might disrupt a potential romance? Or was she simply washing her hands of the Lerners—of him—once and for goddamned all?

She said, "My client should be here any minute."

Mickey couldn't read her. They stood on opposite sides of the mat, two strangers. Mickey bent down and picked up his keys and wallet, which he opened. "The massage was very nice," he said miserably, extracting some bills.

"That's not necessary," Donna said without inflection.

"I won't hear of it," said Mickey. For ten or so minutes he figured twenty dollars—a little extra on account of Nelson. "I insist. Payment for services rendered, absolutely." He regretted that it had all come down, somehow, to money; and yet so much seemed to hinge on her acceptance of it.

"No," said Donna, eyeing his hand, and it seemed to Mickey that there was some horror in her plea, that if he persisted she might let out a scream.

There came a knock at the door, and at once the tension deflated; the arrival of an inquiring third party seemed to put them in temporary cahoots.

"Yes?" said Donna.

The door opened and the girl with the ropelike hair stuck her head in. "Your two o'clock is here," she said, and retreated, closing the door.

Donna looked at her watch. "I'm sorry," she said. "But I have to get back to work."

It seemed incredible to Mickey that she was turning him out like this. For there *was* something between them—he'd felt it—the way her hands touched him, that tenderness, her fingers, her breath. And yet here he was, folding his wallet in pathetic defeat. "I'm sorry about all of this," he said stupidly as he stuffed the wallet in his pocket. He turned to remove his coat from the hook. "The truth is, I did come here to talk, but not about Nelson." He wondered why he said it; it all seemed so pointless now.

"Talk?" said Donna. "About what?"

Mickey turned to her. "I just wanted to apologize for—well, I think we were supposed to get together one time," he said feigning a fuzzy recollection. "Just after Thanksgiving."

"Oh, yes," said Donna, as if it were something she too had forgotten. She glanced at her watch. "Yes. I just assumed something came up."

"It did," said Mickey. "I had to get away. It was a crazy time. I should have called you."

Donna eyed him curiously. "You came to apologize for that?" she said, in what seemed to Mickey a softly pitying tone, as if for his having been so delusional as to think she'd been crushed.

"Well," Mickey said. His instinct was to get the hell out of there as fast as possible, but his huge mortification held him weighted to the spot. "At the time," he said, now feeling his nerve spring up in him like a cornered rat, thinking too that in a way he had been freed by her indifference, that it no longer mattered, that he could say anything he damn well pleased—"I was very confused. I know it sounds crazy, but I was attracted to you—no, I don't mean that *that* was crazy, it wasn't, you're an attractive woman, and I'm not trying to flatter you or seduce you or anything like that, I'm just stating the facts. I thought you were good-looking and warm and bright and I'd be lying if I said I wasn't a little interested. And to feel that way about someone so soon after losing my wife, well, you can imagine that I felt pretty guilty about it, though any person might say it was a perfectly natural thing, me being needy and so forth and looking to latch onto someone. But as fine as that may sound I really don't think it was the case. And so I sort of went off the deep end a little bit—it wasn't just you, of course, it was a lot of things—and decided to just get away from everything and everybody, and try to find a little peace."

Mickey exhaled.

He had launched into this speech, it was true, in the belief that he had nothing to lose, but along with that there had been—and only now did he realize it—a small but potent expectation that his candor would somehow be rewarded. He stood there, defenseless, waiting for something to happen.

Donna looked at him, and Mickey could see in her eyes that though she was moved, she was determined, on principle, to stick to her guns. "I'm sorry," she said bravely, "that things have been so difficult for you. I hope the time away did you good."

"And I hope I didn't shock or offend you," Mickey said. "I'm sorry if I did."

"No," said Donna readily. She threw up a tense smile. "I'm not offended." Again she checked her watch. "I'm sorry, but I do have someone waiting outside." There was the slightest pause, in which it seemed she might suggest they take this up another time, but her smile collapsed and was then immediately and brightly reestablished, as though the plug to her face had jiggled momentarily in the wall.

"Right," said Mickey. "Come to think of it, I should get back to the store." He hesitated, still waiting for that elusive something to occur. "Lots of work to catch up on." He thought to make some last, tantalizing comment about Nelson being welcome back should things fall through with the nursery, but that would only remind her—as if she needed to be reminded!—of his own mismanagement, of the general muddled incompetence that had brought him here unannounced in the first place.

Believing wildly that there remained one final scrap of dignity to be salvaged—it required that he walk the hell out of there right now—Mickey raised his chin and unfocused his eyes so that he could appear to look gamely into hers. "Good-bye," he said, then turned to the door, fully expecting that she would stop him. Instead he found the doorknob in his hand, the door pulling back, and himself walking through the office with vicious poise, exiting like Shaw from a triumphant stage. But inside he was reeling, and when he landed three stories below in an afternoon of gathering white clouds, he had no memory of descending the stairs.

He tore open the door of the van and threw himself into the driver's seat. It was all the kid's fault, he told himself as he jabbed the key in the ignition and twisted its tiny neck. The engine croaked to life, then howled as Mickey smashed the pedal with his foot. If only Ben had been straight with him, had told the truth! But no: he'd lied, a bald-faced, flat-out lie, and because of it Mickey had walked blindly into Donna's office and gotten his deserts.

And so it was over before it even began. He'd done what he could up there in Donna's office—he'd put himself on the line. But there'd been too much damage to overcome.

He slammed his fists on the steering wheel. He'd come home from Paris with a full heart and had been met with nothing but lies and deceit and sorrow. His own son! His own son had undermined him, had wrecked his finest plans.

Dejected, Mickey was left to grapple with the notion that he had raised a monstrous child. The young man in whom he'd been so eager to discover the hope and promise of youth, whom he'd wanted so badly to embrace as an image of himself, had become corrupted by ambition and power. Qualities like honesty and gratitude and good sense—all the things that Mickey had tried to instill in him throughout his childhood—had been tossed out the window. How defensive and protective he'd become at a few well-meaning suggestions! How proud of that computer!

Mickey grabbed the gearshift and pulled; and as he sent the old van barreling out into the street, he suddenly recalled something Emi had said, years ago, during her first pregnancy: how she feared that the child, were it a male, would remind her of her father, the collaborator, the heartless industrialist who'd made his fortune off the blood of others.

And yesterday: hadn't he seen, in Ben's dark, gleaming eyes, the first faint lights of ruthlessness?

It was crazy: there he was on the plane coming home, worrying himself sick that he'd been a derelict father, that Ben was in some way crying out for him, only to find that the kid had been living the life of Riley, computer and all, cutting shrewd deals and summarily axing his workers. Oh, he'd been self-sufficient all right! But what hurt Mickey most was that the kid had probably wished his father had never returned, that he'd stayed abroad forever. And then to withhold crucial information—to cost him his chances with Donna! Oh, it would have been one thing had the kid been, when Mickey first saw him there behind the desk, the picture of neglect—he might forgive him, then—but damned if he hadn't walked in on a small-time tycoon, who, even at this moment, up there behind the door of his bedroom—Mickey could see it—was plotting his father's deposal.

Mickey bore down on the road. He wasn't sure which end was up

anymore. But in a secret place in his conscience, so secret he was
barely aware it existed, he wondered if he weren't inflating the imagery a little so as to avoid the fact of his own desertion.

Ben stared out his bedroom window at the rooftops, the wires and
bare branches, the cold white sky. Rattner's voice had been oddly conspiratorial, as though he and Ben were now brothers in doom. "Nelson put a gun to my head last night," Rattner had told him over the
phone. "I don't know if you've had any trouble, but I thought I should
call and warn you. But don't, I repeat *don't* under any circumstances—
do you hear me, Lerner?—don't you dare breathe a word of this to
anyone. Not even the cops. He'll kill me otherwise. I'm not kidding,
Lerner. He put a gun to my head last night and fired. Missed my head
by an inch."

It had taken everything in Ben's power to cover his own terror—he
knew that Mickey was watching him—and when he hung up the office phone (dropped it, really, he was so insensible with fear) he saw
his father in yet another light entirely. The man had gone from being
a benefactor for whom Ben had been so anxious to make good, to a
defector who had left him in harm's way, to an unwelcome invader
who, raving about ovens and bricks and baskets, had failed to recognize his accomplishments, to finally a kind of unwitting protector, his
one shield against Nelson. With Mickey back, Ben could stay cooped
up in his room with the gun in his hand instead of being an open target at the bakery. And he would no longer be all alone in the house at
night.

And yet he had his doubts as to whether Mickey would ever literally protect him, defend him, should the worst come to pass. Hadn't
Mickey always kept him more or less at arm's length, as though he
were embarrassed of him, ashamed? And to think that all he'd wanted
to do was please the man, make him proud! Why had he even made
the effort? For it was obvious, now, that his work had been over-
looked. Mickey wanted to change things. Change them! And the
worst thing of all was that he would never have come home in the first
place had it not been for the arrests. The police must have contacted
him in France. But suppose they hadn't? Would he have just stayed
over there forever?

Ben looked down at the gun in his hands. He tried to recall any signs of his father's pride, his approval. Hadn't he said, last night in the kitchen, that he, Ben, had done a real bang-up job? And before that, at the bakery; hadn't he said he wouldn't turn everything upside down? And hadn't he been impressed with the computer, and the Lazarus decision, and how everything in the office was so neat and orderly? Wasn't it just possible that he was a lot more pleased than he'd let on, that between his exhaustion and all the hoopla over the arrests, and then the changes at the bakery, he'd simply been too overwhelmed to react? Wasn't it possible that he was in fact bursting with pride, but that maybe he'd felt a little funny—a little jealous—about how things had come along so well without him?

But if he *was* proud, Ben thought; if he *was* pleased by his son's achievements—but no, it was too awful a thought. And yet what if he found out about Nelson, found out that Nelson had been fired, that Ben had maybe mishandled things, and that Nelson now had a possible vendetta against the bakery? Would that cancel all the good he had done? What would Mickey think of him then?

And what was to stop Nelson from showing up at the bakery while Mickey was there, and telling him what had happened? Or worse—coming in and shooting the place up? Wasn't *that* possible too?

Ben felt a new fear—that Mickey himself was in danger. Should he warn him? Tell him what had happened? Explain his side of the story before Nelson had a chance to act? Or was that taking too much of a risk? Suppose Nelson just faded from the picture?

No: he couldn't tell Mickey the truth about Nelson. How could he ever admit that he'd bungled the situation, that he'd hemmed and hawed and waffled and displayed all sorts of weakness, whereas Mickey had never parted on bad terms with an employee in his whole career?

He needed to see his father right now, he decided, needed to get another reading of the man's feelings, his thoughts. It was impossible to sit still any longer without knowing exactly how Mickey felt about him.

It was already four in the afternoon. Ben got dressed and placed the gun in his coat pocket, just in case Nelson should decide to surprise him along the way. It was a good thing Rattner had warned him, he thought. Rattner, of all people, looking out for him.

There was snow coming; Ben could smell it, a hint of smoke in the air. By the time he reached the end of the alley his ears stung, but his hands were warm inside the gloves that Donna had given him.

The bakery came into view. Ben crossed the street and stood at the far end of the parking lot.

He looked in all directions: no sign of Nelson. He walked around the lot and crept up to the bakery from the side. At the edge of the window he turned and peeked in. Behind the counter stood, not Mickey or Morris, but Lazarus; he was reading his tattered book, rocking back and forth, lips parted. The new counterman? A white skull-cap lay on his head like a snowball smashed home by a Gentile.

Morris would be at lunch, Ben figured. Mickey would be back in the office.

Lazarus looked up as he entered. It was strange seeing Lazarus under these circumstances; just a few days ago he'd been signing the man's paychecks. Now he himself was in limbo, and Lazarus was waiting on customers.

"Good afternoon," said Lazarus.

"Hi," said Ben. "What are you doing here?"

"Morris called me and asked if I would come in and give a hand. He was all alone, he said, it was getting busy, and can I come in and help? So here I am. Meanwhile he went to eat lunch."

Ben nodded. There wasn't much warmth between them; Lazarus had serious reservations about the child of a woman who would choose to be cremated.

"Is my father here?" said Ben.

"No," said Lazarus. "He was here an hour ago, then he went out to make a delivery at the nursing home." There was a hint of rebuke in his voice. "He should be back any moment." He returned to his book.

Ben went to the back. The work area looked the same as it had yesterday—the tables, the mixers—but the office had already begun to return to its former disarray: papers and mail lay piled on the desk. It was like entering a patient's room and smelling urine: a kind of senile incontinence seemed manifest in the renewed chaos of receipts and bills and notices.

There came a sound from outside—the van doors sliding open. Ben rushed to the front of the store, where he saw, through the window, a sight that ripped his heart: the figure unloading cargo was not the strong, silver-haired man in a starched white shirt whistling a tune as he made short work of a few empty boxes, but rather, a bent, gray, weatherworn man in trousers and work gloves, snorting steam, his muscles straining with each unwieldy lift and heave.

Ben pictured him fighting traffic in a heap of rattling metal, hauling boxes in his arms or rolling them on the dolly through garbage-stinking delivery entrances. It was a far cry from bricks and baskets, wheat fields and mills, all those ideas that he had spoken about so passionately the day before.

Ben went outside. He could hear Mickey grunting as he reached into the van to pull out the empty boxes.

"Dad."

There was no response.

Ben cleared his throat and tried again. "Dad?"

Mickey looked up. His face was red with cold and exertion. But there was something else there too. Something had happened.

"Need a hand?" Ben said.

"No," said Mickey. He threw the work gloves into the back of the van and looked away.

"You sure?"

"Yes."

Ben shivered. What was it? Had Morris said something to him about Nelson? Had Rattner called?

Mickey tossed another box.

"I want to help," Ben said. He reached inside the van for the last box.

"I don't need help!" Mickey yelled. When Ben pulled out the box, Mickey grabbed it with his bare hands.

But Ben kept hold of the other end; for some reason he could not surrender it. "Let go!" said Mickey. He tugged, ripping a corner of the box. Ben held on and pulled with all he had, causing Mickey to lose his footing. They were now on the far side of the van, out of view of the bakery windows.

"Let me help!" said Ben. He was confused by the struggle, but at the same time could not divorce himself from it; he'd rather rip the box than give it up.

He staggered forward as Mickey yanked at the box, then was thrown back into metal. The force of the crash electrified him. The box fell away from his fingers and flew up in the air with the swing of Mickey's arm, landing on the other side of the van.

"What did I do?" Ben said.

Mickey looked fiercely into his eyes, and suddenly he resembled his former robust self. "Why didn't you tell me?" he demanded. "Why didn't you tell me you fired Nelson? Why did I have to hear it from Nelson's mother?"

Ben could barely speak. "I—I was going to tell you!" he said, staggered that his worst imagining had in fact come to pass. He felt he might fall to his knees.

"You lied to me. Why did you lie?"

"I—"

"What happened!" said Mickey. "Tell me what happened!"

Ben was near tears. "Nelson made a threat to Jay Rattner," he blurted. "He threatened to kill him. I had to do something, Rattner was ready to cut us off, I had to—"

"Why didn't you call me!" Mickey said. "I told you to call me if there was any trouble. Why didn't you call me and tell me what was happening!"

"Why," Ben shouted back, "did you leave me?"

There was a silence, in which Mickey stared at him with wild, uncomprehending eyes. Ben hardly knew what he had said—the words had shot up as if from some exploded core—but he could see that he had struck a nerve in his father, who himself had fallen speechless.

"You should have been here," Ben said, and he felt the trembling of another eruption. "Then you could have handled it yourself. You could have saved Nelson." He glared savagely at his father: "And why wouldn't you—you liked him better than me anyway!"

And he realized that, crazy as it sounded, it was true. Mickey had always treated Nelson gently and with fatherly approval.

"Benjie," Mickey said. His eyes were now pleading for understanding.

"You were always nicer to him," Ben pursued. "Like when—" He broke off, pained by the image, then took a breath and came out with it: "Like when you'd teach him stuff about boxing." He looked away, ashamed of his outburst, but still he saw them there, on the bakery floor, the two of them exchanging playful blows, Mickey instructing, Nelson nodding. And himself standing in the shadows, watching.

"Turn around," came Mickey's voice. It was calm but firm. "Look at me."

Ben turned to his father.

"Put your hands up," Mickey said. "Like this." He crouched and held his fists against his temples.

Ben was hesitant—he didn't want to be pitied—but there was a cold-nosed puppy inside his rib cage that in spite of him leaped to the call, yelping scrappily through the bars.

"See," said Mickey. "You want to keep your hands up and move from side to side, like this. See that? With your shoulders, your head." He caught his breath. "Bob and weave. Move. Duck. To the left, to the right. A little fake. See that?" He was panting now. "Punch comes—you're moving. Don't drop those hands."

Ben held up his fists, mimicked his father's stance. "How do you jab again?" he said stupidly.

"Step into it. Your right foot. And then you shoot your arm out and turn the fist over." Mickey demonstrated. "Jab," he said. He did it again. "Jab!" He dropped his hands. "Go ahead and try it." He stood within an arm's length. "Throw one," he said, and pointed to his jutting chin. "Right there."

"But I'll hit you," Ben said.

"Jab," said Mickey.

"But—"

"Come on!"

Ben thrilled to his father's command. He swallowed his fear and then, when neither of them could have been expecting it, thrust out his gloved fist—and felt his shoulder nearly pop from its socket. He'd punched at nothing: the target had disappeared.

"See that?" said Mickey. "Now you try it."

"What do I do?"

"When I jab," said Mickey, "you duck to the side. Your feet stay planted. Upper body we're talking. When I jab"—in slow motion he guided his pink brick of a fist toward Ben's face—"you move."

Ben moved to the right, and the fist whispered past his ear.

"That's it," said Mickey. "Now a little faster. Ready? Keep your hands up. Here goes: jab!"

Ben moved—the fist whizzed by. Close! Ben felt a tingle at the destruction which he'd barely eluded. "Again," he heard himself say. "Faster."

Mickey planted his feet. "Ready? And jab—"

There was a flash of white light and then a dazzle of dark colors. Ben found himself on the ground, blind, half his face ringing with pain.

"Benjie! Jesus. Are you okay?"

He felt his father's hand on his arm; quickly he got up, too stunned to cry out.

"Jesus—why didn't you get out of the way? Here, let me look at it—"

Ben flinched, turned his head. "I'm okay."

"Why didn't you move?" said Mickey. "I'll run and get some ice—"

"No," said Ben.

"Go home and get some ice on it," Mickey said. "Christ, I'm sorry.

I didn't mean to get you like that. You didn't move. Here, let me look—"

Ben backed away. His chest heaved; he was afraid he might cry. "I'll put some ice on it," he said, then turned and bolted across the lot like a cat on fire. He weaved through the parked cars and rushed heedlessly into the street, sending up a chorus of horn blasts and squealing rubber, and when he reached the other side he ran even faster. The pain in his face had concentrated itself into a hot, throbbing point under his eye, and as he ran through the alley he carried that pain in the palm of his hand, holding it as though it were something rare and precious and alive.

Once home, he rushed upstairs to the bathroom and looked into the mirror. Half his face was swollen and turning colors. The eye was a slit. He touched it reverently.

He honestly could not say whether he'd had time to elude the punch or not; all he could remember was the sound of his father's voice as he called out his name—*Benjie!*—that thrilling note of concern and compassion which for an infinitesimal instant had glittered in the air.

In his room he undressed, drew the shades and crawled onto the bed, grabbing the covers and yanking them over his body so that he was wrapped tight and warm inside them. The pulse of the pain became a metronome, ticking in time with his heartbeat. He cupped the bruise in his hands: he would carry it with him to sleep, a beating light in the darkness, a warning of danger to all in his dreams who sought to do him harm.

Floating languidly just below wakefulness, he perceived a weight beside him, a heat, which he knew must belong to his father.

"Can you hear me?" came the voice.

Ben felt himself nod. He plunged a little deeper toward sleep, imagining himself barely visible from above, a shadow, a sinking shape in the dark, lapping water.

"I'm sorry," said his father's voice. "I'm sorry for all the things I've done to hurt you. I just want you to know that you mean more to me than anything else in the world."

The words dove bravely down into the darkness and Ben swam alongside them, reaching out in fear and fascination to touch the broad white belly of their meaning. It was then that he felt a brush of rough warmth against his cheek, and the light pressure of a dry but tender flesh which sent him twisting bashfully downwards and with a shudder into a pocket of rare warmth. There was a faint click, and then slowly the presence receded. Ben tried to reach out to it, struggling up to the lambent, spangled surface, only to fall back deliciously from the light.

25

The muscles in Mickey's arm tensed and bulged as he scraped the starter from one bowl into another. He'd prepared it last night before going to bed, and now, eight hours later, the mixture was desirably fragrant and fizzy, and gloppy as quicksand. In the second, larger bowl he mixed in careful measurements of water (the bottled stuff, from some underground source in Maine), yeast and organic flour that he'd purchased from his vendor yesterday afternoon.

It was almost six in the morning; a light, tapering snow fell outside, white ashes spinning in the troubled air, the ground growing old with a hoary white moss. By noon, Mickey figured, it will have all but melted away.

The kitchen glowed with fluorescent light, the only light in the world: it was Saturday and the bakery was closed.

The mixture in the bowl thickened; Mickey had to give it his all to move the wooden spoon. The dough was ready to be slapped onto the table and kneaded, but Mickey was reluctant to surrender his grip on the wood. He stirred and stirred.

It wasn't clear if the kid had been awake or not, but somehow Mickey knew that his words had reached him. To what effect remained to be seen. As with Donna Childs, he'd told the truth; finally, that was all you could really do.

Still, he wondered why the kid hadn't moved out of the way. It was as if he'd *wanted* to be hit; as if he'd wanted his father to *feel* what it was like to hurt him.

Mickey emptied the dough onto the kitchen table, and set out a bowl of flour.

When he looked up, he saw Ben standing in the doorway, wearing the blue bathrobe that Mickey had given him a few years ago. His eye was black, blue, green.

"Jesus," Mickey said. "You might want to get some more ice on that thing."

Ben shrugged. "I will." His hands were in the pockets of the robe. It made Mickey wonder how long he'd been standing there.

Mickey dipped his hands in the flour, then dug the heel of his palm into the soft, sticky dough and pushed it forward.

"What are you doing?" said Ben.

Mickey stopped. It occurred to him that he ought to be embarrassed, that a kid might think it strange to come downstairs at dawn and see his father in a white apron, playing with a blob of dough. "Making bread," he said. As the gluten strengthened he had to involve more of his body, bending his knees, rotating his shoulders.

Ben came closer. "What are you going to do with that bowl of flour?"

"I have to add it in. A little at a time."

Ben picked up the bowl. "Now?" He tilted the bowl and let some flour fall over the mass of dough. Some of it landed on Mickey's wrists. It felt cool as talc.

"Is that good?" said Ben.

"Yes. But you don't want too much; that'll dry the dough out." He stopped himself, thinking that Ben might be mocking him. He kneaded more vigorously.

"How long do you have to do that?"

Mickey stopped, took a breath. "Until the dough is ready."

"How long is that?"

"Usually about fifteen minutes."

"You should get a mixer."

Mickey ignored that. He sprinkled in more flour and continued.

Ben shifted his weight. Despite his qualms he stared at Mickey's hands like a fascinated child, and Mickey began to study them that way too; they seemed so skilled.

A minute passed.

"Can I try it?" Ben said.

Mickey stopped and looked at him. The eye was a mess, but he tried to see past it. "You want to try?" he said.

"Sure."

Mickey dipped into the bowl for more flour. "Are your hands clean?"

Ben went to the sink. Mickey listened to the rush of water. A cautious joy took root.

"Okay," said Ben. "They're clean."

"Okay," said Mickey. "First thing, you put your hands like this. Then you dig in with your feet and really use some elbow grease." He rolled the dough. "Got it?"

"Yeah."

"Get some flour on your hands. That's it."

Ben positioned his hands. Mickey wanted to grasp the wrists and guide them, but feared his touch might cause Ben to recoil.

The dough rolled, slowly.

"Good. Now pull it back," said Mickey. He took the dough blade from the table and put it in the sink.

"It's hard," said Ben.

"It takes muscle," said Mickey. He returned to the table and sprinkled in some flour. "Elbow grease. Come on now."

Ben took a breath.

"Work it out," said Mickey. "That's it. Good."

Ben kept at it. Mickey could see that something was kindling inside him—the child's wonder of creation. It was as if the dough had called him from his bed, down the steps and into its softness; he was becoming immersed in it, his one good eye marveling at the changes brought forth by his hands.

"It's getting smoother," he said.

"That's the idea," said Mickey.

"Less sticky."

"That's the idea."

Mickey held the bowl of flour and sprinkled at intervals. He remembered how he'd taught Emi to eat steamed crabs at this very table—how they'd communicated so much and said so little. "You got another ten minutes," he said. "Then you can do a little test. Poke the dough with your finger. If it pops right back, it's done. And remember—careful with how much flour."

Mickey went to the kitchen door and looked out. A pink opaline light had spread over the yard; the clouds were breaking up; the snow on the ground was in tatters.

Between the cherry tree and the flower bed lay a plot of earth, a neat little expanse which suddenly suggested itself as a potential site—Mickey dared to picture it—for a wood-fired oven. Hope came back to him like feeling to frozen fingertips: he imagined not only building the oven with Ben—the mortar, the bricks, the good clean work in the crisp air—but also the feasts they could make there in all seasons: corn, squash, shrimp, turkey, potatoes, clams, apples; they could even roast chestnuts, and the fragrant smoke would be the talk of the neighborhood.

"Dad?"

Mickey turned. "Yes?"

"I think it's ready."

"Good," said Mickey. He walked over.

"Now what?"

"Now we let the dough rise."

"It's gonna be good," Ben said.

Mickey smiled at the kid's innocence. "It'll only be as good as we are," he said. He shaped the dough into a ball. "Take that oil there and rub the inside of that big bowl. Use a paper towel. That's it." When the bowl was greased Mickey filled it with the ball of dough. Then he turned the ball over to lightly grease the top. "Okay. Get me a dish towel from the drawer and wet it and wring it out so it's damp."

Ben did this. "Here," he said, holding out the towel.

Mickey took it and felt the slightest resistance; he had to yank a little. A fear passed through him.

"Now we cover the dough," he said. He was aware of Ben behind him. "And we let it sit."

"How long?"

Mickey turned. Ben was inspecting the webbing of dough still caught on his fingers. "Three hours," Mickey said.

Ben looked at him. "Three hours?"

"Until it doubles in size."

"Like my face." He smiled.

Mickey looked away. "And we can't disturb the bowl. The dough could collapse."

"Three hours."

"Good things come to those who wait," said Mickey. He placed the bowl atop the refrigerator. "The temperature should be close to perfect up there. Don't touch the thermostat."

"I won't."

"Meet me back here in three hours," said Mickey. "Okay?"

"Where are you going?"

"Just out back. Maybe I'll take a jog."

"I think I'll go back to bed," said Ben.

"Wait," said Mickey. He opened the freezer and took out some ice cubes and placed them in a plastic bag. "Go and get that swelling down." He handed Ben the bag.

Mickey waited and listened to Ben's footfalls on the stairs. Then he took off his apron and went outside.

The cold felt good. He picked up some frosted stones from around the flower bed and laid them out on the ground, outlining the foundation of his prospective oven.

The house was quiet; Ben must have been asleep. Mickey took the bowl down from atop the refrigerator and uncovered it. The dough had progressed admirably. He wished Ben would come down, so that he could show him the bloated dough and explain to him the next step, which was to dump the dough back onto the table and deflate it by flattening the center by hand. Mickey did this himself, satisfied that it was still a team effort. He formed the dough into a ball again, then returned it to the bowl and covered it.

Thirty minutes later he put on his apron and dusted the table with flour. He turned out the dough, deflated it and divided it into two parts, both of which he kneaded for several minutes. Then he packed them into balls: these would be round loaves. Peasant stuff.

Ben appeared in the doorway, holding the melted ice pack. "Did I miss anything?" he said.

"No," said Mickey. "You're just in time to help. Can you grab two towels and two medium-sized bowls?"

Ben dropped the bag of water into the sink and did as he was told.

"Line the bowls with the towels," said Mickey. "And rub a little flour into the cloth."

"Like this?"

"Yes." Mickey placed the raw loaves into the bowls and dusted the tops with flour.

"Now what?" said Ben.

"Now we cover them with towels and wait another two hours."

"You're joking."

Mickey shrugged. "Rome wasn't built in a day."

"Yeah. It was built in five hundred years."

"Well, we won't have to wait that long, fortunately."

"What happens after we wait another two hours?"

"Then we bake," said Mickey.

"How long will that take?"

"Five hours."

Ben's chin dropped. "What?"

Mickey laughed. "Forty-five minutes, tops."

Ben went to the refrigerator and poured himself some orange juice.

Mickey sniffed his hands. Fresh dough. Back at Dulac's there were times when he'd thought he'd never get enough of that smell.

"I think I'll go downstairs," said Mickey. "Maybe listen to some music. See what your mother left down there." He looked at Ben. "You're welcome to join me."

The kid turned his head. "That's okay," he said. "I'll just meet you back here in an hour and a half."

It was like a promise between lovers: Mickey's heart soared.

Perhaps the strangest thing of all about being home was to enter through the basement door without knocking and walk down the steps into silence.

Mickey looked around: the shelves, the desk, the music stand, the chair; everything was covered with a bluish film of dust, and Mickey could almost sense, in the walls, the floor, a soft, fading return to a previous incarnation—the wood-paneled clubroom of his adolescence, where the pennants of all the football teams were tacked in the shape of a pinwheel to the ceiling and the phonograph needle snapped and popped over the shoobie-lahs of some forgotten doo-wop sensation whose bass vocalist Mickey had sung along to in the mirror, using his old bicycle pump as a microphone.

Even his wife's most intimate items—her clothes, her shoes, her jewels, probably too her violin, which was locked away for safekeeping—no longer vouched for her ownership; they had become almost absurdly themselves—a shoe, a blouse—and nothing more. It was as though she had never invested herself strongly enough in the object world to have inspired a proper afterglow. Even her blood, Mickey suspected, had it still been there on the sidewalk, would have had very little to say for itself.

There was a single disc in the player: the sixth symphony of Tchaikovsky, recorded some twenty years ago when Emi was still with the orchestra. It was one of the few symphonic recordings she ever made. Mickey figured out the knobs on the stereo, then took a seat in

Emi's chair and read the accompanying notes. It was Tchaikovsky's last major work, a dark piece whose mood was similar to that of a requiem. "Without exaggeration," Tchaikovsky said, "I have put my entire soul into this symphony." He died nine days after conducting the first performance in St. Petersburg.

Mickey closed his eyes and listened. He might have put on one of her chamber recordings, a sonata perhaps, so that he could hear her voice distinctly, but it was more interesting somehow to try and pick her out in a crowd. The first movement began in a low whisper as a bassoon rose up through a fog of what sounded like double basses, and already Mickey could feel the tension, the anticipation of the violins, whose forceful entrance a few moments later caused him to clutch at his thighs. The theme mounted to a nervous climax, then faded; and then a lone voice—was it hers?—prepared the way for a great romantic swell of strings. Mickey's thoughts drifted in and out of the music, which had by now quieted down considerably; and then he was nearly startled out of his chair by a sudden and unexpected knife of strings: terror: his heart had stopped. Then the suspense grew, the chord was struck again and again, now spilling over into a fast, frantic, almost demonic restatement of the theme, a frenzy in which Mickey suffered visions of impending violence—only to relent (Mickey exhaled slowly), then build, relent, build, now with great bombast, and relent again, and then, on the wings of the string section, swell melodiously before dwindling with a plucked pulse of a countermelody down to silence.

Listening to the subsequent movements, Mickey was amazed at the range of moods and emotions that the composer had squeezed into one cohesive work. There was a whole lifetime of pain and terror in this music, but also of joy and sorrow and wit; but above all there was beauty. Mickey was amazed at how much sense it all made to him now, compared to when he had first heard it twenty years ago. He listened with great sensitivity, taking in every note, every surprise, whisper, frolic, every worrisome brassy plunge. And all throughout he listened for Emi, riding with her in the dark through the snorted steam and hoof claps of some glacial Russian winter. He did not realize that his face was awash in tears.

When the final movement went out like a winking ember—when the theme from the first movement had been resurrected, only to be extinguished in strands of thin, gloomy smoke, fading, fading—when silence had seamlessly taken over and made its own great statement, Mickey felt as though he had arrived with his wife at the very edge of the world, and felt too that even now, at this very moment, her soul remained in the swirl of that music, still flying out over the cobble-stones and black forests of a snowy purple night.

He had found her; he knew where she was.

In the kitchen he lined the oven rack with the thick terra-cotta tiles that he'd bought at the housewares store. He preheated the oven to about as hot as it could get.

Ben arrived on schedule, fully dressed. The eye looked improved.

"Finally," Ben said. "The moment of truth."

"Yes," said Mickey. He floured up a large cutting board and turned the raw loaves onto it. "Now," he said. He took up the dough blade. "You do one, I'll do the other."

"Do what?"

"We have to cut lines in the dough," said Mickey. "It's called scoring. Cut in about a half inch. Make any design you want." He handed Ben the knife.

Ben looked at the ball of dough. Then he inserted the knife and carved a plain X.

"Is that it?" said Mickey.

"That's it," said Ben. He seemed pleased with the simplicity of it, the directness of statement. He placed the knife on the cutting board instead of handing it over.

Mickey picked up the knife. "Now let me see," he said. He was a little drained from the music and had no ideas. He shrugged and drew a circle, as a kind of counterpart to the X.

"Hmm," said Ben. He took the blade and filled in the circle with eyes, a nose, a line for a mouth.

"He doesn't look too happy," said Mickey.

"Look where's he's going," Ben said.

Mickey laughed. "Okay. Now see that spritzer bottle on the counter there? Fill it up with cold water."

Ben did.

"Okay," said Mickey. He opened the oven: the heat rushed out and filled the kitchen. "Now as soon as I slide these loaves onto the tiles there, I'll need you to spray the sides of the oven until we get a lot of steam. Ready?"

"Yeah."

Mickey slid in the loaves; Ben sprayed. A dense, sizzling fog developed. Mickey shut the door to trap it.

"Now it's up to the oven," said Mickey. He thought to hold out his hand and shake on a job well done, but something—superstition, maybe—told him to wait until the loaves were baked. "I think I'll do some digging outside. The ground's softened up from the snow." He paused, then said, "Care to join me?"

"Maybe in a few minutes," Ben said. "I'll clean up some of this stuff."

"Okay," said Mickey.

From the small shed next to the backdoor Mickey grabbed the garden shovel, then proceeded to the far end of the yard. On the way he stopped to check the feeder. It was empty, but not for long. The birds had some real good bread coming, at least a few crusts of it, and Mickey liked to think that even they would notice the difference in the quality.

The snow had melted: the garden was nothing but a long bed of mud. It was the sweetest smell in the world, Mickey thought, and with the sun on his shoulders and the sky a deep blue with puffs of clouds that mimicked the cloud-shaped loaves of snow still in evidence on some lawns, there was every reason—even in January—to feel giddy with anticipation of spring.

He struck the ground. It was good to come out over the course of the winter and pay attention to the soil, to chop it, turn it. Of course, the planting wouldn't be the same this year—he and Emi had made a ritual of it, and it seemed almost a sacrilege to plant anything without her. Still, he looked forward to the work, to the harvest, to those muggy days of summer bright with hidden color among the vines.

The mud wasn't very thick; at the attack of the shovel it crumbled and broke into little dry clods.

Maybe Benjie would help him plant this year. They could build the oven, brick by brick, and then plant the food that would eventually be offered there. But then he cautioned himself against hoping for too much.

He turned around to face the house, almost expecting Ben to be standing at the door, watching him. But the door was a blank on account of the sun, as were the windows. And yet Benjie was in there, cleaning up. Mickey could hear it: the tinkle of dishes and cabinets that had been, upon Emi's arrival in his life, such music to his ears.

He could smell the bread.

A sound caused him to turn. A man was in the alley, walking toward him. His hands were in the pockets of his oversized coat; his face was obscured by a large hood. Mickey's heart stopped for a moment—this one looked like a character—but then he saw the face and realized that it was Nelson. His initial wild hope was that Nelson had been sent by Donna armed with some hopeful message, but then he remembered having invited him to stop by. Mickey waved to him.

But something was wrong; Mickey recalled what Ben had said to him yesterday, on the bakery lot, about Nelson having threatened Jay Rattner. Mickey had forgotten about it—there'd been so many other things on his mind—but now the idea worried him.

Nelson entered through the gate. "Hey, Mr. Lerner," he said. He stood just a few feet from Mickey. "I've got something for you." His right hand dug deep in the coat pocket.

What was it? Nelson came closer to him, the one hand still digging while the other reached out to clasp Mickey's shoulder as if in greeting.

A voice called out: *"Don't!"*

Mickey turned. Ben stood on the porch, pointing what looked to be a toy gun, and the next thing Mickey knew there was a loud *pop* and Nelson dove to the ground, and then another *pop* that kicked up some mud just a foot from where Nelson lay, and Mickey shouted his son's name, this was no joke, no toy, it was real, Jesus God it was real, and Ben froze, and as Mickey dropped to his knees beside Nelson, who was motionless, he could feel—was he imagining it?—a stinging in his gut, no, a burning; and when he looked down he saw that there was a stain on his sweatshirt.

"Shit," he muttered. The stain grew. Mickey wasn't sure if he should fall forward or just sit there and stare.

He covered the spot with his hand. The burning got worse.

Nelson breathed. His eyes were closed, his hands covered his head. On the ground by his feet, Mickey noticed, were several packets of seeds from the Green Garden Nursery. "I didn't come here to hurt anybody," Nelson said.

"Put the gun down," Mickey told his son. There'd be time for questions later, he thought. Or maybe there wouldn't.

"Dad." Ben approached, staring openmouthed, the gun dangling in his hand. "No."

Mickey grimaced. "We'd better turn off the oven," he said, "and drive me to the emergency room."

26

The bullet had passed through the colon, causing among other things a flood of contaminating waste to escape into his bloodstream. As soon as he arrived at the emergency room he was rushed into surgery.

Bleeding freely and painlessly in the car (they had decided not to wait for an ambulance), Mickey had had his doubts. To die now would not have surprised him in the least. Why else should he have gone through so much, learned so much, if not to have it all pulled from underneath him? Why shouldn't he be robbed of the next twenty or so years of his life, during which he could have used his experience, his wisdom, his love, to make something, even a small thing, better than what it had been?

He'd closed his eyes and held the dish towel to his wound as Nelson next to him in the backseat and Ben behind the wheel argued as to why all of this had happened, Mickey ascertaining feebly and with wavering concentration that Nelson had given Ben the gun for protection just after Emi's death, and that Ben, what with Rattner's story ringing in his ears, had thought Nelson had come to do harm, and so to save his father had fired in a panic and with bad aim, Nelson meanwhile ducking for cover, Nelson who with a new job had simply come to hand out plant seed and say hello.

Mickey felt woozy. Inside him there was a bullet. And this bullet was the seed of dying: it wouldn't grow, but it would bring all the life that enclosed it folding inward to shrink upon its heat. And yet as he slumped over the burning hole, pressing the towel against it, he felt, too, that he'd been implanted with something else—a difficult sort of love, well-intentioned yet errant, the clumsy, reckless yearning of the young.

They'd gone in and cut out the damaged section of intestine and then put the two new ends back together. They did a lavage and recovered the bullet, which was handed over to the police crime lab for tests. Later, in the course of vomiting on his sheets in the blinding white recovery room, Mickey had been told by the surgeon, a handsome young man from India with black eyes, that he was a lucky son of a gun, no pun intended, and to expect among other things a nifty scar from his sternum all the way down to below the navel.

They'd be watching for abscesses, infection. Pills he would have to take, antibiotics, like it or not. The painkillers were optional, but Mickey was quick to see as how one or two might be helpful. The best thing was that he wouldn't have to worry about one of those colostomy tubes—they'd sewn him right back together just as clean as you'd like. Still, a bowel movement was nothing to look forward to. It would be a long time, months perhaps, before he could sit on the toilet and enjoy.

A few days later he woke up from an unnaturally long sleep that had been brought on, he was sure, by the goddamned pills. Morris was seated next to him, reading the paper.

"How long have I been here?" said Mickey.

"A few days," Morris said. "You'll be out in another week, maybe less, if you start doing what you're told." Then, like a father: "If you get a better attitude."

"My attitude's fine," said Mickey. He stared for a long while at the ceiling.

It was a nice room, as hospital rooms went, large and private, in fact it was the deluxe room on the floor. Everyone should have a room so nice, Mickey reflected. Of course, he was paying good money for it. A big color TV projected down on him, and through a doorway was another room with a sofa and chairs and another television. Ben had

PAUL HOND

slept on the sofa every night since the surgery: he ran the bakery by day, and, afterwards, he came here.

A lot had happened over the past few days. There'd been a whole to-do over the gun, the police were involved, and Mickey in his fresh bandages had called Detective Flemke from the bedside phone the minute he was wheeled there from the recovery room and groggily told him what happened, stressing that it was purely an accident, that these were both good kids, even saying that Nelson was practically a son to him (and in his postoperative stupor it did not seem an exaggeration), and that with all the grief they'd endured already, to say nothing of his own uncertain condition, the last thing his family needed was legal trouble.

Flemke coughed into the phone and then indicated that they, the police, would have to question Nelson about the gun, which of course could lead to some problems for Nelson—"No way around that," Flemke said—and problems for Ben too, if it turned out the gun could be traced to any crimes for which Ben or Nelson could be a suspect. Mickey moaned at this news. "But," said Flemke, "if the story's as clean as you say, then your son might be looking at a little probation or community service," and then he coughed again and added, "or if he's lucky, maybe even not that," which Mickey in his delirium took as a wink, that Flemke would possibly pull some strings on his behalf.

But it was Nelson who was most lucky. Ben had explained it all to Mickey the other evening: because Nelson had no previous criminal record, and was cooperative and well-spoken and employed, the police were inclined to accept his story, which was that, in order to protect himself from neighborhood thugs, he'd bought the gun off a local dope fiend named Withers, who wasn't unknown to the police, and who, when the cops found him thin and dying in a city shelter, told them not only that he'd sold a gun to Nelson, but that he'd done other things, great things, that might also be of interest to law enforcement.

"Here," said Morris. "I snuck this in special." He held up a greasy brown bag with a receipt stapled to it.

"Uh-huh," Mickey said dully. He wasn't hungry. "What time is it?" There was a mellow blue daylight in the window, between the blinds.

"It's just after three," said Morris.

"Maybe," said Mickey, "we should call Ben, see if you ought to run over to the store and give him a hand."

"He's been doing fine," Morris said, a little glumly. "Been doing just fine on his own."

There was a pause in which both men silently acknowledged the quiet passing of a torch.

"Anyhow," said Morris, "when I was picking up the food I ran into Joe Blank and his wife. They were having lunch."

"Lunch?" said Mickey.

"Place was packed and jammed," said Morris. "It's New Year's Day, ya know."

"That right?"

Morris nodded, an old man sitting alone on a national holiday. Well, not entirely alone. "Happy New Year, Mickey," Morris said, and pushed the glasses up on his nose.

And so it was New Year's. There was a time, a while back, when Mickey would close the store on New Year's, but when the King holiday was established, he decided to close up on that day instead. You couldn't have two off days in January, and New Year's was better for business, what with the football parties, and people wanting to eat. Besides, it gratified him to close on King Day, giving him as it did the feeling that he was striking a blow for racial unity. Morris had other opinions. "Martin *Looter* King, they ought to call him, all the tumult he caused." But he enjoyed the time off just the same.

"Joe Blank asked about you," Morris was saying. "Asked if you were still overseas."

"And?"

Morris touched his glasses. "I said as far as I knew, that's where you were." He looked at Mickey. "Did I do right?"

"Yes," said Mickey.

"He thinks you met a woman." Morris sat back, his legs arthritically spread. Two rings of pale, ashen flesh showed between his dark socks and the cuffs of his trousers. Mickey could not remember the last time he'd glimpsed his uncle's private skin. He forgot that the old man had feet, an ass. A stomach.

"And I told Shirley you went away to the woods for a couple of weeks. A cabin in the woods."

"Good," said Mickey. No one needed to see him like this, he'd decided. Already he'd lost weight. He was weak, tired. He looked like hell.

How was it possible? Never in his life had he been hospitalized. Never in his life had he missed a day of work on account of illness. He'd prided himself on that, and it depressed him to no end, that his health had been taken from him.

It seemed a thousand miles away, that beaming health, no, farther,

as impossible and far away as Dulac's cellar. He could not imagine recovering. That he might ever jog again, or bend down in the garden,
or lift a rock, or drive a shovel, or press his palms into a fat thigh of
dough—it was inconceivable to him. Health was another country. He
couldn't even go to the toilet without hurting, couldn't even laugh,
for Christ's sake, without lighting up with pain, and he could at least
thank God there was so little to laugh at. Morris had tried, the old
goat—told a string of racy jokes, not one of which Mickey thought was
particularly funny, and all of which he'd heard a dozen times. Oh, he
didn't mean to make himself sound hopeless; the human body was capable of repairing itself in remarkable ways, and obviously there were
many people who had overcome worse conditions. He supposed Emi
would understand—she'd been very aware, painfully aware, of being
at "the height of her powers," and almost certainly would have preferred death to a sad decline; and if he himself had quit his first love,
boxing, too early—and any fighter worth his weight in jockstraps
would have been delighted to retire on a second round knockout—he
feared, now, that he'd arrived, suddenly, on the other side of his prime:
not a physical prime, but a spiritual one. It seemed to him that ever
since he'd found himself bereft and in agony in the pit of Dulac's cellar, he had been rising rapidly from the bottom toward some high
summit of bliss, the height of which, he felt, had been reached, after
so many highs and lows, just the other afternoon, with the bread in
the oven and the shovel in his hands, his son cleaning up in the
kitchen and his nostrils alert to something of April flitting in the air,
of the browning crusts of the loaves, of the mud of the flower beds and
imaginings of the brick and mortar with which he would build his
own temple of fire. Yes; it seemed that his world, while not perfect,
while far from complete, had attained, in that moment, a kind of rick-
ety athletic grace, rugged and flawed and beautiful, recalling both the
noble musculature of youth and the crackling joints of wisdom getting out of bed, the moment where the best of a person and the best
of his life become one, and he stands there waiting patiently for the
feeling to pass, hoping that it doesn't but knowing that it must; and in
between this fraction of an instant between hope and knowledge,
there lies—imperceptibly, almost—a brief commune with death, a
nod, an understanding, never otherwise admitted, that it is only with
its permission that we can feel these marvelous things.

Was this not the height of being? And yet at the time, squeezing at
his purple berry of a wound as the car seemed to hit every bump in
the road, he'd been resentful, had thought that in dying now he'd be

gypped out of what had seemed to him at that moment a bright future, or at least a hopeful one; he hadn't seen the whole picture,
hadn't seen the arc rising to its apex and catching the light. For he had
been in the light. He couldn't see that it was a life cut not short, but
cut, God willing, like a diamond.

How brilliant to have been taken away right then!

But now, lying helpless on stiff, stale institutional sheets, Mickey
felt he had traveled too far, had missed his stop, gone past it and into
the gloomy unknown. And with Ben having established himself with
flair at the bakery (Morris, too, had given the kid high marks), and
having proved himself, at a young age, a sharper, more resourceful
businessman than his father—well, what was a man to do? What was
left?

Mickey closed his eyes; he couldn't bear to look at his uncle, who
was sitting there, gazing at the smooth white hands on his lap.

When he awoke, it was night, or at least early evening. The sky was
black; the bedside lamp was on. Morris was still sitting, just as before,
only his eyes were closed and his glasses rested on the soft, inconse-
quential mound at the crotch of his trousers. Yet something was different in the room. It agitated Mickey; it was as if something were
missing, or had been replaced. He couldn't be sure what it was.

He could smell the dinners being delivered up and down the ward.
Mickey had told the nurse from day one that he would not be eating
any of this poison. Between Ben and Morris bringing him wonton
soup and crab cakes from all the best places, and him not even hungry in the first place—he was getting by mostly on liquids, it was easier on the kishkas, he only prayed he wouldn't get constipated and
really have to push—well, he didn't need their idea of supper, and as
far as the painkillers went, they could keep them too. What was pain
to him? Better to feel something than nothing at all.

When the meal delivery subsided, Mickey's nose—and it was the
real source of his power now, this nose, it was damn near the only
thing that moved on him—picked up on another scent; and when he
turned his head he saw, on the nightstand, what at first struck him as
a trick of his imagination.

"Morris," Mickey called.

There was no answer.

"Morris."

Morris opened his eyes, then quickly put on his glasses.

"Where did those come from?" Mickey said, indicating with his head the striking arrangement of wildflowers in a tall glass vase that must have arrived while they were both asleep. There were stalks of spiky blue delphinium, young golden sunflowers and, most prominently, a fistful of purple-pink heather, whose tiny bell-shaped flowers seemed to be awaiting a breeze, that they might jingle with some secret message or song from the fields.

But even as Morris reached over to pluck the small card from the lip of the vase, Mickey had a strange, uneasy feeling about the identity of the sender.

Morris held the card a few inches from his glasses and read: " 'Heard you had a little gardening accident. Hope these will help you get better.' "

Mickey awaited more. "And?" he said.

"That's it," said Morris.

"It isn't signed?"

Morris looked more closely. He shrugged. "It isn't signed."

"Let me see it," said Mickey. He reached out. Morris put the card in his hand.

Mickey looked it over. He was aware of a tingling in his toes. The handwriting itself—a leaning script like blown grass (a feminine hand, he thought, though he was no expert)—gave him a shiver, as of a sudden pulsing intimacy. He read the message several times, slowly, uncertain if it was meant to be humorous or cryptic or even threatening, or just plain innocent and warm. It could be read in any of these ways, Mickey thought. And if the flowers gave the words a softness, if they canceled any threat (for a moment he had feared it was Shirley, letting him know she was on to him, that she'd done a little investigating), then the lack of a signature imbued them with something undeniably personal. In that absence of words lay a whole other message entirely, a message that Mickey couldn't begin to interpret.

Who else would possibly know that the incident had happened out in the yard? That it happened at all?

Mickey turned the card over. Written across it was the insignia of the Green Garden Nursery.

The bandages became lighter; a strength returned to his hands. Yes, he thought: he'd known it all along.

Nelson must have told her. Told her *something*. But what did it matter? The flowers—they were here. And the card.

But why no signature? What was she telling him, or not telling him? Did she expect him to know it was her? Was it some kind of signal, a wink? Was it shyness? An oversight?

Mickey looked at the telephone, there by the vase.

"Who is it from?" Morris said.

"I think it might be from Nelson's mother," said Mickey.

"Nelson's mother?"

"You've met her."

"And she forgot to sign her name?"

"People forget," said Mickey. "Sometimes they forget."

"Sometimes they forget on purpose," said Morris, but Mickey could see from his uncle's blank expression that the comment meant nothing.

"Maybe I should call," Mickey said.

"Maybe you should call and ask her," said Morris.

Mickey looked at the card again. *Hope these will help you get better.* Hope? The word seemed strange to him, like a name he once knew, a woman.

"It couldn't be anyone else," Morris said, proud that he'd kept the news so airtight under his hat, as per Mickey's instructions. "No one knows a thing."

"Should I call?" said Mickey, more to himself. He glanced from the card to the phone, and back to the card. "What if they're not from her?"

"So then you say hello," Morris said.

Mickey breathed deep. Christ, he wanted to get the hell out of here. Get these bandages off and get a shower and dress up in his own clothes. Talk on his own phone. Make his own dinner.

"I think I'll take a walk," said Morris. "They got a nice salad bar on the first floor." He stood up, wobbled a moment. "You ought to get up and walk, Mickey. Instead of lying there all day and night. You want anything from downstairs?"

"No," Mickey said. "Benjie ought to be here soon."

He watched as his uncle shuffled past the bed, an old man headed out to ogle the nurses and get lost in the marvelous possibilities of the salad bar.

"Morris," Mickey said. "Before you go—can you hand me the bag you brought? The food?"

Morris turned back, picked up the bag and set it on the bed next to Mickey. "There's utensils inside," he said.

Mickey closed his eyes for a minute, then opened them. Morris was gone. The food would be cold by now, Mickey thought. That was okay, he was supposed to avoid hot food.

He reread the card. *Get better,* it said.

The phone rang. Mickey felt the shrill peal of metal in his gut.

He reached over and picked up. "Hello?"

"Dad. It's me. Just letting you know I'm on my way over. You need anything?"

Mickey gripped the receiver. A blaze of gold from the sunflowers caught his eye. "I'm fine, Benjie," he said.

He wished there was a radio around, that he could listen to some music, something to further encourage his waking senses; he wanted to raise his hands and conduct from his bed, command a minor orchestra. And so he did: he raised one hand, thumb and forefinger touching, and over his body threaded the rise and dip of some old, nameless symphony.

He recalled how the Tchaikovsky had dwindled so peacefully to its conclusion instead of ending with dramatic finality, with the grand, decisive blasts that marked many symphonic works. Audiences in Tchaikovsky's time hadn't been ready for that kind of ending, that long decrescendo, like an exhaled breath, into silence, air. Perhaps they did not see themselves that way. But Mickey understood. The end must come, be it in a violent flash, or slowly, like the long, crumbling death of a tradition. But let it come like sleep, Mickey prayed; let the strings lower us softly, let the bassoons linger in the dark.

ABOUT THE AUTHOR

PAUL HOND was born in Baltimore. *The Baker* is his first novel.

ABOUT THE TYPE

This book was set in Berling. Designed in 1951 by Karl Erik Forsberg for the Typefoundry Berlingska Stilgjuteri AB in Lund, Sweden, it was released the same year in foundry type by H. Berthold AG. A classic oldface design, its generous proportions and inclined serifs make it highly legible.